Pamela — Thank you for [illegible] a [illegible] wanting to [illegible] return [illegible] Latter [illegible] Chris[illegible]

ALL FALL DOWN

CHRISTINE POPE

DARK VALENTINE PRESS

This is a work of fiction. Names, characters, places, and incidents are either the product of the author's imagination or are used fictitiously. Any resemblance to actual events, places, organizations, or persons, whether living or dead, is entirely coincidental.

ALL FALL DOWN

ISBN: 978-0615697260

Published by Dark Valentine Press

Cover art by Nadica Boskovska. Cover design and book layout by Indie Author Services.

To learn more about this author, go to
www.christinepope.com.

DEDICATION

To the healers in this world and all others…

CHAPTER ONE

The slavers came for us in the night.

We should have been safe. After all, the village was located more than twenty-five miles from the invisible line that separated my homeland of Farendon from neighboring Seldd. No one had ever heard of slavers venturing so far within Farendon's borders before—but, as they say, there is a first time for everything.

I slept restlessly. Perhaps I should have been more accustomed to sleeping in strange places, but even after several years of traveling the countryside and plying my trade, I still found getting any kind of rest the first night or two in a new village or town difficult at best and sometimes downright impossible. And Aunde, poor hamlet that it was, with barely a hundred souls to call its own and a tavern hardly worthy of the name, could only offer a physician of the Golden Palm a rough pallet laid down in front of the dying fire at that same tavern. No one else in the village had the room to accommodate me, or at least they claimed they didn't.

The villagers mainly lived in one-room cottages and scraped out a rough living growing barley and raising sheep. Not surprisingly, the majority of them were somewhat overawed by my presence. The innkeeper possessed some worldliness, having once made the great journey to Lystare, the capital city where my order had been founded, but to the rest of them I was as alien and exotic as if I had washed ashore from the far-distant southern land of Keshiaar.

As I turned once more, trying in vain to find a comfortable position on the lumpy, straw-filled pallet, I heard shouts and the unmistakable slap of running feet on the hard-packed dirt outside. With a frown, I abandoned my useless attempts at slumber and sat up, reaching over to pull my cloak about me. The air was chill, with the first bite of autumn that promised harsher days to come, and I had gone to bed still wearing my gown and chemise. At least my current clothed state saved me the time of pulling my garments on, and I pushed the scratchy woolen blankets away and stood.

Through the darkness I saw the bobbing lights of lanterns and torches moving with impossible haste toward the tavern in which I had made my rough bed. I had barely focused on the dark shapes of the men who carried them when I heard the voice of Frin, the innkeeper, behind me.

"Slaving bastards!" he whispered fiercely. "You must hide yourself, Mistress Merys."

Slavers? I thought, but I did not waste time with arguments. "Where?" I asked, even as I knelt to gather up my precious satchel, which was filled with the various instruments and herbal concoctions vital to my profession.

"Here," he replied, and gestured for me to follow him

into the kitchen. A faint outline showed against the bare boards of the floor, and he bent down to unlatch the door to a root cellar.

No sooner had I gathered up my skirts and begun to make my way down into the fusty-smelling darkness, however, than the door to the kitchen burst open, slamming against the wall with such force I was sure the hinges must have been bent.

A rough voice called out something in words I could not understand, and then three men swarmed into the small room. One barked something at Frin, who shook his head. I had no idea whether he merely could not comprehend the other man's dialect, or whether the innkeeper was only trying to disavow my presence. One of the remaining men seemed to spot me immediately, however, for he advanced to the rough stairs of the root cellar, where I had only been able to descend a few steps before they caught up with me.

Even in the darkness I could see the man's beard split in a grin, and he called out something to his compatriots. His left hand shot out and grasped me by the upper arm, and then he hauled me up into the kitchen.

I should have been terrified, but instead I felt strangely calm. Perhaps it was merely that—up until then, at least—my profession had always accorded me deference and respect. Perhaps I kept myself from giving in to terror by feeling somewhere, deep down, that this was merely a horrible misunderstanding. As soon as these marauders could be made to understand who and what I was, of course I would be released immediately.

I had just begun to lift my left hand toward the man who held my other arm in order to show him the rayed sun tattooed on my palm when he barked something at me and threw me to the kitchen floor. I dropped the satchel I had clutched so desperately the whole time, and even as the three invaders moved toward it, I pushed myself across the dirty wooden floor, one hand reaching to secure its precious contents before they could take it from me.

Of course, my attempt was in vain. With a laugh, one of the other two men plucked it from beneath my desperate outstretched fingers and then opened it. His laughter died away quickly enough, and he stared at me with puzzled, angry dark eyes.

"*Senth ka rendish*?" he demanded, and I shook my head.

"I fear I don't speak your language," I said. No doubt they had thought that a satchel which was obviously worth so much to me must carry something more valuable than a collection of dried herbs and stoppered glass bottles.

The man who had pulled me from the cellar steps said, in an accent so harsh I still had difficulty understanding him, "What is this…rubbish?"

"I am a physician," I said, and this time I managed to open my left hand before me so the tattoo of the sunburst would be obvious to all, even in the dimly lit room. "Those are my medicines and salves."

Although my heart pounded so heavily in my breast I was sure they could all hear it, I felt some measure of pride that I had managed to keep my tone calm. Surely once they realized who I was, they would let me go.

The one who had spoken in my own tongue spat a few words at the two others. Again the one who held my satchel laughed, and then he tossed it at me. Caught off-guard, I barely had time to grab the handle before the battered leather bag smashed into the wall behind me. Even so, I could not help feeling a wave of relief flood through my veins. Surely now they must let me go….

But that apparently was not to be. My relief was as short-lived as it had been intense, for in the next moment the man who could speak the common tongue grabbed my arm once again and pulled me toward the door.

Poor Frin, who had stood mute and appalled throughout this entire exchange, finally took a step forward.

The man who held me gave him a brief look. "You are not worth taking, old man," he said. "But you may still live if you keep your mouth shut."

"Don't worry, Frin," I said, making sure my voice remained steady. The last thing I wanted was for the elderly innkeeper to give up his life in a futile attempt to rescue me from the slavers' grasp. "I'm certain I will be able to get this sorted out."

And I fastened him with a determined glance, willing him to stand back and allow matters to run their course. He nodded slightly, used enough to my authority after even the few days I had spent in the village. During that time I had tended to the outbreak of tertian fever which had brought me there in the first place—as well as setting the odd bone or two and placing poultices on the various sores and weak chests to which any farming village was prey. I could only hope he would have the wit to send word that I had been captured to Lystare, where the Order of the Golden Palm had its guild house. Surely as soon as they knew of my fate they would send someone to ransom me….

Frin offered no further protest as the slavers hauled me out of the tavern's kitchen and on into the open area that served as a meager village square. More armed men awaited us there, as well as a large wagon already filled with the younger, more able-bodied denizens of Aunde. From the wagon came the sound of weeping, but that was the only protest the captives seemed able to make.

Of course, what did I expect? For them to grasp their pitchforks and scythes and handily dispatch these invaders? Aunde's inhabitants were simple farming folk; Farendon had not been at war for more than fifty years. They probably knew less of battle than I did, I who had traveled beyond my country's borders into lands where men still did wage war upon one another.

Frowning, I wondered at the boldness of these men who had invaded Aunde. For years the Selddish slavers had made incursions into the borders of my land, but never as far as this. The two countries lifted their hackles at one another and growled occasionally, but the rulers of Farendon had not, at least in my lifetime, considered the loss of a few hundred peasants each year enough provocation to spill the blood of thousands more soldiers. The raids continued, and occasionally the king of Seldd sent reparations in the form of gold or grain or the exquisite linen fabrics for which his country was known, but no one seemed to care overmuch.

Except, of course, the folk who were taken into slavery.

Rough hands shoved me up into the wagon, where I took my place on the hard wooden floorboards, surrounded by my fellows in misery. The other captives seemed to roughly number half women, half men, and I saw no one older than their mid-twenties. Unlike me, many of them were still clad in their night wear, and they shivered in the cold.

Next to me sat a young girl, probably no older than sixteen. I thought I recognized her. Although she herself was healthy enough, her younger brother had had a mild case of the tertian fever.

"Elissa?" I whispered, and she looked over at me, startled, her eyes showing white-rimmed in the darkness like a frightened mare's. Then I could see her thin shoulders relax slightly as she recognized me.

"Mistress Merys?" she asked. "Not you!"

I lifted my own shoulders in a resigned shrug, and then moved closer to her. "Here," I said. "I was fortunate enough to have my cloak with me when I was taken. Why don't you pull that one end around yourself, and we can try to stay warm together?"

She nodded gratefully, and then lifted one side of my cloak and wrapped herself into it. Poor thing—I could feel her shivering as she moved closer to me, and I had no doubt it had little to do with the chilly night air. I couldn't free her, but at least I could offer her this small comfort.

The slavers called out a few words to one another in their own tongue, and then I felt the wagon slowly begin to move. Its unsprung weight bounced heavily on the rutted road below us. The boards on which I sat bit into my thighs, and I found myself wondering how far we would have to go before we could be free of the wagon's discomfort. Although a few wild thoughts of escape crossed my mind, I knew any such attempt would be useless; the slavers numbered five, and they were all mounted. I knew I could not possibly hope to outrun them on foot, especially in the dark and in unfamiliar country.

In my own travels, I rode a sturdy little sorrel mare. I found myself missing her more and more as the weary miles pressed on. At some point in our journey Elissa nodded off, her head falling against my shoulder in the utter weariness brought on by despair. I wished I could have shared in her oblivion, but I sat wakeful as the night wore on, even as the other occupants of the wagon slowly fell into sleep one by one.

I could tell the slavers moved as quickly as the cumbersome wagon would allow them. There was no possibility of reaching the border before daylight, so I surmised they must be headed toward some sort of camp or stronghold they had set up within my own country. Fortunately for them—and unfortunately for the inhabitants of the border areas—this was a wild, rough region, scarred by low-lying ranges of hills with deep, uninhabited valleys in between. The soil was poor and for the most part not worth cultivating. Its only utility lay in its appeal to the roving bands of brigands and slavers who frequented its wastes.

Sure enough, we ground to a halt in a narrow valley dotted with scrub oaks. I could see little in the pre-dawn grayness; a fog had come up in the night, and it quenched even the torches the slavers carried. They rousted us out of the wagon and into the dubious shelter of a rocky overhang. Evidently it had been used for this same purpose in the recent past: Sour straw lay littered on the hard-packed dirt ground, and I saw scraps of fabric and bones from past meals scattered amongst the dirty twists of hay.

Nose wrinkling, I helped Elissa out of the wagon as best I could and then stood some ways apart from the rest of the group. Used to conditions not much better than this, the villagers eased themselves down onto the straw and seemed prepared to continue with their sleep as best they could. Even Elissa found a spot up against the far wall of the overhang and curled herself into a ball far smaller than I would have thought possible.

For myself, I stood at the edge of the enclosed area and watched as the slavers slowly brought the wagon around to a staging area under a tree and then unhitched the horses. Evidently they were in high spirits—I heard them laughing and trading what sounded like good-natured barbs with one another.

"No sleep?" came a voice from the foggy grayness off to my right, and I turned to see the slaver who had pulled me from Frin's kitchen.

"I slept in the wagon," I lied.

He gave me a knowing nod, as if he were all too aware that I had been as wakeful during the long ride here as I was now. "Too good for our accommodations?"

Eyes narrowing, I looked back at him. He had the sort of face one could pass a hundred times in a crowd and not truly notice, neither ugly nor handsome. For some reason, he seemed more amused by me than anything else. "It's filthy," I said, at that point not much caring whether he took offense or not.

He did not. Instead, he threw back his head and laughed, showing off teeth far better than they should have been. "I could tell you were a fine lady. What in all the hells were you doing in a rat hole like Aunde?"

"I'm not a fine lady," I protested. "I'm a *doctor*. Dirt spreads disease. And I was in Aunde to treat an outbreak of tertian fever."

"A doctor, eh?" He studied me for a moment. "One of those healers of Inyanna?"

"Certainly not," I replied, my tone sharp. "They pray to their goddess for healing. Members of my Order use science to heal the sick, not superstition."

"Science," he repeated. Then he shook his head and spat on the ground. "There won't be much use for that where you're going."

And with those dark words he strode off, leaving me to watch as he disappeared into the billowing fog, which seemed to grow thicker as daylight approached. Frowning, I pulled my cloak more closely about me and brooded over his parting shot.

Where exactly were we going? Of course no one had bothered to tell us of our destination, but I guessed that from here we would be taken to the great slave markets of Myalme. The city was located about two days' ride from the border that separated Seldd from Farendon. On all the continent, only Seldd still practiced the barbarism of slavery, and it was a land that held itself close, aloof from most of the trade and politics that connected the lands from North Eredor to the west to Purth toward the east. Ringed on three sides by the impassable ranges of the Opal Mountains and the heavily forested slopes of the Razorback Hills, Seldd was a land unto itself.

Although members of my Order traveled as far as Sirlende to the west and the hot reaches of Keshiaar to the extreme southeast, they avoided Seldd. The slavers held little respect for status or learning—as I had already found—and there was too much danger of capture. Traders who did venture within the borders of Seldd traveled in large groups accompanied by well-paid mercenaries so as to avoid presenting too tempting a target.

This was why Seldd still spoke its own language when most of the folk on the continent shared a common tongue, albeit one that had its own dialects and accents. Obviously some of its inhabitants spoke my language, but I foresaw difficulties ahead if I ended up in some backwater far from a city or trade route. Still, there was no use worrying now about what might or might not happen in the future.

Suddenly I could feel the weariness in my limbs, the dull ache in my head from fatigue. Filthy or no, the straw began to look quite inviting. Besides, my cloak would shield me from the worst of the dirt. Finding an empty spot next to Elissa, I sank down onto the ground and arranged the excess fabric from my cloak to cover her as well. Then I leaned my head against the stone wall and drifted off into an uneasy slumber.

Some hours must have passed by the time I awakened, for a hazy sun stood well past its zenith. Apparently the sounds of the slavers approaching to hand out a meager meal were what had roused me. I opened my sleep-gummed eyes and saw the men passing around a few loaves of coarse bread and what looked like half a wheel of cheese. To their credit, the villagers took the food silently and parceled it out so that everyone could have their fair share.

Elissa handed me a thick piece of bread and a slab of blue-veined cheese. She ventured a quick, half-hearted smile. "At least they're not starving us."

"Of course not," I replied. "We're valuable merchandise. We're of no use if we're half-dead of starvation."

As soon as the words left my mouth, I regretted them. Elissa's full mouth quivered a bit, and I could see the tears start in her long-lashed dark eyes.

More than once during my training I had been taken to task for my bluntness. It was not seemly in one whose purpose was to soothe the ill, but I had always found it difficult to keep my tongue fully in check. I had hoped that I'd improved somewhat over the years, but obviously I still had some ways to go.

"But don't worry," I went on briskly. "I'm sure you'll find a very good situation. A pretty girl like you would most certainly make a fine lady's maid."

At that she did perk up a bit. I supposed for a girl from a forsaken little hamlet such as Aunde, even slavery might not be so bad if she found a place in a great house. Certainly I wouldn't mention my fears that instead she could end up being worked to death in the endless flax fields that formed the basis of Seldd's economy, or, only slightly better, toiling in one of the weaving houses where the flax was spun into linen until she went blind from the unending close work. To tell the truth, I wasn't sure whether those fears were for her alone or for myself as well. I had skill and would be an asset to any large household…if I could convince my new owners that it was in their best interests to keep me as a house slave and not as another back to be broken in the flax fields.

But perhaps it wouldn't come to that. I could only hope that Frin would have the presence of mind to report my capture to my superiors. I was certain they would do whatever was necessary to secure my freedom. After all, they had more than ten years invested in my training. At twenty-five, I still looked forward to decades of plying my healing art throughout the various kingdoms of the continent, and since all of my earnings save what I required for certain personal necessities were given over to the Order, I could not imagine that I would be left to rot in Seldd.

Of course I had been warned by my superiors not to venture too close to the border. As much as the people who lived in those regions needed our help, we physicians simply could not risk capture by slavers. And I had thought I was being careful. Another village, even closer to the border than Aunde, had requested my help, but I had had to decline, even though it pained me to refuse aid to those in need.

Why this particular group of slavers had become emboldened enough to venture farther into Farendon than any others, I couldn't say for certain. Perhaps the inhabitants of the other villages were becoming too wary. Perhaps they had abandoned their homesteads and farms altogether. One would have thought that at some point the slavers' depredations would become too great to bear, and that our leaders would be forced to act. But our king was the lazy, pleasure-loving son of yet another indolent monarch, and I supposed war over the rights of a few peasants was something to be avoided at all costs.

Elissa had continued to watch me closely as I sat silent, brooding over my own thoughts. At length she ventured, "What does a lady's maid do?"

Glad I could take her mind away from the squalor and uncertainty of our present situation, I explained her possible duties as best I could. Of course I had no maid while taking my training in the house of the Order, but my sisters and I had had a personal servant who attended to us before I left home at fifteen, and who continued to do so for my siblings after I was gone. So I was able enough to describe how she would take care of a lady's wardrobe, and help with her hair, and run errands for her.

"No kitchen work, and no work in the fields," I said, and I could see Elissa's slender shoulders relax a bit.

"That sounds better than what I was doing in Aunde," she replied, looking down at her reddened and chafed hands. "I'm quick with a needle, though, and I suppose I could learn to dress hair." She touched the long dark braid that fell over her shoulder and was quiet for a moment. I watched her thin fingers smooth their way over her hair, as if for the first time really contemplating the intricacy of the weave of her braid.

"You're filling her head with nonsense," said another of the captives, a narrow-faced man of about my own age. "It's to the fields with all of us."

"You don't know that for sure," I said calmly enough, although what I really wished to do was snap at him to not frighten the others any more than they already were. "We all have our own skills, our own talents. Seldd requires slaves for much more than simply working in the fields."

Elissa's face had again grown tight with worry at the young man's words, but she seemed to relax slightly as she listened to my reply. "What Mistress Merys says is true," she added. "We have no way of knowing exactly what our new masters will want with us."

He scowled, then gave Elissa an appraising look.

I could tell he was probably about to make some misguided comment as to exactly what a slave owner might want with a girl as pretty as Elissa, so I said hastily, "And we won't know until we're there, so there's no need to borrow trouble. Besides," I added, "we don't want them to see us quarreling, do we?"

The young man lifted an eyebrow, but then he obviously saw, as I had, that a group of the slavers had approached our makeshift holding area. Mouth thinning, he brushed at the dirt on his breeches and stood, even as Elissa and I followed suit.

Five men came toward us, led by the man with whom I had spoken earlier. He gave us a casual glance, and then said, "We're moving out. Come along."

There being nothing else we could do, we followed him out from underneath the overhang and then climbed back up into the wagon. He took a seat up front, next to another man who waited there as he held the reins of a team of horses that waited patiently, anticipating our departure. The remaining three men mounted their own horses and fell in around us as we began the next step of our journey.

Where that would take us, or to whom, I had no way of knowing. All I could do was huddle into my cloak, Elissa close by my side, and pray to whatever gods might be listening that I would have the strength to face whatever came next.

CHAPTER TWO

In the end, our journey took the greater part of three days. For the first day—while still within the borders of Farendon—we traveled from dusk until the sun began to show on the eastern horizon, when we made camp in some well-hidden glade or ravine. Then, once the sun had set, we took to the wagon again, to spend the evening hours slowly rattling our way farther from home. But on the second day I knew we must have crossed over into Seldd, for the slavers allowed us only a few hours of rest before we set out in the mid-morning to continue our journey.

At first I could see no real difference between this country and my own. Here, as in Farendon, the trees were just beginning to turn, their leaves showing bright hues of ochre and crimson. The weather held at least; although the fogs returned the second night, after that the days were mild, the evenings clear and cool but not yet cold. Then, on the third day, I saw the first of the great flax fields stretching out to either side of the road, as well as the hunched dark figures of the slaves who worked them.

I could tell when Elissa first noticed them as well. She had been staring off into the distance, a dreamy look on her face, when suddenly she stiffened, a frown creasing the skin between her delicate brows.

"The fields...." she whispered, and pulled my cloak more closely about her, even though the day was fine and clear.

By then I was weary enough that no ready words of encouragement found their way to my lips. I merely patted her on the shoulder and gave her a small smile, hoping that would be reassurance enough. I had no more idea than anyone else of our true destination, and platitudes that had been simple enough to utter a few days ago now appeared to me completely useless. All we could do was wait and see what happened.

Toward the evening of the third day, we approached a low-lying city that clustered around the edges of a dark, brooding lake. Although of course I had never been there before, I knew it must be Myalme, a regional center of commerce—and the nexus of the Selddish slave trade.

If I remembered my geography correctly, the body of water on which Myalme was situated was called Lake Nureine. Several large rivers flowed into the lake. Seldd was not a densely inhabited country; uncounted miles were taken up by the unending fields of flax and barley and wheat. So Myalme, although one of the three greatest cities of the realm, looked small and provincial when compared to the stone towers and wide cobbled streets of Lystare, the capital of my own land.

The slave markets were situated on the outskirts of town, at the eastern end of Lake Nureine. Somehow, the air did smell different here—damper and faintly tinged with the scent of fish and human waste. It was to be expected, I supposed. The slave markets were filled with the miserable wares of the trade, and so many people packed together in such primitive conditions couldn't help but stink. Still, I found myself trying to breathe through my mouth, all the while praying that we wouldn't be here long.

Fortune seemed to be on my side. The slavers were met by a well-dressed, fleshy man who threw Elissa and myself a look that made me shiver and draw closer to the young woman. She, thankfully, had not seemed to notice. Her fearful attention had been drawn to a large platform at one end of the open space in which the wagon had stopped—clearly it was the place where the slavers displayed their wares.

The newcomer then engaged in what sounded like protracted and somewhat heated negotiations with the leader of our slavers. Once or twice the slave leader gestured vigorously in our direction, and finally he came over to us where we waited in the wagon.

He stopped in front of Elissa and myself, made a few more jabbing motions with his forefinger, and then paused.

I held myself very still, refusing to meet either one's eyes. If the damned man tried to open my mouth to show off my teeth, I most certainly would give him a bite he wouldn't soon forget.

Fortunately, it did not come to that. The well-dressed newcomer looked us over from head to toe, then gave the rest of the captives a quick but keen glance. At last he nodded.

The slaver was too much a professional to heave a sigh of relief, but I caught the sudden release of tension in his shoulders. Then, as he apparently noticed me watching him, he gave me a quick wink. I looked away, an unwilling smile threatening to pull at one side of my mouth. I always knew that my sense of the absurd would get me in trouble one day.

I watched as the well-dressed man handed the head slaver a heavy bag, presumably filled with the local coin. Then he stepped to one side as the slaver approached the wagon and pointed at Elissa, two of the more likely-looking young men, another pretty girl probably a few years older than Elissa, and myself.

"You there," he commanded in his rough accent. "Come along now—it's your lucky day."

"I find that difficult to believe," I commented, even as I bent to retrieve my satchel.

"Believe what you want, my tart-mouthed friend." He stepped to the side as, wearily, one by one, we climbed down out of the wagon. The remaining captives watched us with a combination of worry and envy. "But I figured you'd prefer a private transaction to public display." And his gaze shifted briefly to the slave platform at the edge of the courtyard before sliding back to me.

Privately, I was inclined to agree with him, although I remained silent.

"Listen up, you," he went on, this time directing his words to those of us who had apparently been just been sold. "Master Dorus will be back for you shortly. You've just been sold to Lord Shaine of Donnishold. That's probably more than you lot deserve, but there you have it." Again he gave me that knowing grin, and this time I lifted an eyebrow at him. The grin widened further. "Too bad I can't be there to see what he makes of you."

"I'll be sure to write and let you know," I shot back.

Again he refused to take offense. No doubt the heavy money pouch hanging from his belt had done much to improve his humor. "I'm sure you would, darlin'—if only I could read!"

My lips parted to issue another retort, but we were interrupted by the arrival of Master Dorus with another wagon, this one lighter and better built, with a covering of heavy canvas stretched over a framework of curved beechwood. Accompanying Master Dorus—who I assumed must be the steward to Lord Shaine—were two more men, both wearing studded leather doublets and short, businesslike swords at their belts. No doubt they were there to serve a dual purpose of guarding Master Dorus and his cargo…and to ensure that said cargo stayed put and didn't try to wander off in the night.

Dorus fixed us all with an unmoving stare, and without a word we climbed up into the wagon. I didn't fancy sharing such close quarters with him for the journey (however long that might take), let alone being a member of his household. His dark eyes were cold, opaque, and the tightly graven lines around his mouth spoke of a harsh, unforgiving nature. I wondered at the unseen Lord Shaine, who would entrust such a man with his slaves and the management of his estate. Then I tried to tell myself that such dislike for a person on sight was certainly contrary to the teachings of the Order, which preached tolerance and respect for all living things.

Of course, tolerance probably came more easily to those who hadn't been sold into slavery.

At least the interior of the wagon was clean, and neat rolls of bedding had been placed there for us. Perhaps we were slaves, but it was apparent to me that we had fetched a good sum, and as valuable property we would at least be given the basic necessities.

We all settled ourselves down as best we could. No one spoke. I could tell that Dorus' presence had unnerved the rest of them quite possibly more than it had me. He hadn't said one word to us, so I had no idea whether he spoke the common tongue or not, but none of us seemed inclined to test whether he had that knowledge.

Although the canvas covering of the wagon shielded us from the elements, it had the disadvantage of hiding the passing landscape from our view as well. Of course, night fell soon after we left the slave districts of Myalme, so most probably we would not have seen much.

An hour or so after we were on the road, Dorus passed back to us a hamper filled with what proved to be fairly tasty meat rolls, as well as some dried fruit and several flasks of water. We shared the meal in silence, and then, one by one, we dropped off into slumber, lulled by the meal and the endless swaying motion of the wagon.

At some point during the night we must have stopped, for when I awoke and peered out the opening at the back of the wagon, I could see we were in a small village. The buildings had been fashioned of a dark-gray native stone and looked dour under a lowering early morning sky. At the edge of my vision I detected one of the two guards, who stood off to the rear of the wagon. No doubt we had stopped so that Master Dorus could pass the night in a real bed at an inn. Of course we slaves would not be offered anything besides the makeshift beds we had on the wagon floor.

At the same time I became uncomfortably aware that the call of nature had exerted itself somewhat forcibly on my bladder. Surely they wouldn't expect us to relieve ourselves here in the wagon. It was far too clean for that.

I managed to catch the guard's attention and, through the use of some awkward hand gestures, somehow conveyed my need to him. By the end of the exchange I could feel myself flushing, which, I told myself, was ridiculous. After all, as a physician I had to deal with all sorts of bodily functions on a daily basis. Somehow, though, it was quite different when the functions involved were my own.

Still, the guard allowed me to clamber out of the wagon and follow him to an outdoor privy located behind the inn. I took care of my business as quickly as possible and then allowed myself a deep breath of cool morning air once I was back out in the relative freshness of the courtyard.

By the time I returned to the wagon, the rest of its occupants had roused themselves, and the guard was forced to perform privy duties for the entire group. I couldn't help but allow myself a small, unnoticed smile at his obvious chagrin. As a man-at-arms to a lord, he most likely felt that such work was far beneath him.

Two servants—or possibly they were slaves as well—emerged from the rear of the inn bearing bowls of some sort of porridge. I didn't recognize the grain from which it was made, but it had so little taste it couldn't really offend. It seemed nourishing, however, and I ate with good appetite. If I had learned anything over the past few years as I traveled about the countryside, it was to eat when food was offered. No matter what the day had in store for us, it would be better to face it on a full stomach.

After another interval, Dorus finally emerged from the inn and took his place on the front seat of the wagon. The two guards mounted their own horses and fell into place behind us as we continued on down the road.

It was difficult to gauge the passing of time, as the sky had clouded over to a uniform gray, obscuring the sun. At least rain had not yet begun to fall. We again passed the time in silence, broken only by another makeshift meal at midday, when we were given strips of highly seasoned dried meat, some cheese, and surprisingly good bread, no doubt purchased at the inn, for it tasted fresh.

The forced inactivity began to prey upon me. I couldn't remember a time when I hadn't been doing at least three things at once. During my training I had interminable lessons in herb lore and anatomy, accompanied by practicums where we went into the countryside to gather herbs and other natural substances for medicines, or studied the inner workings of the body through dissections (frowned upon by the priestesses of Inyanna, but viewed by the city elders as a convenient way to dispose of the bodies of executed criminals). And life in the field was no different. I was used to rising early to compound my medicines and see to the patients in my care, patients whose complaints could range from the simple nausea of early pregnancy to lung ailments to the variety of diseases that had plagued men since the beginning of time: pox, mumps, a variety of fevers, ague.

For lack of anything better to do, I tried to calculate how

long it might take for Frin to travel to Lystare and inform my superiors of my capture. By all rights he should have been able to take my mare, abandoned in Aunde, but there was no guarantee one of the other inhabitants might not try to lay claim to so rich a prize. Very well, I would allow that he would might have to walk. The tiny hamlet had not even been noted on my maps, but I had estimated it lay a little more than a hundred miles from the capital city. Walking at a brisk pace, a man might be able to achieve that distance in a week—possibly less, if he were able to obtain the occasional lift from a passing carter or merchant. Still, it would probably be some time before anyone with the means to do anything about it learned of my capture.

And once they did, what then? Even if Frin had managed to commit the faces of the slavers to his memory, they had been very careful not to call one another by name during the raid. Their anonymity would no doubt protect them from any sort of reprisals. No, my only chance of salvation lay in someone traveling to the slave markets of Myalme and making inquiries there. Even then I was none too sanguine about my chances for rescue. Our sale had been a quiet, underhanded transaction. We hadn't even been placed on display for the general round of buyers to see us. Who would ever know that a small group from Aunde, including a displaced physician of the Golden Palm, had been sold there one evening?

As if to mirror my dark mood, the skies chose that moment to open up. For a few moments it seemed as if the heavy canvas that covered us would be enough to protect us from the deluge, but that hope proved short-lived. Once the material was soaked through, it began to drip upon me and everyone else in the back of the wagon. The other occupants scrambled to grab their blankets to protect themselves as best they could, while I once again offered the meager protection of my cloak to Elissa.

From a storage trunk located immediately behind the driver's seat, Dorus produced a broad-brimmed felt hat, which he grimly clapped on his head. However, he did not stop, instead slapping the reins across the horses' backs to increase their speed as best they could in the rapidly liquefying mud of the roadway.

His haste led me to wonder whether we were drawing near to our destination. I hoped so. No matter what awaited us at the end of our journey, surely it couldn't be any worse than the increasingly sodden misery in which we all sat. Beside me, Elissa began to shake with the cold. The poor girl had been taken in only her shift, which of course was completely unsuitable for the wet, cold weather.

There wasn't much I could do besides let her burrow up against me in a vain attempt to combine our body heat. Although I was better dressed than most of the other captives, in a plain but well-made gown of wool with detachable sleeves and a stout chemise of medium-weight linen, the garments didn't do me much good once they were soaked through. At least I had been wearing my sturdy calf-high boots when the slavers captured me. They protected my feet much better than the low indoor shoes most fashionable women wore. But dainty slippers served no purpose in the rough life I normally led, and I saved such fripperies for the times I was back in Lystare and briefly engaged in the social whirl that seemed to swirl endlessly around my town-bound family.

An increasing darkness outside the wagon told me that night would soon be upon us. I huddled in my cloak and wondered how much farther we had to travel. Certainly Dorus didn't intend to keep driving on through the night? At some point the horses would need to rest. Besides, even in Farendon it was not entirely safe to journey on the road after darkness fell, and Seldd was a much wilder, less civilized place.

But then the wagon shifted as we turned down a fork in the road. Beneath us the ground felt rougher, the way even more rutted—if possible—than the main road had been. I leaned away from Elissa to look past Dorus' shoulder, but the falling rain and approaching dusk revealed nothing but a thick darkness. Then I saw a wavering orange glow that must be torchlight, shimmering through the rain. Slowly a high stone wall came into focus, a wall in which was centered a sturdy wooden gate. On either side of the gate stood a guard dressed very much like the men-at-arms who rode with us.

Their swords remained in their scabbards. Obviously they recognized Dorus and his wagonload of fresh slaves. The casual way in which they greeted him made me wonder how often the steward was dispatched to Myalme to bring in another group of workers for the estate.

The flickering torchlight did little to reveal our surroundings. We were now in some sort of courtyard; I could hear the wagon wheels rattle against stone, not churned mud. Shadowy forms of tall buildings seemed to rise around us on all sides, but I could not make out any architectural details, save to note that the castle—if that was truly what it was—apparently had been constructed of the native dark-gray stone that seemed to be the chief building material in Seldd.

The wagon ground to a halt. Elissa looked up at me with wide, dark eyes. I wished I had more words of encouragement for her, but at the moment I felt quite as frightened and cold and uncertain as she looked. All I could muster was a fleeting smile that was little more than a grimace, and I could tell it did nothing to reassure her. She bit her lip and looked away.

Dorus climbed off his seat and made his way around to the back of the wagon. At the same time, the two guards who had had outrider duty the entire trip dismounted and flanked him.

"Out, then," he said curtly.

Although his accent was thick, I had no trouble understanding him. Well, that answered one question of mine, anyway. I was glad I had held my tongue throughout the journey. He was not the sort I would have wanted listening in on my private conversations.

Awkwardly, our muscles stiff from the protracted journey, we climbed out of the wagon. The rain still beat down, but as we were all soaked through anyway, it didn't seem to make much of a difference whether we were under the dripping canopy of the wagon or the open air. At least the ground under our feet was rough flagstones and not ankle-deep mud.

From somewhere beyond the wagon several more figures appeared, a man and a woman. In the flickering torchlight it was difficult for me to make out their features, but they seemed to be somewhere in late middle age. They spoke a few words to Dorus in their native tongue, and he gestured toward the rest of the group from Aunde, pointedly not including me with the other captives.

The woman nodded, and waved her hand toward the others even as she spoke a few words that none of us could understand. But her intent was unmistakable. She obviously wanted them to follow her.

Elissa gave me a quick, frightened look. Confused, I began to move along with the rest of them, even though I was fairly certain I had been excluded from her direction.

Dorus spoke immediately. "No. Not you."

Halting, I looked over at him but remained silent.

"This way." And he pointed toward the main keep and began to walk in that direction, the rain sluicing off his broad-brimmed hat as he did so.

I had no choice but to follow, my mind racing with questions. Why would I be separated from the rest of the captives from Aunde? Hadn't I been sold as a slave along with all of them? Why then would I not be taken where they were? Although I had no way of knowing for sure, I guessed that the man and woman were taking the other slaves to their quarters. It was far too late in the evening to be setting them to any tasks.

But it certainly was not slave quarters I entered now. The shadowy form of the main castle keep swallowed up the two of us as we entered. Immediately there was respite from the relentless rain, but inside it was hardly warmer than it had been in the courtyard. Thick candles shuddered in their sconces as the draft from the open doors blew down the hallway ahead of us, and I shivered.

The narrow corridor opened up into a larger hall, and in here at least a fire burned brightly in the enormous carved granite hearth at the far left side of the chamber. Evidently we had arrived not long past the evening meal, as I saw slaves still working to clear away the wooden plates and bowls and wipe down the three long tables that stood in the center of the hall. I received a few curious looks as we passed, but this room was apparently not Dorus' final destination.

At the end of the hall opposite the hearth, a narrow flight of stairs curved up and out of sight, apparently leading to a tower of some sort. It was in that direction which Dorus headed, with me trailing ever more uncertainly in his wake.

I usually prided myself in being of a practical turn of mind, of not giving myself over to fancies and speculation. Certainly that sort of behavior was not desirable in one who had to work with the sick or injured. In those situations one had to attend strictly to the here and now, or the patient would inevitably suffer. But I could feel my stomach growing tighter with dread as we mounted the stairs. For what purpose was I being led to this tower? I counted myself a woman of the world, and I knew how much at these people's mercies I was. If I were to be used in the worst way a woman could be, this seemed to be the place to do it.

Dorus paused on a landing, in front of a sturdy iron-barred oak door. He knocked, saying a few words in a questioning tone.

The door opened, and a thin-faced boy of probably no more than sixteen or seventeen looked out. He seemed to answer Dorus' question with another question, and he looked at me with some uncertainty.

Then I heard another voice from inside the room, this one deeper and with the unmistakable tones of command. The boy stepped away from the door, and Dorus entered, indicating that I should follow.

Not knowing what else I could do, I did as instructed. Behind me the boy closed the door, and I jumped slightly. Then I straightened and moved forward with exaggerated dignity, hoping that no one had noticed my uneasy start.

The chamber was circular, as was to be expected in a tower room. It had no fireplace, but a brazier to one side helped a bit to offset the chill of the damp night. Faded hangings depicting hunting scenes hung on the stone walls, in another attempt to ward off the cold. On the floor was a surprisingly fine rug of Keshiaari weave. Two chairs flanked the high arched window on the far side of the room. From one of them rose a man.

He was quite tall. I am not a slight woman, but the top of my head probably would not have even brushed against his chin. His nose had obviously been broken once and set badly. He wore a simple dark tunic, although a wool mantle held with a fine brooch of carbuncles and gold added a note of somber elegance to his appearance.

I waited as he stood silent for a moment, staring at me. Although I would not consider myself vain—I had always been called the "handsome" Thranion daughter, as opposed to the "pretty" one—still I would have preferred to have a chance to change out of my filthy and sodden gown, to wash my face and hands and hair, before being subjected to this sort of inspection.

He spoke then, in the common tongue. His accent was considerably better than Dorus', although he still tended to burr his "r"s and add too much emphasis to other consonants. "Dorus tells me you are a physician."

Even as I took in the words I could feel a wave of relief

wash over me. So this was why I had been hustled away from the other slaves. The chief slaver must have informed Dorus of my claims to be a member of the Order of the Golden Palm, and he had known that my skills would be needed here at the estate.

"Yes, I am, my lord," I replied, lifting my left hand to show the many-rayed sun tattooed on my palm. I could only hope that he would understand what the tattoo meant.

Likewise, I was uncertain as to how I should address him. Dorus had of course not warned me that I would be meeting the lord of the manor. However, "my lord" seemed safe enough—and I seemed to recall that Seldd had a different system for its land-owning nobles than my own country of Farendon. In Seldd, there was a king, and then a vast group of nobles who held their own ancestral lands, all of whom were simply called "Lord." There were none of the intricate hierarchies of my own kingdom, with dukes and barons and baronets and counts and who knows what all else, each with his particular form of address. I could still recall how incensed a particular duke had become when I had accidentally addressed him as "your Excellency" instead of "your Grace." Luckily, I was the only person who could soothe his young wife's morning sickness, and she had kept him from throwing me out in the street. Still, I couldn't help but reflect that the Selddish way was much simpler.

"I am Lord Shaine," he said. He studied me for a moment longer and frowned. "Are there many women in your Order?"

"Some," I answered slowly. So that was it. Still, I was used to that sort of reaction, even in Farendon. Just because the founder of my Order had been considerably more enlightened in terms of seeing women as capable as men didn't mean that the rest of society necessarily viewed the matter the same way. I could only imagine Seldd, backward as it was, would be even more prejudiced. I lifted my chin and continued, "Not as many as there are men, of course. Oftentimes it is difficult to convince one's family that training with the Order is a respectable alternative for a woman."

"But not in your case."

While I did not feel entirely comfortable discussing such matters with a complete stranger—and one who technically owned me—I decided candor was the best policy. "Not when my father had two other daughters' dowries to take care of, my lord."

That comment elicited a smile and a show of white if somewhat uneven teeth. "Well enough." Then his expression sobered, and he said, "Then let us see if you can help yet another patient."

I grasped the satchel I had held in my right hand all this time and nodded.

"This way," he instructed, and then added, his gaze flickering over to Dorus, who had stood to one side throughout the preceding exchange, "That will be all, Dorus."

The steward inclined his head, but I caught the narrow dark glare he gave me before he turned to leave.

Still, whatever the cause of the steward's hostility, this was not the time to be worrying about it. Lord Shaine pushed aside one of the faded hangings, revealing another door that led to a smaller set of stairs. I followed him up the narrow steps, clutching my satchel grimly and hoping that I wouldn't trip. There was no handrail, and I could only imagine that a stumble here would do little to reassure Lord Shaine of my competence.

At the top of the stairs was another door, which he pushed open, even as he said, "Auren? I've brought a physician." Then he moved into the room, and I entered behind him.

The room was smaller than the chamber we had just left, but more elegantly furnished. Another fine rug covered the floor, and the hangings looked newer. The furniture had touches of elegant carving, and a pewter vase holding some last straggling autumn blossoms sat on the bow-legged table next to the bed. But noticeable beyond all that was the sweet-sick smell of diseased flesh.

I looked down to the bed to see a pale-faced girl of probably no more than thirteen or fourteen, her black-smudged brown eyes enormous in her thin face. She gave me a listless glance and then shut her eyes again, as if she hadn't even the strength for so slight an effort.

Lord Shaine's face was expressionless, but I could see the tension in his shoulders as he looked down at the girl. Then he glanced over at me and simply, "This is my daughter. You will heal her."

CHAPTER THREE

For a moment I could only stand there, staring at him. His tone of voice invited no argument or comment. Still, this was what I had been trained for...although I feared, from the smell in the room, that I might have been brought here too late to do any good.

"I will examine her," I said. "But I will need a basin of hot water and some soap first."

"For what?"

I set the satchel containing my medicines down on the stone floor and spread my dirty hands before him. "How do you think her wound became infected in the first place?"

He scowled, the line between his brows becoming more pronounced as he did so, but to his credit, he did not waste time arguing with me. Instead, he turned and shouted something down the stairs.

Assuming he had called out to the young slave I had seen earlier, I made my way to the dresser on the side of the room opposite the bed and set my satchel down on the scarred wooden top. For necrotic tissue, I carried little with me that might help, although I had a tincture of poppy mixed with other herbs that could at least help her with the pain. For these sorts of injuries, the Order advised packing the wound with honey, as it seemed to inhibit the spread of infection and often actually aided in the growth of new, healthy tissue. Maggots were helpful as well, since they would eat away the diseased flesh and leave the sound portions of the limb alone.

As I had thought, it was the young slave boy who came up the stairs carrying a basin of faintly steaming water, as well as a thick bar of yellow soap and a rough linen towel. I indicated that he should set the items on the dresser next to my satchel. He did as I instructed, and then disappeared back down the stairs. Ignoring him, I went to work scrubbing my hands, using a small brush I carried in the satchel to get the grit out from under my nails and the embedded dirt from my cuticles.

Lord Shaine looked on in silence as I performed my ablutions. Once I was done, I set the damp towel to one side and picked up the small bottle that contained my tincture of poppy.

"Auren?" I asked, casting a questioning glance at her father.

He nodded, even as she wearily opened her eyes and gave me the unfocused look of one long lost in pain and fever. I would need to give her some willowbark tea as well, but for now the management of her pain was the most important thing.

"Take a sip of this," I said, tipping the bottle against her dry lips.

She swallowed, and gave a little gasping cough.

Lord Shaine started forward. I raised my hand in a quelling gesture.

"It's all right," I said quietly. "Her throat is a little dry from the fever."

Pausing, he looked at his daughter, and back over at me. I met his eyes steadily, willing him to understand that I would never bring harm to anyone in my charge.

Then I said, choosing my words carefully, for I did not wish to offend him, "Perhaps it would be better if you waited downstairs, my lord. It may be difficult for you to see—"

"I will remain here," he said at once, his deeper tones overturning mine with an unshakeable sound of certainty. "I have seen wounds on the battlefield."

"But not your own daughter's," I replied.

"Enough. Go on with it."

I allowed myself a sigh, but did not waste my breath on any further argument. If he thought he could manage the sight, so be it.

With care I took hold of the bedclothes and pulled them away. The girl wore a heavy linen shift that stopped at midcalf, and I could immediately see the bulky bandages that covered her left leg below the knee. Delicately I began to unwind the bandages, forcing myself to ignore the ever-increasing smell of the suppurating flesh. Finally I was done, and the wound revealed.

It was not quite as bad as I had expected, but it was still bad enough. Somehow she had gashed the inner side of her calf, opening up the flesh. Someone had obviously tried to stitch it up, with clumsy and straggling threads still visible through the puffed, angry flesh around them, but of course the wound had not been properly cleansed first, and infection had set in.

Working slowly and carefully, I felt around the site of the wound, probing with my fingers. A few times I heard a quick intake of breath as Auren gasped, but for the most part the poppy had dulled her senses enough so that I was able to carry on with my examination. Behind me I felt rather than heard Lord Shaine wince, but he remained silent, allowing me to do my work.

Although I could see the red streaks emanating from the wound, I did not think it was so far gone that I would have to remove the limb. Surgery was necessary, of course, but I felt I could cut away most of the dead tissue from the fleshy part of her calf and then pack the wound with honey. It would scar terribly, and she would most likely always walk with a limp, but at least she would walk.

Finally I turned to look up at Lord Shaine. He was pale beneath the neat beard that shadowed his jaw, but his gaze was steady enough.

"I'll have to operate, but I believe I can save her leg," I said.

He shut his eyes briefly. "Thank the gods. The local healer said he would have to take her leg at the knee."

"And that still might not have stopped it, particularly if he was the one who performed the initial surgery," I snapped. Of course I felt for Lord Shaine, but witnessing the careless handling and downright stupidity of untrained healers always made me feel a bit wild. I wanted to make a few pointed remarks about how the physicians of the Order could have been here in Seldd offering aid, if it weren't for the country's barbaric practice of enslaving anyone who didn't have the means to protect him- or herself. But starting a senseless argument now would serve no purpose. Besides, perhaps if I were able to impress him enough now, he would feel more inclined later on to free me....

"I'll need more hot water," I said then. "And the rawest pure spirits you have."

At that request he gave me a sharp look, brows drawing down over his eyes. For some reason I noted that they were a clear, deep blue, quite unlike his daughter's. "What on earth for?"

"To clean my instruments," I explained, then stood and went to my satchel. I pulled out the sharp cutting knives, the finely serrated bone saw. "We believe that infection is caused by dirt and lack of hygiene. Alcohol can do wonders for cleaning wounds and surgical implements."

He still hesitated, giving me that narrow-eyed look, and I said, in tones as cutting as my knives, "Do you value the contents of your cellar more than your daughter's leg, my lord?"

His mouth thinned, and he replied, "You would do well to remember who it is to whom you are speaking."

Again I had to step on my tongue to prevent myself from tossing a retort back in his face. I took a breath, then said, fighting to keep my voice mild, "My only concern here is to help your daughter. I have sworn a vow to succor the sick. To that end, however, I must make certain requests."

Lord Shaine was quiet for a moment, seeming to consider my words. Of course he was most likely used to getting his own way in things; he had about him an air of command that somehow managed to avoid shading into arrogance. "I will see to it," he said at length, then stepped forward, laid a hand briefly on his daughter's pale brow, and turned and left the room.

I let out a breath I hadn't realized I had been holding, and went on about my tasks. From a far corner of the room I borrowed a small table that could serve as a staging surface for my various instruments, and set them out on a clean piece of linen I also carried in my satchel.

The heat from the girl's body was palpable, but I dared not give her any of the willowbark tea to settle her fever until I was done with the actual surgery. While the tea would help her febrile state, it also would thin her blood somewhat, and I feared she would bleed too much as it was. Still, I set the bottle containing the powdered leaves to one side in preparation for the moments after the surgery.

I had two vials of honey left, enough to pack the wound initially, but I knew I would have to procure more, and soon. There was no way for me to know how well-stocked Lord Shaine's larders might be, but honey was a common enough foodstuff, and I would have to hope for the best. Likewise, I often used spiderwebs as wound dressings, but I had had no time to restock my supplies after the last surgery I had performed, as the summons to Aunde had come almost immediately following a surgery I had undertaken to remove an enlarged appendix. Since I was now in the heart of flax-producing country, I had to assume the one thing Lord Shaine could supply was ample amounts of clean linens.

Lord Shaine returned, carrying a squat smoked-glass bottle that held a liquor so potent I could smell it from where I sat. Several lengths of clean linen were also draped over his left arm. He handed the bottle of liquor to me in silence, and placed the stack of cloths on the table next to my implements.

"Thank you, my lord," I replied, then turned away from him to carefully pour the bottle's contents over the array of knives I had laid out on the table by Auren's bedside. I'd found a small bowl that would serve well enough as a catch basin, and the excess liquid fell into that. The fumes stung my eyes, and I blinked the tears away. Now more than ever my vision must be clear and unobscured.

I lifted the largest of my three knives, then said over my shoulder, "You really should not stay for this, my lord—"

"Proceed," he commanded immediately.

Allowing myself the smallest of shrugs, I turned to the girl who lay before me. All I could hope now was that if he became sickened by the proceedings he would step outside, or at the very least vomit into the chamber pot that sat in the far corner of the room.

Distractions could kill. I had been trained to focus my mind solely on my patients and the best means to cure them. Fatal errors could occur when we physicians allowed ourselves to think of our patients as individuals rather than the latest in a series of problems requiring a solution. This way of thinking had come to me with difficulty, and even now I tried not to think of how young Auren was, how fragile her pale features against the fall of dark blonde hair—idly, I wondered if she took after her mother, as Lord Shaine's hair was brown, although his was of the medium shade that often is lighter in its youth. But no. Time for all that later, after she was healed. For now, the task of stopping the spreading infection lay before me.

The first cut was deep, slicing firmly into the soft flesh at the side of her calf. Blood welled up immediately, but I was ready for it, applying pressure with my left hand even as I continued to make the cut. The smell of putrefaction grew stronger for a moment, but by this time I had become inured to the various stinks the human body could produce. I continued my work, carefully moving through the muscle, avoiding the arteries as best I could. At one point I dimly heard a gagging noise from behind me as I removed a large piece of flesh and dropped it into another bowl, but I kept on, ignoring the distraction.

As I had thought, the infection had not yet spread all the way to the bone, and so I was able to keep the vital musculature that attached to the shin more or less intact. I had to work quickly, however, as she continued to bleed freely, and in her weakened state, too much blood loss could be just as fatal as the infection itself. But a few moments later I was satisfied that I had removed all the diseased tissue, and picked up my needle and catgut suturing thread.

My needlework had always been fine, even as a young girl who stitched nothing more important than a spray of flowers on a pillowcase. Indeed, during my training with the Order, more than one instructor had commented on the neatness of my stitches, to which I had replied that at least my parents had taught me one thing which could be of use to me as a doctor. And indeed it had—the needle flashed in and out, drawing the sound flesh together even as I paused frequently to blot away the blood that continued to flow from the open wound. Her leg looked sadly misshapen—concave where it should have been convex—but the body has an amazing capacity to repair itself, and Auren was young and appeared to be otherwise healthy. In six months or so, no doubt she would be back on her feet, this episode only a memory of an evil dream.

Once I had completed the stitching, I poured a little more of the pale spirits Lord Shaine had brought me over the wound, making sure that any stray infection which might try to redevelop would be thwarted. Then I took one of my precious bottles of honey and spread a very small amount over the wound before I gathered up some fresh linen, tore it into strips, and began to re-wrap the leg.

Some blood seeped through the stitches, but not much. I had sewn up worse wounds than this—a jagged slash by a boar to one man's thigh came to mind—and I did not expect it to give me too much trouble. Then again, I knew I must guard against over-confidence. Too many times I had seen patients who appeared to be on the mend have sudden, catastrophic relapses, and I knew it would be some time before I could breathe completely easy about Auren's recovery.

No sooner had I completed wrapping the leg and begun the weary task of removing the blood-soaked sheets from beneath the girl's limp form than Lord Shaine spoke.

"She will—she will live, won't she?"

I turned to face him. His countenance was scarcely less pale than that of the girl who lay as if dead on the bed behind me, but, to his credit, he had not vomited, and he had stayed to the end. I didn't know how many other men would have had the strength to do that.

"It's very early yet, my lord, but I see no reason why not." I discarded the bloody sheets I held and knelt in front of the dresser, finding the fresh bedclothes I sought in the bottom drawer. Then I returned to the bed and began to stretch the clean sheets across the feather mattress.

Lord Shaine made no move to help me, not that I really expected he would. He watched as I worked, then asked quietly, "What is your name?"

Only after I had finished my task did I look up at him and smile. "Merys, my lord," I said. "Merys Thranion, of Lystare."

"Thank you, Merys." The grave blue eyes scanned my face briefly, and he added, "Thank you for saving my daughter."

I bent my head, accepting his thanks. Probably it had taken no small effort of will for him to extend that courtesy to one who, although possessed of special gifts and training, was still only one of his slaves. I said, "I'm only glad that I got here in time, my lord."

"As am I," he replied, and he looked to the bed where his daughter slept, her face almost as pale as the bleached linen on which she lay. "As am I."

His gratitude was unmistakeable. I could only pray that I might continue to build on it as the days wore on.

It soon became apparent to the household that Lord Shaine had accorded me a special place in it. That first night I spent at Auren's bedside, since the hours immediately following a surgery were the most crucial. Her fever rose, as I had feared it might, but the willowbark tea kept it from ascending into the dangerous area where brain damage and death might occur. After that I was given quarters in a small room located directly above hers. Apparently Lord Shaine valued my services enough that the slave quarters would never be my home.

Once I realized I would be awarded at least a modicum of dignity, I began to feel a little better about my situation. Oh, of course I still wondered how I might make my escape, or whether my superiors at least might come to my aid, but I knew I would not leave Auren until I had assured myself that she would make a full recovery. In the meantime, though, I had my privacy, and the regard of the lord of the manor—no small feat, all things considered.

Most of the other slaves did not speak the common tongue, and so I was reduced to pointing and other vague hand gestures to get my wants and needs across. I supposed while I was there I should make the effort to learn their own language, and most of them put up with good enough humor my clumsy attempts at learning the vocabulary. My accent, I fear, was not very good, but since part of my training had involved the memorization of the various medicinal herbs and the parts of the body, I picked up the words readily enough.

Two days after her surgery, Auren opened her eyes and looked at me with something resembling lucidity. She said a few words in Selddish, and I spread my hands in frustration, then said, in broken words, "No speak…."

What looked like the beginnings of a smile pulled at her pale lips. "Are you from Farendon?" she asked, her accent distinctly better than her father's.

"Yes," I replied, relieved beyond measure that at least we would be able to communicate. "I'm a physician."

She raised her eyebrows at that comment but said only, "My leg hurts."

"I expect it does," I responded mildly.

"But not as much as it did before," she added, as if worried that she might have offended me. "Did you come here to take care of me?"

"I suppose you could put it that way," I said. Then I frowned, thinking it through. "I've never had a chance to ask for certain—I was brought here with some other slaves, but I don't know whether it was a lucky chance that brought me to Dorus' attention, or whether your father sent him out specifically looking for someone who was a healer."

Pushing herself up against the pillows, Auren regarded me critically for a moment. "You don't look like a healer."

"Actually, the members of my Order prefer to be called physicians. And what precisely is a healer supposed to look like, anyway?"

"Well, the healer from the next village is a skinny old man with a dirty beard. I didn't like him." She crossed her arms over her small breasts, "And the midwife who comes to deliver the slaves' babies is round and fat. You're neither—you're actually quite pretty, aren't you?"

"Pretty" is usually not the word used to describe me, I thought. I had inherited my father's height and the lean elegant bones of his face as well. Then again, perhaps Auren's vocabulary didn't include the word "handsome."

"Well, thank you, my lady," I said, deciding to accept the compliment.

She nodded seriously, and leaned over to touch the

bandaged length of her lower left leg beneath the blankets. "So you didn't have to cut it off."

"No, thankfully."

"I was afraid it would be gone when I woke up. Everyone said it would have to come off." Her tone was matter-of-fact, as if she were speaking of someone else's leg. "Even when I woke up and could feel it hurting, I wasn't sure it was still there. Old Wilm the miller lost his foot to frostbite before I was even born, but he says he can still feel it itching sometimes."

"That does happen," I admitted. "We call it 'phantom pain.' The body is remembering something that's no longer there."

Auren was silent a moment, her dark eyes considering. "So how did you fix my leg?"

Trying to decide how much it was appropriate to tell her, I paused. Then I looked at her serious little face and said candidly, "I had to cut away part of the muscle, the part where the infection had taken root. Then I stitched you back up."

Again she sat quietly, thinking over my words. "Will I be able to walk?"

"I see no reason why not. You may limp a bit, but it shouldn't keep you from living a normal life."

"And dancing?"

"Dancing?" I repeated, wondering whether she had much opportunity for that here in her father's dour castle.

"That's how I shall meet my future husband," Auren explained. "Everyone gathers at the castle—the sons of the local lords—and we dance. Then everyone decides who will marry whom." Frowning, she added, "Who would want to marry a girl who limps?"

"You're a very pretty girl, my lady," I replied, thinking she seemed a little young to be worrying about whom she would marry. "I'm sure a slight limp wouldn't bother any young man who liked you."

Her frown deepened, as if my words had done very little to convince her. Then she asked, "What about riding?"

"Of course. It would probably be easier for you to ride than walk."

"If Father lets me, that is," she said. "That's how it happened."

"You fell while riding?"

"Yes," she replied. "But it wasn't an ordinary fall—I take those all the time. Father thinks I'm too wild, but why bother trotting down dull old paths when there are all these stone walls around here to be jumped?"

"Why," indeed. I was beginning to see that Auren was what my mother used to call "a handful."

Still, the girl was friendly enough, and her high spirits weren't my concern, after all. "So what happened?" I asked.

"I saw a wall a few miles from here—and Cloud and I cleared it, but then he put his foot wrong when we came down the other side. I fell off—which I've done a hundred times before—but there was an old tree stump there, and I fell against it and tore my leg open."

Doubtless filling the wound with splinters, dirt, and the gods knew what else. No wonder it had become infected.

"Luckily, Cloud only sprained his ankle. Father was so angry with me—he said I could have broken Cloud's leg, and then he would have had to be put down." She lifted guileless eyes to mine. "At first I wasn't sure if he was angrier that I had hurt myself or my horse."

"Surely you must be mistaken," I said lightly. I was fairly certain she didn't really mean what she said—she just wanted to see my reaction.

A lift of the thin shoulders beneath the plain white linen of her shift. It was obvious she had dropped weight during her illness—from her frame I could tell that normally she would be a tall, well-built girl, broad-shouldered like her father. "I know he's unhappy that the only one of his children who lived was a girl."

Uneasy, I ventured, "My lady, I don't think —"

"Oh, it's true enough. Ask anybody." She watched me for a moment, then said, "You probably wouldn't, would you? You have that sort of face."

"What sort of face?" I asked, hoping that I might distract her from more disturbing topics of conversation.

"The polite kind. You look like a lady. Were you?"

I permitted myself a slight smile. "Not exactly. My father is a wool merchant in Lystare. That's the capital of my country."

"I know. At least Father made sure I always had a tutor. That's why I speak common so well."

"That you do," I agreed, inwardly marveling at her volubility. Then again, it didn't seem as if she had many people here in the castle in whom she could confide. From what I had seen over the past few days, most of the household staff was made up of slaves from my own country; Seldd's neighbor to the east, Purth; and even a few fair-haired South Eredorians, none of whom had seemed particularly inclined to conversation in my brief meetings with them. Already I was seen as being somewhat apart from the rest of the slaves. I might not be any freer in a legal sense than the rest of them, but I slept apart, in my small tower room, and I took my meals in my chamber as well and not the large common room that adjoined the slave quarters. A few of the household staff were natives of Seldd and therefore free—Dorus and Ourrel, Lord Shaine's personal manservant.

"A merchant," Auren echoed, and tilted her head to one side. "I've heard that merchants are rich. Are you?"

I almost laughed at her audacity, but instead tried to look slightly disapproving. "That's not the sort of question you ask of strangers, my lady."

"But you're not a stranger, are you? After all, you've been living here for several days now, correct?"

"That is true," I admitted.

"Father often scolds me for being too free with my tongue," she said then, and scowled. "As if I can help it."

"You could, you know," I commented. "You just have to stop and think about what you're going to say before you say it. I often find myself in the same predicament."

"Really?" Auren raised her eyebrows in disbelief. "You seem quite reserved."

Only because you've hardly let me get a word in edgewise, I thought, but I merely smiled. "Well, I've had a few more years to school myself in discretion. My father used to tell me if it was in my head it was most likely on my tongue a second later. But I've managed to gain a closer guard on my words as the years have passed."

"That doesn't sound like very much fun," she said, her tone sour.

Here was where I should have made a speech about politeness and tact. But I was not her governess, and in some odd way this outspoken woman-child reminded me of myself, from not so very long ago. "No," I admitted, "many times it isn't. But neither is getting into arguments with people, which is often what happens if you always speak your mind with no regard for what other people might think or feel about what you're saying."

She was silent for a moment, appearing to consider my words. Then she said, "How long will my leg hurt like this? It's starting to itch."

"That's a good thing," I replied. "It means you're healing—your muscles are knitting together as they should. But it will probably keep hurting for quite some time."

"So I probably shan't be able to go riding again before winter." Her tone was fretful.

I had to remind myself that she was recovering from major surgery, and that this was the first time since the operation she had been able to sit up and hold a conversation. Probably she was hungry as well. Over the past few days I hadn't been able to get anything more nourishing into her than a few spoonfuls of beef and barley broth.

"What about some dinner?" I asked, attempting to change the subject. "You need to eat—it will help you get better more quickly."

"I suppose so," she answered, not very graciously. "As long as it's not Merime's mutton stew. I hate that."

"I don't know what they were planning for this evening's

meal," I said. "Let me go check for you. Is there anything in particular you would like?"

"Roast chicken, or at least chicken pie. Some bread. And cheese?" This last was said on a rising note, as if she wasn't sure I would agree to something so rich for a convalescent.

But I knew there was nothing I need interdict for her in terms of her food—she needed good, nourishing meals, but I saw nothing wrong with any of her choices. "I'll see what I can do," I replied, and rose from my chair at her bedside.

"Thank you, Merys," she said gravely, although I thought I caught a brief glint in her eyes. Then she added, her expression much more serious this time, "I am glad you are here."

Oddly enough, given my current situation, I wanted to reply that I was glad to be here as well. Instead I gave her a brief smile and left the room, my expression sobering as I made my way down the narrow steps that led into the great hall. I had heard nothing of Elissa, and as for myself…

After all, how I could be happy to be here, when I was only a slave?

CHAPTER FOUR

THE DAYS BEGAN TO SHORTEN. From my vantage point in the tower, I could see the slaves take to the fields to harvest the flax that seemed to be the main crop produced on Lord Shaine's lands. The golden sheaves appeared to my untrained eye to look much like wheat, save that after the flax was bundled, the workers laid the cut sheaves in water—to loosen the seed, Auren informed me. From here it would be taken to market in Myalme, or further still to Soren, the capital of Seldd.

Auren was up and about much sooner than I would have liked, but my protestations that she would over-tax her injured leg fell on deaf ears. At least I was able to extract from her the promise that she would not attempt to ride again until I said it was safe, and I had to admit that being cooped up in a small chamber, no matter how comfortable, held little appeal to me and even less to a girl as lively as Auren.

I also managed to prevail in suggesting that perhaps it was time for Auren to have her own maid. Apparently she had made a similar request to her father some months ago, and he had dismissed the idea, telling his daughter she was too young yet to have a maid waiting on her day and night. But after this latest accident he appeared to recant. Possibly he had realized that having someone watching after Auren day and night was not necessarily a bad thing.

Elissa seemed a perfect choice, and Auren agreed readily enough when I suggested the girl to her. The fact that Elissa had no experience working as a lady's maid did not seem to bother her in the slightest.

"After all," she told me in confiding tones, "it's not as if I have much practice being a lady, either. Perhaps we can learn together."

So Elissa was given a pallet to sleep on in my own chamber, and if I regretted the loss of my privacy, I did not regret at all saving the girl from the fields. When she came to move her meager belongings into my own tower room, she grasped my hands in hers and said in an intense whisper, "Thank you, mistress. I feared I would have to work in the fields forever."

"I told you I would try to help," I replied. "I'm sorry it took as long as it did. But you seem to be safe now."

"Yes," she said, taking in the sparsely furnished room we now both shared. But at least it was clean; I had seen to that first thing. No doubt I had offended both Dorus and Seyla, the chief female slave who appeared to manage the household servants, but on such matters I was inflexible. And since I kept the room clean myself, and did not add any extra burden to the household staff, I could not see why it should make a difference if I were overly fastidious about the state of my surroundings.

Luckily, Elissa and Auren seemed to get along well enough; I often heard them chattering away in the common tongue. Elissa, to her credit, also showed an interest in learning Selddish, and I think it gave Auren great pleasure to take Elissa in her charge and teach her her native tongue. Elissa proved her worth in other ways—certainly Auren's hair went from resembling a bramble bush to sleek and smooth, with intricate braids and coils. She began to look like a lady, and although she walked with a definite limp and would continue to do so for some time, I had no doubt that Lord Shaine would have any problems finding her a suitable husband when the time came.

For myself, I worried I would be idle once Auren healed well enough to move about on her own, and I wondered what my fate would then be. I soon found I needn't have plagued myself with formless fancies. A great estate such as Lord Shaine's had its daily round of mishaps, from the slave who managed to almost slice off two fingers from his left hand while harvesting the flax to the scullery girl who somehow spilled half a kettle of scalding water down her front.

I made my way about the estate, stitching cuts, spreading salves, even delivering a child to one of the slave women. At first I found myself silently disapproving—who on earth would be foolish enough to bring a child into such conditions? But then I realized that to deny these people even the momentary pleasure these illicit couplings produced would be to deprive them of possibly the only happiness they could achieve. Sad that a child should be born into slavery, of course, but I learned that such children actually received better treatment than their parents. A child born into slavery was not necessarily fated to be a slave forever. At the age of sixteen he could buy his freedom, if he could prove that he had worked enough in the intervening years to have earned a sum equal to his cost on the open market. It seemed, again, strange and barbaric to me, but at least it was better than having self-perpetuating generations of slaves.

It was Ourrel who explained these things to me, in his quiet yet unflinching way. He was a tall, grave man, a native of Seldd with an impeccable sense of dignity—a far more suitable candidate for steward than dour and heavy-browed Dorus, in my opinion.

Ourrel added, "Do not think, Mistress Merys, that we do not know what the rest of the world thinks of us. More than once I have heard his lordship say he wished he had more power to change things, and I am inclined to agree with him. However, if he were to free his slaves wholesale, word would spread quickly enough, and it would cause unrest on the estates of those who see no reason to discontinue the old ways. So we do what we can here to make the lives of those in service not quite so difficult. Perhaps you think it is not enough, but even free men cannot always do as they wish."

To these revelations I could only nod and murmur that I understood. Whether this was the complete truth or not, I couldn't say, but Ourrel's words made me think less harshly of Lord Shaine, and my respect for both men grew as a result.

Of Lord Shaine I saw little, but I supposed that was to be expected. Once he had reassured himself Auren was well on the way to health and that there would be no relapses, I saw him very little in her tower room. His reserve troubled me somewhat, for I could not help but contrast him with my own jovial, good-natured father. However, if I had learned anything over the years, it was that the world possessed as many types of men as it did diseases to lay them low, and I could not judge Lord Shaine simply because of my own personal experience.

It was during one of my rounds in the kitchens, a little more than a month after my arrival at the estate, that I made a disturbing discovery. Merime, the head cook, suffered from shortness of breath and chest pain. While her surest remedy would have been to shed some of the twenty-odd stone she carried about every day, I held my tongue on that matter and instead treated her with an infusion of foxglove that had worked very well in the past for patients who had heart conditions.

But it was not Merime or her condition that troubled me. She took the medicine with good enough humor and thanked me for it. Then, out of the corner of my eye, I saw the same young slave who had brought the water up to Auren's chamber skulking in the corner near the hearth. He had the sort of hangdog, half-guilty expression of one who does not want to attraction attention yet at the same time desperately craves it.

I noticed immediately the blue-black bruises on his upper arms beneath the short sleeves of the dark linen tunic he wore, a garment far too skimpy for the chilly late autumn weather, even if he spent most of his time in the considerably warmer confines of the kitchen. Then my eye was drawn to the pinched, frightened look on his face, the shadows under his eyes that were almost as black as the bruises on his arms.

"You there!" I called, using the common tongue, for I was fairly certain he had come here as a captive, as had I. "Please come over here for a moment."

He looked as if he wanted to bolt but instead took a few halting steps in my direction.

"What's your name?" I asked, for it was obvious he would not speak unless addressed first.

He jabbed his toe into the stone floor, staring down at the ground and avoiding my eyes.

"You speak when you're spoken to, boy," scolded Merime, who had been looking on with some bemusement, as if she couldn't comprehend why I was bothering with a young man who didn't seem to be in any immediate need of medical attention.

"Raifal, mistress," he answered, looking as if he very much wished to be someplace else.

"How did you get those bruises on your arms?" I inquired, already fairly certain of the answer…or at least the answer he would try to fob off on me.

"I'm clumsy," he said, his voice a dull monotone, as if repeating an oft-recited but not entirely understood lesson. "I bang into things."

I wanted to retort that no one was that clumsy, but I knew I would have to tread carefully here. "As a healer, I've seen a lot of bumps and bruises. But it seems a little odd to me that you would only have bruises on one part of your arms if you're continually bumping into things."

He looked stricken then, his jaw tightening even as he glanced away from me. His gaze flickered for a second toward Merime, and he hung his head, remaining silent.

Obviously he would say nothing else in front of the cook, and I couldn't very well ask her to leave her own kitchen. The spacious pantry immediately behind me seemed the most convenient solution.

I unlatched the door and indicated that he should follow me inside. Merime raised an eyebrow at me but said nothing; I had earned her goodwill by easing the pain of her heart condition, and at least at the moment she seemed inclined to trust me…which was more than I could say for Raifal. He entered the dim, herb-scented room with me, but the whites of his eyes showed in the semi-darkness, reminding me of a frightened horse about to bolt.

Pitching my voice low, just in case Merime should decide to press an ear to the pantry door to hear what transpired within, I asked, "Who has been hurting you, Raifal? I want to help you, but I can't if I don't know what the situation is."

Again that tightening of the jaw, but I could also see his lower lip tremble. He was, after all, very young, fifteen or an under-grown sixteen. "He said if I told anyone he'd kill me."

I willed myself to stay calm. But I had seen this kind of abuse before. The bruises on Raifal's upper arms were just the sort left by a pair of man's hands as they grasped an unwilling victim. Choosing my words with care, I asked, "Has he hurt you…other ways?"

Silence, and a quick averting of his eyes, was my only reply.

His lack of response was answer enough. Fighting the sick anger that rose in me, I then said, "Raifal, I can't make him stop if I don't know who it is."

"You can't make him stop," he answered, his voice thick with rage and unspent tears. "No one can." He gave me a contemptuous look. "Who would listen to you? You're just another slave, just like the rest of us."

The words were a slap in the face, but I forced myself to remember that he was angry and afraid, and had most likely suffered the very worst sort of abuse. "Yes, but I'm also the slave who healed Lord Shaine's daughter," I replied. "That gives me an advantage, don't you think?"

He said nothing, but gave a small lift of his shoulders. Not exactly encouraging, but at least it wasn't an outright denial.

Hardening my voice slightly, I said, "And if you say nothing, what then? Do you think he'll ever stop?"

The boy's hands balled into fists, another indication of the impotent anger he must surely be feeling. Then he whispered, "No."

"Then let me help you. That's what I've been trained to do. But I can't do anything if I don't know who your tormentor is."

"Do you—you promise if I tell, then you'll get him to stop?"

I took a breath as I felt the relief sweep over me. "I promise, Raifal." Even as I said the words I worried that I might not be able to uphold my vow—but what else could I do? Without information, I was as helpless as he.

He was silent for a long moment, obviously torn by worry and guilt. I wanted to lay a soothing hand on his arm, but I guessed he would spurn my offer of comfort. For someone who had suffered the way he had, a touch would only be cause for further torment. Instead, I only waited in agonized silence, wondering what on earth I would do if he refused to offer up the name of his abuser.

But then he said, so softly I could barely catch the words, "It is Dorus."

Anger washed over me, so intense and sudden that I knew if the steward had suddenly appeared before me, I could have killed him with my bare hands, I who had sworn a vow to preserve life at all costs. As much as I wanted to give in to my rage, though, I knew I must remain calm at all costs.

"It was very brave of you to tell me, Raifal," I said, before the silence could grow too terrible. "Can you try to stay out of the steward's way for a while so that I can go find Lord Shaine and speak with him?"

He swallowed and then nodded. "Mostly he would come for me in the night, anyway. Merime needs me to fetch the meat for dinner from the smokehouse—that will keep me away for a while."

"Good," I said, and pushed open the door to the pantry.

Merime stood at the large scrubbed oak table in the center of the kitchen, chopping leeks, but I could see the avid curiosity in her light blue eyes.

Ignoring her gaze, I said, "Run along to the smokehouse, Raifal."

The boy all but bolted from the kitchen, gratefully accepting the opportunity for flight I had given him.

I turned to the cook. "Merime, do you know where I might find Lord Shaine?"

She lifted her fat shoulders. "Am I his lordship's keeper? At this hour—possibly riding the fields. Or he could be in his study."

It was little help, but I knew she was right. I had assumed she might know a little more of his movements simply because of her lengthy tenure in the household, but in truth Merime rarely ventured forth from her culinary domain. Dorus would most likely know where to find Lord Shaine, but of course the steward was the last man on earth with whom I wished to speak at the moment.

If his lordship were in fact riding the fields, surveying as his slaves brought in the last of the flax harvest, then I was definitely out of luck. My exalted status had given me free run of the castle and its outbuildings, but I most certainly would not be allowed to take a horse from the stables, and given the estates' vast acreage, I could walk from now until the end of the week and still not locate Lord Shaine.

But he could be in his study, and it would not seem out of place for me to seek him there, especially since the chamber was located in the same tower as Auren's room, and my own as well. I made my way across the great hall, noting as I did so an unusual bustle. Several slaves were in the process of mopping the stone floor, and the hangings had been taken down, presumably to be removed to the courtyard for a good beating. Obviously his lordship expected guests this evening. I was surprised Auren hadn't said anything to me about having visitors, since she usually managed to keep me informed of the goings-on about the castle, but perhaps she was unaware of the impending festivities as well.

I wondered uneasily whether this was the most appropriate time to be confronting Lord Shaine. Surely the news I had to impart would be most unwelcome. But I had promised Raifal I would do everything I could to help him, and better that I should see Lord Shaine now, while the hot anger still burning in my breast gave me the courage to bring up such an unpleasant topic.

Never before had the steps up to the first landing where his lordship's study was located seemed so short. I paused for a long moment outside the door, gathering my breath. Then I lifted my hand and knocked.

A moment of waiting silence that seemed to go on forever, and at last I heard Lord Shaine's voice from inside. He spoke in Selddish, of course, but even I could understand the simple command. "Enter."

No help for it, then—I had not been given the luxury of delay by his absence. I lifted the latch and entered the room, hoping that I didn't look overly flustered.

He seemed somewhat surprised to see me. The level brows lifted for a second, but he said evenly enough, in the common tongue, "Mistress Merys. Is there a problem with my daughter?"

For a second I just stared back at him, and then I shook my head. Of course—what reason would I have to disturb him in his study, other than something to do with Auren?

"No, my lord. She is well. I believe she is out enjoying a short walk through the herb garden with her maid." These short excursions were something I encouraged, once I had determined the leg was healing well and that Auren would not be overtaxing the limb by walking on it. Now that the muscle had begun to knit itself together, it was important for her to keep it from atrophying.

Lord Shaine laid aside the quill he had been holding and regarded me with a frown. "What is it, then?"

Now that the moment had come, a horrible awkwardness seemed to take possession of me. Suddenly I felt as I had at my first "grown-up" dance, when I was taller than most of the boys by a head, and my feet had seemed huge. For some reason, I couldn't decide what to do with my hands, so I let them hang by my sides, feeling as useless as the rest of me did.

I cleared my throat. "My lord, I would not have disturbed you if this weren't a matter of the gravest importance—"

"Well, what is it?"

Nothing in his face or manner indicated anything except an impatience to hear what I had to say and be done with it. I supposed I should be glad that he hadn't simply ordered me out of his study once he realized my presence there had nothing to do with his daughter.

"It's about one of the servant boys—Raifal."

Lord Shaine's face remained expressionless. I wondered whether he even knew Raifal by name. "Yes?"

There being no easy way to say it, I decided to just give him the simple truths of the matter, not couched in euphemism or polite words that would soften the ugliness of the situation. "He's being abused by your steward." Somehow I could not bring myself to say Dorus' name.

The slightest tremor seemed to go through Lord Shaine's frame, but if I had not been watching him carefully, I probably would not have even noticed it. When he spoke, the words came slowly, as if he considered each one with care before he uttered it. "That is quite an accusation. Why would you think such a thing?"

"Because the boy told me so himself." I waited for a

response from Lord Shaine, got none, and pressed on. "My lord, I noticed the boy when I was down in the kitchen, attending to Merime. His arms are black and blue between the shoulder and the elbow. I spoke with him in private, and he finally confessed to me that it was your steward who had used him so—and worse." I took a breath to collect myself; the previous words had tumbled out of me like a stream in spate. Then I added, "He also told me that Dorus threatened to kill him if he ever told anyone about the abuse."

He continued to watch me closely for a moment longer. Then he said, "You're a brave woman, aren't you, Mistress Merys?"

"I beg your pardon?"

"I don't know how many of the other slaves would have had the courage to come to their master with this sort of information."

I flinched at the words "other slaves," but I refused to let him upset me. If that was all he saw me as, regardless of the service I had provided for him and his daughter, so be it. "Perhaps none of the *other slaves*—" and I made sure I gave the words extra emphasis, even as I scowled at him— "has sworn an oath to protect others from harm. But I have. I could not let this go on, once I had learned of it."

Whatever else he was, Lord Shaine was not stupid. He gave me a sharp look, then said, "And what would you propose that I do about it?"

"You should dismiss him. Immediately."

At that Lord Shaine gave a short, humorless laugh and stood, pushing his chair away from the desk with an abrupt, angry gesture. "You make it sound so simple."

"It is."

He took a step toward me, then another. Although I would have liked nothing better than to move away from him as he came closer, I stood my ground, lifting my chin as I did so. Whatever else, I would not let him see me cowed.

Stopping a few feet away, Lord Shaine said, "Tell me, Mistress Merys, did you notice the preparations in the hall downstairs?"

Wondering what he was driving at, I replied, "I did."

"It so happens that tonight three of the neighboring lords and their families are dining here. Families, I might add, that include sons who are of an age to marry my daughter. Do you see?"

Indeed I did, and I began to comprehend his predicament. Probably he had not mentioned it to Auren because of her tendency to become over-excited by things. Although I knew little of managing a great house such as his, I did know that a steward was certainly necessary to coordinate such an important event. Still, as much trouble as it would cause, Dorus needed to go.

"I understand, my lord. But do you not think that for one evening Merime and Ourrel might manage things between them?"

Scowling, he replied, "And after that, what? Do you have any idea how difficult it is to find a competent steward? Dorus has been with my family for more than twenty years. And I'm supposed to dismiss him based on hearsay from two of my slaves?"

"I am not your slave!" The words tore themselves from me before I even knew I was going to say them. Aghast, I looked away from him. What he would do in response to such effrontery I could only imagine. He would certainly be in his rights to strike me, or order me whipped for that kind of insolence.

He did neither. Instead, he watched me narrowly, and asked, "Were you not sold in the markets of Myalme? Did my steward not bring you here as my property?"

"I will admit that I was kidnapped from Aunde, in my homeland," I retorted. "And money exchanged hands for my person. So by your barbaric laws, perhaps that makes me a slave. But I was not born a slave, and I still do not think of myself as one. I doubt I ever will."

"Think what you like," he said. "But that doesn't change your status here in Seldd."

"As you say, my lord." Even as I said the words, I was surprised by my boldness. I had no idea why this streak of defiance had suddenly chosen to manifest itself, save that I suddenly realized how weary I was of knowing I was not free to leave this place whenever I chose, or that people such as Raifal and myself had no rights under Selddish law. It had been foolish for me to try to save him. There was nothing I could do for either of us.

"And if I dismiss Dorus, what then?" Lord Shaine asked suddenly, startling me. "Would you offer to assist Merime and Ourrel? Do you know anything of how a great house is run?"

I stared at him for moment, hardly comprehending what it was he had just suggested. Then I said, "I'm afraid I do not, my lord. But I am a quick learner."

"Why does that not surprise me?" He regarded me for a moment, and I found myself wondering exactly how it was he had broken his nose. Certainly if I had had the task of setting it, I would have done a much better job. But oddly enough, I found that I liked its off-center appearance. It gave his face a character I found interesting.

"You won't regret this, my lord," I said then, for I could see the concern begin to creep over his features.

"Oh, I think I will regret it a good deal, Merys."

It was the first time I had ever heard him call me by my given name without the title of "Mistress" preceding it. I decided to take the new informality as a good sign.

"However," he went on, "neither will I condone that sort of behavior in my house. There have been…rumors…over the years, but no one ever had the courage to accuse him directly."

"You knew?" I asked, feeling the anger begin to rise in me once again.

"I said there were rumors. Nothing definite, nothing brought directly to my attention. I do nothing without good reason, Merys. That includes dismissing a long-time servitor without evidence or cause."

"But you will do it now," I said, my tone firm, unquestioning.

"But I will do it now." He looked away from me then, as he watched the flames in the hearth leap for a space. "For some odd reason, I trust you. I don't believe that you would have come to me with this if you hadn't been certain."

"Oh, I was certain," I said, and shivered a bit. Unfortunately, I had seen this sort of thing before, although the last time was at the household of a baron in my own kingdom, and the victim a girl barely twelve years old. The horror of that situation had compounded itself when the girl found herself pregnant and tried to get rid of the child herself. I had been able to keep her from bleeding to death, but I knew that she would never bear another child. Whether that was a blessing or not, I would never know. As soon as she was well, the girl had been sent on to another household, and the entire scandal hushed up. The situation had sickened me, as it would have anyone with the slightest sensibilities, but since the girl had been removed from her predator, there had been very little else I could do.

But seeing it here once again, and with no chance of saving Raifal but ridding Lord Shaine's household of Dorus, I had known what must be done. That Lord Shaine was man enough to remedy the situation without blaming the boy or even me for being the bearer of bad news spoke volumes about who he was, and he was raised in my estimation all the more for doing so.

His keen eyes had apparently caught my shudder, for he asked, his tone gentler this time, "You have seen this sort of thing before?"

"Yes, my lord. A girl of twelve. She conceived a child and tried to rid herself of it. She almost died."

"Thank the gods at least we did not have that to contend with here," he said, and his tone sounded very weary. Then he went on, "It appears we have much to do. Send Ourrel to me. I will have him fetch Dorus. Probably it is better that he know as little of your role in this as possible."

"Thank you, my lord," I replied, thinking of Dorus' narrow dark eyes and the evil glance he had given Elissa and me when he had first seen us in Myalme. At the time I had worried merely that he had unwholesome designs on either or the both of us. Now I thought perhaps it was a dislike of the female sex that had made him look upon us so unfavorably.

"And after you have done that, see if you can round up my daughter and that decorative but not very useful lady's maid you suggested for her." His eyes caught mine, and this time his expression was rueful and a bit amused. "We have a feast to prepare for."

"Yes, my lord," I said, with a completely uncharacteristic meekness. Then I gave him a small curtsey and fled the chamber, all too aware of his keen gaze following me as I left the room. Still, I felt triumphant as I descended the stairs in search of Ourrel. If nothing else, at least this was one matter in which I had persuaded Lord Shaine to see my side. Perhaps, in time, I could make him see how wrong my presence here was, and how it would be better for him to free me.

Now if only I could push away the pang of sadness that thought caused, for in my tenure here, I had grown attached to so many of them: Auren and Elissa, Merime, even the overly correct Ourrel and the enigmatic Lord Shaine. I guessed it was simply because I had spent more time here than almost any other location since the time I'd left the training house of the Order to make my way in the world. It was normal that I should form such attachments…which was why we were told never to stay more than a month or so in each place. Otherwise, we would feel overly responsible for our charges, and not have the strength of will to move on to wherever we were needed.

At least, that was what I told myself.

CHAPTER FIVE

I NEVER KNEW EXACTLY what transpired between Dorus and Lord Shaine. But within an hour of my own conversation with his lordship, the steward had left the castle, taking with him a good riding horse from the stables and leaving behind a swirl of rumors and speculation. For my own part, I was merely glad that the furor of preparations for the evening's festivities kept me safely away so there would be no possibility of crossing paths with the villain.

Merime had the kitchens well enough in hand, and Ourrel stepped in to oversee the final decoration of the hall, but Elissa was definitely over-matched by the strong-willed Auren, who was none too happy to learn at such a late date that her future husband might be arriving in the next few hours.

"What was Father thinking?" she fumed, leaning on her crutch as she watched Elissa pull a variety of gowns from the wardrobe. "Why now? Look at me!"

I assumed she meant the crutch, which she still needed to help her get up the stairs or over the rougher patches in the gardens. Indoors she could do well enough without it, but I feared pointing out that fact would not meet with a particularly favorable reception at the moment.

"Perhaps he was trying to be accommodating to the other families," I suggested. "There could be snow any day now."

"How do you know?" she asked scornfully. "Can you smell it?"

In fact, I almost could. Although I was hundreds of miles from my own homeland, I had done enough outdoor traveling through all seasons to feel the change in the air, to sense the shift in wind currents—indeed, Auren's deprecating words notwithstanding—to smell the increasing dampness in the atmosphere.

"What about this one?" Elissa asked, a note of desperation in her voice. She held up a lovely high-waisted gown of deep blue, its neckline and detachable sleeves covered in a twining pattern of leaves and flowers.

"Blue makes me look sick," Auren replied, her scowl deepening.

I wondered why she had the dress at all, if she disliked the color so much, but now was not the time for argument. Giving a quick glance at the time-marker candle that burned steadily on the girl's dresser, I saw we had little more than an hour to get her ready by the time Lord Shaine had specified.

With a small shake of my head, I stepped past Elissa and began taking inventory of the contents of the wardrobe. Auren actually owned a fairly impressive collection of gowns for a girl her age, although I would never have known that from the way she dressed on a daily basis. I wondered at the variety, then speculated perhaps her father had begun amassing clothing as part of her dowry.

At any rate, I found a fine damask gown in a warm dark green that would do very well with the girl's honey-colored hair and brown eyes. Lifting it out of the wardrobe, I said, "This one is lovely."

I could tell from the mulish look in Auren's eyes that she wished to contradict me, but instead she gave an exaggerated sigh and said, "Oh, very well."

Elissa and I exchanged a relieved glance, and I handed the gown to the girl, who dropped it over Auren's head and then set about tightening the laces that closed it up the back. The sleeves were separate and tied on with a complicated system of ribbons that required my assistance. I recalled wearing such things in my father's home before I took up the life of a traveling physician, but Elissa, straight from a farm in Aunde, had little experience with such fripperies.

With that task accomplished, I was able to sit back and watch as Elissa went on to dress Auren's hair in a complicated series of braids and coils, all of which she accented with a few brass and cabochon garnet hair combs. When she was done, Auren looked quite elegant and certainly some years older than the fourteen she possessed.

The effect was marred somewhat by the limping steps she took once she arose from her seat, but I hoped Lord Shaine would have the good sense to leave dancing off the evening's entertainments and allow Auren to remain seated. At least that way her prospective suitors would be able to admire her pretty face without the distraction of the limp.

We had agreed that I should escort Auren down to the hall, as at least I had the experience of attending social functions such as this one and could be counted on not to make too many missteps. Also, since I had been brought here with my luggage intact, I actually had a decent gown to wear. It was something I carried with me for the odd cases where I had to attend the wealthy or the titled and my usual brown linen working gown simply wouldn't suit.

Adjusting my steps to Auren's halting ones, I followed her down the stairs. Custom required the lord of the hall to greet his visitors separately, and that was the reason I escorted the girl now, and not her father. As we drew closer, I could hear the sounds of laughter and voices raised in greeting. They echoed in the large chamber, and the contrast with its usual calm was startling. Normally the meals held there were quiet ones; Lord Shaine had no other family besides Auren that I knew of, and it was only in the past few weeks that she had been fit enough to join her father there. Some other members of the household, such as the more senior men-at-arms, took their evening meal in the great hall as well, but still the tone was sedate, especially compared to some of the more boisterous estates I had visited over the years.

At the bottom step Auren paused, then threw a stricken look at me over her shoulder. "There are so many of them," she said slowly. The bravado of earlier had completely disappeared from her tone.

"But you told me yourself that you've met most of them before," I pointed out. "What is there to be frightened of?"

"None of them have seen me since—since—" And she paused, staring down at her injured leg, now safely hidden beneath folds of glinting damask. A look of disgust quickly passed over her features and was gone.

I could understand her dismay. After all, she had been a healthy, vigorous girl, a stranger to serious illness or injury, and now she saw herself as marred forever. The wound was healing, and healing better than even I had hoped, but she would never be as she was before the day she took that tumble from her mount.

"It's all right, Auren," I said gently. "Everyone knows what happened to you, and they all understand. Indeed, I've heard everyone thinks you're quite the remarkable girl to have survived your injury as well as you have."

"They do?"

Heartened by the lift I heard in her voice, I replied, "Yes, they do. And you look so lovely that I'm sure no one will even notice your limp."

She faced forward again, then paused. "But I want to do without this when I enter," she said, and handed me her crutch. "I've been practicing without it. I can make it to my place at the table."

I'd heard that determined tone before and decided it was better not to disagree. Besides, I could keep the crutch with me and give it to her later on in the evening if she required it.

"Very well, my lady," I said. "Now go on. Your father is waiting."

With a lift of her chin, she stepped down from the bottom stair and slowly began to make her way across the hall to the dais at the far end where her father and his guests waited. I could tell from the extreme care with which she walked that the journey was a difficult one, but even to my eyes her limp did not look too pronounced.

Good girl, I thought, then moved my gaze from her laborious progress across the floor to the visitors who awaited her.

They were a varied group, to say the least. Of course I immediately noticed Lord Shaine, who stood several inches taller than anyone else in his immediate vicinity. He looked quite splendid in a high-necked doublet of a dark wine color, with just the slightest traces of embroidery around the collar and the cuffs of his close-fitting sleeves. To his immediate left stood another man who appeared to also be in his early forties or so, but there the resemblance between him and Lord Shaine ended. This man was much shorter and inclined to fat, and for some reason he had chosen a cut velvet doublet in an unfortunate shade of ochre that did little to enhance his ruddy complexion. I guessed the boy who stood by him must be his son; the young man, although probably not even twenty yet, already seemed as inclined to fat as his father.

Frowning slightly, I looked on to the rest of the group, hoping that they would be a little more promising. The second family—for the mother seemed to have come along with this one—certainly had a more appealing mien on first inspection. Both parents at least were fairly slender and inclined to be tall, as was their son, who looked somewhat dashing in a black doublet slashed with red. It was only on closer scrutiny that I noted the son's close-set eyes and the furrow that had already begun to dig its way into his brow, young as he was. Still, one couldn't judge character simply on the ill fortune of having one's eyes set too close together, so I decided to give him the benefit of the doubt and move on.

The last members of the group were a slight but still lovely woman of late middle age, and a young man who seemed the oldest of the three prospective suitors. Probably he was very close to my own twenty-five years. That might have been a problem, save that I had seen girls no older than Auren married off to men twice their age and more. Compatibility never counted as the highest priority, or even a priority at all in many of these cases. Rather, it was simply who made the best offer or presented the best chance for advancement. At least this young man had apparently inherited his mother's good looks. I assumed that was who she was, as they had similar coloring, both dark-haired but with fair skin and even, regular features.

Apparently noticing my inspection of him, the unknown young man shot a dazzling smile in my direction. Caught off-guard, I could feel the color rise in my cheeks, and I looked away quickly. I guessed he had no idea I was in fact one of the slaves. My gown was far too good, and I had had Elissa dress my hair while Auren took her bath. Still, I had not come here to attract attention, and I quickly made my way across the far end of the hall to see if I could offer any help to Merime. Auren was now in her father's hands.

But Merime, surrounded by what seemed to be five times more kitchen slaves than the household normally possessed, brushed me off when I appeared.

"Goodness sakes, no," she said breathlessly, even as she waved a young woman carrying a pair of wine bottles past her and out the kitchen door. "Bring your fine dress in here? And unless I'm mistaken, you've as little experience in roasting a side of venison as I do sewing up wounds. Stay out there, and make sure Lady Auren keeps out of trouble."

With a sigh I nodded and returned to the hall. At least this time I appeared at the opposite end from the place where I had last entered, and my presence was somewhat masked by the arrival of Lord Shaine's senior men-at-arms, the master of the horse, and the falconer, all of whom had status enough to be invited to such an event. Along with them came several tens of people whom I did not recognize but who probably were the retainers of his lordship's guests. Of course they would sit at the lower tables, but at least they helped to fill up the room and make me a little less conspicuous. Possibly I could even take my place among them during the actual dinner portion of the feast, although I was not certain how my presence would be received. Perhaps it would be better if I simply ducked back into the kitchen at the appropriate time and stole a few morsels for myself.

For now, however, I used the shifting crowds to provide concealment as I watched the group on the dais. Quite formally, Lord Shaine had taken Auren by the hand and appeared to be introducing her to all of their guests. Her back was turned, so I couldn't see her face, but I could guess what her expression might be as she greeted the plump lord and his equally chubby son. I assumed that the quelling presence of her father would force to her to maintain at least a semblance of politeness, however.

After she had made her courtesies to all of them, the company took its place at the high table. I could tell, even from this distance, that she had definitely lingered in her greeting to the handsome young lord who had flashed me that brilliant smile. Not that I could blame her. If I had been in the same situation, he most likely would have been the one to whom I pinned my own hopes.

The rest of the crowd took its cues from those at the high table, and all around me people began to seat themselves at the less exalted but equally loaded lower tables. Merime had certainly outdone herself this time. Certainly in my admittedly short tenure at Lord Shaine's estate I had yet to see such a feast produced. I glimpsed roast venison, and partridges and pigeons cunningly displayed with their feathers still attached. Bowls full of tubers sweetly cooked in honey sauce sent a rich aroma into the air, and my stomach growled in response. Best for me to escape into the kitchen now, before anyone noted my anomalous presence in the hall.

Luckily, no one seemed to take notice of me as I slipped back into the kitchen. With most of the servers occupied at the feast outside, Merime's kingdom looked oddly deserted, although the disarray I beheld certainly told its story of the feverish preparations for Lord Shaine's feast.

"Hiding?" the cook asked, as she stepped away from the hearth, where she had been giving the glowing coals a sharp prodding with the poker. "Can't say as I blame you. I'll be glad when all those high and mighty lords take themselves off again."

"It is a lot of extra work, I would imagine," I ventured, feeling oddly guilty, even though I knew that Lord Shaine would never have expected me to work in the kitchens, slave status or no.

"You don't know the half of it," she replied, grimly wiping her hands on her grease-spattered apron. "Still, I don't imagine you came in here to listen to me complain. Looking for a bite?"

"If you have any to spare—"

"Listen to her! 'If you have any to spare'—we'll be feeding the staff for a week on the leftovers from this feast. Pull up one of those stools over there, and I'll see what I can cobble together for you."

What Merime "cobbled together" for me turned out to be sizable indeed. A large portion of pheasant breast, a hunk of venison big enough to feed me for several days, helpings of various side dishes, and a large chunk of her special "sour" bread all appeared as if by magic on an oversized silver plate, which she set down before me with a look of satisfaction. The finishing touch was wine served in one of Lord Shaine's special glass goblets, the ones that normally sat on a high shelf under lock and key.

I felt overwhelmed by her hospitality but recovered myself enough to say, "Thank you, Merime. Certainly I never expected anything so fine."

"You should be having it, though, with what you've done for that girl—and the rest of us." Her broad, pleasant face grew uncharacteristically grim. "No one else would have had the courage to go to himself the way you did. And for ridding us of that adder, I do thank you."

No need for me to ask who the "adder" was. "I only wish I had found out sooner," I said.

"Well, but you noticed at least, which is more than I can say for myself. Sure, that Raifal always had a hangdog look about him, but he's not been a slave overlong. Hadn't had time to get used to it like the rest of us, that's what I thought."

Struck by her remark, I paused with a mouth full of wine and then remembered to swallow. "Can one get used to it?" I inquired.

"That would depend on the person, I suppose." Tilting her head to one side as she regarded me carefully, she went on, "I don't suppose you ever would. You come from the quality, I can tell."

"I'm just a merchant's daughter," I protested.

"There are merchants and merchants," she said equably, "just as there's nobles and nobles. Were you born in a big house? Did you have servants? Did you ever have to worry about where your next meal was coming from?"

"Well," I said, hesitating. Her remarks took me aback. I had never thought much about our own wealth, separated as my family had been from the nobility. But she was correct. We weren't nobility or even gentry, but we had always been more than comfortable, and in fact probably possessed more actual wealth than many who had a title in front of their names. "The house was rather large," I admitted.

"Hmph," was her only response, but I could tell she thought she had scored a point. "Anyhow," she went on, "it's easy enough to tell that you're used to dealing with the quality, whether noble or just rich. Most of us were taken from farming stock. I've been here for twenty years…and most ways it's been a better life than I would have had back home in Farendon."

"How can you say that?" I exclaimed.

"Easy enough. Back home the most I could have had was another farmer's son for a husband, and backbreaking work all day to hold on to a few miserable acres. Here I have my own place, and an important one, too. Freedom?" She sniffed. "What would I do, if someone were to come in to tell me I was free? I'd tell them to get the hell out of my kitchen!"

She told the truth, or at least her own truth. I couldn't argue with her. After all, I knew nothing of the life she'd lived before coming here, and I had seen how much influence she wielded in her small domestic demesne.

"But you—" she said. "Well, you had your own power, of a sort, didn't you? Order of the Golden Palm, woman young as you? No wonder you chafe here like one of Master Breen's new-caught falcons. Lucky we are to have you, that's the gods' own truth, but even I can tell you were meant for grander things than this."

The delicious food suddenly tasted like sand in my mouth. I knew her words to be true. They brought to light the feeling of unease that had underlaid my every waking moment here, ever since I knew Auren would heal and that by rights I should have moved on. But I couldn't. I was as trapped here as one of the falcon master's half-tamed birds.

"They'll come for me," I said, giving the words a firmness I did not precisely feel. "As soon as they know I was taken, they'll send someone to ransom me."

"You think so?"

"They must." *They must*, I thought, *for if I'm left to languish here forever I most certainly will wither and die, like a bloom denied sunlight for too long.* "These things take time, after all. And whoever comes for me must wait for the convenience of a merchant train large enough to avoid capture by the slavers."

"Is your Order so wealthy, then?" Her face expressed nothing but curiosity, but I wondered if I had made a mistake in confiding my hopes of rescue in her.

"Not overly so," I replied cautiously. "But those who are able do give donations to the Order in exchange for our services, and we have many wealthy patrons." Not to mention my own family, I thought then. Surely my father will do whatever he must to see his daughter returned to her homeland.

"Then I will pray to the Goddess that she sees your way safely home," Merime said.

I did not want to tell her the Goddess and I had parted ways some years before. I had followed the path of science and learning, not of faith, but if Merime wanted to believe that her prayers would find a home, then so be it.

Unsure of how to respond, I instead took a few more bites of the excellent food Merime had set before me. "Perhaps I should see how Auren fares out there," I said, after an uncomfortable pause.

"Perhaps you should," she agreed.

Since it would have seemed rude not to eat a bit more, I helped myself to a few more forkfuls of roast pheasant before finally pushing the plate away from me. "That was wonderful, Merime," I said. "Thank you again."

Apparently somewhat mollified, she retrieved my plate and nodded, but her expression was still somewhat guarded. It wasn't the first such reaction I had had from a follower of Inyanna. I could only hope that the goodwill I had built up through my various other works was enough to compensate for my unabashed heresy.

Out in the great hall, the feasting seemed to be winding down. Servers still moved amongst the tables, but it was obvious that most of those attending had eaten their fill and now merely nibbled at the items which had pleased them the most.

At the head table I saw Auren seated at her father's right, and the pinch-faced young man seated in turn at her own right hand. I wondered how he had been accorded the honor of being placed next to her, and thought with a twitch of my lips that perhaps they had had to draw straws to see who would win that exalted position.

I could tell the plump lord was not exactly happy with his son's placement at the far end of the table. Then again, he should have known that one such as his son, even if he proved to be kind-hearted and noble, was not the sort to stir romantic fancies in a young girl. Of course, romance had very little to do with such connections, but it seemed to me Lord Shaine showed a solicitousness toward his daughter that would extend to her choice of a husband. Perhaps she could not have anyone she chose, but at least she would have the final determination as to whom, in the limited pool of those deemed eligible, she would finally wed.

Even as I stepped quietly into an inconspicuous, shadowy corner of the hall, I saw a group of musicians move toward the open area in the center of the room and begin to arrange themselves for the next stage of the evening's entertainments. Silently I thanked Lord Shaine for his cleverness. With the musicians placed so, there would be no question of dancing. In accordance with his wishes apparently, the first song was an old ballad, sweet and sad, but certainly not lively enough to invite tapping feet or thoughts of dance.

I listened to the tune, common enough in my own land as well—though with slightly different wording, and a different language, of course—and thought of how two lands could be at once so different and so similar. The climate here differed little from that of my homeland, although the situation of Lord Shaine's estate not far from the foothills of the Opal Mountains made for conditions a little more chilly and damp than at home in Lystare. Dress and other manners, again, were not so dissimilar. Perhaps they were a bit plainer here in Seldd, but certainly not so exotic as to invite comment.

Yet of course a huge difference existed between the two countries. Slavery had not existed in Farendon for hundreds of years; Seldd was the last holdout on the continent in clinging to the barbaric custom. Pressure from its neighbors had not altered Selddish policy, and that seemed unlikely to change any time in the near future.

I thought then on Merime's words regarding the Goddess. Like me, the cook was a native of Farendon, and apparently had kept her native religion all this time...although, to be truthful, I couldn't see much difference between what was believed in Seldd and in my own land. Names differed slightly, and the myths that had sprung up around the gods had changed a bit with their migration across the continent, but the pantheon remained mostly intact. For myself, what I had grown up believing and what I had come to think as an adult were two entirely different matters. During our training, no one had tried to persuade any of us acolytes that belief in Inyanna; or Thrane, lord of the land beyond death; or even Mardon, ruler of the heavens and the sunset and dawn, was mistaken. Instead, through study of the body, and the application of scientific principles—and learning as well of the beliefs of other lands, such as Eredor and the Sirlende—I came to believe, as many of my Order did as well, that as frail mortals we could not possibly begin to understand the true powers which controlled our world. We gave them names and demesnes in order to make them more human, but who...or what...had caused the world to come into being and ordered the kingdoms of plant and animal surely was as far beyond our comprehension as we were beyond the understanding of the insects that crawled beneath our feet.

Lost in thought as I was, I did not immediately notice a lull in the music. At the high table the players shifted a bit. Lord Shaine stood, and his other guests took that as a cue to rise from their seats as well, although I noticed Auren remained seated.

The door to the kitchen banged open, and two young slaves I did not know emerged, carrying a huge iced cake on what looked like an impromptu stretcher. They took it to a side table that already groaned with various sweetmeats and fruits, along with heaping bowls of nuts. Obviously the dessert course was upon us.

I tried to shrink back further into the shadows, but my efforts apparently were in vain. To my dismay, I saw the handsome young lord disengage himself from the group at the high table and move in my direction, purpose evident in every step.

To attempt to flee at this point would be too obvious. Instead, I held my ground and fixed what I hoped was a neutral and correct expression on my face. Perhaps I was wrong. Perhaps I flattered myself in thinking I was the reason he left the group at the high table and headed toward the back of the hall.

But no. Even as I tried to think of a good way to make my escape, he paused a few feet away from me and gave me another one of those dazzling smiles.

"It would require a darker corner than this one to hide you, I think," he said, speaking in fluent if heavily accented common.

"My lord?" I replied, trying to keep both my expression and my voice bland.

Apparently undeterred, he went on, "I could not help but ask Lord Shaine who that glorious creature in the wine-colored gown was. Imagine my surprise in learning that you were one of his slaves."

Glorious creature? I didn't know whether to blush a darker wine than my gown or possibly burst out laughing. Still, this was not the first time I had come up against a practiced flirt. Even amongst those who studied to become part of the Order were men who seemed to take pursuit of the fairer sex even more seriously than the pursuit of knowledge.

"That is true, my lord," I said gravely, but I feared that I could not help but let a smile tug at one corner of my mouth.

Unfortunately, he seemed to take that ghost of a smile as encouragement to continue further. "How on earth did you come to be here?"

"Much as any of the other slaves, I fear. Taken in the night and sold in the markets of Myalme."

His fine eyebrows lifted. "And that is all that you share with them, I wager. You're no more like the rest of that—" and he waved a hand to indicate the servers working to clear the tables— "than my matched pair of bays are like a set of draught horses."

Despite myself, I felt the color rise in my cheeks. Although his attention was unwanted and uninvited, it was also flattering. Few women would be completely immune to such words, even though they were highly inappropriate.

"You are too kind," I said, lifting my eyes to meet his, "but I fear I have no more status than any of the rest of them. Once, perhaps, things were different, but—" I spread my hands in a helpless gesture, and I could see his gaze sharpen as he caught the tattoo on my left palm.

"So you're the one who doctored Lady Auren?" he asked, and I nodded. "We had heard of you, but somehow I had envisioned you as some old crone dispensing salves and poultices."

I wasn't sure what offended me more—the use of the term "crone" or the thought that a physician of the Order was good for no more than mustard packs on rheumy chests or lotions for stinging nettles. "It is true that I am still young for my work," I admitted, once I was certain my voice would not reveal how his words had infuriated me, "but the Order would not have granted me the status of a traveling doctor if I were not ready for it."

"Of course not," he said quickly, and I wondered if I had let some betraying anger creep into my face.

"Ill luck brought the slavers to the village where I had been working, but ill fortune turned to providence, as otherwise I would not have been here to take care of Auren." I realized as I said the words that I should have referred to her as "Lady Auren," but he appeared not to hear the slip.

"By all accounts you've done a marvelous job," he offered. "Her limp is hardly noticeable."

I looked past him to the head table, where Auren still sat. She laughed at something the pinch-nosed boy next to her said, and I decided I must revise my opinion of him somewhat. Surely Auren would not find him so amusing if he were at all tedious and mean-spirited. Certainly he was closer to her in age than either of the other two, and that counted for much.

He followed my gaze, then looked back at me with a knowing smile. "I am remiss," he said. "I have not yet introduced myself. I am Lord Arnad of Sleane. And you are?"

"Merys Thranion…lately of Lystare," I added.

"Lady Auren seems to have made a great impression on my young Lord Larol—and he on her."

"Disappointed?" I asked, even though I knew I skirted the bounds of propriety with such a question.

"Hardly. One must follow the forms, but I had no great interest in joining my fortunes to Lady Auren's, considerable though hers might be." His voice softened, becoming uncomfortably intimate. "My tastes run to more…mature women."

Again the flush rose in my cheeks, and I wondered what on earth I could do to remove myself before the situation became even more compromising. I tried to tell myself that most of these strangers surely had no idea of my true status here—in my wool velvet gown with its embroidered bands at the neck and hem, the fine linen of my shift showing through the slashed sleeves, I must have looked no more a slave than the rest of them. Still, whatever Lord Arnad's intentions, they couldn't possibly be honorable, and handsome as he might be, that sort of dalliance was certainly the last thing on my mind.

I hardened my tone to the sort of brittle flippancy I had heard my older sister use on unwanted suitors. "Indeed? Well, that must be welcome news to all the spinsters in the area."

For a second he just stared at me, as if not truly comprehending my words. Then he gave a laugh, if a somewhat forced-sounding one. "Indeed." One muscle along his jaw tightened, and I could see his eyes narrow a bit, as if he were thinking something over. "Do you weary of this place?"

"My lord?" I could only pray that the tendril of fear which had begun to trail its way up my spine had not found its way into my voice. I wasn't sure what he was thinking, but I had a feeling it would not be much to my liking.

"Come with me," he ordered, as he gripped one of my arms and began to pull me through the crowd.

Wrenching myself from his grasp was out of the question. He was a lord, and I was a slave, and even if I still had been an independent member of my Order, I had no idea what protocol required in a situation such as this. Instead, I quickened my pace to keep up with him, moving to his side so that it at least would appear that I walked beside him and wasn't being dragged along like some chattel.

He paused in front of the dais, dropping his hand from my arm. Lord Shaine lifted surprised eyes to the two of us, his gaze resting on me for a second. Around him the other nobles halted in their conversations as well. Auren frowned, a forkful of Merime's spice cake lifted halfway to her lips.

"Lord Shaine!" Arnad called out, and I winced. Must his voice be so clear, so carrying?

"Yes, Lord Arnad?"

I felt suddenly as if every eye in the hall was fixed upon us. I could not meet Lord Shaine's gaze but instead looked off at some neutral spot on the wall. Whatever Lord Arnad was planning, I knew I would not like it.

Taking a breath, Arnad announced, "I would buy this slave from you, my lord!"

CHAPTER SIX

For the longest moment, silence reigned in the hall. I felt it ringing in my ears.

Then the awful quiet was broken by Lord Shaine's mild tones. "I am afraid, Lord Arnad, that she is not for sale."

Arnad made an impatient gesture. "She has rendered her services here, Lord Shaine, and your daughter now thrives. I have need of her skills on my own estate. Shall we say five thousand *renads*?

From somewhere behind me I heard a gasp, but of course I dared not turn to see who had made the startled sound. Five thousand *renads*? I knew Shaine had paid barely that sum for all five of us captives from Aunde, and we had fetched a good price, according to the whispers of the other slaves. An odd pecking order existed amongst the workers on the estate, based not solely on one's duties but also on how much one had cost.

Lord Shaine's expression did not flicker, although I noticed that Auren had given him the briefest worried glance, as if she were uncertain as to how he would react to such a proposal. "As I said already, she is not available—at any price." He didn't even look at me, but instead kept his gaze fixed on Lord Arnad.

I could feel the watching eyes of the hall fasten on Arnad and myself as we made our odd tableau before the high table. Never before had I been the center of so much unwanted attention, and the blood slowly rose in my cheeks, although I tried to stand as still as possible and keep my face as expressionless as Lord Shaine's. How I wished that I stood next to him, instead of here next to Arnad. Our proximity, I feared, would make it seem as if I were in agreement with his preposterous proposal. I did not wish for anyone to think I had a hand in his offer or wished to go with him.

The tension seemed to radiate off him in waves. I had no idea why he had fixated on me. Perhaps it was merely because I presented a novelty. Now, however, I got the distinct impression that this developing contest of wills between him and Lord Shaine had very little to do with me.

"Lord Shaine," Arnad said, and although his voice remained pleasant enough, the tightness of his mouth belied the even tone of his words, "I am offering you a fortune. Surely she can be replaced easily enough."

"And I am not in need of a fortune, being already in possession of one." Deliberately, Lord Shaine lifted a flagon of wine and poured a good measure into a pewter goblet. Then he raised it toward Arnad, offering it to him. "Come now, my lord. Have a drink, and let us forget this foolishness."

"Foolishness?" Arnad's eyes narrowed, and he said cuttingly, "I think you forget yourself, Shaine."

The dropping of the honorific was not lost on me…nor on its target. The merest shadow of a frown passed over Lord Shaine's features, but he remained calm. Instead, he looked over at me and said briefly, "Perhaps it would be best if you retired for the evening, Merys."

Relieved beyond measure that he had offered me a way out of the awkward situation, I lowered my head and replied, "As you wish, my lord." Not daring to risk a glance at Arnad, I gathered up my skirts and fled toward the entrance to the tower. All around me people backed out of the way, staring at me as if I were some sort of legendary monster that had been dropped in their midst.

At least Arnad made no attempt to stop me. Perhaps he had realized that seizing me in Lord Shaine's hall, in front of so many witnesses, would make an already awkward situation completely untenable. Whatever the reason, I was able to make my escape unmolested. I ran up the stairs, my low indoor shoes slapping on the stone, my breath coming in great heaving gasps. It was not until I had achieved the relative safety of my tower room that I realized how my heart pounded, how the blood throbbed in my face and my throat.

Not knowing what else to do, I sat down on the bed and stared out the narrow window until my breath had calmed itself somewhat. The view was blurred by the bubbled glass, but at least I thought I could see the vaguest glimmer of Taleron, the larger of the two moons, as it made its way up over the foothills to the east. Tears began to burn, unshed, in my eyes, but I blinked them away. Weeping would accomplish nothing. At least I had gotten away before the situation grew any worse.

That thought led me to wonder what further words might have been exchanged after I had gone, but I probably didn't want to know. I was sure that Lord Shaine would eventually gain the upper hand, but what sort of lasting scars might such a confrontation create?

All at once I was reminded of how much a stranger I was here, how little I knew of Lord Shaine and his connections to his neighbors. Had he and Lord Arnad been friends before this? Did Lord Arnad have a reputation for a hot temper and an eye for women? I guessed that was quite possibly so, but no one had thought to give me any warning to stay away from him. Then I shook my head. Blaming others served no useful purpose. How could anyone have guessed that I might have attracted such unwanted attentions from him?

Slowly I felt my body begin to still, the blood cool in my cheeks. Much as I would have liked to discard the heavy gown I wore and take my hair down from its uncomfortable pins, I thought it better to wait. The evening was still in its youth, and perhaps I would be needed after the guests had gone.

To keep myself from going mad with waiting, I retrieved some neglected darning from the low side table Elissa and I shared for various oddments. Then I lit a second candle with the one I had left burning against my return, and set to work.

Somehow the simple task allowed me to focus my thoughts elsewhere than the ugly little scene I had just left. My tower room floated far enough above the hall that I could simply shut it and its occupants aside. No doubt at some point I would have to face the consequences of what had happened, but for now I was content to sit in the candlelit confines of my chamber and think of simple things. I needed to beg some time from Merime in the kitchen to make more of my valerian salve against the onset of winter chilblains. At some point I would need permission from Lord Shaine to go out and gather various herbs that must be harvested before the onset of winter rendered them unavailable for months. And I had noticed that the castle's store of soap was woefully inadequate.

So I went on, thinking of various simple problems and their solutions, until finally the door to my chamber opened, and Elissa looked in, somewhat fearfully.

"Oh, you haven't gone to bed," she said. Relief was evident in her tone.

"No, I thought I should wait in case either you or Auren had need of me." I laid the darning aside.

"Lady Auren's already in her bed," Elissa said. "Quite a night she had of it, what with being betrothed and all."

I closed my eyes in a brief silent prayer of thanks. At least Arnad's demands hadn't interfered with what had been, after all, the principal reason for the feast.

"So, she and—?" I paused, for I couldn't recall the name of the young lord who had been seated next to her at dinner, and I had never heard the plump lordling's name mentioned at all.

"Young Lord Larol," Elissa supplied. "I heard from the other slaves that that's what they expected. They're of the same age and have known each other all their lives. Besides, what girl could really be interested in Lord Noren, after all, and Lord Arnad—" There she paused, and her flush was apparent even in the gold-tinted candlelight.

"Well, then," I said. "I'm pleased to hear that everything managed to work itself out."

"More or less, mistress," she agreed, her tone uncertain. "Oh, but what a row Lord Arnad and Lord Shaine had—not shouting, you know, the way my ma and da used to, but still."

Wearily, I asked, "So what happened?"

"Oh, they exchanged a few more words, and then Lord Arnad decided to leave in a huff, and took all his slaves and retainers with him. Word is in the kitchens that Lord Arnad has always had too high an opinion of himself—although I have to say he is very handsome—and Lord Shaine never had much use for him."

Then at least I hadn't caused a rift in a long-standing friendship. I had seen Arnad's type before, young men born to wealth and privilege and gifted with pleasing countenances, men who thought that everyone and everything should bow their way. This was the first time I had been at odds with such a man, however, and I fervently hoped it would be the last.

Hesitating for a moment, Elissa looked away from me, then said, "But his lordship would like to speak with you."

"His lordship?" I echoed, and the worry that I'd thought I had dispelled began to wash over me once more.

"In his study. Now." A frown creased her pretty brow, and she added impulsively, "I'm sure it's nothing, mistress! Perhaps he just wanted to make sure you were all right."

Hardly the sort of concern a master would afford his slave, I thought, but I didn't bother to protest. Feeling even more drained, I stood and said, "Well, I suppose I shall see soon enough."

There being little else for her to say, she stood in mute worry as I passed her by and descended the two flights of steps to Lord Shaine's study. I knocked, even as I said, "My lord? It's Merys."

This time I did not receive the usual command to enter. Instead, the door opened after the space of a few heartbeats, and Lord Shaine stood there, unsmiling. "Come in," he said, and turned, leaving me to follow him after I had shut the door behind me.

Two chairs had been pulled up to the low-burning fire in the hearth. He indicated that I should take one, and I sat, feeling distinctly uneasy. It did not help matters that he remained standing.

His were not the actions of a man toward his slave. How many of the other household servants had ever been seated in his presence? I shot him a quick, sideways glance, but once again I could not read his expression.

Not knowing what to say, I sat silently and waited. He gathered up a filled wine goblet and handed it to me. "You look as if you could use this," he said.

I knew I could not protest. Instead, I took the goblet from him and allowed myself a few sips.

"Rather an interesting scene, didn't you think?" he asked suddenly, turning and fixing me with a sudden gaze. I had a sudden thought of one of Master Golan's beetles back at the Order's examination room, skewered to a bit of parchment with a pin.

Still, I did not want Lord Shaine to see me cowed. "It depends on how one defines 'interesting,' I think," I replied, and sipped at my wine once more.

"Perhaps 'uncomfortable' is a better word," he said. Then he lifted his own goblet to his lips and drank, more deeply than I had of my own wine.

"My apologies, my lord, for any disruption of the evening, but truly I had no hand in the matter. Lord Arnad acted quite—" I paused for a moment, searching for the right word— "precipitately."

The straight, wide-set brows dropped a bit as he considered. "That one will do, I suppose. And although I was able to fend off that 'precipitate' young man, it was not done without inviting the attention of everyone in the hall, as well as his 'ill regard'—his words, not mine. But of course you were not there for the conclusion of the scene, were you?"

"No, my lord, having left upon your counsel." Now I could sense his anger; he was a man who kept his emotions in check for the most part, but in this matter the control had slipped just enough for me to see the rage beneath it. "I did nothing to invite his attentions, Lord Shaine. Indeed, if I had known that he was the sort to thrust those attentions upon the nearest halfway appealing female, I should have taken greater care to stay out of the great hall."

"Indeed," he said. "And now I have to contend with the questions and the rumors—why on earth would Lord Shaine not consent to sell one slave, when offered such a ridiculous price for her? Could it be that he has some greater reason for keeping her than merely as a nursemaid for his daughter?"

Head bowed, I stared down into my goblet, gazing into the deep garnet-colored liquid as if I could find answers there. These were the questions I had dared not ask myself. Truly, if I were no more than a slave to him, then why would he have cared whether I left his household or not? But I had never gotten the slightest hint that he had any more regard for me than as the one who had saved his daughter's life.

During my time at the estate, I had gleaned as much as I could regarding his lordship's history, not that there was any more to it than the same sad story I had heard many times before. The marriage had been arranged, of course, but he and his young wife had apparently cared for one another. She suffered a miscarriage. Then she gave birth to Auren, and all seemed well. True, an unmarried girl could not inherit, but they would find her a strong husband, and the estates would be safe. Besides, plenty of time remained for Auren to have many brothers. A boy was born, a boy who died when only five days old. Then another boy. Sickly, he barely lived for three months, and perished, chest heaving and face blue from what I guessed must have been a malformed heart. The third son lived only a few hours, and this time he took his mother with him in death.

Lord Shaine never remarried. No one knew whether it was because he had loved his wife so much that he could bear to see no other in her place, or because he dared not risk seeing the death of yet another child. Auren had always been a vigorous and active girl, and obviously Lord Shaine had pinned all his hopes on her. No wonder he had been so desperate when she was injured. The loss of his only remaining child surely would have been incalculable. Some whispered that he was unwise in his adamant refusal to remarry, for he was cousin to the king, and as such should have been more concerned with furthering his bloodline. Perhaps, but I could not find it in my heart to condemn him for his choice.

I opened my mouth to speak, but he held up his hand.

"Let me set your mind at rest, Mistress Merys." Once again he sounded very formal. "My concern for you is only what I would have for someone who most certainly saved my daughter's life...and also for a well-born, educated woman who deserves better than to be the latest toy for Lord Arnad's bed."

Startled, I stared at him, unable for a moment to find any words. Oh, I had been fairly certain of Arnad's intentions, but to hear them spoken of so openly—

Lord Shaine must have noticed my shocked expression, for his mouth pulled into a grim smile even as he said, "I had assumed you were a woman of the world. How could you not be, if you have truly spent the last few years traveling and seeing all manner of human disease and injury?"

I made a dismissive gesture. Of course he was correct. Sheltered I certainly was not, and although I had never experienced the act myself, I knew everything about relations between women and men...as well as everything that resulted from such relations, from childbirth to the pox.

"You were not mistaken, Lord Shaine," I said at length, knowing he expected some sort of reply. "It is true that as a physician there is very little I have not seen over the years. Please forgive me if I seemed at all shocked or surprised by what you said. I know you were only trying to protect me."

That statement seemed to mollify him, as I had hoped it would. He took another sip of his wine—a smaller one this time. "Luckily, Lord Arnad's temper is as changeable as it is quick. I have no doubt that by this same time next week he will have found something else to rouse his ire, or his interest." Lord Shaine watched me closely, but this time with a slightly amused crinkle at the corner of his eyes. "If he doesn't lay siege to my castle within the next few days, I will consider us safely past this crisis."

I could tell he did not mean for me to take him seriously, so I ventured a fleeting smile. "I am very sorry, my lord, if any of this upset Auren—"

He shook his head. "I believe she was more worried for you. It seems she's formed quite an attachment over this past month." His expression darkened somewhat, and he added, "That is yet another reason why I would not willingly see you go from this place."

"I have no intention of doing so, my lord," I replied, feeling a liar even as I said the words. Truly, I would not have gone with Lord Arnad of my own accord, but I still hoped and prayed that someone would come soon to secure my freedom.

"Very good, Merys." For a brief moment he looked abstracted, his gaze far away from the genteelly shabby room, and then he said, "I just wanted to make sure you understood why I handled the situation as I did."

"I do, my lord. And I thank you once again."

"Then that is all. You must be weary."

"Yes, my lord." I bowed my head, and then turned to go. But even as I made my way to the door, I caught him looking at me with a slightly baffled gaze, as if he had possibly meant to say more but somehow hadn't quite managed to do so.

What he had desired to say, I wasn't sure and perhaps didn't want to know. All I did know was that I had managed to survive another encounter with him with both my dignity and my position intact. I could only hope that in the coming weeks there would be nothing else to mar the fragile understanding which had come to grow between us.

Not long afterward, winter closed in upon Donnishold. An early snow howled down past the shoulders of the Opal Mountains, enclosing Lord Shaine's estate in its icy grip. The wind seemed to find its way in through new chinks in the ancient stone walls and around the warped wood that enclosed the much later-period glass windows with which the castle had been fitted. I recalled that when I had been a young girl I had thought a castle a most romantic place to live, especially when contrasted with my father's handsome but oh-so-prosaic townhouse of modern construction. But now, having experienced the discomfort of a castle, I recalled with some fondness the stout wooden floors, the tightly glazed windows, and the hypocaust of my family home.

"It heated the floors?" Auren asked in some astonishment one day, after I had rubbed my chapped hands for what seemed like the hundredth time and made an unkind comment about the heating arrangements in her father's castle.

"Yes, and the walls on the ground floor. One could sit comfortably without having to be wrapped in shawls and cloaks."

We all sat in her chamber, Auren and Elissa and I. At least she had a hearth, whereas Elissa's and my chilly room could be heated only by a brazier. And having three bodies in such a small space also did much to help ward off the drafts.

My handiness with a needle had been put to good use in assisting with Auren's wedding gown. One of the other household slaves whose talents lay in such areas had already draped the glinting gold-threaded damask over her and cut out the basic pieces, but it fell to me to embroider the traditional musk roses over the bodice and the full detached sleeves. I held one of those sleeves now, and was glad of the extra layer of warm fabric draped across my lap.

"No wonder you complain of the cold so. Although," she added slyly, "one would think that someone who has to travel to treat sick people all the time would be better able to live with it."

"I can bear it, if I must," I replied calmly. "But that doesn't mean I enjoy it."

Auren stared back at me for a moment, dark eyes wide, and then she began to giggle. I noticed that she laughed more readily these days, and more and more she walked about the house and the grounds without the aid of her crutch. She looked forward to the summer, when her betrothed would come to her here and take his place at her side. Since he was a younger son, and she an only daughter, he would become the heir to Lord Shaine's estates and take on the family name. That was how these things were managed in Seldd, so the line would always continue unbroken.

I was just gladdened to see her nearly healed and light of heart. Certainly the dark weather had done nothing to dampen her spirits. I only wished I could have said the same for myself.

With winter upon us, my chances of any sort of rescue before the spring thaw began to seem more and more remote. Of course some limited trade continued through the winter months, but those who didn't have to travel chose the wiser course and stayed home whenever possible. Perhaps someone from my Order could bribe a merchant and his train to make the perilous journey into Seldd at the time of the snows… perhaps not. I supposed that it would depend greatly on how valuable they deemed me.

Lord Shaine did not allow his slaves to sit idle through the winter months, although the flax had been harvested and the vegetable gardens gleaned of all they could produce before the first frosts descended. Beyond the slaves' quarters sat three long, low buildings in which the flax was processed and then woven into fine cloth that would be taken to market once the snows had melted. Recently he had expanded this enterprise into dyeing the cloth as well, and on days when the snow held off, I could see the lengths of fabric drying on numerous ropes stretched between the buildings. The lively shades of blue, green, red, ochre, and amber were bright notes against the muddy snow, incongruous gleams of color in an otherwise dull landscape.

Again I found myself impressed by Lord Shaine and his clear mind. All around us the world was changing, slowly but certainly. More and more people came to the cities, to work in the new iron foundries and factories where all sorts of goods were being produced: pottery, furniture, wagons, textiles, tools—the list was endless. In a way, his lordship had created his own factory here, where he could directly profit from the production of the fine linen for which Seldd was known. Apparently he was the first of the local lords to attempt such an undertaking, but I had seen several of them (although thankfully not Lord Arnad) come to visit the estate and tour the facilities here.

That hotheaded lord had taken himself off in a huff. Word trickled back to us that in an act of retaliation he had apparently hired Dorus as his new steward, but although this news produced in me a vague uneasiness, I could not think how Dorus' new position would make a difference to those of us who remained at Lord Shaine's estate. No doubt the erstwhile steward had been privy to some of his lordship's private matters, but that was a matter of concern to Lord Shaine, not me. And of course I worried for the slaves at Lord Arnad's estate, for I did not think it would take long before Dorus' old habits reasserted themselves. I was also fairly certain Lord Arnad would not champion their rights the way Lord Shaine had those of his own servants. Still, there was little I could do about it now, and since Lord Shaine had taken the news in stride, I attempted to do the same as well.

Suddenly restless, I laid my embroidery aside and went to the window. The glass here was of a better quality than that in my own chamber's window, and I had a fine view of the courtyard. The skies had lowered again, and I somehow could sense that snow would begin to fall again very soon. For now the weather held, although it was bitterly cold, so chill I could see the vague mist of my breath as I stood there, looking out through the faintly streaked glass.

Because of the cold, the courtyard was mostly deserted; two men-at-arms huddled in their cloaks near the main gates, and as I watched, I saw one of them stamp his feet against the chill and blow on his gloved hands. Miserable duty, no doubt, and I did not envy them, even though they were free and I was not. Farther off I caught a sudden flicker of color as two slaves strung a length of vivid blue fabric between the dyeing house and one of the weaving buildings. They worked as quickly as possible, bare fingers probably numb in the freezing air. I thought then of how lucky I had been in my reception here, slave status or no. That could have been me, shivering in the cold while performing back-breaking work for no pay but a few meals and a place to lay my head.

Then I saw the men-at-arms suddenly snap to attention. Looking past them, I spied a largish party of men on horseback approaching the castle gates. Numbering ten or so, they led several heavily laden pack animals with them, and they did not appear to be armed beyond the usual short swords any man traveling the roads would carry.

My heart began to pound—foolishly, I knew, because this could just be an ordinary caravan of merchants, chancing travel at this season because of the higher prices they could command. Then again, Lord Shaine's estate was remote. Auren had told me that often they saw no outside visitors save their nearest neighbors for the entire winter. So why these travelers now? Could my rescue finally be upon me?

"What do you see, Merys?" Auren asked, and I turned, hoping that my face would not reveal any betraying excitement.

"It appears that a caravan of merchants is approaching the castle," I replied, trying to keep my tone level, indifferent.

"Really?" She tossed aside the pillowcase she had been embroidering—indifferently, as it was obvious her skills were shaky at best—then hurried over to the window, her limp hardly noticeable in her excitement. I barely had a chance to step aside before she brushed past me, wiping at the foggy window panes so she could gain a better view. She peered out for a moment, then announced, "We should go down to the hall to greet them."

"As you wish," I replied, with a curl of the lip. Perhaps it was her duty as the *de facto* lady of the castle to offer such hospitality. I was more inclined to think she merely desired anything that would break up the mundane routine of her day. Not that I could blame her—the days of inactivity, with only the occasional chilblain or cough to require my skills, had begun to wear on me as well.

Dorus had not yet been replaced. Lord Shaine's personal servant, Ourrel, still supervised the daily routine of the castle, so it was he whom we first encountered when we descended the stairs. Elissa stayed behind, to continue the necessary but tedious darning of Auren's stockings.

Ourrel's dark eyes lighted on Auren and me for a moment, and he inclined his head ever so slightly. "My lady," he said to Auren, "how kind of you to come and greet our visitors."

Brushing the compliment aside, she said breathlessly, "Who are they? What have they brought with them?"

He ignored the rudeness—obviously he was used to the impetuosity of fourteen—and replied, "Traders from Purth, my lady. As to their goods, we are not sure yet. I'm sure they would be more than willing to share that information with you and your father."

As he spoke, I saw Lord Shaine enter the hall from the courtyard. I guessed he had been in the dyeing house and had come in as soon as he received word of his visitors. A few flakes of snow dusted his dark hair and the shoulders of his cloak; the merchant train seemed to have arrived just in time.

As if my thoughts were a summons, they began to make

their way into the hall. My count had been correct: They numbered ten. None of their faces were familiar, and I felt my heart fall. And Ourrel had said they came from Purth, not Farendon. Hoping that my disappointment had not shown on my face, I watched as the leader of the merchant group bowed deeply before Lord Shaine.

He murmured something polite, although I could not make out the words. But the merchant leader bowed once again, then said something to one of the others in his group. That man nodded, and I watched as they opened up one of their packs to reveal lengths of gleaming foreign silks. Another man opened his pack, showing fine pelts: fox, mink, beaver, ermine.

I began to suspect that they must have gotten wind of Auren's upcoming nuptials at some point in their travels, as these were the sorts of luxury goods that even a household such as Lord Shaine's would only purchase in limited quantity. But to further expand the dowry of an only, beloved daughter—

"Goddess," Auren breathed, and her dark eyes glowed as she took in the fabulous contents of the merchants' packs. Without a backward glance toward me, she hurried over to her father's side and laid a hand on one of the mink pelts, a rich glossy brown that would do very well with her honey-colored hair.

A period of good-natured haggling ensued, although I was certain Auren would get the best of Lord Shaine eventually. He smiled down at his daughter, obviously happy in her reflected joy, not paying attention to the lead merchant or the sudden, furtive look the man gave his subordinate.

More quickly that I would have thought possible, the man drew the long knife he wore at his belt and, just as Lord Shaine bent over to more closely inspect the mink pelt his daughter lifted toward him, drove the blade into his side.

CHAPTER SEVEN

I BELIEVE I SCREAMED. I can't remember for sure—I only know that after a heartbeat's-breadth of sickened shock, I moved without hesitation across the stone floor of the hall, even as Ourrel outpaced me on his longer legs.

Until then I hadn't realized that Ourrel always wore as well the short, leaf-bladed sword common to Seldd. He gave a shout and drew it now, and lunged savagely toward the leader of the merchants. The man had barely withdrawn his own knife from between Lord Shaine's ribs before he suffered the same fate he had brought down on his victim. The steward's sword plunged into the man's side, driven deep by Ourrel's headlong rush to succor his lord.

At that point—only a few seconds had passed, but they felt like an eternity—Auren finally realized what was happening and let out a despairing wail. Lord Shaine sank to his knees, hands clutched against his lower ribs as bright blood began to seep out between his fingers.

The leader of the merchants (hired assassins, more likely) staggered backward, a look of surprise etched on his sharp features. Probably he had not expected to meet with any sort of resistance. At the same time men-at-arms crowded into the hall from the courtyard, no doubt drawn by Ourrel's shout. By then I had reached Lord Shaine's side and dropped to my knees beside him, reaching for the fastenings on his doublet as I did so.

Auren continued to keen, arms wrapped tight around herself as she stared down at her father. But I could not waste any attention on her, nor on the clash between the remainder of the so-called merchants and Lord Shaine's men.

The world had shrunk down to just him and me. Fingers racing with desperate speed, I pulled away his bloodied clothing, moving his hand as I did so. "I'm here, my lord," I said. "You must let me see the wound."

His blue eyes were slitted with pain but still lucid. "Is Auren—"

"Auren is fine, my lord. You must let me help you."

He nodded, his face pale and tight with pain.

Once I had his clothing pulled away from the wound, I was better able to see exactly how bad the damage truly was. He bled freely, so I grasped a corner of his linen shirt and tore, pulling loose a strip that I could press down against the knife cut. As far as I could tell, the blade had missed the ribs and slid in just beneath the lung but not caught it. Otherwise, I would have been hard-pressed to save him. Punctured lungs were tricky, and I had never before had the opportunity to attempt to repair one.

Luckily, it did not seem as if things had come to that pass. Without my aid, Lord Shaine would have bled to death, but as it was, I thought I might be able to save him.

Pressing my hand and its makeshift bandage of torn shirt against his wound, I risked a glance over my shoulder at Auren. She stared down at us, eyes huge in her suddenly pale face. Past her I could see Lord Shaine's men-at-arms making quick work of the rest of the merchants, and I gave a brief prayer of thanks to whatever powers might be watching over us that the men had been as quick to respond as they were.

"Auren," I said.

The girl gazed at me vaguely, her eyes not really focusing. I worried that she might be going into shock.

"Auren," I repeated, making my voice louder this time, "you must run up to my chamber and get my satchel of medicines. You know—the dark brown leather bag I keep by the side of my bed?"

She nodded, but somewhat uncertainly.

"Ask Elissa if you can't find it. She'll know where it is. Run!"

That last word finally seemed to penetrate the veil of shock which had wound itself around her, and she grasped her skirts in both hands and ran toward the steps, disappearing up into the tower.

I couldn't waste any more time worrying about her. Lord Shaine reclaimed my attention, and I pressed more firmly against the wound in his side, even though I could tell the pressure pained him. The lines around his eyes tightened for a moment, and the cords in his neck stood out as he swallowed.

Some patients like to know everything about their condition. Others want only reassuring words, no matter how bad it might be. I guessed Lord Shaine was of the first type and said, "It looks to be a clean wound, my lord. He missed the lung, and the bone as well. As soon as I have my kit, I'll sew you back together in no time."

He nodded. "Arnad," he whispered. "Bastard. Stake my life on it."

Haven't you done that already? I thought, but said only, "Time for that later, my lord. Don't try to speak."

His only reply was a scowl, but I knew for the moment at least he would heed my words.

Auren chose that moment to return, closely trailed by an aghast Elissa. Auren thrust my kit at me and asked, "He's not—is he—?"

"He's going to be fine, Auren," I replied, setting the satchel down on the floor and pulling out the bottle of alcohol I had stowed in there a few weeks earlier, along with one of my smaller needles and a length of catgut. Lord Shaine flinched as I cleaned the wound, but he made no sound.

As I worked, I noticed Ourrel come up behind Auren. At his shoulder was Master Marus, chief man-at-arms. Their faces were grim and tight with worry, but I knew the immediate danger was over, both here and for my patient as well. Even as I slid the needle in and out of Lord Shaine's flesh, working as quickly as I could against the ongoing blood loss, the other men-at-arms were at work as well, pulling the bodies of the would-be merchants out of the hall and unceremoniously dumping them in the courtyard.

"How is he?" Marus asked at length. His face seemed a little pale, but he managed to keep from averting his eyes.

"Stop…talking…about me…as…if…I'm…not…here," slurred Lord Shaine. His skin grew whiter by the moment as blood loss and shock combined to bring him closer and closer to unconsciousness.

"He'll survive," I said briskly. "A clean wound, no major organs touched. He's very lucky—or the assassin was incredibly unlucky. Look at it how you will." A few more stitches, and then I was done. I lifted a roll of clean bandages out of my kit and began wrapping them around Lord Shaine's midsection. Soon the line of neat stitching was hidden from view.

"The gods smile on you, my lord," said Marus, and he forced a smile.

Shaine nodded, but I could tell he hadn't the strength to utter any more words.

"He needs to be put to bed," I said. "If you two can assist?"

No one made any comments about being ordered around by one who was, after all, merely a slave. Both Ourrel and Marus knelt down on the blood-stained stone floor and then lifted Lord Shaine's tall form, carrying him out of the great hall and up into the tower. His own sleeping chamber branched out from the study, its door hidden beneath one of the faded tapestries that lined the outer room. Auren ran ahead and yanked the tapestry out of the way as the two men carried him inside, while I hurried past them so I might pull back the heavy embroidered counterpane and other bedding. They laid him down as gently as they could, but I could still hear a hissing sigh of pain escape his lips before he was safely placed against the thick feather mattress.

"He looks dead," Auren whispered, staring down at the limp form of her father.

"But he's not," I retorted. "And I intend to keep him that way. If you could help me with his boots—"

Together we tugged and pulled off his high scarred boots, but since it was so cold, I thought it better to keep his stockings on. I needed to remove the rest of his bloody clothing, but I certainly didn't require an audience for that.

"Thank you," I said, for Ourrel and Marus both stood there awkwardly, as if not sure what to do next. "I can watch him from here. If you could bring up some water?"

Ourrel tore his gaze away from his master's still, white face and said, "Of course. Do you need anything else?"

"At the moment, no," I replied. What Lord Shaine needed now more than anything else was rest. Of course I would remain by his side, to make sure the stitches held and to be there to attend to his needs when he awoke, but Marus and Ourrel had much to do—and Auren needed to be kept safely out of the way.

"See that Lady Auren goes back to her rooms," I went on. "If I need anything, I'll send for it. For now, I just need to make sure he survives the night."

They nodded, but Auren looked down at me with a familiar stubborn expression on her face. "I don't see why I can't stay here with him."

"He needs rest, Auren," I replied. "And I am a physician. It falls on me to watch over him. If he calls for you, I will come and fetch you directly."

She didn't much like my words, that I could tell, but at least she offered no further argument and went meekly enough as Ourrel and Marus herded her out of the room. I could hear the sounds of their footsteps as they departed—Auren's lighter tread as she ran up the stairs to her own chamber, the heavy sound of Ourrel and Marus making their way down to the hall.

What they would do next, I had no idea. If Lord Shaine's half-wild words in the hall were correct, and Lord Arnad had been behind this, then what now? Would Lord Shaine retaliate? The men had been hired thugs, I was almost certain, and how it could ever be proved that Arnad had hired them, I did not know. But this was not the sort of iniquity that could be left unanswered. Wars had been fought over less.

But it was also winter, and war would only come with the arrival of spring. In the meantime, I had Lord Shaine's health to worry about.

He lay motionless, eyes shut, hands still on either side of him, for I had tried to avoid putting any pressure on his wounded torso. I could barely see the rise and fall of the embroidered coverlet above his breast. But he breathed at least. Arnad's plot—if that were truly the reason behind Lord Shaine's injury—had been foiled.

It began to grow dark. The room was unfamiliar to me, but I located a trefoil-design candelabra on the large table that stood against the far wall and lit it from the dying embers of the hearth. Before the fire could sink any lower, I stirred up the coals and added a few more logs from the willow basket which sat to one side of the stone fireplace. Once I had reassured myself that the fire would last a few hours longer, I returned to my seat at Lord Shaine's side.

His color looked a little better, but that could merely have been the reflected glow of the restored fire. I thought of how recently I had held a similar vigil over the sickbed of his daughter. The circumstances then had been very different, however; they had both been strangers to me, and my concern for Auren had been simply the disinterested desire of a physician to see her patient recover.

But now—*now*, I thought, and I sighed. Their faces and voices had become as dear to me as if they were members of my own family. I could not imagine what I would do if my reassuring words proved false, and Lord Shaine did not survive the night. Caught by a sudden impulse, I leaned forward and laid my warm hand on his cold, limp one. The pulse beat still in his wrist. At least I could feel it, weak as it was, and forced myself to take heart from that. Lord Shaine was a vigorous, healthy man of barely forty summers. There was no reason he couldn't live another twenty or thirty, as long as I was here to see that he took no other harm.

I knew I shouldn't be thinking such things. I knew I should be trying to get myself away from here, back to a land I understood, where I was respected and no man's chattel. How on earth could I be considering staying here to watch over Lord Shaine, a man who had survived several decades without any assistance from me?

The answer had been there for some time, even if I had been too foolish to see it. Even in that tense little interview following my run-in with Lord Arnad, somehow I had hoped against hope, wondering whether he would say the words I had longed to hear: *I would not let Lord Arnad take you, for I love you myself and could not bear to see you go.*

What an idiot I was. As if a man of Lord Shaine's importance could ever come to care for someone like me. Even if I were not his slave, even if I had come here of my own volition, as a physician of the Order offering my services, still I had been born humbly, the daughter of a merchant. Oh, occasionally those of the nobility might stoop to marry one such as me, but only if their fortunes had failed and they needed to bolster their sagging finances with an infusion of merchant gold. Lord Shaine did very well for himself and could have had the pick of every eligible young woman in the region, had he desired it. Obviously he wished to expend his energies in other areas. Love was not something that mattered much to him, as far as I could tell.

I felt the strength of his hand, even cold and still as it lay beneath mine. Perhaps this would be the only time I could touch him so, pretending that I had every right in the world to keep my hand on his. If anyone intruded, they would probably just think I touched him to ascertain whether he had a fever or not. No one would ever think I held his hand because I couldn't bear not to.

This was madness. I should fall to my knees right now and pray to the gods—whoever and whatever they might be—to deliver me from this place before I found myself even more lost than I already was. In matters of the heart, I knew myself to be as green as Auren. Oh, once when I was still training at the house of the Order in Lystare, I had found myself attracted to one of the young men there, someone who was a year or two ahead of me and impressively worldly, at least to my unschooled eyes. But the farthest I had ever gotten in the infatuation was a brief kiss in the courtyard of the school before we were found out and threatened with expulsion if such a thing were ever to happen again. The kiss had been pleasant, but certainly not worth risking my future career over, and that had been the end of it.

Once I was out in the world, I had taken care to present myself as aloof, coolly professional, not the sort to be pursued or encourage such attentions. Not that I felt myself to be the sort of woman to attract the undue notice of men, as always I contrasted the strong bones of my face and my unfortunate height with the more conventional prettiness of my sisters. But a woman journeying alone always had to take care, even in Farendon and Purth, where members of the Order were respected and appreciated. I thought I had divorced myself from my heart, but apparently it was not content to be cast aside so coolly.

I looked down at Lord Shaine and wondered if I had done anything yet to betray myself. I didn't think so—I had trained myself in professional courtesy and detachment for so long that, until these past few moments, I had not even understood that what I had merely thought was respect toward a man of intelligence and determination was actually far, far more. But now I knew, it was only a matter of time before I revealed my feelings. And what then?

I could not imagine. At best I could probably hope for a sort of bemused pity, the sort that would lead him to tread carefully around me, and eventually seek to have me removed to a different situation. Perhaps if things got bad enough he would finally regret not allowing Lord Arnad to take me off his hands.

No, that I would never believe. As to what would happen next, once Lord Shaine was well enough to assess the situation and decide what action to take...again, that lay well beyond my scope. I probably had a better education than anyone on the estate, Lord Shaine included, but my only training in war had been the means to treat the wounds it caused.

My studies of Seldd (what I could recall of them, at any rate) had painted a bloody picture of minor squabbles between local lords. The king rarely interfered in these disagreements, preferring to let the matters be solved through strength of arms. So there was a very real chance that once the spring thaws came, Lord Shaine would lead his men against Lord Arnad. If he won, Arnad's lands would be forfeit, and added to Shaine's own holdings. But if he lost—

I tried to tell myself it would not come to that. For one thing, Lord Shaine had just made a valuable ally by betrothing his daughter to the middle son of his neighbors. Lord Larol's father would be duty-bound to add his strength to any conflict between the two other lords, for if Lord Shaine lost, then their own son would also lose his right to marry Auren and one day become chief of Lord Shaine's lands. Besides, although Lord Shaine never seemed to trade on his connection with the king, still it might be a deterrent to open warfare if Lord Arnad lacked sufficient allies. There was also the strong possibility that his involvement in the matter could never be proven, and Lord Shaine would simply have to go on as if nothing had ever happened. It wouldn't be the first time. Bitter feuds had bubbled under the surface for years, only to erupt decades later when someone finally made a misstep and gave an excuse, however slight, for the grievance to be addressed once and for all.

I felt as if I must do something or go mad with all the

thoughts that waged war in my head. Carefully releasing my pressure on Lord Shaine's hand, I stood and made my way over to the window. I stepped carefully so as to avoid making any noise that might disturb him. As it was, I almost tripped over the fringed edge of a rug I had barely noticed in the dimness of the room, but I caught myself in time.

Across the courtyard a bonfire burned in the night, angry orange and yellow flames licking at the darkness. For a second I watched, puzzled, wondering what on earth could be burning. Then I realized it must be the corpses of the false merchants that burned. Of course it was the only practical way to dispose of the bodies now that the ground had frozen solid, but still the sight bothered me. Thugs and killers they might have been, but in Farendon burning was reserved only for the corpses of animals. Even the lowest killer is allowed his place in the sheltering earth. Wintertime funerals were always preceded by a ritual fire burned on the final resting place—both to honor the gods and to soften the earth beneath.

But those dead men would not have such care afforded to them, and I turned away, more troubled than I had thought I would be over the treatment of these would-be killers. I was still young enough to be affected by the indifferent cruelty of men. I hoped that I would never grow so callous or cold that these sorts of things would lose the power to move me. Better to hurt than not to feel at all.

"Merys." Lord Shaine's voice was weak, but clear enough.

Immediately I left my post at the window and went to his side. Looking down, I saw that his eyes were open and lucid enough, though bright with pain. "My lord?"

"Was anyone else harmed?"

"No," I replied. Somehow it did not surprise me that he was concerned for everyone besides himself. "You were the obvious target. But Ourrel and Marus and the rest of your men-at-arms made short work of the intruders."

"Good men," he said, and closed his eyes. When he spoke again, it was without opening them. "So once again you were there to patch up the wounded."

"It's what I do, my lord."

"Still...." A long pause, and then he said, "You are necessary here. You do realize that, don't you?"

Was this his way of rationalizing my enslaved state, or were his words a plea? Had he somehow seen the restiveness beneath my outward calm, realized that it was only a matter of time before I attempted escape through one means or another? Or had he somehow guessed at my feelings, and now tried to find the only words that would keep me here?

"I have done you some service, my lord, that is true." As I spoke I laid my hand across his brow. His skin felt warm to the touch, but not abnormally so. Just as quickly I removed my hand. I did not want him to think that the gesture had been anything more than an attempt to ascertain his temperature.

"Much more than that, Merys, as you well know." He opened his eyes, but instead of looking directly at me, he remained flat on his back, staring up at the stone ceiling. "Sometimes I wonder how we got along without you."

Those words threatened to bring the tears to my own eyes. I blinked and glanced away from him, even though I knew at the moment his attention was not directed toward me. Willing a calm into my voice that I most certainly did not feel, I replied, "But you did—and well enough, from what I can tell. But I'm happy that I could make some difference."

The phrase "...while I was here" floated in my mind even as I made my reply to him, but I hoped Lord Shaine wouldn't notice that my sentence sounded rather unfinished.

Apparently he did not, for he made a slight movement on his pillow and then said, "It pleases me to hear that you are happy. This life has not been too difficult for you?"

In many ways, my life here was easier than it would have been if I had continued to practice my calling in the manner for which I had been trained. Here I slept in the same comfortable bed every night. I always knew I would stay relatively warm and well-fed, and I never had to worry about brigands on the roads. But at the bottom of everything lay the knowledge that I was not free to leave whenever I wished.

I forced a smile and turned back to him. "Not too difficult, my lord. But you should be resting, not talking."

"Doctor's orders?" he asked, and in the dim candlelight I could see a tiny lift at the corner of his mouth.

"Indeed," I replied, my tone as severe as I could make it.

He gave a small chuckle and then winced. I was sure his stitches must have given him a twinge. "Perhaps you're right."

Somehow resisting the urge to reply, "I'm always right," I merely smiled. I began to turn toward the table where I had set the candelabra, but Lord Shaine reached up and caught my hand. Startled, I paused, looking down at him.

"I am glad you are here," he said simply. "Don't ever forget that."

My heart pounded at his touch. Not trusting myself to answer, I gave his hand an answering squeeze, then nodded. He released my fingers, his hand falling limply back onto the bed, as if he had had only the strength for that one small gesture.

But it was enough. I gathered my wits sufficiently to go and blow out the candles; the fire would provide illumination for a while, and what Lord Shaine needed now more than anything else was rest. He had shut his eyes again, and I could see he already drifted in that twilight between sleep and waking. Moving quietly, I stepped to the door and let myself out. Once I had shut it, I laid my cheek against the age-blackened oak for a few seconds, thinking of the man who slept within, feeling still the touch of his hand on mine. He wanted me here, needed me. I realized suddenly that I found myself understanding Merime for the first time.

I, too, had begun to realize that there were some things more important than freedom....

CHAPTER EIGHT

MIDWINTER CAME UPON US QUICKLY. Here in Seldd, the celebration of the ancient holiday did not differ greatly from its observance in my homeland. Merime and her kitchen staff busied themselves in a frenzy of baking and stewing, Ourrel supervised the decoration of the hall with greenery and flowers carefully dried the summer before, and everyone plotted to keep their gifts secret from their chosen recipients. This was no easy task, given the crowded nature of the castle and the way we were forced indoors, day after day, by the inclement weather. Indeed, the snow fell so heavily Auren fretted that her betrothed and his family would be unable to make the journey. Lord Shaine would play host this year, since the estate was to be young Lord Larol's new home in the coming summer.

But come they did, arriving a day early in order to take advantage of a break in the weather. Their arrival sent the household into an even greater uproar, and even I was drafted to help with airing out rarely used chambers and making sure there was sufficient linen to accommodate all of the visitors. They came with a sizable train: Lord Larol, of course; Lord Marten, his father; Lady Yvaine, Larol's mother; a younger sister named Alcia; and a group of ten of their own servants. Of course there was no real need for them to bring so many of their own attendants with them, but I'd had enough experience with the nobles of my own land to know that they continually played games in order to impress others with their wealth and standing. Although Lord Shaine probably knew to a copper *graut* the worth of Lord Marten's estates, it was necessary for Marten's family to appear as important as possible.

By this time Lord Shaine had regained his feet. The wound had taken no infection and healed cleanly, although he had been bedridden for the better part of a week before I deemed it safe enough for him to get up and resume his duties about the castle. No further words of a personal nature had been spoken between us. Indeed, as time wore on, I began to wonder whether those soft words had meant what I thought they had, and whether the touch of his hand on mine had been only a dream.

To be sure, I had had enough to occupy myself during those weeks. In addition to the extra work required to prepare for the Midwinter festival, one of the slaves had broken her ankle when she slipped on the kitchen steps, Elissa had contracted a putrid sore throat, and one of Master Breen's falcons decided to rip open the cheek of the young slave who assisted in the mews. I poulticed and patched and soothed, dispensing medicines when I could and advising bed rest when no other cure presented itself. All were grateful for my care, and indeed they healed better and much more quickly than they would have without my intervention.

Sometimes I thought of Lord Shaine's words to me. Although I knew that all of these minor hurts could have been survived had I not been here, at least I still could provide service, do something to help make these people's lives a little easier. I tried to tell myself that it made no difference whether I plied my trade on Lord Shaine's estate or about the countryside of Farendon. I had been trained to succor the sick, and that I did here.

Auren had improved steadily as well. She looked forward to the feast of Midwinter Night, for she knew her father had hired in a special troupe of musicians to provide dance music; I had advised that I thought she was able to begin dancing once again.

On that one night, master and slave would mingle freely in the great hall and celebrate the closing of the old year and the coming of the new. It had been so in my own home, though of course we had no slaves. But the servants had put aside their cares for that one evening and taken their turns on the dance floor. Even now I recalled the novelty of dancing with the boy who mucked out our stables and the tall young man who was the assistant cook. I didn't know how much things would differ here, but Lord Shaine had made one thing clear: I was to be included in the celebrations.

Elissa and I had plotted together and made a lovely embroidered hood in deep brown wool, trimmed in mink, for Auren. The contents of the false trader's packs had at least been some compensation for the injury they'd done to Lord Shaine, and he gifted me with some of their stores. I took the brown wool and a mink pelt for my gift to Auren. During the winter evenings, Elissa had stitched the fabric and then given it to me for the coiling embroidered design of leaves and flowers I picked out in warm green and copper threads. For Elissa I had embroidered two fine linen handkerchiefs, and for Merime I stitched a handsome new apron in bright blue linen to match her eyes.

I wished to give Lord Shaine a gift but was at a loss as to what would be appropriate. Despite his status, he wore plain, simple clothes. If one hadn't known better, on first sight Ourrel might have been mistaken for the lord of the manor, since he always took care to wear well-tailored doublets picked out with embroidery or elegant trim. I hadn't the means or the opportunity to buy his lordship anything, and that bothered me as well. In the past I had always possessed a fair amount of pocket money. The Order paid me an allowance, and often my patients would give me what they could in exchange for my services, even if it were only a few copper pennies. Because of this I had never wanted for anything I might need—and I always was able to purchase supplies and other necessary items as the need arose. Now, however, matters were quite different.

Telling myself that my lack of funds was of no consequence, I had finally out of desperation decided to give Lord Shaine a fine brooch of chased silver and amber that had ridden around in my satchel for several years. One of my patients had given it to me in payment some time back, but I'd never had the opportunity to wear it, as the piece was a bit bulky and masculine for my taste. At the same time, I hadn't wanted to sell the brooch, and so it had traveled across Farendon with me, securely wrapped in a piece of flannel. Lacking any other more appropriate packaging, I kept it in its flannel but was able to secure a piece of red ribbon to tie around it and make it a bit more festive. Perhaps it would be considered inappropriate for a slave to give her master such an expensive and slightly intimate gift, but I had nothing else to offer.

But now all the preparations were finally complete, and I watched as Auren fairly danced with impatience as we waited in her chamber for the call to join the festivities in the great hall.

"It must be sunset," she said, peering out the window at the gray sky outside. "How could anyone tell, after all?"

"It's not yet the fifth hour of the afternoon," I replied, after giving a quick glance at the hour-marking candle that sat next to her bed. "It will be here soon enough."

She looked lovely, in a gown of warm, dark red that suited her honey-toned coloring. To celebrate her betrothal, Lord Shaine had gifted her with a set of cherry amber and gold jewelry. The blood-tinted cabochons glowed at her throat and in the carefully arranged masses of her hair, beautifully complementing the velvet she wore—yet another prize from the abandoned packs of Lord Arnad's would-be assassins.

Truly Auren looked older than her fourteen years. I had been somewhat surprised that she and her young betrothed would be wed so soon, but it seemed it was the fashion to marry early here in Seldd. Neither my brother nor either of my sisters had married until they were at least twenty, but to be twenty and yet unwed in Seldd was to be positively hopeless. What Auren thought of me, still obviously free at the advanced age of twenty-five, I dared not think.

Auren turned away from the window with a sigh, obviously disgusted by my apparent lack of excitement. "You'd think you'd never been to a Midwinter ball before," she remarked.

"I've seen my share," I replied placidly. "Which might, if you stopped to think about it, account for my calm regarding the matter."

"But a ball held just for you, to celebrate your betrothal?"

"I'll admit I've not had that honor."

Seeming to realize her misstep, Auren put out a hand, and said, "I didn't mean it that way—"

"I'm sure you didn't." I took care to keep my tone light. "Don't think I didn't have the opportunity, my lady. It was only because I decided to serve the Order that I didn't marry." My words were only partially true. I had no doubt that my family would have secured a good match for me, if that had been how I chose to lead my life, but there hadn't been anyone in particular who showed an interest in me.

"Of course," she replied, and she appeared almost subdued. Then her expression grew brighter, and she added, "You are looking very well, Mistress Merys."

I wanted to laugh, but instead received the compliment as graciously as I could. Once again I wore my wine-colored velvet gown, only a few shades darker than Auren's, as I of course had nothing else remotely suitable. At least the color suited my warm brown hair and fair skin, though I had no jewels to complement the ensemble.

Poor Elissa did not fare quite so well, even though we had rushed to make her a new gown with the length of fabric that had been her own gift. All the household's slaves had received yardage to make a new set of clothes, but it was stuff that had been rejected as being unsuitable to take to market, poorly dyed or with defects in the weave of the fabric. It was all serviceable and strong and new, if not exactly becoming.

Elissa's gown was a dark green that contrived to make her look a little sallow, even though it could not detract from the delicate bones of her face. And at least it fit well enough, although privately I still thought she looked too thin.

At last we heard the jangling of the bell from the hall, Ourrel's signal that all was finally ready. Auren practically threw open the door to her chamber and raced down the stairs, her flat-soled shoes making slapping noises on the stone throughout her precipitous descent. Elissa and I followed at a rather more sedate pace, although we attempted to move quickly enough so that Auren wouldn't be completely out of eyeshot.

The hall was a riot of color and noise and movement. Swags of evergreen and pale waxberries decorated the dark beamed ceiling, hung from the walls, and trailed down either side of the great hearth. More candles than usually could be seen in the entire keep had been brought into this one room, and the heady smell of beeswax warred with the more toothsome aromas emanating from the kitchen. Young Lord Larol and his family were already there, clustered about the table against the far wall that gleamed with pewter goblets and dark glass vessels holding various vintages from Seldd and beyond.

Ignoring all propriety, Auren ran toward her betrothed, holding out her arms. I was glad to see that he ignored a disapproving look from his mother and took Auren's hands, lifting them to his mouth and kissing each one in turn. In fact,

I couldn't help smiling as I watched Larol offer his affianced bride a cup of warm spiced wine, all solicitous attention. His parents might as well have been on one of the moons for all the regard he paid them.

"Oh, it is lovely, isn't it?" breathed Elissa, as she looked around the hall in some awe. Then she hesitated, and I stopped to turn and look at her.

"What's wrong?" I asked.

"Are you sure—I mean, is it truly allowed?"

Poor girl. She still couldn't believe that for the Midwinter feast the household slaves were allowed to spend time with their betters. I supposed that, as the daughter of a freehold farmer, she had never had the chance to celebrate Midwinter in a lordly household such as this, and so she had no real concept of the idea that for one night at least she would be included in the doings of the more elevated folk. Some of the household slaves—such as Merime and her staff—of course had to keep at their work so that the rest of us might feast, but they would have a day of rest tomorrow, while others of the household handled their duties.

At any rate, Elissa was always keenly aware of her place… not that Auren ever let her forget it. I doubted it was malice on Auren's part that led her to adopt such an arch tone whenever she addressed the other girl. After all, Auren had been raised to be waited on by slaves her entire life, and I supposed she knew no better. And Elissa, who had the sort of nature that always sought to please and not resist, meekly accepted whatever unreasonable demands Auren might make of her.

I, on the other hand, held a much more ambiguous place in the household. True, I was counted among the slaves, but

I was free to make my way about the estate, always looking for those who might need my assistance and care. Very seldom was I asked to take on any duties other than those I would have had if I'd come here freely, doing the business of the Order. Indeed, Auren seemed somewhat in awe of me at times. My healing of her leg had cemented her goodwill from the beginning, but my saving of her father had placed me in some exalted category that very few other people occupied. And since Lord Shaine always treated me with respect as well, the other members of the household followed suit. Sometimes I felt more like an honored if captive guest than a true slave.

Knowing how unsure of herself Elissa was, I tempered my smile and replied gently, "Of course it is, Elissa. It is the custom. You should go and enjoy yourself." I glanced about the hall, spying several young men who worked as household and field slaves clustered in an awkward group down near the fire. "Look, there's Raifal, and Clem, and—I don't know the name of the red-headed one. Go on over."

She gave me a doubtful look, but as she was not one to argue, she did as I bade her and headed off in their direction. Her shyness would be short-lived, I hoped—after all, she worked with many of them every day as she ran errands for Auren and assisted with other duties as necessary.

I watched as Clem gave her a winning grin, followed by a rather doubtful but no less friendly smile from Raifal. The poor boy had been long in his recovery from Dorus' depredations. No one spoke of what had befallen him, but in a household such as this, secrets were difficult to keep for very long. Everyone afforded the boy such extra care as they could manage, even as Raifal remained silent and withdrawn. I could only hope with time he would come to understand that not everyone was a predator.

Master Breen, the falconer, greeted me with a smile and a welcome goblet of warm spiced wine. "You're looking well this evening, Mistress Merys," he said. "Happy Midwinter."

"And to you as well, Master Breen," I replied, taking the goblet from him, grateful for his open warmth. He occupied a high position in the household, and I knew that our visitors would probably take their cues from him. Perhaps it was silly of me to fret over my reception, but I knew my own place in Lord Shaine's home was quite irregular, and I had worried beforehand that young Lord Larol's family and retainers might not see me in quite the same light as those who knew me well.

"And how does this compare to celebrations in your homeland?" he inquired, and again I was thankful for his easy manner. He was a vigorous, stocky man only an inch or so taller than I, with mid-brown hair and brown eyes. Indeed, I always thought of him as being brown all over, since he usually bore a deep tan from his time spent out of doors, and the leather doublet and heavy gloves he wore were invariably brown as well. Even this evening, when he had put on what passed in him for finery, the shade of his garments was a deep brown verging on black—the color of new-turned earth in spring.

"Quite similar," I replied. "The greens and berries are a little different, of course. But we decorate the hall, and invite the servants to join us—for, as you know, slavery is not practiced in Farendon."

"Of course," he echoed, but he did not rise to the bait—not that I had expected him to. His manners were too good for that.

"It's much the same wherever I've gone throughout the northern part of the continent," I went on. "Although in Purth they have taken up the odd custom of bringing in some sort of evergreen tree—sometimes a fir, or a pine—and then hanging decorations made of painted parchment and tin on it. It tends to create quite a mess, but it does look festive."

He raised a brown eyebrow. "Interesting. I'm not sure if I'd mention that one to Lady Auren—she'd be sure to want to try it, and then everyone would have more work than they do already."

Laughing, I replied, "I hadn't thought of that. I'll make sure to keep it to myself, then."

He nodded good-naturedly, the lines around his eyes crinkling a bit as he smiled.

And then *his* voice— "So are you keeping Merys all to yourself, Breen? I wanted to introduce her to my guests."

Master Breen bowed. "I wouldn't presume to keep her from you, my lord."

I looked up to see Lord Shaine watching the two of us. His face betrayed nothing, but I was afraid I couldn't say the same for myself. Heat rose in my cheeks even as I said, much more coolly than I felt, "Master Breen has been good enough to make an outsider feel welcome."

"Outsider?" Lord Shaine echoed. "After you've been here an entire two months? Nonsense."

Not knowing exactly how to reply to that, I merely lifted my shoulders, even as I noted how well Lord Shaine looked this evening. He had discarded the plain linen garments he usually wore in favor of a black wool doublet embroidered in warm shades of bronze and olive and taupe, and his shoulder-length hair had been pulled back into a neat club at the base of his neck.

Then I found my voice enough to say, "Outsider compared to those who have been here all their lives, my lord."

"True enough." His gaze shifted to Master Breen, and he went on, "If I may steal Merys away?"

"Of course, my lord."

I gave Master Breen a brief curtsey and followed Lord Shaine across the hall to the spot where Lord Larol and his family stood. As we crossed the floor, I could feel the eyes of the company upon us. Perhaps they wondered why Lord Shaine would show such honor to one of his slaves. For myself, I merely lifted my chin a little higher, determined not to reveal any discomfort or unease in being so singled out.

We stopped in front of the family group. I could see where young Lord Larol had gotten his close-set eyes and slightly pinched nose, as they were echoed in his mother's face. But at least his features were redeemed by the pleasant expression he wore. I could not say the same of her.

Lord Shaine seemed to disregard her stare of disapproval as he said, "My lords, my ladies—this is Mistress Merys, who healed Auren's leg and treated my own knife wound."

I swept a deep curtsey; my early training had not yet deserted me. Possibly not expecting a gesture of respect worthy of court, Lady Yvaine lifted her eyebrows.

Lord Marten at least looked somewhat impressed.

"Mistress—Merys, is it? I see you have done much for which we have cause to be grateful."

"Oh, yes," agreed Larol, who took Auren's hand once more and gave it a small squeeze. She flashed a quick smile up at him, her cheeks coloring a bit.

"I'm only glad that I was able to assist them, my lord," I replied, my tones so demure that I saw a look of amusement flit across Lord Shaine's face before he schooled his features once more into impassivity.

"Merys, as you can see, is quite modest," he offered. "But we were very lucky to have one with her training amongst us."

"What kind of training?" Larol's younger sister Alcia put in, looking briefly surprised at her own audacity in asking such a question.

"I'm a member of the Order of the Golden Palm," I replied. "In my homeland of Farendon, it's a place which trains people in the medical arts and then has them travel the country, always helping those in need. Some prefer not to travel, and stay in the main Order house in Lystare, performing research and serving as instructors. It was while conducting such research that one of our members discovered an inoculation against smallpox, not ten years ago."

"An in—a what?" Auren asked, clearly surprised.

"You get a shot in your arm," I explained. "I could show you the mark, but I have too many sleeves in the way." Both Lord Shaine and Lord Marten chuckled, although Lady Yvaine still looked displeased. "At any rate, once you've had an inoculation, you don't have to worry about getting smallpox."

"Impressive," Lord Shaine said. "Could you do that for the people on the estate?"

"Not at this time, unfortunately. I was not carrying the vaccine with me when I was taken, and only those back in Lystare who are skilled in such matters are able to produce more."

"A pity," he said, then shook his head. "It is this sort of thing which frustrates me. That such learning exists, and yet we here in Seldd are unable to take part in it."

A few pithy comments on his country's isolationism and barbaric dependence on slavery rose to my lips, but I knew better than to utter them. Lord Shaine, I felt, was a man better than the country which had raised him, and it was only natural that he should strain against the limitations it placed on him and those he cared for.

Instead, I only gave a philosophical shrug and said, "Perhaps one day—"

Alcia's eyes were shining. Perhaps this was the first time she had ever encountered a woman who had an identity apart from mother, sister, wife…or slave. I obviously fascinated her, for she asked, "Does it hurt? The inoc—inoculation?" She struggled with the unfamiliar word and then looked quite pleased with herself for finally getting it out.

"A bit, yes," I admitted. "And it does leave a small scar—but nothing like what getting the actual pox could do." Despite myself, I gave a small shiver. I had seen villages ravaged by the pox in Purth and the remoter areas of Farendon. Although the Order had done its best to make sure the vaccine got out to everyone, in some cases places were simply too remote—or superstitious fear kept others from receiving the healing gift. And when it came, the pox left scarring, injury, and death in its wake.

"It seems you have quite the treasure here, Lord Shaine," said Lady Yvaine, although her sour tone belied the implied praise of her words. "I can see now why Lord Arnad wanted her so badly."

Once more my cheeks flamed with color, and I had to clench my hands within the heavy velvet of my skirts to prevent myself from throwing a retort back at her. I knew her words had been calculated to wound. For whatever reason, she had decided I was an enemy...or a threat.

Lord Marten had the good grace to shoot a look of annoyance at his wife, while their daughter's eyes opened even wider, and poor Larol suddenly seemed very interested in the toes of his boots. Auren's dark brows drew together, but Lord Shaine forestalled the outburst by saying, with far more equanimity than I could have mustered,

"Indeed, Lady Yvaine. I believe the gods smiled the day she was brought to us."

Fairly caught, it was all Lady Yvaine could do to muster a sickly smile. I could tell she wanted to lash back out at Lord Shaine, but causing a scene with her son's future father-in-law—at a Midwinter gathering, no less—would doubtless cause a rift that might take years to heal.

"In fact," he went on, blue eyes pensive, as if he had no idea how irritated Lady Yvaine actually was, "I have often thought that perhaps it would be best to free her."

That comment made me turn abruptly to look up at him. He seemed serious, as far as I could tell. Surely he wouldn't play such a cruel joke upon me. But why on earth would he make such a statement in front of Lord Marten and Lady Yvaine?

The woman's gaze slid toward me for a moment, as if she wanted to gauge my reaction to Lord Shaine's words before replying. "I don't see how it would be in your best interests to free someone who has proven herself so valuable," she retorted.

"Of course, it would not," he replied, imperturbable. "But it would certainly be in her best interests, would it not?" And with that parting shot he offered me his arm, and I could do nothing but take it and follow after him as he led me away from the spiteful Lady Yvaine and the rest of the startled and bemused little group.

A moment passed before I was able to find my voice. Only after he paused with me near the hearth did I manage to say, "Did you really mean that?"

"I did." He took a sip of his own wine, but I noticed he watched me closely even as he did so.

"But—but why?" I faltered. Of all the things I had expected to come to pass this evening, being offered a chance at freedom surely was the last.

"Because the value of my daughter's life—and my own, I suppose—is far greater than the trifling amount I paid for you. Because the more I thought on it, the more wrong it seemed. And because—" He paused, and his eyes were unreadable. "Because you wish it."

That I had, for so long it seemed there had never been a day when I didn't think on how I could achieve that goal. Lately, though, ambivalence had begun to creep in. I hated being chattel, of course, hated the thought that I could not have any say in the decisions which would affect my life. But suddenly it had become very difficult to envision a life that did not include staying on at Lord Shaine's estate. Staying close to him, even though I hated to admit it, even to myself.

I hoped the blazing fire could excuse the flush I felt in my cheeks. I, who had never lacked for words, who always had been ready with an easy answer or calming words for my patients even in the worst times of crisis, could suddenly think of nothing to say. Instead of facing him, I looked out into the crowd and watched as a laughing Auren took Larol by the hand and led him to the dance set that had begun to form in the center of the hall. The group of musicians, who were situated off to one side just past the hearth, launched into a lively tune, and soon the floor was filled as more came to join them in this, the central part of the festivities.

Lord Shaine's sharp eyes missed very little—if anything—but he remained silent as I stood there for a long moment, searching for the words that had abandoned me. But when the silence grew too awful, he said gently, "Of course, even if I freed you this night—which I have a mind to do—it would not be safe for you to leave until the spring thaw. I could only ask you to stay as an honored guest until then."

A flood of relief washed over me. It was not necessary, then, to utter words that might shame me, or at the very least make things horribly awkward between us. I could reclaim myself, and still have time to understand where things might go next. I still had no true idea whether his solicitousness grew from a general respect for me, or from a more personal regard.

"My deepest thanks, my lord," I said. "That sounds so inadequate, doesn't it?" And I managed a shaky laugh.

"I understand," he said, smiling a bit. "But now, if you would oblige me?" And he offered me his hand.

For a moment I just stared at him blankly, and then I realized he wanted me to enter the dance with him. Even though my heart pounded and my mouth felt suddenly dry, I knew I could not refuse. So I laid my hand in his and allowed him to lead me out to join the rest of the revelers.

From there the evening seemed to pass in a blur. We danced, not just that once, but several times, to the point where Master Breen good-naturedly chided Lord Shaine about keeping me all to himself. After that I took a turn with Breen, and with Ourrel, and even with young Raifal, who proved himself to be light of foot but unable to meet my eyes. Later on I saw him talking with Elissa and was heartened to think that perhaps his diffidence was confined only to my presence. I knew the dreadful secret he carried, but of course I hadn't spoken of it to anyone else. Very likely other members of the household knew, but I was the only one to whom he had made a direct confession, and perhaps he could pretend to himself that I was the only one who possessed the whole truth of what had happened between him and Dorus.

Everywhere was light and merriment and music, the faces of people who had put aside their cares at least for this one night. And my heart felt lighter than any of theirs, for Lord Shaine had told me that I was to be free.

At length I paused to catch my breath after a particularly romping piece known as "Gray Mare." I was dizzy enough already, so I decided to satisfy my thirst with a drink of well water and not more spiced wine. As I stood by the refreshment table, fanning myself with one hand and taking frequent sips from my goblet with the other, Lord Shaine approached me again. We had passed one another in the last dance set, and he seemed to be just as exhausted by it as I. Along the edge of his forehead his hair clung damply to his brow, and I could see the shine of sweat on his skin.

"Was I imagining things, or did the musicians keep speeding up the tempo of that last one?"

"Not your imagination, my lord," I replied with a laugh. "Lady Auren's idea, I'm afraid. Perhaps at fourteen I wouldn't have had as much difficulty with it, but—"

"It's even worse at forty," he said with a grin. "My daughter does seem to delight in setting up mischief. I had hoped that young Larol would have the handling of her, but I'm afraid it's already apparent who'll run things in that pairing!"

By his expression I could see he wanted to look rueful but wasn't succeeding very well. I knew just how proud he was of his pretty, high-spirited daughter.

Then he stepped into the center of the room, goblet held high. "Gentles!" he called out. "The blessings of this house upon all of you. Happy Midwinter!" He lifted his goblet and drank, and everyone followed suit. I began to regret the lack of wine in my goblet, but he certainly hadn't given me enough warning to get something more appropriate to drink.

"I have an announcement to make," he went on. "Several, actually. Of course you all know that Lady Auren was recently affianced to Lord Larol. The date of their wedding has been set—look for another celebration here on the tenth day of summer!"

Following his words came another cheer, and again everyone lifted their goblets and drank. I sighed and took another sip of water.

"Also, our present good fortune is due in no small part to the ministrations of Mistress Merys, a physician of the Order of the Golden Palm. My daughter now walks because of her, and I would not be speaking to you now if it were not for her skilled care."

I heard Master Breen say, "Hear, hear!" and after a barely perceptible pause everyone cheered and clapped. Everyone, that was, except the sour-faced Lady Yvaine. Perhaps she thought a slave unworthy of her applause.

"Because of the services she has rendered this household, I wish to give her a special Midwinter gift." He turned toward me, extending a hand, and I had no choice but to step out from my relative refuge near the table of food and drink and into the center of the hall to stand at his side. A smile crinkling the corners of his eyes, he said, "Mistress Merys, I give you your freedom."

A moment of silence then, until someone—I believe it was Master Breen, bless him—began to clap. Then everyone else added their cheering to his applause, some of the slaves even calling out my name and hallooing boisterously. Again I could feel a blush heat my cheeks, but somehow I managed to recover myself enough to smile at them all and raise a hand in acknowledgment.

Lord Shaine beamed down at me, and I knew he wished me to say something.

"Thank you, my lord," I said then, directing my words to him but pitching my voice loudly enough so that everyone in the hall could hear me. "This is a most wondrous gift, and I do thank you for it. And do not fear," I added, turning away from him slightly and addressing the watching crowd. "I will stay with you here for the rest of the winter, to see you all safely through to spring."

Again everyone cheered and I looked away, to see Lord Shaine staring down at me with a peculiar expression on his face. Something about his mouth softened, and his lips parted, as if he were going to say something else.

What he had been about to say, I would never know. For the great double doors to the hall were flung open, and the two men-at-arms who had been unlucky enough to be assigned guard duty this night hurried in.

"My lord," said one of them, and even across the hall I could see how pale his cheeks were beneath the leather-covered helmet he wore. "My lord, it is the plague!"

CHAPTER NINE

THE HALL WENT DEATHLY STILL. For a soul-freezing moment in time, I stood there, heart seeming to have stopped in my breast.

The Lord Shaine spoke, and it was as if light and color suddenly flowed back into the room. "What do you mean, Graf?"

"My lord, there is a man at the gates. We did not let him in." Graf swallowed, and his gaze shifted from Lord Shaine to me. I supposed it was natural that he should look to the healer for guidance. "He has come from Lord Arnad's estates, and he says the plague is there."

"The true plague?" I asked, for in some regions the practice had arisen of calling any terrible disease a plague. But there was only one pestilence truly deserving of the name….

"Truly, Mistress," he replied, and I could see the convulsive movement of the knot in his throat as he swallowed. "They are requesting our help."

Silence again, as I looked away from him to Lord Shaine, whose jaw tightened slightly before he said, "Take us to him."

Then he turned and addressed the rest of those watching, whose expressions ranged from fear to horror to simple curiosity. "This should not mar our Midwinter celebrations. Go on, and let Mistress Merys and me attend to this problem."

He waved at the musicians, who scrambled to fetch their instruments and resume playing. For a moment I feared no one would follow Lord Shaine's direction, but then young Lord Larol held his hand out to Auren, and led her to form yet another set in the center of the hall. After a brief pause, more couples followed their lead, and Lord Shaine and I were free to follow the two men-at-arms outside.

It was bitterly cold, and I wished I could have run upstairs to retrieve my cloak. Still, at least the sky was clear for once, although somehow it felt even more chill than when it was covered in overcast. Lord Shaine and his guards moved quickly, however, and at least our rapid pace served to keep my blood moving, warming me somewhat.

The gates were shut. I followed the three men up a narrow set of stairs in the guard house, to a window that overlooked the rutted, muddy lane which led up to the keep. From there I could look out to see a man waiting for us as he sat astride a horse whose sides heaved and gleamed with sweat. Obviously he had ridden hard to get here.

From behind Lord Shaine's shoulder I studied the stranger as best I could. His face looked pale in the darkness, but I could see no outward sign of the disease upon him. I gave Lord Shaine a questioning look, and he nodded briefly. Stepping up to the window, which was open to the icy night, I called out, "I am Merys, the physician you seek. Are you ill?"

He shook his head. "No, mistress. That is why I was sent. So many are ill—Lord Arnad, his lady mother—most of the slaves—" His voice broke, and he fell silent for a time, obviously struggling to regain his composure. "It came upon us four days ago—brought, we think, in a trader's train that came from Purth. They seemed well enough when they arrived at the estate, but one of their company fell ill within a day of reaching us, and then it began to spread—"

"I understand," I said. Then I glanced back at Lord Shaine, whose face seemed almost too still. My own mind seemed to race frantically as I tried to recall everything I knew about the plague.

The last outbreak had been almost five centuries ago, immediately following the great mage wars. At the time it was said the plague had come as a punishment from the gods, to further show their disapproval toward those who had dared to harness unearthly powers for unholy uses and then whom the gods had pleased to lay low. Beginning in the deserts of Keshiaar and moving slowly northwest, the disease had spread from town to town, farm to farm, laying waste to everything in its path. In some villages, I had read, the citizens had died to the last man. Finally the plague burned itself out, having devastated most of the eastern half of the continent, although it never made inroads into North Eredor or Sirlende.

My only experience of the disease was through what I had read, of course, for there had been no outbreaks since that time of pestilence. I knew it could be highly contagious, and that it appeared in one of three forms. The first involved swellings of the glands in the groin and neck, accompanied by fever, headache, and a sore throat. This was the most survivable form of the plague, and my texts had advised that the patient might survive if the swellings were lanced, releasing the disease from the body. The second form involved the lungs, resulting in a form of pneumonia, and was almost always fatal and highly contagious. The third variation—rarely seen—involved the poisoning of the blood. No one knew why some victims would sicken with one form over another, but if the plague infected one's blood directly, then the victim would be dead within the day, covered in blackened hemorrhages.

Gathering my breath, I asked, "Do they have the swellings and fever, or has anyone been coughing, as if they have the ague?"

"Swellings and fever mostly," he replied, "although Lady Margon began coughing as I left."

In which case she would probably be dead before I even arrived. I could do nothing for her, but there were many more who might survive—if given the proper care.

"I must go, my lord," I said quietly.

"And risk yourself?" he asked. His deep blue eyes were somber but unsurprised. Somehow he had known I would make this request.

"It is what I was trained to do," I replied. "I would not be true to my Order if I did not offer what aid I could."

If I had expected him to offer any further argument, I would have been disappointed. He merely nodded ever so slightly, then asked, "And what do you require of us?"

Thinking furiously, I said, "As much raw alcohol as I can take with me. Bandages. And an old set of boy's clothes."

At that he raised an eyebrow, and I explained, "I can ride more quickly astride, and whatever I wear over there will have to be burned once I return. Better that it should be old and of little worth."

"We'll see to it directly," he replied and nodded at Graf, who gave a quick bow and disappeared from the chamber, no doubt to carry out his lord's wishes.

I turned and called back out the window, "I will be ready to ride within the hour."

Even in the flickering light of the torches that illuminated the open area before the gates, I could see the relief in the stranger's face. "Thank you, mistress."

I could only hope that his relief would be justified. For myself, the beginnings of sick worry began to cramp my stomach as I realized exactly to what I had committed myself. This was what I had trained for, of course—to go into the disease-ravaged areas of the world and bring hope and succor with me. But this was no mere outbreak of tertian fever or measles or even smallpox—this was the plague, the most evil and mysterious disease the world had ever known, and I was afraid.

Fear was not something I usually experienced in my work, save the ever-present worries I had for my patients' survival. For whatever reason, I had always been remarkably immune to the ailments that struck others with frightening regularity. Oh, I had been known to suffer a mild ague in the winter if I were careless about staying warm and dry, but I had treated patients with a bewildering variety of illnesses and had never caught a one of them. My instructors used to say I had obviously been chosen by the gods for this vocation, since my constitution made me unusually well-suited for attending those whose every breath carried contagion.

But the plague….

Its mystery and virulence had given it near-mythical proportions by this time, and the fact that it had resurfaced now after so many years worried me greatly. I feared that the luck which had carried me up until now might be sorely tested in the days ahead. But at least I could do everything in my power to make sure it did not come here.

"Some instructions," I said, looking directly at Lord Shaine.

"I see that less than an hour of freedom has given you the courage to assume command," he remarked, but I could tell he teased me gently. There was no anger in his words.

"This is an area in which I am suited to take command," I replied. "After I have gone, make sure the gates stay shut. No one is to enter, and no one is to leave. It's only through the strictest of quarantines that you can escape this disease. If I return—" He startled at that, I could tell, and I swallowed and continued, "When I return, I will stay apart from you all until several days have passed and we can be sure I have not contracted the illness. From what I can recall of my studies, the incubation period is no longer than five days."

"So you have studied this pestilence."

"Yes, what written accounts have survived. We have been lucky—very lucky—that it has not resurfaced ere this time. Why now, I do not know, but—" I raised my chin to look at him. His face was half in shadow, the only illumination the flaring torches. This Midwinter was a moonless one.

He did not reply directly. Instead he gave a rueful smile

and said, "So it appears we will all have to suffer Lady Yvaine's company for some time."

"I'm afraid so, my lord. At least you all will—I shall be safely off tending to plague victims."

That comment elicited a small chuckle, as I had hoped it would. "I keep thinking at some point you will stop surprising me. So far that day has yet to come."

"I would hope so, my lord!" And with those words I gave him a slight curtsey, then turned and left the guard room overlooking the courtyard. I had much to do, and little time to do it in.

I did not bother to pack much—merely my kit and such personal necessities as I might require. A grubby set of boy's clothes had been found for me, and I changed out of my velvet gown quickly, then hung it in the wardrobe. Already the evening where I had worn such finery seemed as if it had passed in another life. Auren remained in the hall with Larol's family, trying her best to keep the guests distracted from the hideous news, but Elissa fled to our chamber to await my arrival. In fact, it was she who had begun packing for me, thus expediting my departure.

After watching, white-faced, as I carefully plaited my loose hair and pinned it around my head, she burst out, "How could you be going there, mistress? After what he did—what he said—and to go to the plague!"

None of this was very coherent, but I understood her well enough. It was for reasons such as this that we had been admonished over and over again during our training with the Order to maintain as much detachment as possible. Personal connections could only cloud the relationship between a physician and his or her patient.

"Would you have everyone there die, Elissa?" I asked gently, for I knew she was very young and probably understood little of the sort of responsibility I had taken on myself when swearing my life to the Order. "I have no very high opinion of Lord Arnad myself, but surely his slaves and other members of his household are blameless." Save Dorus, I thought, with an inward wince. A very uncharitable part of me fervently hoped he would be dead by the time I arrived.

"I suppose not."

I smiled at her then, and clasped my satchel shut. The close-fitting breeches and loose doublet I wore felt odd, but I knew they were the most practical thing for me to wear. They also smelled faintly of perspiration, but I couldn't mind that now. Besides, I knew I would face far worse stinks than these by the time I was done.

I gathered up my cloak and wrapped it about myself so that the guests might not see my inappropriate attire, and Elissa followed me as I made my way back down to the hall.

Lord Shaine had obviously been waiting for me; he stood near the steps and made a movement toward me when I appeared.

"All prepared?"

"As much as I can be," I replied.

"There's a horse waiting for you in the courtyard. I did not know how experienced a rider you were, so I took care to see that he is strong but docile."

His solicitude moved me greatly, and I smiled. "Thank you, my lord. I have ridden a great deal, actually, but it relieves me to know that I won't have to be worried about my mount."

"And I suppose there is no hope of dissuading you."

We might have been alone in the hall. He looked only at me, as if the chamber weren't filled with guests possessed by varying degrees of curiosity and fear. I could feel the fear myself, but I had to push it far back in my mind. It would be all too easy to lose my resolve, to try to hide myself here with everyone else and let the pestilence take everyone it wished, as long as it did not take those for whom I cared.

"None, my lord," I said finally. At least my tone had a resolve I currently did not feel.

"Then the gods go with you," he replied. The barest pause, and then he turned away.

I could only stand there, watching wordlessly as he went to rejoin the crowd. Had he meant to say something else, something of a more personal nature? I couldn't say. That hesitation I noted might have meant nothing at all, save an inability to say something more profound than the simple words he had given me.

There was nothing for it. I could not waste time with tormenting myself over his every word…or even his omissions. I had made up my mind, and it was time to go. I turned, and did not look to see who watched my departure.

Graf waited in the courtyard with the horse that had been readied for me and held him steady while I mounted, not that it was truly necessary, as the gelding was more than placid and barely flicked an ear at me as I took an unaccustomed seat astride. But the man-at-arms held the bridle as he guided me out through the courtyard, past the now-open gates, and into the freezing darkness where Lord Arnad's man awaited me.

I discovered soon enough that his name was Brit. He had been a slave, but Lord Arnad had apparently offered him his freedom and five hundred golden *ranads* if he would ride to Lord Shaine's estate and beg my assistance.

"I can only hope that I might live to spend it, mistress," he said, as we jogged along in the freezing night. Normally we would not have started until dawn, but even moments were precious now. We could not wait.

"You will," I replied. "For when we reach Lord Arnad's estate, you will stay far away from everyone. If you've managed to avoid the infection this long, then we must do everything we can to keep you away from it."

"No arguments here, mistress!"

At that I did manage a laugh, but then we fell into an uneasy silence, both of us consumed with our own thoughts.

I should have been reviewing everything I had ever heard or read about the plague. I should have been planning contingencies and deciding on a course of action for the time when I arrived at Lord Arnad's estate. At the very least I should have been paying attention to the road, which was the barest muddy, rutted track between snow banks. But I did none of these things. All I could think of was the steady regard in those calm blue eyes as Lord Shaine bade me farewell. Did he care after all? Had he wanted to let me know something of his feelings, lest I disappear into the depths of the plague and become lost to him forever, but had somehow found his tongue tied?

I did not know. The only thing I knew for certain, as we

plodded on through the freezing dark toward a sort of death I had never imagined, was that never before had I so much wanted to live.

At first, nothing seemed amiss at Lord Arnad's estate. Instead of an ancient keep such as the one which brooded at the heart of Lord Shaine's lands, Arnad's home was of newer construction, probably no more than a century old, with half-timbered walls and elegant mullioned windows. It had not been built to withstand attack, but instead as a comfortable home for the landed nobility who had lived there for generations. Very probably it had been built on the site of a much older structure.

Smoke should have been curling from the chimneys that protruded in random patterns from the steeply pitched roof, but I saw none. Even with the sun now rising, the temperature hovered around freezing, and of course fires should have burned to keep off the winter chill. But if there were no one alive to light the fires, or keep them burning—

I kicked my heels into my horse's sides, spurring him into a startled canter. Brit lagged behind for a moment before he caught up with me.

"What's amiss?" he asked breathlessly as he clung to the pommel. Obviously he had far less experience on horseback than I did.

"Far too much, I'm sure," I replied, slitting my eyes against the freezing wind and praying for any sign of life from Lord Arnad's home.

But I saw none. We came into a large courtyard bordered by what appeared to be the stables and the slave quarters.

The entrance to the main house was some ten yards directly in front of me.

I dismounted, and began to unfasten the straps that held my medical kit. "See if you can put the horses in the stables—but look sharp. If there's anyone inside, stay away, and see if you can find some other covered place to wait for me." Once my satchel was free, I opened it and drew out two long strips of tightly woven linen, then handed one to Brit. "Tie this over your mouth and nose—like so." And I fastened my own mask over the lower half of my face, not so tight that it would impair my breathing, but also not so loose I would have to worry about it slipping.

Brit gave me a dubious glance, then looked down at the strip of cloth he held. "What's this for?"

"To keep out the infection," I replied. I had no time to explain to him the Order's theories on airborne contagion—and indeed we did not know for sure how exactly disease was passed on. But experience had proven that protecting one's air passages in such a way greatly reduced the spread of disease.

At any other time, the alacrity with which Brit tied the mask to cover his mouth and nose might have amused me. Instead, I just shook my head. "Remember, stay away from anyone you see, even if they don't look ill."

He nodded, then took my horse by the reins with one hand and his own mount by the other. They walked slowly off in the direction of the stables, with Brit giving me one last uneasy look over his shoulder as he did so.

No help for it. He was safe enough for now, and I had work to do. Grasping the worn handle of my satchel, I turned and made my way to the front door of Lord Arnad's home.

It pushed open at my touch, and I stepped inside, blinking a little at the sudden dimness after the bright snow-lit day outdoors. The interior was almost as freezing as the outside air, and after a second I found myself glad enough of it. Otherwise, the smell would have been unbearable.

Probably at one time it had been a pleasant room. At the far end of the hall stood an enormous grey stone fireplace, its hearth now choked with unswept ashes. Unlike Lord Shaine's stone hall, this room had a floor of age-darkened oak, and a series of fine mullioned windows on the opposite wall. They let in a harsh stream of white morning sunlight that was unpitying in what it revealed.

The bodies lay huddled on the floor. A few had obviously succumbed as they sat at the long tables that stretched out in the center of the floor. Slave, noble, retainer—it had not mattered in the end. They all surrendered to death together.

I forced myself to take a breath, to swallow against the convulsive choking that seemed to seize my throat. These all seemed dead, but I had to make sure.

"Is anyone there?" I called out into the heavy stillness. "I am a physician. Brit brought me here."

Silence for the space of a few heartbeats, and then I heard a low answering groan from the far end of the room. I hastened in the direction of the sound and paused, staring down at the ruin that was Lord Arnad.

Whatever happy confluence of symmetry that had once made him so handsome was now gone. His skin had a yellow, waxy cast, and that same jaundiced tone was reflected in the whites of his eyes. The skin underneath them looked bruised, the shadows purple-black. His mouth was slack and caked with dried spittle and black flecks that were probably blood. I heard his labored breathing from several feet away.

Knowing there was little I could do at this point, still I moved forward and sank down on my knees at his side. He had collapsed on the floor next to the head of the table. I had no way of knowing whether he had tried to maintain his status of lord of the hall until he was too ill to stand any longer, or whether he simply hadn't the strength to go any farther than this.

"My lord?" I asked. "Can you hear me?"

A rattling breath, and the slightest movement of his head. It might have been a nod.

"It's Merys," I went on. "I've come to help. You sent Brit to fetch me."

Again that slight shift in the angle of his head. The bleary eyes seemed to focus on me for a few seconds. "Too late," he said, the words hardly more than a breath.

I feared he was right, but I had to at least try. From within my satchel I retrieved a pair of thin kidskin gloves and drew them on. Then I set to work on the fastenings of his doublet. When I saw what it revealed, I knew there was nothing I could do.

In the earlier stages of the disease, it is possible to lance the plague boil and drain off the infection in that manner. But in Lord Arnad the infection had already spread. On his pale and clammy skin I saw the telltale bluish rings across his flesh that meant it had begun to move through his blood. He might still breathe, and he might still have the power of speech, but he was already dead.

With a sigh I settled back on my heels. It was times such as these that I wondered why I had the learning I possessed, if it were still not enough to save the afflicted. Perhaps if I had even gotten here a day earlier, I might have been able to save him. As it was—

Feeling my mouth settle into a grim line, I reached once more into my satchel. The thin vial I found held a heavy derivative of the wild poppy that grew far to the south, in Keshiaar and beyond. A little would ease his pain. A bit more, and he would leave this world in gentle oblivion, a passing far more desirable than the wracking convulsions the plague would bring.

"Two sips of this, my lord," I said, marveling at the steadiness of my voice.

He did not have the strength to sit up to accept the drink, so I slid one hand behind his head to lift it up slightly. Then I tilted the vial almost to his lips—taking care not to touch them—and watched the blood-colored liquid trickle into his mouth.

"Better," he breathed, red-rimmed eyes closing as the drug began to take effect.

I knew when the life left him, could feel the sudden limpness of his body against my hand. Gently I laid him back down against the wooden floor, even as I fought to keep the tears from rising in my eyes. It was all I could do for him, and I wanted to scream out against my impotence.

After a few moments of silence—the only tribute I could offer—I stood and surveyed the hall. I saw no other movement, no other signs of life. But I had to make sure.

Moving slowly, I crossed the hall once more, to ascend the wide double staircase that dominated the other end of the room. I took the stairs to the left, choosing them at random, and climbed slowly, the weariness of the sleepless night and despair at what I had found weighting my limbs, making each step feel as if it were ten times as high as it really was.

But up on the second floor all I found was death as well. More slaves. Arnad's mother collapsed in a pool of bloody dried mucus. A pretty dark-haired girl who looked to be Arnad's younger sister. She seemed almost asleep at first; at least she had died in her own bed, the covers pulled up carefully to her neck. It was only on closer inspection that I noted the dried blood at the corner of her mouth, the black-blue splotches indicative of massive hemorrhaging marring the white skin at her throat.

Everywhere I looked I saw only death, until, overcome, I staggered back down the stairs and out into the bright sunlit courtyard. I pulled the cloth from my nose and mouth and drew in huge gasping breaths of the icy air, feeling as if I were about to suffocate. Then I began to cough as the chill caught at my throat.

Brit's voice, tentative. "Are you all right, mistress?"

I turned to see him peeking out around one corner of the stables. "I'm fine," I said, realizing even as I said them how much of a lie the words were. Still, I didn't know what else to say. "But they're all dead."

"All?" he asked, his voice cracking.

Belatedly I remembered that this had been his home, even if only as a slave, and there most certainly had been people here to whom he had been close. But hiding the truth from him would serve no purpose. I nodded, then looked back up at the house.

There had to be at least fifty corpses in there, and even if the ground were not frozen solid, Brit and I were too few to ever hope to bury them all. It had to be the fire, much as I hated the idea. My spirit quailed at the thought of moving all those bodies down to ground level for disposal. I had to think of a better way....

After staring at the building for a few moments, I nodded to myself. Of course. The disease had tainted every corner of the home. There was only one way to be sure.

"Brit, I need fire—torches, or lanterns."

"But why—" Then he must have noticed the grim set of my mouth, for he said in faltering tones, "You can't be thinking—"

"But I am," I replied. "We must fire the house. All inside are dead. It's not fit to live in."

Reluctance palpable in his every movement, he looked from me back to the building that had been his home, and to me once more. Something in his eyes seemed to harden then, and at length he nodded. "I'll see what I can do," he said, and darted off back into the stable.

Within a moment or two he re-emerged, two glass-paned lanterns dangling from one hand and what looked like a tinder box in the other. He set his burdens down on the ground, struck sparks from the flint he pulled out of the tinder box, and set both lanterns alight.

"Now what?" he asked.

I guessed that once we got the fire started well enough, the half-timbered structure would burn on its own, what with the wooden floors and exposed beams. But it would probably need some help to really catch.

"The kitchen," I said. "We can use wine or spirits to set it off."

Again that dubious look passed over his features, but he did not argue. I supposed that a lifetime of following orders kept him from questioning me. I certainly did not wish to re-enter the house, but we had no choice.

I reached up to re-tie the mask around my nose and mouth; Brit's was still in place, so he waited silently until I was ready and then followed me as I moved around the side of the house. I guessed that there was a separate entrance to the kitchen somewhere in the back, and I did not want to return to the main hall until it was necessary. Sure enough, the kitchen and sculleries stood out somewhat from the main part of the house, attached on one wall but freestanding on the other three sides.

The door stood slightly ajar. I reached out to open it the rest of the way and choked back a gasp as the corpse that had been propped up in the doorway fell over in a heap.

"I can't—" said Brit, looking down at the dead body, his eyes showing white with fear.

"I can't do this alone," I snapped, shock lacing my words with more tension than I had wished. Then I deliberately softened my tone, for I reminded myself that while these were merely corpses to me, to him they were people he had known, perhaps loved. "I'm sorry, Brit—I do need you to help me. Please?"

I fancied I could his heart pounding from where I stood. Then he nodded slowly, and I took a breath, forcing myself to step over the woman's body in the doorway.

Nor was that corpse the only one. I saw two more, young girls this time, both huddled over the heavy wooden table that was pushed up against one wall—probably where the chopping had been done.

Gagging noises came from behind me, and I stopped and took a few steps back, laying my hand on Brit's arm. "It's better if you don't look at them," I said gently. "Where's the door to the cellar?"

Thankfully he had not vomited into his mask, or I would have had to work fast to clear his airway before he choked on his own bile. Above the linen, his face looked almost as pale as the fabric that covered its lower half. Without speaking, he pointed at a stout door of barred oak set into the floor a few paces away.

I went to it and squatted, grasping hold of the heavy black iron ring to pull it open. A dark square yawned beneath me, and I was thankful for the already lit lamp I held. The stairs below were narrow and steep, and I was equally glad for my stout boots and the fact that I wore breeches and not my customary long gown.

The cellar smelled of damp and stone, overlaid with an odd musky odor. But at least I could not sense any of the ever-present scents of decaying bodily fluids and decomposing flesh that had settled like a miasma over the rest of the house. I descended carefully, holding the lantern aloft. The last thing I needed was to trip and fall down here, with only Brit's dubious aid as insurance.

Bottles glimmered in the lantern light, racks covering all of the cellar walls save the one into which the steps were cut. Then I saw movement in the darkness, and a rough voice cried out, "Who's there?"

He sounded faintly familiar, but I could not think who it might be, hiding there in the cellar. I said, holding the lantern up closer to my face, "My name is Merys. I'm a physician—Lord Shaine sent me here to help."

Then he stepped forward into the lantern light, and I could see him clearly.

He was Dorus, Lord Shaine's erstwhile steward.

CHAPTER TEN

Shocked as I was by his unexpected appearance, I could only stand there, staring at him.

His eyes narrowed. "Merys," he said. "Merys, the interfering bitch. Merys, the one who had me sent here—to this!" He flung out a hand, as if to indicate the plague-ravaged house above us.

I took a step backward. While I wished to retort that he had brought this on himself, what with his crimes against Raifal and the gods knew how many others of Lord Shaine's household, I knew better than to give my tongue free rein. "Are you ill?" I asked, using the calm, matter-of-fact tones I usually adopted when working with patients. "Any fever? Nausea?"

"None of that, damn you," he spat back. "I hid down here as it began to spread."

No time to wonder at the capriciousness of fate, that would slaughter so many innocents above and yet allow this beast in man's form to continue to draw breath. I could see the hatred in his eyes as he stared at me, and I began to be afraid.

"The very air here is tainted," I said. "You cannot remain in this house."

"I'm done with your commands, bitch." He stepped toward me, and again I moved back up another stair, all the while wondering whether Brit could reach me in time if I called for his aid—and whether he would be of any use even if he did get there before Dorus could lay hands on me.

Then I had no time to wonder, for Dorus lunged forward and grasped my left leg a little below the knee, jerking me forward and causing me to lose my balance. I slipped and plunged down the remaining steps, straight into him.

He caught me, but there was no mercy in his touch. His hands grasped me around the upper arms, and he flung me down onto the stone floor of the cellar. By some mercy I was able to retain my hold on the lantern I carried in my right hand, but still I hit the ground hard, the breath knocked out of me by the sudden viciousness of his movements.

Then he was down on top of me, knee pressing into my solar plexus as I gasped for air. I am not a small woman, but he was far taller and heavier than I, and, the occasional childhood skirmish with my brother notwithstanding, I had no idea how to defend myself against such an attack.

"Are you mad?" I gasped at last, once I had recovered enough breath to speak. "I came here to help!"

"I don't need your help," he snarled. And his hands moved with shocking swiftness from my arms—now that he held me down with his sheer weight—to my throat.

The terror that surged through me gave me a strength I didn't know I possessed. Apparently he hadn't yet noticed the lantern I still held, and once my arm was free, I raised it as quickly as I could and swung the heavy glass and metal object into the side of his head.

The blow connected with a sickening crunch of bone, and he let out a shocked cry. Blinding anger seemed to flow over me and guide my arm as I drew it back and struck him once more. This time the lantern's glass shattered, and the heavy tin itself dented slightly. Dorus slumped to one side, the sickening pressure on my lungs finally removed, and I pushed him the rest of the way off me with my free hand even as I used my legs to shove myself backward, away from him.

Gasping with pain and fright, I slowly stood. He remained where he was, blood slowly flowing from the wound at his temple. I didn't know whether he was dead or merely stunned. At the moment, I didn't care.

"Mistress Merys?" Brit's voice came from somewhere above, sounding shaky and frightened. "Are you well?"

"I'm alive, if that's what you mean," I muttered, reaching up to touch my throat. It felt sore and tender; no doubt bruises had already begun to form.

Obviously he couldn't hear me, for he asked again, "Mistress?"

"I'm all right, Brit," I called back. "Don't come down here—I dropped a bottle and there's glass everywhere."

"Yes, mistress."

I took a breath and then looked around. Dorus showed no signs of stirring, so it was best I went about my business.

A rack off to my right held some of the same clear spirits Lord Shaine had given me for cleaning wounds. No doubt it was highly flammable.

I lifted two bottles—one to use to aid in burning the house, and the other to bolster my medicinal store—off the shelf and turned to go. But my conscience stopped me. I knew I could never burn the house down over the head of a living man, no matter what sort of monster he might be.

Setting the bottles down on the floor, I kneeled once more and pressed two fingers against the artery in Dorus' throat. I felt nothing, and so shifted my fingers slightly. Still nothing, and I knew then that he was dead.

I wished I could have felt something. Surely I should have been horrified at what I had done—my whole being was focused on saving lives, not taking them—but sadly, I could not find the nobility in myself to care. He had attacked me, after all, I who had only come here to offer assistance. Why should I mourn the departure from this world of a man who clearly would have taken my own life without a second thought?

Moving slowly, I stood once more, torn muscles and bruised flesh protesting even as I did so. I gathered up the bottles of spirits and made my way back up into the kitchen.

One look at me was apparently enough to cause Brit to cry out, "Mistress Merys? What happened?"

"Your steward and I had a difference of opinion."

"My steward—you mean, Master Dorus was down there?"

"Was," indeed, I thought, but I only nodded. Then I added, "He was fevered—taken by the plague. He's dead."

I wasn't sure what Brit's reaction would be, but I hadn't thought it would be what came next. His mouth tightened a bit, and then he only said briefly, "Good."

Oh, Brit, not you as well? I knew there was nothing I could say. Still, I had to admit I was glad Dorus was dead. I would have preferred the plague had taken him before I ever reached this place, but if the gods desired that my hand be the means for retribution, so be it. All I knew now was that I wished to be quit of this cursed house as soon as possible.

Brit gave my broken lantern an askance look, but he forbore asking any further questions. I uncorked one bottle of spirits, spilled some on the wooden table, and dropped the lantern upon it.

The flames that rose up immediately were almost frightening in their intensity, hungry yellow and orange with a blue-white heat at their center.

"Go, quickly!" I called to Brit, who hurried after me as I ran from the kitchen and back outside.

Perhaps the fire in the kitchen would have been enough. But I needed to be sure—I needed to know that Lord Arnad and all those who had died around him would not be left to rot with no more care afforded them than an animal that had died on the side of the road. So I ran back into the great hall, where I spilled more spirits on the center table there.

"Now, Brit!" I commanded, and he tossed the lantern on the table. Again the fire took hold quickly, and I stayed just long enough to see the flames lick their way down the table legs and then catch in the wood flooring.

I hoped that would be enough. We both hastened to the door and stood outside in the courtyard, waiting to see the results of our handiwork. For a few long moments, it seemed as if nothing had changed. Then I heard a sudden whooshing noise, like the sound of a suddenly indrawn breath, and a great gout of flame rushed up out of the main chimney. Flames began to show through the windows, and suddenly the glass shattered, bursting outward like the shards of a thousand dying suns.

We turned and ran for the stables, which apparently had been unoccupied except for some very worried and half-starved horses. I wasn't sure what to do with them, but I knew we couldn't leave them here. So we hurried to clumsily tie them together in a long train, and then both Brit and I remounted, hastening our horses out of the stables—not that they needed much urging, as the smell of smoke was already making them restive and difficult to control.

Turning our backs on the devastated estate, we departed down the broad, flat avenue that led up to the main house. Only once did I turn to look over my shoulder, just in time to see the western part of the main wing collapse entirely, the fire having just swallowed up the roof.

No one came to see what had happened. Brit and I might have been alone in the world, save for the ragged line of horses following behind us and a few crows that circled lazily overhead, ominous black shapes in the hard blue sky.

Our horses were weary, and I knew that the short hour we had stopped would not be enough to rest them sufficiently to carry on all the way back to Lord Shaine's manor. But I was also afraid to beg lodging at a strange house or inn, for I did not yet know how widespread the plague was in this area. To be sure, it had devastated Lord Arnad's estate, but Brit had said the disease had been carried there by a group of traders from Purth. It all depended on how many other places those traders had stopped, and whom they might also have infected along the way.

In the end we found a deserted shack a few hundred yards off the road. Nose and mouth still swaddled in my protective linen, I looked inside to see if anyone was there. But the building appeared to have been abandoned for some time, long before the plague was even a whisper of fear. Weary from the sleepless night and the horrors we had just experienced, we got the horses into the shelter of a dilapidated barn even more ramshackle than the little house itself. There was not much grain to go around, but we were able to feed and water each of them and give their necks a reassuring rub before Brit and I finally collapsed on the brushed dirt floor of the shack.

It was in a brooding quiet that I handed him some of the road rations I had brought along with me: strips of the same highly spiced dried meat I had eaten during my journey to Lord Shaine's estate, a tasty mix of dried tanisberries and nuts that Merime had made up specially for the holiday, a loaf of heavy-grained bread that cried out for butter and honey, though we had none. I poured some spring water for Brit and drank deeply myself. Although the mask over my nose and mouth had kept the worst of the smoke from my lungs, still my throat felt raw and tight. But perhaps that had more to do with my dark thoughts.

I knew that there was nothing I could have done. Even if Brit had come to us a day earlier, I could not have saved at least half those people. Perhaps Lord Arnad; he had not been as far gone as the others. But even that was questionable. The feeling of impotence rose up in me again, and I felt hot tears start to my eyes, though I blinked them angrily away. Weeping would not save the dead. Tears would not change the fact that I was helpless in the face of the greatest pestilence the world had ever known.

Oddly, I felt nothing for Dorus. The man was dead, and by my hand, and yet my only reaction to his death was a sort of relieved numbness. At least he could no longer prey on the innocent, could no longer leave a trail of ruined lives behind him. That I had sworn an oath never to hurt another and to devote my life to healing seemed strangely immaterial. If nothing else, I had acted in self-defense. I had tried to help him, attempted to ascertain the state of his health. He had replied by striking out at me. I had had no choice but to react. Perhaps I had overreacted, but I challenge anyone else in my place to have done anything differently.

These thoughts ran through my head as if I had already been brought in front of a tribunal. I knew logically that no one need ever find out what had transpired at Lord Arnad's estate. Certainly Brit would say nothing. Dorus' death was only a source of relief to him, as no doubt it would be to many others. And Brit had not seen me actually strike Dorus. Only I knew for sure the manner of his passing.

Brit seemed as little inclined to conversation as I. By tacit consent we remained silent, and after we had eaten we wrapped ourselves in the blankets we had brought along with us and curled up to sleep. By necessity we slept back to back, sharing each other's warmth, but there was no intimacy in our closeness. We might have been a hundred miles apart.

As always I found it difficult to sleep, but I forced myself to lie quietly so as not to disturb the young man who lay beside me. After a while the weariness of the preceding day and night finally overtook me, and I slid down into darkness.

Dreams haunted my sleep, dreams in which I wandered through the kitchens at Lord Shaine's estate and desperately looked for something of vital importance. What it was never became clear, even though my actions grew more and more frenzied. I went out behind the kitchens, into the area where Merime and the kitchen staff disposed of refuse. In my dream I sank to my knees, digging through the midden as I tossed aside bones and the tops of carrots and all other sorts of organic waste.

"Why isn't it here?" I cried. "What has she done with it?"

And with those despairing words ringing through my head, I awoke, eyes wide open in the unfamiliar darkness. For a few seconds I could not think of where I was, but then I heard Brit's calm breathing beside me and remembered the shack where we had taken refuge. Luckily my own unrest had not disturbed him, and I settled back down against the bundled cloak I had substituted for a pillow, willing the deep, cleansing breaths back into my lungs. A nightmare, but one that seemed oddly compelling while at the same time vague. What on earth could have been so important that I would dig through the garbage heap to find it? And why those images, after all the death and despair I had just seen? It could have been much, much worse, after all.

And with that thought in mind, I closed my eyes once again, and this time fell into oblivion untroubled by any fragments of the daytime world.

We awoke early, before the sun had even begun to lift beyond the horizon. The dirt floor was cold and hard, and both Brit and I had slept long enough that we knew we had the strength to continue our journey. If we made good time, we could be back at Lord Shaine's estate by late afternoon. Although I knew quarantine awaited both of us once there, at least we would be in familiar surroundings.

During the afternoon and night we had slept, the sky had darkened once more, with low clouds blowing in from the northwest. They promised more snow, and I hoped it would hold off long enough for us to reach our destination. Otherwise, we would be hard put to cover the remaining miles before nightfall. But our luck held somehow. Although the day grew greyer and greyer, and a biting wind sent its searching fingers even through our heavy cloaks, the road remained dry and hard, untouched by snow.

At some point in the mid-afternoon we finally saw the gray towers of the keep rise up in the distance. Brit and I urged the horses to a faster pace, now that we were certain the end of our journey was at hand. In less than an hour we had reached the front gates, and I heard Graf call down to us, "Mistress Merys! What news?"

I had dreaded this moment, but my reply was firm enough. "All gone, Graf. We came too late."

His first response was a muttered oath, but then he asked, "And you? Are you well?"

"Neither of us has any sign of the disease so far," I replied. "But it does not always show immediately. Has Lord Shaine set up quarantine quarters for us?"

"Yes, mistress. We emptied the smaller of the two dye huts for you." And after he made that reply I heard him call out to the other guards to open the gates.

He met us as we dismounted, but I noticed he took care to stand some distance away, and he had wrapped a strip of linen over the lower half of his face, as I had instructed. But I saw his eyes widen in surprise as he took in the additional horses we had brought back with us.

"I didn't know what else to do with them," I said. "I didn't want to leave them there, although we set loose as many others of the livestock as we could. I thought they would be worth something."

"Indeed, mistress," he agreed. "It would have been a waste of good horseflesh, and we'll see that they're well tended to." He signaled two of the other guards, and they took hold of the horses and led them off in the direction of the stables.

Brit and I then followed him to the smaller of the two dye huts, which had been made as comfortable as possible with the addition of two camp beds, a low table, and a considerable amount of warm bedding. The only source of heat was an open fire pit, and there was a smoke hole that unfortunately let in a good deal of freezing air, but if we kept the fire stoked sufficiently, we should be able to manage well enough.

"I'll have Merime send over something warm," he said, speaking to us through the open doorway as Brit and I disposed of our packs and other belongings.

"Thank you, Graf," I said. "Make sure it's left

outside—we'll claim it after the person who brings it is safely gone."

"I know his lordship will wish to speak to you as well," he went on. "But perhaps it would be better if you ate first."

I thanked him again, and he disappeared around the corner. Shutting the door, I turned to see Brit already occupied with building up the fire. He looked up at me, dark eyes somewhat nervous.

"How long do we have to stay in here, mistress?" he asked.

Well could I understand his worry. The thought of being trapped in here for days with little occupation did not appeal to me, either, but there was no help for it. I simply could not run the risk of exposing the rest of Lord Shaine's household to the plague while there was even the remotest chance we might have carried it back with us.

"At least four days, Brit," I replied, somewhat wearily. It somehow sounded even worse when said aloud.

He winced but had the good grace not to make any complaints. At least we were both still alive—no thanks to the plague, or Dorus, for that matter. When we arrived here, I'd had a heavy knitted scarf wound around my neck to keep out the cold, so the bruises I felt there but hadn't yet seen were safely hidden.

As promised, the food arrived—heavenly game pie and a complicated sweet made with cake and nuts and swirls of honey. We both made short work of it, and I had to smile at my own lack of table manners. My mother, I'm sure, would have been appalled.

Accompanying the food had been a jug of water newly drawn from the well, along with a flagon of hard cider.

Replete, Brit and I drank slowly, savoring the moment. At least now we were both warm and well-fed, as comfortable as our situation could make us. And I felt well enough. Now that my feet had unthawed and my stomach had stopped protesting its empty state, I could assess the rest of my well-being and ascertain that, so far, I could detect no symptoms of any illness.

I was about to ask Brit how he fared when a knock at the door forestalled me. Brushing the crumbs from my breeches, I went to the door but did not open it. Instead, I put my face up to the crack and asked, "Who is it?"

"Lord Shaine."

A flush rose to my cheeks, and I was suddenly glad that the door stood between us. "My lord."

"Graf told me what you encountered."

Oh, but I had only told him the barest bones of the story. I had seen no need to fill his head with horrors—and I saw no reason to do that with Lord Shaine here and now. "Yes, my lord. We were too late. All we could do was get out of there as quickly as we could in the hope of avoiding contagion."

A silence from the other side of the door. It was hard for me to gauge his reaction without being able to see his face.

"And so you left everything as you found it?"

I swallowed. At the time what I had done had seemed the most logical course, but now I wondered what Lord Shaine would think when I told him I had fired the house and everything—everyone—in it. "Alas, no," I replied slowly. "There was no way Brit and I could have given everyone a proper burial—and the state of the house, the contagion—" I sighed, and said in a rush, "We burned the place to the ground, my lord. I could not leave them there to rot, and I could see no other way."

This time the stillness that resulted from my words stretched out for so long I began to wonder whether he planned to reply at all.

"You did what you thought best," he said finally, and I heard the weariness in his voice even though I could not see his face. "Perhaps, when this is all over, you may have some angry distant relatives to answer to, but—"

I hadn't even thought of that. Still, I couldn't imagine anyone wanting to live in that house after fifty some-odd corpses rotted away in it. At least the land was still valuable—or would be if enough people could be found to work it. That, however, was none of my concern. I said as much, to which Lord Shaine replied,

"You may be right. And of course I will defend your actions in the event anyone challenges them. But enough of that." He paused, then asked, with a subtle shift in tone, "And how goes it with you?"

One hand went to my bruised throat, and again I was thankful for the heavy wooden door that separated us. "I am well enough, my lord. Both Brit and I so far are not showing any symptoms. But of course I won't know for sure for several days."

"Of course," he repeated. "Is there anything you need, while you wait?"

I longed for books, for a piece of half-finished embroidery—anything that might fill the empty hours. But to handle something was to risk infecting it, and I knew I could not take that chance.

"No, my lord," I said at last. "We will have to be patient. I don't want to—to touch anything until I know for sure."

A silence in which he might have nodded. I had no way of knowing for sure. "We will keep constant watch on you, Merys."

His words had the air of a farewell about them, and I fought the disappointment I felt rising in my breast. Of course I could not expect him to stand here and talk with me all day. He had his own concerns and duties to attend to.

So I said merely, "Thank you, Lord Shaine." And I pressed one hand up against the lintel of the door, wishing I could see his face just for one moment.

But I did not get that longed-for glimpse, of course. He said, "We will talk again," and after that came such a prolonged silence that I knew he had gone, and that Brit and I had been left here to ourselves once more.

I will not recount those days here. They were wearisome enough to live through the first time. Suffice it to say that Brit and I told each other tales of our respective lands, dozed a good bit, spent long hours staring at the fire, dragged out our meal times so they would fill as much space as possible. But in between were the empty hours and minutes where we did little but sit and wait, wondering when and if our bodies would betray us.

That day never came. After four days had passed, and neither of us had yet shown any sign of disease, I deemed it safe for us to finally leave our self-imposed isolation. To be safe we burned the clothes we wore and the bedding we had used; we turned our backs on one another to hide our nakedness until we could gather up the new garments that had been left for us outside the door. And then, finally, we walked back out into the fresh air once more, and stood there for a long while, reacquainting ourselves with the feel of the breeze in our hair and the pale winter sun on our cheeks.

Lord Shaine approached us then, and smiled. "It is good to have you with us again, Mistress Merys," he said formally, and his gaze shifted to Brit, who stood off to one side, fidgeting and looking worried. "And Brit—you have a home here for as long as you need it. No one will challenge your freed status. Master Breen wondered if you would be interested in assisting him in the mews?"

"Oh, I would, my lord," Brit exclaimed. His plain face glowed. To be trained in the arts of falconry would one day accord him a high standing in another household. Lord Shaine could not have thought of a better place for him.

"Well, then," said Lord Shaine. "Run along to Master Breen, and tell him I sent you. I must return with Mistress Merys to the house."

Brit bowed his head and then turned and ran off in the direction of the mews. I could feel myself smile as I watched him leave. Poor boy, he had done his best over the past few days, but I knew the forced inactivity and constant worry about whether the plague boils would begin to show at any minute had worn on him.

Of course, it had worn on me, too.

But now I was free, with Lord Shaine watching me, and the wind in my hair once more. I had the absurd impulse to whirl about in the courtyard, to open my arms to the half-clouded winter day and embrace its beauty. But of course I did no such thing. Instead I followed Lord Shaine back into the keep, where I was immediately surrounded by Auren and Elissa, Merime, and even young Lord Larol.

"So are you truly all right, mistress?"

"Father said they were all dead. Is it true?"

"How could you not get sick, when everyone else did?"

For a moment I could only stare at their faces, confused by the babble of voices after my long isolation.

Lord Shaine held up a hand. "One at a time, I beg you. Mistress Merys has been through quite an ordeal, and we need to give her time to think things through."

I shot him a grateful look and then smiled. "I'm fine. But the sad news is true as well. The plague took the entire household. My Order teaches precautions to take to avoid the spread of infection, and that is why neither Brit nor I took ill." I looked past their inquiring faces to Lord Shaine and asked, "And have we had any other news of the world?"

"Some, and none of it good." His mouth thinned. "A rider came to our gates the morning after you left. No, of course we did not allow him in," he added, in response to my sudden worried look. "I spoke to him from the second story of the guard house. But the plague is spreading—it has gone forth from here and on into Myalme, where the devastation is great. Or so we are told."

He fell silent, and I could see his brooding gaze take in the young people who stood by him, the slaves who lingered just within earshot but far enough away so as to be unobtrusive. The hall looked much as it always did—although some straggling greens still decorated the fireplace, the only reminder I could see of the Midwinter celebration—and I thought then of what an island of safety it was. So far we had survived. Could we continue to maintain our isolation and come through this unscathed?

"But we are safe," I said firmly. We could not allow ourselves to be overcome by doubts and fear. We all had to remain strong.

"Yes, we are safe," he repeated, and his expression softened a bit as he looked on his daughter and her betrothed.

The remainders of the Midwinter decorations jogged my memory, and I held out a hand to Auren. "My lady, in all the confusion, I quite forgot to give you your Midwinter gift. Would you come with me and receive it, although it's quite late?"

"More presents?" she asked, her face lighting up. "It sounds like that celebration in Keshiaar, where they give presents for seven whole days! Have you ever heard of that?"

"I believe I read something of it once," I replied with a laugh. "But you will have to do with only one from me, I'm afraid. And you, too, Elissa," I added. "I have something for you as well."

"Me?" she asked, her delicate face flushing.

In answer I held out my hands to both of them, and they gaily followed me up the steps to my tower chamber. I caught a glimpse of Lord Shaine's approving look before we left the hall, and I knew he must be glad that I had found some way to distract them from the rumors of plague and death.

Auren and Elissa waited in Auren's chamber as I bade them to stay there while I climbed the extra flight of steps up to the room Elissa and I shared. It would have been far too crowded in there for all three of us.

The gifts lay where I had left them, securely wrapped in an extra length of fabric and pushed up against the wall at the head of my bed. As I drew them out and pulled the linen away from them, I saw the brooch I had placed there as well, awaiting a time when I could give it to Lord Shaine. That opportunity had not yet presented itself, although perhaps I could find a time later tonight when we could be alone. But for now I slid it down underneath my pillow and gathered up the two girls' gifts. Then I hurried back down the stairs to Auren's chambers, where they both impatiently awaited my arrival.

Both girls showed their appreciation for their gifts, although in very different ways. Auren tore away the linen wrappings that held the hood I had made for her, took one look at the rich brown fur trim and elegant embroidery, and immediately leaped out of her chair, throwing her arms about my neck before I could stop her.

"It's beautiful!" she exclaimed. "It's the best Midwinter gift I've gotten!"

Somehow I doubted that, although I knew her current enthusiasm was genuine. Auren lived in the moment; of course it was the best present she'd gotten, because she'd received the others days ago, and they had already lost their novelty.

I managed to disentangle myself from her clumsy embrace and said, "I'm very glad it pleases you."

She reached out to stroke the soft fur that framed the hood, and then ran a finger over the leaves I had embroidered along the fur trim. "You do such lovely work."

Elissa spoke for the first time. "Yes, mistress, truly you do." She looked down at the embroidered handkerchief I had given her. Of course her gift was not quite so extravagant as Auren's, but I suddenly got the feeling that the little piece of embellished linen was the fanciest thing she had ever owned. The light in her eyes dimmed a bit. "But I have nothing for you."

Truly I had not expected anything, and I said gently, "Midwinter is about giving, not receiving, Elissa. That you are pleased with your gift is enough for me."

Elissa's words seemed to have affected Auren as well. "I wanted to give you something, mistress," Auren said, "but I could not decide what would suit you best."

Luckily I had always found Auren's heedlessness to be a source of amusement rather than irritation. So I smiled and replied, "Did not your father already give me the greatest gift your family could give, the gift of my freedom? Surely I have no need of anything else."

"That's right," she replied. "In all the confusion, I had forgotten." A frown troubled her brow. "So you will be leaving us?"

"Not until spring. I would not wish to travel so far in winter, and besides, now there is the plague...." My words trailed off. For a brief moment I wasn't sure whether in the remotest corner of my soul I was happy that the plague had trapped me here for the winter. At least no one would question my decision to stay.

Both of the girls looked distressed by my words, and I realized that for a few moments they had probably forgotten about the plague. Still, I could not pretend it did not exist.

"But we are all well and safe here," I said, echoing the words I had stated earlier down in the hall. "And now I think

I smell Merime's pigeon pie. It must be time for supper. We should make ourselves ready."

Auren immediately set the fur-trimmed hood down on her bed and stood. Elissa folded up her handkerchief with exquisite care and tucked it into her bodice, but then she shot me a nervous glance, looking from me to Auren and then back.

For a moment I wondered what ailed her, and then I suddenly understood the reason for her diffidence. This would be the first time I entered the hall as a free woman. I somehow doubted that Lord Shaine would have me sit at the high table, but I also felt certain that I would no longer take my place among the more exalted of the household slaves, the ones who were lucky enough to eat at the long table in the kitchen instead of out in the drafty slave quarters.

At that thought a sudden wave of nervousness passed over me, but I knew better than to betray my own unease. I could not control what would happen, after all.

Instead I forced a smile, then said, "Let us go down." I could not allow them to see how important this meal was to me.

I could not allow them to know how much I cared.

CHAPTER ELEVEN

I SHOULD HAVE KNOWN my fears were baseless. As soon as Auren and I entered the hall, Lord Shaine stood up from his seat at the high table and came toward us. "If you would do me the honor, Mistress Merys?" he asked, and gestured toward an empty seat several places down from his own massively carved chair.

Nodding, I took the seat he specified, trying to ignore the sharp-browed glare Lady Yvaine shot at me. Though of course I could not have expected to be seated immediately next to Lord Shaine—that honor had been given to Auren, who sat on his right, and Lord Marten, who had the place to his left—still the position I occupied put me on a level with her ladyship, and I could tell Lord Shaine's solicitude toward me had definitely raised her ire. But of course she could not publicly voice her disapproval, and so instead she settled for a few more baleful glances in my direction before the servers arrived with the food.

This was no feast such as Lord Shaine had offered his guests at Midwinter. Young Lord Larol and his family might be with us for an extended time, and Lord Shaine apparently had decided not to bother with the niceties for such a lengthy period. The meal we ate was simple enough—Merime's pigeon pie, a dish of sweet tubers and onions, bread and butter.

In Farendon, we have a saying: "The most welcome visitor is unwelcome after four days." I could tell that held true here as well. Lord Shaine might feel duty-bound to keep his daughter's affianced groom and his family safe here at Donnishold, but I got the impression it was a duty he found more and more of a burden each day. His expression was pleasant enough, but he seemed little inclined to speech, and there was an uncharacteristic restlessness in the way he played with his knife and fork.

Although I certainly understood how he felt, I knew there was little he could do to remedy the situation. It might be weeks or even months before it was safe enough to resume contact with the outside world. It actually worked in our favor that the estates of Seldd were so isolated from one another; as long as we were careful, we could avoid contagion. Lord Shaine and his overseers had made sure that we had sufficient stores to last out the winter. The men would still go out and hunt when the weather permitted in order to augment the mounds of smoked meat, poultry, and fish that had already been laid down against the coming of the cold season. Now it was simply a waiting game.

Even as I sat and ate the simple but filling food, however, I felt uneasy. It somehow seemed wrong to sit there and feel warm and safe and satisfied when so many others might be suffering and dying at that very moment. Had I not taken a vow to succor the sick? Should I not have immediately left this place once I knew I was free of infection, and gone out into the world to see what little relief I might bring?

And how much could you do? the practical side of my mind asked. *You are one woman, and they must number thousands of sick. Surely you are not arrogant enough to think you could help them all?*

No, of course not, but the Order had taught me that one life saved was a multiple blessing, for of course each life touched many others. Who was I to remain safely here in Donnishold, sheltering myself from the plague? How could I ever face my peers again if they should learn of my cowardice?

How could I ever face myself?

I set down my fork, knowing I had no stomach for any more of my meal. Around me the conversation ebbed and flowed—carried on mostly between Auren and the Lady Yvaine as to the preparations for the wedding, with a few asides contributed by Larol and his sister Alcia—but I found I could not participate in it. Instead, I stared off toward the dark doorway at the far end of the hall, the one which led to the keep's main corridor and the entrance to the castle. Did I possess the courage to walk down it one last time, to face horror and death and the very real possibility that I would never see this place again?

Several times I noticed Lord Shaine's keen blue-eyed gaze resting on me, but as he sat several places away, of course he could not engage me in conversation without the rest of the table listening in. No one else seemed to notice my abstraction, and it was with an immense feeling of relief that I saw the kitchen slaves come in at last to clear away our table settings.

At this point in the evening, Lord Shaine would usually retire to his study, and Auren often would come up to the tower to join Elissa and me for an hour or so of needlework before we went to our respective beds. Unfortunately, I had no idea of how the evenings had been spent in my absence, now that the household numbered young Lord Larol and his family.

So I waited, hands folded in my lap, as the table was emptied and I watched Auren to see what happened next, hoping that I might take my cue from her. To be honest, I mainly wished that I could slip away, quiet and unnoticed, so I could go to my room and decide what I should do. My conscience told me I should prepare to leave the next morning, after I had gathered together as many supplies as I could, but I already felt myself resisting that course of action. What difference could one day make, or two? Such a mission would require rest, and preparation, and was not something to be undertaken lightly.

But those were specious arguments, and I knew it. Better that I should admit to my fear. Fear can be healthy, after all, if it makes one more cautious. However, I knew there was more to my reluctance than a simple desire to avoid the misery and death which surely awaited me beyond Donnishold's borders. I hadn't imagined that small but telling hesitation as Lord Shaine had bade me farewell before I departed for Arnad's estate. Could I really leave this place without knowing anything of his true feelings for me?

The others at the high table stood, and I did so as well,

watching out of the corner of my eye as Larol and Auren stepped closer to the hearth, their fingers intertwined. They shot a few furtive looks in their respective parents' direction. No doubt they plotted to see if they could slip off to a secluded corridor where they might share a few stolen kisses. Lady Yvaine fixed her son with a disapproving glare, however, and Larol blushed suddenly, while Auren seemed to find something of absorbing interest in the wilted greens that still adorned the mantel. I surmised that the two lovebirds weren't feeling quite brave enough yet to face her ladyship's wrath.

Meanwhile, Lord Marten and his daughter wandered off in the direction of the hearth as well. His lordship didn't seem to be particularly perceptive, so his movements most likely betrayed only a desire to stay warm in the drafty hall, and not any particular interest in his son's and future daughter-in-law's doings.

No one seemed to be paying any attention to me, so it seemed the perfect opportunity for me to slip out of the hall unseen. I stepped down from the dais and began to move in the direction of the tower stairs. But I had only gone a few paces when Lord Shaine's voice stopped me.

"Mistress Merys."

With some reluctance, I turned. He stood next to his seat on the dais and regarded me carefully, a half-amused look on his face. "Away so soon?"

"I thought I should leave you to your family's company."

He glanced at Larol and Auren, and at the other members of Larol's family who clustered near the hearth. "They seem to have some occupation for the moment. I would speak with you privately."

At his words my heart began to beat more quickly in my breast, but I merely bowed my head and said, "Of course, my lord," then waited for him to step down off the dais and come to stand beside me.

Gesturing toward the doorway, he indicated that I should follow him, and I did so, feeling increasingly puzzled. I would have thought he might prefer to speak to me in his own chambers, as we had done so many times before, but instead he led me out through the corridor, on into the open courtyard.

It was bitterly cold. The stars glittered like chips of ice against the night sky, but I saw thin ribbons of cloud beginning to drift overhead. From that harbinger, along with a shift in the wind's direction, I guessed that another storm had begun to move in from the east. The signs did not bode well for my travel plans. I knew little of Seldd's geography or its roads, such as they were. I had reached Lord Arnad's estate without incident only because I had a native to guide me. What would I do in a midwinter snowstorm, if I found myself stranded far from everything I knew?

Lord Shaine paused just outside the entrance to the keep. A faint breath of air from inside the hall followed us, like a ghostly memory of summer's warmth. The freezing air in the courtyard seemed to settle on my body, heavy as a leaden cloak. Although I could not deny a small thrill at being here alone with him, I knew we could not stay outside for very long.

"You seemed very far away at supper," he said.

A little startled, I risked an upward glance at him. Only one torch relieved the darkness, and so I saw little in his face—just a chance gleam from his eyes, and exaggerated shadows below his brow and cheekbones. "Perhaps I was," I admitted. "I have much to occupy my mind."

"Such as?"

Did I dare to tell him the truth of my thoughts? But how could I do otherwise? I owed him honesty at least. "My lord, I cannot stay here."

My reply appeared to surprise him. He shifted slightly, and stared down at me. "A few days ago you seemed determined to stay the winter," he said, and I could discern nothing from his tone. "May I ask what has happened to change your feelings on this matter?"

"I have had time to think," I replied simply.

"Think on what?"

The cold from the freezing stones on which I stood seemed to be working its way up my legs, leaching all warmth from me. I crossed my arms in a vain attempt to slow down the chill that threatened to overtake my entire body. "That I cannot hide here in safety when there are so many who need my help."

He didn't waste time asking me to explain myself. When he spoke, his tone sounded strangely gentle. "And do you sincerely believe you can make that much of a difference, one woman working alone?"

At his words I opened my mouth to protest, and he held up a hand, requesting my patience. "I do not mean to belittle your skill, Merys," he said. "I of all people know how much healing you hold in those hands of yours. But how much good can two hands—even ones as skilled as yours—do against a great evil such as the plague?"

A question I had already asked myself, and one for which I had no ready answer. But still I replied, "More good than these two hands could do here, sitting idle." Hoping I looked braver than I felt, I gazed up at him. The uneasy light in the courtyard rendered his familiar features almost unrecognizable. I might have been speaking to a stranger. Paradoxically, that notion gave me the courage to go on. "I swore an oath, my lord, an oath to tend the sick and the wounded, wherever they might be, and whatever illness they may be suffering. It is a very simple oath, actually, one which has no provisions that allow the healer to avoid his duties simply because he fears for his own life. This is a risk we all must take, we who swear our lives to the Order. I cannot abandon my vows now, just because the thought of what lies beyond these walls terrifies me."

I fell silent then, wondering if I had said too much. Certainly it was the longest speech I could ever remember uttering in his presence.

For a moment he did not speak. Then he said, "You are an extraordinary woman, Merys."

His words of praise brought the blood flooding to my cheeks, and I stammered, "Oh, no, my lord. That is—I do only what I have been sworn to do, what I know I must—"

"Are you contradicting me?" he inquired, and although the words might have been stern, I could tell from the amused tone of his voice they had not been intended that way.

"No, my lord," I said meekly, and he laughed outright at my uncharacteristic humility.

"Enough of that," he remarked. "So is there nothing I can say to dissuade you?"

There were many things I wished to hear him say, but I knew I did not have the courage to articulate any of them. I merely looked away from him, glad of the uncertain light.

"Well," he said, then paused. "I will say them anyway, even if they do nothing to change your mind. Auren needs you. The people of Donnishold need you. Would you abandon them to their fate, to succor strangers who know nothing of you?"

The hope that had begun to blossom in my heart seemed to wither and die. What a fool I was, to think he had any regard for me save how I might serve him, serve the people I could tell he loved, even those who numbered among his slaves. Each word seemed like a barbed dart, causing agony with every syllable, driving home the knowledge that he meant far more to me than I did to him.

He watched me closely. No doubt he expected some sort of reply, but my tongue was a dead weight in my mouth, my throat dry. I cleared my throat.

"My lord—" I began, but a new voice interrupted me, saying,

"Mistress Merys!"

Gathering my ragged composure as best I could, I turned to see Wilys, the master of horse, approaching from within the keep. He had not been at supper, as far as I could recall, and so must have first gone inside looking for me.

I stepped away from Lord Shaine, who said nothing. But I could sense him standing there behind me. I could only hope that my face had not betrayed me, that he had not been able to read any of my disappointment from my expression. I was glad then of the poorly lit courtyard. Perhaps the shadows had sheltered me.

Somehow I forced my features into more placid lines and turned to Wilys. I managed to ask in Selddish, for I knew his grasp of the common tongue was shaky at best, "Is anything amiss?"

The gods only knew what he must have been thinking, to see me and his lord huddled in an obscure courner of the courtyard. But of course he would say nothing. A t any rate, whatever it might have looked like, the exchange between Lord Shaine and myself had been entirely innocent. Too innocent, unfortunately.

Wilys frowned. "Mistress, one of my stablehands has been taken ill. I need you to come look at him."

"Of course," I said immediately. This was, after all, my duty, and even if I had determined to leave Donnishold, I could not turn my back on someone who needed me here. This would delay my leave-taking, no more. A contemptible part of my mind hoped that the stableboy was quite ill, taken with an infection of the lungs or something else that would require me to stay for some days. Anything that would prevent me from having to say farewell to Donnishold and the man who had impossibly claimed my heart, even though I knew it was not mine to give.

I had thought myself well beyond such entanglements, but the gods had apparently deemed otherwise. I could not stop to marvel at their cruelty, however—I had someone who needed my assistance. "I need to fetch my supplies," I said. "What are the sick boy's…." And I trailed off, realizing I didn't know the Selddish word for "symptom." "How does he ail?" I finished lamely.

"Fever, and his breathing sounds bad, like a winded horse," Wilys replied.

That could describe a number of things, unfortunately. Well, I would know for myself soon enough. "Wait for me," I told him, then fled, not daring to meet Lord Shaine's eyes.

As hastily as I could, I mounted the tower steps to my room. Elissa slept already, her face a pale blur in the dark chamber. By that time I knew the room's layout so well I had no need of a candle; I merely knelt by my bed and pulled the satchel out from its hiding place underneath.

Auren met me at the bottom of the stairs, Larol's family ranged behind her. They must have noted my precipitous dash up the tower's stairs.

"Is something wrong?" she asked. Although she sounded calm, I could see the worry in her eyes.

"Nothing you need to trouble yourself with," I replied, and uttered a silent prayer that my words were the truth. "One of the stablehands has fallen sick, and Master Wilys has asked me to look in on him."

Auren still looked troubled, so I added, "It is the season for coughs and fevers, my lady. I find myself surprised that I haven't been called in for such a thing ere this night."

At my words, she nodded, and said, "This is true, mistress. Why, last winter we were all laid up with a fearful ague. I wish you had been with us then!"

I said, "Well, I am here now. But now I must go to attend this boy—"

"Of course," she replied at once. "I did not mean to keep you."

Her manner seemed almost too grave, too courteous, but I thought I knew the reason why—the disapproving Lady Yvaine stood only a few paces behind her, listening to our every word. No doubt she would be quick to note any misstep.

"No harm done, my lady," I said, and gave her a reassuring smile. "It is your right to inquire as to the health of your household." These last words I said in a slightly louder tone, so the Lady Yvaine could not help but hear them. I certainly did not envy Auren her future mother-in-law.

But after that I made a quick curtsey, then hurried back out to the courtyard, where Wilys and Lord Shaine both waited for me. Lord Shaine sent me one long searching glance before he nodded, then turned and went back inside the keep. How I wished I could have followed him. Instead, I nodded at Wilys, indicating that I was ready.

Without speaking, Wilys led me toward the stables. The slaves who worked there slept on the premises, in a small lean-to built up against the south side of the building. I supposed this was so they could be immediately on hand in case any of their charges should require special care during the night. For all their outward sturdiness, horses could be remarkably fragile creatures.

The stablehands numbered five, not counting Wilys, their master. The four boys who were not ill loitered in the stable proper, looking uneasy. I did not know them very well, as they spent the majority of their time in the stables or in the training yard, making sure all of Lord Shaine's valuable property remained in top form. The red-haired one looked vaguely familiar, however, and I remembered that I had seen him in the hall during the Midwinter feast.

"In here, mistress," said Wilys, and pushed aside the

heavy leather curtain that served as a door for the stable-hands' quarters.

It was a mean, small room, crowded with too many bunks for the space. But the two lanterns which illuminated the place showed it was neat and reasonably clean, no small feat for a chamber shared by that many young men. I supposed that Wilys kept a close eye on all of them to make sure they did not dirty the room overmuch.

The sick boy lay on the bottom bunk nearest the door. I went to him immediately, kneeling down on the cold stone floor next to his bed.

He did look very bad, face pale and somehow sunken, a sheen of sweat covering his thin features. I heard immediately his rapid breathing, and began to run down a mental list of possible maladies. So many diseases presented first with fever, but for his breathing to be that labored, yet with no cough? Typhoid, possibly, in its early stages, but there had been no other cases on the estate that I had known of. Indeed, aside from the usual chills and bumps and bruises, Lord Shaine's people were a remarkably healthy lot.

The boy muttered something I couldn't quite make out, and I said in Selddish, "I am Mistress Merys, the healer. Can you understand me?"

"Hurts," the boy said, and pushed at the rough blanket that covered him.

"Hurts where?" I asked. "Does your head hurt? Your chest?"

He shook his head, and grasped the blanket once more and shoved it off him. It was certainly not warm enough in there for him to do such thing, especially when wearing a thin linen tunic such as the one that covered his slender form, and I automatically reached out to cover him up once more.

"No!" he protested, attempting to slap at my hands. "Hurts there."

The blow felt as if it had been delivered by a very small child, so weak was he. With a sigh, I folded the blanket back so that it would only cover him up to mid-thigh. Tenderness in the belly?

"Does your stomach hurt?" I asked, praying that perhaps he had merely ingested some food which had turned, or water gone bad from standing too long.

A feeble head shake. Then he pointed at his groin.

Trying to ignore the feeling of dread that began to tighten my throat, I grasped the edges of his tunic by my fingertips and lifted.

For a long moment I could only sit there and stare at the swelling in his groin, at the bruised lump that had distended and distorted the pale skin there. Some part of me wanted to stamp its feet and cry, It's not fair! like a small child given a punishment she felt she did not deserve. Hadn't I taken every precaution? Hadn't I done everything in my power to ensure neither Brit nor I carried any trace of the disease?

All my cautions seemed to have to been for naught. Suddenly feeling unutterably weary, I replaced his tunic with as much care is I could, then rose to my feet. Wilys and the other stable boys watched me, fear already showing in their faces, although I had said nothing. Perhaps my own features had already betrayed me.

The plague had come to Donnishold.

CHAPTER TWELVE

"He is very ill," I said. Somehow my voice remained cool and calm, although I was neither of those things at the moment. "And I very much fear that some of you will be ill soon as well."

"It is the plague?" asked Wilys.

I did not know the word itself in Selddish, but his meaning was clear enough. "Yes," I replied.

The man's face drained of all color, and the stableboys shifted and murmured amongst themselves, but at least none of them tried to bolt. So Wilys had that much control over them.

"You must all stay here," I went on. If I focused on what to do next, perhaps I could keep a tight rein on the panic that had begun to coil in my belly like a restive snake. "I can't do anything about the contact you've had with the other members of the household, but we absolutely must make sure no one else is exposed any more than they already have been."

"How long?"

I admired him then, admired him for the stoic way in which he faced me—and his fate. I didn't bother to ask him what he meant by the question. "Usually the first signs of illness appear within three or four days of exposure. Of course, I have no way of knowing how long it has been since each of you was exposed." I swallowed, and wondered if the judges back in Lystare felt this way when they handed out a death sentence. Of course, in those cases one hoped the condemned man was guilty of the crime that demanded his life, whereas I knew Wilys and the young men—boys, really—who clustered around him were completely innocent. A deep breath, and I continued, "It will be much as it was with the stableboy here. A fever. Difficulty breathing. Swellings in the groin and armpits, and possibly the throat."

"And then—until it is over?"

His voice shook somewhat, but Wilys broad, pleasant faced was resigned. And somehow that angered me, that he should think himself dead while he still lived and breathed.

"It may not be," I told him, and an expression of surprise passed over his features. The stableboys looked at me askance. "I was too late for Lord Arnad's people, but I am here for all of you now. There are things that can be done—even for him." I gestured toward the limp form of their stricken comrade. "The important thing is for all of us to remain calm, and for you to remember that I have been trained in these things."

Brave words. A few of the stableboys' faces brightened a little as they appeared to take what I had said to heart. Wilys' features remained stolid and unmoving, but he gave a little nod. Perhaps they believed me more than I believed myself.

After all, they had seen me save both their master's life and the life of his daughter. They knew I had stopped infections and eased coughs. Very likely they had no idea how pernicious a thing the plague was, and how, as it had lain dormant for so many centuries, I had no practical experience in how to treat it. I had read books and a few surviving accounts. I knew how to recognize the symptoms, and I knew of a few measures, such as lancing the plague boils to release the infection inside. But all of that counted for very little in the long run. I knew that some of the people watching me at that moment would die, and most likely many of the people who lingered inside Lord Shaine's keep, still blissfully unaware of the doom that had fallen on us all.

Not him. Dear gods, I can bear it if at least I don't lose him.

Immediately I was ashamed that such a thought had even passed through my mind. I was here to help everyone, not just the man I had come to love.

"I need you all to think of whom you've had contact with, and tell me their names," I went on. "I will pass word along that those people will need to be separated as well. I'll ask Lord Shaine to turn the larger of the dye huts into a—" I stumbled for a second or two as I realized I didn't know the Selddish word for "quarantine"…if indeed there even was one, "—a place where people can be kept apart from the others."

The stableboys began whispering amongst themselves, and produced far fewer names than I had expected. Perhaps that wasn't so odd; they did tend to be isolated out here away from the main keep. Still, the list was long enough, and included half of the men-at-arms, as well as most of the kitchen staff. Wilys repeated many of the same names, but added Master Breen to the count, and my heart sank a little. The falcon master did not always take his supper in the great hall with the family, but he had been there often enough that there was a chance they had all been exposed.

Flushing furiously, the eldest of the stableboys said he'd also seen Irinna, one of the young women who worked among the dyers.

"Seen her?" jeered one of his comrades. "Funny way of putting it. Stuck your tongue down her throat, more like."

The stableboy turned even brighter red, and I sighed mentally. So I would have to add this Irinna and her companions in the dye hut to the list of possibly exposed people. At this rate, there would be very few in the stronghold who wouldn't be under a cloud of contagion.

A knock came against the doorframe of the stablehands' sleeping quarters. I heard Ourrel's voice say, "Mistress Merys?"

"Don't come in!" I called out. At once I went to the door, but I opened it only a crack. "Stand back, Ourrel. The plague is here."

Silence. Then, "Gods help us."

"Let us hope they can," I said crisply. "Tell Lord Shaine one of the stableboys is ill, and I have no doubt that the rest of them have been exposed. And I as well, so I will have to remain here."

I could not see Ourrel's face, but there was no mistaking the slight tremor in his normally deep, calm voice. "Of course, Mistress. How may I be of service?"

"I'll need my satchel, and some changes of clothing—Elissa can see to that." I paused. "Perhaps you should fetch something to write with. I have a list of people who may also have been exposed."

"No need for that, mistress. Just tell me."

Then I recalled the times I had seen him working with Lord Shaine, when Ourrel could tally up long lists of sums in his head and somehow keep track of his master's requests and instructions without ever having to take notes or write down pieces of information. A handy skill. "Very well," I told him. "Here they are." And I rattled off the names, and said a quarantine area should be set up.

"It will be done, Mistress Merys. I will also have extra food and blankets brought out. And a pallet, so that you need not sleep on the floor."

I thanked him, and he left. At once I returned to the sick boy, who had fallen into a light, feverish doze. Carefully I lifted his tunic so I could once more inspect the swelling at his groin. It was a smallish lump, not quite the size of an egg, with angry red edges. From what I could recall of my studies, lancing the bubo only seemed to be successful when it was further advanced, and more of the sickness had centered in the infected node. I had no idea how long that would take, but it was clear I would be performing no surgeries on the boy tonight.

"He is resting," I told Wilys and the watching stableboys. "And we should all rest, too. How do you feel? Any light-headedness, fever?"

They all shook their heads, but I knew better than to be relieved. The disease would do as it willed. Just because they hadn't presented any symptoms yet didn't mean that they wouldn't wake up delirious and shaking the next morning, or the next night.

And there was no guarantee the same wouldn't happen to me as well. What they would do if I fell ill, I didn't want to contemplate. Then again, even if the plague had already invaded my body and begun to take hold, I should still have a few days where I could be useful. In the meantime, I would take what measures I could.

After lifting up my woolen outer skirt, I reached down and began tearing strips from the hem of my chemise and one of my petticoats. Wilys looked on, somewhat aghast, as the stableboys laughed nervously. One of them even had a ridiculous glint in his eyes at the sight of my exposed ankles.

"Oh, for goodness' sake," I snapped, and thrust one of the strips at the young man in question. "Tie that over your mouth. All of you," I added, as I handed a piece of linen to each of them. "Like so." And I demonstrated by tying the strip over my mouth and nose.

"What good is this going to do?" the one stableboy who had been caught kissing Irinna asked.

"None of you are coughing yet," I replied, my words somewhat muffled by the linen strip. "That means the contagion is not in your lungs, and therefore isn't in the air. By covering our mouths and noses, we can keep the infection from entering our air passages."

They shot dubious looks at one another, and at me, but no one seemed inclined to argue when I was offering them a shred of hope, even if it was flimsier than the linen which covered the lower halves of our faces.

I heard another knock at the door, followed by Lord Shaine's voice. "Merys?"

Something within me seemed to turn over at the sound

of that warm baritone, but I knew I must maintain my composure. I was a physician of the Golden Palm, not a lovesick girl. Lifting my chin, I made my way to the door, and once again opened it the barest crack. "My lord," I said formally.

I could see nothing of him save a slight glint of his eyes in the reflection from the lantern inside the lean-to. "Is what Ourrel says true?"

"I fear it is. But as of now only one of the stableboys is ill, and rest assured I will do everything I can for him—and to make sure none of the others here catch ill."

His voice was rough. "And what of you?"

"I fear I am exposed as well, and so must endure here for a while. But remember, I survived Lord Arnad's estate, so I am sure I will make it through this as well. I cannot take a chance by returning to the keep, however. You understand."

"I don't understand a thing," he said, and it was clear he made no attempt to hide the bitterness in his voice. "How could this have happened, after all the precautions we—you, that is—took?"

"I fear I have no answer for that, my lord." Indeed, it was a question that still gnawed at me. Truly the plague was an evil thing, to have so neatly circumvented all the safeguards I had put in place. But I had no time to inveigh at the gods, or my own clumsiness. "If I have learned one thing in this life, it is that railing against what might have been does me very little good. Only tell me that you will manage the quarantine, and that I will have all the supplies here that I have requested."

"Whatever you need, Merys," he said at once. "That is the least I can do for you. But if it spreads—"

"Then the quarantine will be set aside, of course." I tried to ignore the traitor part of me that whispered if such a terrible thing were to come to pass, at least I would be free to see Lord Shaine, to have more of him than a disembodied voice outside a door. "But we must hope that never happens. In the meantime, please follow my precautions. Make sure everyone stays in their rooms as much as possible, and have everyone cover their mouths and noses like so." I cracked the door open just the tiniest bit more so he could see the fabric I had tied over the lower half of my face.

"I will make certain of it."

Oh, how I wished to fling open the door so I might have him hold me, feel the comfort of his strength, even though I knew that strength would be of little use against an enemy as evil as the plague. Somehow I retained enough control of my wits to stifle the mad impulse. Instead I said, "You should go, my lord. We know the plague is here, but we cannot say that about the rest of the stronghold. You must return to where it is safer."

He was quiet for a moment, then said, "I fear you are right. But tell me—you will be well. Promise me."

"I promise," I said immediately, even though I knew such a promise was a foolish and empty one. Even I couldn't guarantee my safety.

But that seemed to be enough for him. "Take care, Merys," he told me, and then he was gone.

I closed the door but lingered there, one hand still resting on the door latch. Somehow I did not want to turn around. For once I did so, I would be confronting the reality of my situation—the sick boy on his bed, the other young men who had placed their all too fragile lives in my hands. I took in one breath, and another. My lungs were clear, the air seeping in around the door frame cold and clean. I was alive, and so was everyone else. For now.

Then I turned, and began to explain what we all needed to do.

Because none of the others had yet showed signs of contagion, I had them move out into the stables proper. Luckily the straw-filled mattresses on their bunks were light and easy enough to move. There was some grumbling about having to bed down with the horses, but I pointed out that the horses would actually help them to stay warm, and that I doubted very much whether they wanted to be in the same room when it did come time for me to lance the plague boil. After that they picked up their belongings and moved away with some alacrity, and, despite the situation, I saw a quick grin flit across Wilys' mouth before he sobered once again.

Some time after that Ourrel had several of the household slaves leave a veritable mountain of supplies outside the door—a pallet for me, bread and fruit and several meat pies, flagons of hard cider and buckets of water, piles of fresh linens and sheets and blankets. Moving everything inside took some time, and for that I was glad. I could concentrate on storing the supplies and setting up my pallet on the floor next to the sick boy's bed, even though Wilys tried to persuade me to take the bunk across from the plague-stricken stablehand.

"It is probably safer on the floor," I pointed out. "After all, I have no way of knowing whether the infection has touched that bunk. Not to say that a floor is the cleanest place in the world, but at least it is not someplace where someone has been sleeping."

He could make no argument against that, and finally disappeared into his own room, which was located at the far end of the stables. Most likely he was the safest of all of us, since he had slept apart from the boys in his charge. I had no way of knowing for sure, of course. The plague had already shown itself to be a most capricious disease, and it was entirely possible that all of my careful precautions would be for naught. Still, I had to try. If nothing else, following all the rules I had been taught to prevent contagion gave me some sense of security. The collected wisdom of those who had gone before me must count for something.

But none of them had fought the plague, my mind whispered, as I lay down on the pallet and tried to will myself to sleep.

True, the Order had been founded many years after the last outbreak had ravaged the continent, but that fact couldn't discredit their wisdom, nor the fact that many different diseases could be treated with the same sorts of medications and methods. And at least I could make this fight here, where I knew I had adequate supplies. Had I not spent most of the autumn gathering and concocting medicines to fight the various ailments I knew always descended with the onset of winter? A fever was a fever, after all, whether brought on by influenza or plague.

If not precisely comforted, I did feel somewhat calmer after I had assessed the situation. Besides, I would be of no good to anyone if I allowed myself to be overwrought and deprived of sleep. I shut my eyes and pulled the blankets more closely about me, and drifted into blackness.

The dream was upon me once again. Once more I dug through the midden behind the kitchen door; once again dirt blackened my fingers and nails as I flung carrot tops and peelings aside. Something pale caught my eye, and I seized on it, only to see it was merely a clump of poisonous mushrooms. Tears stinging my eyes, I continued to paw through the mess, my breath coming short with fear and desperation. And then I froze, for I heard a keening cry, a sound so unearthly I thought it must have come from the throat of some wild animal.

It came again, and I sat up in my pallet, clutching the blankets to my breast. For a second or two I could not think where I was, and then I realized I lay on the floor of the stablehands' hut. I had left one lantern lit, and its flickering illumination showed whence had come that horrible cry. The ill stableboy had sat bolt upright in his bed, hands scrabbling at the lump in his grown. Blood and pus dribbled from the wound, and blood marked his sheets with ghostly stripes that looked almost black in the dimly lit room.

At once I scrambled to my feet, even as I heard a clatter of worried voices from the main stables. Wilys burst into the lean-to. "What is amiss?"

"He's delirious," I said, bending over the afflicted stableboy, who was writhing as I attempted to grasp him by the wrists and push him back down against his pillow. "We must tie his hands down before he hurts himself again."

The stable master nodded. "Stop gawking, you!" he reprimanded the young men who had gathered around the doorway, their worried chatter a nervous counterpoint to the unearthly howls coming from their ill comrade. "Go fetch me some rope, and be quick about it!"

Apparently they weren't so unnerved they couldn't recognize a command when they heard it. Two of them darted away and came back with several lengths of rope, probably horses' leads or somesuch. Wilys took it from them and came over to the delirious boy's bunk, then grasped one of his wrists and tied it to the post. I gasped with relief, for in his fevered state the young man was far stronger than I had imagined, and I hadn't known how much longer I would have been able to hold him down. My relief didn't prevent me from tying the wrist I still held to the other post, and as I did so Wilys grasped his ankles and fastened them down as well.

Once I knew the stableboy was secured and could do no further harm to himself, I went to my satchel and fetched the strong spirits I kept there always, along with a clean cloth. After soaking the cloth in the alcohol, I applied it to the wound. The boy screamed again, but there was nothing for it. I could not allow a secondary infection to set in; his fingernails were far from clean.

"Gods, he's possessed!"

"Hardly," I said crisply, although I couldn't fault Wilys for thinking such a thing. To an observer who knew little of fevers and pain and what they might do to the mind, the stableboy's writhing and unearthly howls could seem to be the work of some inhuman invasion, and not the unfortunate byproducts of a disease that cared very little what it might do to one's sanity. "It's only the fever. I must get some willowbark tea down him, to see if I can break the fever. Have you a brazier?"

"In my room. I'll go fetch it."

Why he went himself instead of ordering one of the onlooking stablehands to get it, I wasn't sure. Perhaps he didn't trust them to handle it...or perhaps he merely wished to remove himself from the sick stableboy's presence.

In the meantime, I could do little except continue to dab at the ulcerating lump in the boy's groin. His howls redoubled. With a sigh, I stood and went to light another lantern so I could see better what I was about. In truth, the malignant bulge did appear to have grown in even the short amount of time that had passed since I had fallen asleep. No wonder he'd cried out so and tried, in his delirium, to rid himself of the source of the pain. Red streaks radiated outward from the mass, and it had begun very much to resemble a shiny white egg shoved underneath his skin.

Wilys returned, a sturdy brass brazier in one hand and a sack of coal in the other. Moving quickly, he set up the brazier in a corner as well away from the bunks as he could safely manage, and then struck a flint to catch a spark from the coal. "It'll still be a few minutes, mistress," he said.

"I understand. But in the meantime, could you fill that pan with water? Over there." I pointed to where I had collected the pots and pans in one place, next to a heaped pile of water skins.

He nodded and set to work, and then hung the pan from a trivet and set it over the brazier. As he completed this task, he shot a worried glance toward the boy in the bunk, who still writhed against his bonds. The light from the various lanterns glistened in the sweat that had collected along the young man's brow.

"He looks very bad, mistress."

Well, there was no denying that, but I had seen people who appeared even worse and yet had somehow managed to live. Of course, none of them had had the plague, but I made myself take heart from the fact that over the years I had managed to save several who had, to all appearances, been on their death beds. "How is that water doing, Wilys?"

My question hadn't been meant as a rebuke, but he appeared somewhat chastened as he replied, "Nearly hot, Mistress."

"Good." I selected a few pieces of choice willowbark from my satchel and went and dropped them into the steaming water. Among the other kitchen accouterments that had been sent along were several wooden spoons, and I took one and began to stir the mixture slowly. It needed to steep, but not boil, and I adjusted the trivet slightly so the pan of water wasn't quite so close to the coals, which had begun to glow in shades of orange and red.

Wilys glanced past me to where the boy twisted and turned in his bed. He had stopped screaming, but continued to moan in low, guttural breaths that somehow were more wrenching than the screams had been. "Can you really help him?"

I never paused in my stirring of the willowbark mixture, even though Wilys' question had caused my heart to skip, just for a second. What good, really, was willowbark tea or hot compresses or any of the remedies I might employ against something so pernicious as the plague? But I couldn't let myself doubt. I had to try, no matter how hopeless the cause might seem.

"I'm treating his—" Again I floundered in my poor Selddish, and resolved that I must ask the word for "symptom" from Ourrel or Lord Shaine or whoever might be the next one to check in on us. I sighed, and said, "I cannot cure the actual plague. All I can do is treat the signs of it. But it's those signs that can kill you, whether from the fever, or vomiting, or—" Again I had stop; "hemorrhage" was also not in my limited vocabulary. "At any rate, if I can bring the fever down, he might have a fighting chance."

The stable master nodded slowly, but he looked grim. "And if not?"

I did not reply. The answer seemed clear enough to me, and Wilys was no fool. He knew what would happen if all my tisanes and poultices were for naught. Now it was time to put them to the test. "Bring me a cup," I said.

Of course the stableboy did not want to swallow the tea. From having been dosed with it myself once or twice when I was a child, I knew it tended to be bitter; my mother had always put honey in her willowbark tea, but I had to save my precious stores of honey for infections. I could not use it as a simple sweetening agent. But the boy was certainly not the first patient I had dealt with who did not want to take his medicine, and I coaxed it down, tipping it toward the back of his throat so his gag reflex would cut in and he had no choice but to swallow.

After he had forced it down he did seem to quiet a little. His head fell back against the pillow, and he no longer seemed to fight against the restraints on his wrists and ankles. I knew better than to think this was anything but a momentary victory. In dread diseases such as this, a physician may win a battle here and there but still ultimately lose the war. Still, I was a little heartened to see the boy slip into what appeared to be a natural sleep. Often the defenses of one's own body could be the best medicine. If he slept, perhaps he could gain the strength to fight off the disease himself.

Wilys asked quietly, "He's not…?"

I shook my head at once. "No, he but sleeps. I've cleaned the wound he gave himself, but I shall have to keep an eye on that. I'm hoping that it will continue to rise."

"Whyever for?"

"Because then I can cut it open."

The stable master shot me an aghast stare. "What?"

I explained to him how the poison of the disease could be drained from such a wound, but it was clear he didn't understand, or didn't wish to. Perhaps he was only envisioning having to be my assistant in such a procedure. Obviously he was the only likely candidate for such a role, as I doubted any of the other stableboys would be of much use in the operation.

"It's all right," I said gently. "There may be no need for such a thing, if he can fight off the fever. The plague is not always fatal."

At that Wilys raised an eyebrow. It was true, although one could never predict who would live and who would die. Some people seemed to be immune, while others would come down sick and yet somehow recover. This applied only to the bubonic form, of course—if the disease entered the lungs or the bloodstream, then the victims invariably died within the day. That is what I feared happened to Lord Arnad's household, as almost all of the victims there seemed to have perished from acute pneumonia.

"I'll watch over him," I told the stable master. "You need your rest as well, and this is my task, my charge. If anything happens, I will call for you."

It seemed as if he would protest, but then he nodded. "You know best, mistress." He hauled himself to his feet and went through the doorway to the stables. I could hear him say a few words to the boys who still seemed to be loitering near the entrance, and they appeared to disperse back to their respective beds.

As for me, well, this would certainly not be my first sleepless night, and I guessed it would not be my last. There was a little stool tucked into the corner near the head of the bunk, and I fetched it and sat down. The sick boy did not stir, not even as I touched two fingers against his throat to gauge his pulse. It was weak and fast, but the sweat on his brow had dissipated a bit, and his skin did not feel quite so hot as it had previously. I had to be content with that.

Usually when I sat up with patients through the night I had a book or a piece of handiwork to keep me occupied. I had no books with me, save the notebook where I recorded the various medicinal mixtures I concocted, and I had forgotten to ask for one of my half-finished needlework projects when I gave my list of required items to Ourrel. Just as well, I supposed, as I would have had to burn it once I left this place—*if* I left this place.

I chided myself for that. So far I felt fine, if more than a little weary, but I was used enough to that. Lacking anything else, I catalogued my list of supplies once again, and made mental notes to myself to ask for more alcohol and turmeric, which I had used in the past to treat a variety of illnesses. I had never read anything about turmeric being useful in treating the plague, but it had aided me in the past and could possibly be of some help now. And so I rattled on, trying to keep my mind active, as the minutes and then hours ticked by and the boy slept quietly before me.

It came on so quietly that I hadn't even realized I'd fallen asleep until I lifted my head with a jerk from where it fallen on the rough blanket of the stableboy's bed. Careless, even if I had been weary. I should have asked Ourrel for some tea; the stimulant would have helped to keep me awake.

I could do nothing about it now, however. I leaned forward and laid my hand against the boy's cheek.

Only to find it cold against my touch, cold and still as the bitter morning outside. As I slept, he had passed from this world.

For a long moment I only sat there, staring at his still features. He looked peaceful enough. Perhaps his heart had stopped, or some other organ had failed. It happened that way sometimes, according to the accounts I had read. Better that, I supposed, than to die in convulsions and writhing pain, or drowning in his own mucus. Still…

I reached out and lifted the blanket to cover his pale, quiet face. And then I wept, for I realized I had never even asked his name.

CHAPTER THIRTEEN

We could not bury the body, of course; the ground was frozen solid and would remain that way for some months. Ourrel's men left a pile of firewood near the rear entrance of the stables. Everyone in the household was under strict orders to stay away, and so we sent the boy—whose name was Drym, as it turned out—from this world on a pyre that rivaled those of the barbarian kings of old. And then we could do little but wait and worry, and wonder who would be next.

A day passed in such quiet misery. The stableboys sent furtive looks at one another, as if trying to see who might be displaying any symptoms of the plague. None of them did, so far—they were a thin but healthy lot, as far as I could tell. Perhaps Drym had been the exception, and perhaps the disease would pass the rest of us by. That was foolishness, I knew, but the heart will often hope for what the mind knows cannot come to pass.

Ourrel brought by more supplies, and Lord Shaine came to me in the late morning. I had no words of reassurance for him, save my continuing health, but that seemed to be enough for the moment. He spoke quietly of his sorrow at Drym's passing, and I could only say in response that at least the boy's death seemed to have come to him peacefully enough. I did not bother to mention that it was a far better fate than that which had met those in Lord Arnad's household. There was no use in painting pictures of future horrors. And after a murmured wish that our quarantine would not continue for much longer, he left. He had his own frightened household to keep watch over. After he left, I tried to hold the sound of his voice within my mind, the warm tones that always made me think of a finely tuned woodwind. It was all I could have of him, it seemed.

And on the third day of our quarantine, Wilys came to me with a face somehow pale and flushed at the same time. His steps, which usually seemed so steady, now wavered, and he watched me with frightened, bloodshot eyes.

No, I thought. *Not him. Of all of them, he should have been safe.*

"I have it, don't I?" he asked. And though the expression in his eyes reminded me of a wild animal caught in a trap, his voice sounded calm enough.

"Perhaps," I replied. One touch on his forehead told me he burned with fever. "Any aches?"

"My head pounds, and I hurt here." He reached up and touched his left armpit, but gingerly, as if even the slightest pressure pained him.

I knew what that meant, of course, but I still had to see for myself. "May I?" I inquired.

A careful nod, and he watched with white-circled eyes

as I removed his leather jerkin and then undid the laces on the heavy linen shirt he wore underneath. Sure enough, as I lifted the billows of fabric away, I could see a reddish patch under his arm, vaguely circular in shape. The lump had not yet begun to rise, but I knew it lurked under the skin, a vile eruption waiting to come forth. Carefully I replaced his shirt and said, "Let me help you back to your bed."

"So," he said, his tone heavy. Then he nodded, and straightened his shoulders, even though I could tell the movement pained him. "Should I not come to you here?"

"No," I said at once. "Your bed is already separate from the others, and you will be more comfortable in familiar surroundings. I can move my pallet in there, as well as the brazier and my other supplies."

He watched me for a moment, his face pinched but resigned somehow, as if at least now that he knew the worst he would do his best to face it. "No need to help me, Mistress Merys. I can still walk under my own power."

Slowly he turned from me and made his way back to his own room, while I bent to gather up my pallet and all the other items I would need to nurse him. My hands shook as I tucked my little notebook into the satchel, and I paused a moment to regain my composure. I would be of no use to Wilys or anyone else if I could not keep calm. He was just another in a long line of patients I had cared for through the years. I could not let the fact that I knew and liked him stand in the way of his treatment. Nor could I allow myself to be shaken by the severity of the disease we all faced. My masters at the Order would be most displeased to see me rattled like a young student confronted by her first case of the pox.

Thus having mentally scolded myself, I trudged through the stables with my burden as the stableboys watched me with frightened, pale faces. At least the scent of horses and straw was familiar and almost comforting, bringing to mind happier times and memories of freedom. Of course, I was free now—technically. But the bonds which tied me to this place now were just as strong as the chains of slavery had been.

In an odd way, it was almost a good thing that the stableboys were slaves. The habits of obedience had been so ingrained in them that I guessed none of them even thought of trying to escape, to break quarantine by fleeing this place and seeking to run somewhere away from the plague. They certainly had the means, were they so inclined, as they had access to mounts and tack and a good supply of food and water. If I had been in their place, I would have at least entertained thoughts of escape, but although the fear on them was so palpable I could almost see it rising like some sort of miasma in the pale sun that poured in through the high windows of the stable, none of them did anything beyond mutter to their fellows as I passed them by.

Wilys' room was small but neat, much like the lean-to the stableboys had shared until disease drove them out into the main stables. He had a rope-slung bed with a good mattress that proved to be filled with feathers, not straw, and likewise he had a hearty pile of thick woolen blankets. Besides the bed there was a small table and a chair, and on the table was a lantern. No need for it yet, as his room was also blessed with a window covered with the thin transparent membranes poorer folk used when they could not get glass. But at least it was light.

Not that the light revealed anything besides a very sick man.

The stable master had followed my advice and taken to his bed. The leather jerkin he had been wearing was now draped carefully over the back of the room's single chair, and he had the blankets pulled up to his chin.

"I'm going to make some willowbark tea," I told him, and I saw him shut his eyes and shake his head.

"And that did so well for Drym."

"He was farther along in the disease than you," I said, my tone firm. That was true enough; I still had no idea how many hours the stableboy had sweated with fever in his bunk before someone thought to call me in to look at him. Whereas with Wilys the lump in his armpit had not yet begun to rise, which signaled to me that the disease had not been working for nearly as long.

"Hmph," replied Wilys, but that was all the protest he made.

I busied myself with setting up the brazier and the trivet, and then I placed my satchel and the supplies I thought I would need on the tabletop. It was very neat as well, with a wooden plate, bowl, and cup stacked to one side, along with a small knife with a handle of carved horn. It was true that Wilys seldom came to the hall to dine with the other members of the household, but I hadn't realized that he ate here alone in his room.

It came to me then how isolated so many of the people here on the estate were, even those who counted themselves free. Apparently Wilys had no family, and neither did Ourrel nor Breen, as far as I could tell. They had given their lives over in service to their lord, and the household had become their family.

As it had for me.

No, that was foolish. I had become fond of these people—more than fond, in the case of Lord Shaine—but I had my own family, my parents and siblings and the extended complex network of cousins and aunts and uncles that touched most of the merchant families in Lystare, not to mention family friends and those in the Order with whom I had become close. How could I possibly think of Lord Shaine and his household as more important to me than those who were my own flesh and blood? True, I had spent more hours in company with the folk of Donnishold than I had with my own family of late. The life of an itinerant healer did not allow for much in the way of familial visits, although I did try to see them several times a year, depending on where my travels took me. They were dear to me, so very dear, even if months and months passed without my seeing their faces or hearing their voices. And yet, these people here, from Merime to Auren to the stately Ourrel, had somehow become just as dear, and I knew I would mourn their loss as greatly as if I had lost someone of my own kin.

Reckless of me, and yet I knew it was something I could not have avoided. I had not been blessed with a cool and distant nature, the way some of my fellow physicians in the Order had been. For them it was easy enough to look at a patient as a series of problems to be solved. I had trained my mind to work that way because I knew I must, but my spirit fought against it always. As I knew I must fight against it now as I treated Wilys and all the others who were sure to follow.

In silence I poured some of the willowbark tea into a cup I had brought with me, as the one which sat on his table must surely be infected with the plague as well. He drank the tea without protest, although I saw the slightest flare of his nostrils at its bitter taste. Once he was done, I took the cup from him and set it down on the table; I would wash all the utensils down with alcohol before I used them again.

"And my boys?" he asked.

"All still well, as far as I can tell," I replied. It was possible that one or more of them could be hiding their symptoms from me, but I didn't think that very likely. Already they had become accustomed to my being there in case of any illness, and there was no reason for them to conceal the signs of the disease.

"That…is something."

His speech sounded slurred, and I sent him a sharp glance. He had settled down against his pillows, and his eyes were shut. Yet the sheen of sweat on his brow did not seem quite so pronounced, his color not quite so hectic. It appeared the willowbark had done him some good. Most likely he was only slipping into sleep, which was the best thing for him.

I tried not to think of what had happened to Drym when he had fallen asleep.

There being very little else I could do, I sat and watched the stable master as he slept. However that sleep had come upon him, it was a restless one—he seemed unable to stay in one spot for more than a minute or so at a time, and would twitch and toss as he vainly sought a more comfortable position. I considered waking him, but I knew even a restless sleep was better than none at all. Besides, those disordered movements at least signaled to me that he was still alive.

I wondered how they fared in the castle but supposed all should still be well, as of course either Ourrel or Lord Shaine himself would have come to inform me if anything was amiss. Still, I chafed at my isolation here, even though I knew we had still been very lucky to have the outbreak in the relative isolation of the stables rather than in the keep itself. And I wondered again how the disease had come here at all, when I had taken every precaution I could think of to keep it outside the walls of Donnishold.

Then one of the stableboys came to the door, eyes wide and dark with fear. "Mistress—"

Even though I knew the answer, I had to ask the question. "Is someone ill?"

"Grahm, Mistress—he's took bad!"

Well, I was a fool if I thought the disease wouldn't continue to spread like a fire in a summer-dry forest, but even so my limbs felt heavy with a terrible weight of dread as I stood and cast one more look at the still-sleeping Wilys before I gathered up my satchel, then turned and followed the frightened boy out to the stable.

It was easy enough to see where the afflicted Grahm lay—all the other stablehands had retreated to the farthest position in the stable, while he writhed on the straw in an empty stall. And when I knelt down next to him, at once I saw that he was in far worse shape than Wilys.

His face, too, was flushed, but sweat dripped off it in a river, and splashed in all directions as he thrashed away in the dirty straw, which stuck to his neck and face and the exposed flesh of his forearms below his too-short sleeves. On that exposed skin I could see small dark-colored circles, and my heart sank. He moved, and he breathed, but when the plague spots came, lore stated that death soon followed.

How it could have come on him so quickly, when no one had told me he was ill, I had no idea, but that mattered little now. If one of the horses in the stables had been taken so ill, it would have had its throat slit, and quickly, so it could suffer no further pain. I could not do that to Grahm, of course, but I could help him out of this world in the same way I had aided Lord Arnad.

Grimly I opened my satchel and pulled out the little vial of poppy. For one long, agonizing moment I stared at it, unsure as to whether I could really do this thing. Arnad had been far gone, almost comatose, but the boy before me still moved and breathed, even though every breath was more labored, and his movements had a stiff, jerky quality that showed they were the result of convulsions and not any truly conscious effort on his part. And then he coughed, and coughed again, and a gout of blood spattered against the pale straw beneath him.

Without thinking, I pulled a clean cloth from the satchel and wiped the blood off his chin and mouth. He should at least leave this world with some dignity. His form trembled beneath my hands, seeming as frail as a butterfly's wing. Before I could lose my resolve, I set aside the bloodied cloth and retrieved the vial of poppy, and tipped three or four drops into his mouth.

He did not choke against it, as Drym had with the willowbark tea. No, he swallowed it in one convulsive spasm, and almost at once went limp and quiescent, his lashes long and dark against his livid cheeks.

"Goddess grant you grace," I murmured, although I did not truly believe the words. My mind refused to understand how any deity could send such suffering to her subjects.

I rose to my feet then, and automatically brushed the straw from my knees. With one hand I retrieved my satchel; the other, borne by some unconscious reflex, reached up to push a stray hand of hair off my brow. I did not want to think of what I had just done. My work was to heal, not kill, but the plague had no respect for such niceties. Terrible as my decision had been, I knew it was the right one.

"He is gone," I said clearly. "We must take the body outside and burn it, as we did with Drym."

From a darkened corner of the stable came a shaky voice. "No, mistress, even though you command it."

While I understood their fear, I also knew it to be pointless. All of us were doomed, even though we as yet walked and breathed as normal folk. "Don't be ridiculous!" I snapped, my own desperate fear giving my words an unaccustomed sharpness. "We've already been exposed—all of us. Touching him now will change nothing. I would do it myself, only I am not sure I could carry him so far, and I must go back to check on Master Wilys."

A protracted silence then, one broken only by the faint ghosts of what I guessed must be a whispered argument amongst the stableboys who yet lived. They numbered four now, and I was sure all of them were more than a little discomfited by the fact that they had already lost a third of their small crew. I waited, knowing that in the end I was powerless to force them to do anything they did not wish to do. Wilys, perhaps, could have done so, but he was ill-suited for anything at the moment save lying in his own bed and fighting the infection in his own way.

At length two of the boys came forward, one so slight and thin I wasn't sure whether he would be any great help in removing Grahm's body, and the tall one with the firm chin who had once, in a time that now seemed centuries ago, confessed to kissing Irinna, who worked in the dye hut.

"Thank you," I said briefly, and that was all.

They knew what to do; the taller boy took Grahm by the shoulders, while the thin one grasped the dead stablehand's feet, and together they shuffled him away and out through the large double doors that led to the courtyard. We still had some wood left over, although I did not know whether it would be enough. I would have to ask Ourrel for more when he came to check on us. Luckily the door into the stableboys' lean-to was on the opposite side of the building from the spot we had chosen for the funeral pyres. I had told Ourrel that everyone should stay as far away as possible from that side of the structure.

I knew the boys would tell me if the wood was insufficient, and so I went on, back into Wilys' room, where he still seemed to have slept through everything. A quick touch of his forehead told me his fever appeared to be somewhat lessened, and I took some heart from that. His sleep had quieted as well; his hands lay folded against the dark wool of the blankets. Those hands were browned and covered with scars and calluses. Clearly he was not the sort of master who stood back and allowed his underlings to do all the work. No, those hands had seen hard labor, and they told me as much about the man as his actions and words had.

The window blazed with sudden orange and gold. Apparently the stableboys had found enough fuel to feed this last pyre. I stood in the center of the room, watching the false warmth of that fire limn the small modest room in shades of ochre and russet, and wondered where it would end.

By some miracle, Wilys lived through the night. I slept on my pallet on the floor next to his bed, starting at every sound, but in truth he was far less restless than I. And when a pale wintry sun sent its first tentative rays through the blurred panes of the window, I looked up to see the stable master still quietly, gently asleep. His broad, plain face was peaceful, and the breaths he let out sounded quite normal. Moving with care, I pushed my own blankets aside and stood, then placed a wary hand on his brow. I thought he still had a fever, albeit one greatly reduced from the day before.

He opened his eyes. They were blue—a bright blue, startling against his tanned skin. He looked from side to side, and his eyebrows lifted in an expression I would have found comical if it were not for the fact that I was so grateful he was alive at all.

"How are you, Master Wilys?" I asked.

For a moment he said nothing, but only lay there in his bed and seemed to consider my question. At least, his brow furrowed in quite a formidable way before he replied, his voice sounding quite strong, "I—I am all right, I think."

I wouldn't give in to the relief that passed over me. It happened this way sometimes, according to the accounts I had read. Live or die? Who knew? The gods, perhaps, but they never revealed their secrets.

If they even existed.

"May I see?" I asked Wilys, who looked confused at first, and then nodded and pushed the blankets away so I could take a closer look at the problematic spot in his armpit, where the infection was centered.

Only it wasn't there. Oh, I thought I saw the barest reddish stain against his skin (which was far, far paler there than on his hands and face and neck, which were exposed to the sun day in and day out), but when I laid a gentle finger against that spot, he didn't even flinch, and I could sense no hardening beneath the surface that would indicate the developing shape of a plague boil. Incongruously, I found myself glad that the boil had started to develop there, under his arm, and not in his groin as it had with Drym. Of course I knew all about the male anatomy—one could not preserve maidenly modesty for very long in my profession—but still, awkwardness could sometimes arise when a female physician had to treat a man with whom she'd had social interactions.

"Anywhere else?"

He shot me another of those perplexed glances.

"Any soreness in any other places?" I had read that sometimes the plague could play tricks, that it could travel from place to place within the body. Somehow I did not think that the case here. For one thing, his fever was greatly reduced, which indicated that his own natural defenses had somehow managed to fight off the invader, when for whatever reason the stableboys had been unable to do so.

His hands lifted from their resting place on the blanket and moved to touch his body, beneath the other arm, along his throat, and finally over his groin. He hesitated, then said, "I feel nothing, Mistress Merys."

"You don't?" It couldn't be true. He had to have missed something. "If you will allow me?"

He nodded, and turned his face away as I ran professional hands over his neck, his arms, and his groin. Even though I studiously avoided his gaze, I saw a wash of red pass up over his throat and face, a flush that had very little to do with fever. As soon as I was able, I stepped back. I had been taught to keep my features cool and impassive, but I guessed that at the moment I was not very successful at doing so, for Wilys' own face seemed to light up, and he asked, "Is it gone?"

"I don't know if it's gone, precisely," I replied, "but you do seem to be much better. I have read that it happens this way sometimes. I believe you are a very lucky man, Wilys."

"Thanks to you, mistress."

I didn't bother to disabuse him of that notion. If he wanted to think I had something to do with his apparently miraculous recovery, then so be it. I knew I had done nothing but help to bring down his fever. His own body had done the rest.

At that moment I heard a muffled pounding noise I couldn't quite identify. The tall stableboy appeared at the door to Wilys' room less than a moment later. "Mistress, Master Ourrel is asking for you. He says it's important."

That most likely could mean only one thing, but I wouldn't allow myself to become agitated. I told the stable master to stay in his bed and that I would be back to check on him in a moment. Then I hurried through the stable and back into the stableboy's lean-to. I cracked the door open less than an inch and looked up into the steward's lean, worried face.

For once he seemed to have abandoned the niceties. "Merys, we have need of you."

"What is it?" The fact that he had not bothered with my title was not lost on me.

"It's Merime. She's—she's begun coughing. And she has a fever. She says it's nothing, just a touch of the ague, but it seems much worse than that."

"Coughing," I repeated, my tone flat. The brief euphoria I had experienced at Master Wilys' seeming recovery vanished as quickly as morning mist with the rising of the sun. "Anyone else?"

He shook his head. "No."

Not yet, was what that really meant. For if Merime, who prepared the food for everyone in Lord Shaine's household, was coughing, then it was only a matter of time before others—many others—fell ill. A very short amount of time, if what I had read was true.

"I must go to her," I said, and opened the door fully. Ourrel took a step back, his normal dignity somewhat impaired by his haste to get away from me. "Don't you see, Ourrel? It matters not whether I've been in contact with plague victims here, when someone in Lord Shaine's immediate household is ill. No one is safe. Not I—not you."

He paled as my words appeared to sink in.

"Come," I continued. "We have very little time."

CHAPTER FOURTEEN

Merime had been taken to her own bed in the small room off the kitchens where she had made her home. Even as I entered the chamber she began to fuss, saying it was foolish for me to be there when all she had was a touch of the ague, which came upon her each year at the same time. And then she began to cough, her round frame wracked by convulsions that brought up a phlegmy mass into the handkerchief she held against the lower part of her face.

I had taken the time to once again cover my own face with a strip of linen, even though I had abandoned the precaution after Master Wilys had fallen ill. But none of the stableboys had shown evidence of the airborne type of the plague, and so such measures hadn't seemed necessary. Here, though, they were the only safeguard I could think of. As soon as I entered the building I instructed Ourrel to have everyone do the same. Perhaps it was a case of locking the safe after thieves had made off with the family fortune, but I could think of nothing else to do. I also informed him to spread the word that the residents of the castle should retire to their rooms and not venture forth for any reason. They all might have already been exposed, but I didn't know that for sure, and perhaps the preventive measures I put in place would be enough to save even a few lives.

At least here I had ready access to the kitchen, and at once I put a pot over the fire to boil. The one thing all the plague victims had in common so far was a fever, and so I guessed that brewing up a large batch of the willowbark tea was a logical first step. When I brought a cup to Merime, she shook her head in between spasms of coughing and gasped, "I can't—swallow—"

"Try, Merime, there's a dear," I soothed, and brought the cup to her lips. Truly, she wasn't able to get down more than a sip or two before being wracked with coughs once again, but I waited for the paroxysm to pass, and then slipped down a few more swallows, and continued in such a fashion until she had gotten through half the cup.

She whispered, "No more," and I took the cup away from her lips. It would have been better for her to have the whole dose, of course, but one of the things I had learned over the years was to stop when a patient had reached the end of her endurance.

Although her room was quite warm, backing up to the kitchen and the enormous double hearths there, I still asked her, "Are you warm enough?" For I knew well enough that the actual temperature in a room had very little to do with someone's comfort when they had been overcome by a fever such as that which the plague brought on.

But she only nodded, and slid down a little on her pillows.

Her eyes shut. I knew better than to hope for a miraculous recovery such as Wilys had made, however. When the illness reached the lungs, there was very little I could do except try to ease each patient's suffering as best I could.

Once I had determined she truly was asleep, her breath coming in short pants as if she knew even in sleep that to draw in breath any more deeply was to invite another bout of coughing, I slipped out of her room and back into the kitchen. I had my satchel with me, of course, but ranged in the larder and pantry there were a great deal more supplies I could use to supplement my arsenal. Even so, if the whole household should fall ill, I didn't know how long any of them would last. Still, it seemed best to take inventory now, before any more of Donnishold's residents began exhibiting symptoms.

I fetched my little notebook and went to the pantry, then stood in the open door so daylight could illuminate the various jars of herbs and spices. Just off the kitchen was a small room that Merime and I had begun to share where we both hung herbs to dry, and I would have to take inventory there as well once I was done here. Things had been so scattered for the past weeks that I truly could not recall what I had set out there myself and what Merime had had the slaves gather.

Here was marigold, and feverfew, and stores of licorice root and burdock and dandelion. Almost all of them could be used in one way or another, and I sent an unvoiced thank-you to Merime for her organization. She had made things so much easier for me—even if she might never know.

"Merys."

I turned at the sound of Lord Shaine's voice, muffled now by the strip of linen he wore over his nose and mouth. His dark blue eyes were grave, and more shadowed than they had been two days ago.

Foolish that his voice could make my heart skip a beat, now when I had so many more important things to concern me. Somehow I managed to meet his gaze directly. "My lord."

"Please." He waved a hand. "With all that has come to pass, I think the time has come to dispense with formalities."

"Very well…Shaine." The word sounded oddly raw on my tongue.

He nodded, but his gaze was abstracted, his eyes not meeting mine. "How is Merime?"

"Not well." I hesitated, then realized that I could only give him the truth. I had always been plain with him before this, and I vowed to remain that way, no matter what our end might be. "She has the pneumonic form of the disease." At that remark his brows drew down, and I could tell he did not know the common word I had used. Most of our conversations were held in my native tongue, as he was so much more fluent in that than I in Selddish, but even his scholarship had its limits, I supposed. "It has gone into her lungs. I cannot say why—none of my studies have ever truly explained why the disease manifests in these different ways, or why it should afflict one person in one manner and another in one quite different. But this, I fear, is where the true danger lies. For once it has reached the lungs it has no cure, and it is far more contagious than the type of plague that affected the stableboys, and Wilys."

Shaine's head went up at that, and his frown deepened. "Wilys is ill?"

"Yes, my…Shaine. I thought you knew." I hurried on, wishing to tell him at least one bit of good news, "But he has made a most miraculous turn, and I do believe he will recover. That happens as well, although it is the exception, unfortunately." And I reminded myself that once I was done in the kitchen, I would have to return to check on the stable master. Just because he seemed to be on the mend did not mean I could leave him untended indefinitely. Perhaps I should have him brought into the castle; he certainly ran no risk of being infected anew, and I knew that very soon I would have little enough time to devote to running back and forth between the kitchen and the stables.

"That is something, I suppose." He hesitated, and this time he looked on me squarely, as if trying to inspect me for any signs of illness. "But you are well?"

"So far." I somehow managed a laugh, although it sounded false and tinny even to my own ears. "Don't you know that I never get ill?"

"Never?"

"Oh, once or twice I've had a slight bout of congestion, but nothing beyond that." Again I wondered at such a thing, for usually physicians of the Order would fall ill at least once a season. It was something that couldn't be avoided, no matter what precautions we took. And yet invariably I had always been the one to nurse the others through their rounds of bronchitis and fever and flux. That great good luck, however, certainly couldn't extend to the plague, but I wasn't about to tell Shaine that. Let him think that I was miraculously immune. Perhaps it would give him some strength to face what lay ahead.

At least he looked healthy enough, straight and strong, with no trace of sweat or flush of fever on his features. Again I gazed on his tall form and wished things were different between us, that I could fold myself into those strong arms of his and find some kind of solace there, but I could not change what was. I had to keep my mind trained on the situation at hand.

I went on, my tone crisp and no-nonsense, even though I found I couldn't quite meet his eyes, "Because Merime prepares the food for everyone, I must assume that all in the castle have been exposed in some way. She was careful, more careful than many cooks I have come across over the years, but all it would take is a chance cough into a pot, or her wiping her nose on her sleeve, and the disease would make its way around everyone who had eaten that food."

"So there is no hope for us?"

On someone else's lips such a question might have sounded self-pitying, but he seemed brisk and no-nonsense, only wanting to know how matters lay.

"I would never presume to say there was no hope. Only that now I am not sure how much I can do to stop the spread of the disease, as I have no idea who might have already been exposed to it. And, as I said, once it is in the lungs, there is not a great deal I am able to do, except ease my patients' suffering." I thought then of Lord Arnad, dead at my hand, and poor young Grahm as well. "Still, I believe that keeping people as isolated as possible can only help, and covering our mouths and noses, so that if someone does cough in our vicinity we do not breathe in their illness, is simply the sensible thing to do."

"So it floats on the very air?"

"I believe so. I think that it is passed in other ways when we speak of the form of the disease that infects the blood and causes the lumps in one's groin and armpit and neck." For some reason I felt a bit of heat touch my cheeks as I mentioned the groin, and I hurried on, "We have done much research, but it still seems that the cause for these things lies beyond our grasp. Perhaps one day we will be able to say definitively why a disease is passed in a certain way, but for now I can only follow what has been proven to work in the past. There was a bad outbreak of an influenza strain two winters ago in Lystare, and those of us who muffled our noses and mouths as we are doing now stood a much greater chance of avoiding the sickness than those who did not protect themselves. Since that was what shielded us then, I can only surmise that it will help us now as well."

"You will be our shield," he said, and added, "I cannot help but think that the gods have sent you to us, Merys." Those deep-set blue eyes caught mine, and held. His lips parted, and I waited, wondering if this time he might utter the words I so longed to hear. But then he looked past me, and added in a much more formal tone, "And you will of course let me know if there is anything else you require."

I chanced a quick glance over my shoulder and saw that Ourrel had come in from the doorway to the kitchen gardens. He, too, had the lower half of his face covered. What he had been doing outside, I had no idea, but perhaps he had been performing his own inventory of the last of the straggling herbs and vegetables—a few rows of turnips and sprouts, a patch of rosemary that hadn't quite gone dormant for the winter. At any rate, his presence explained the sudden shift in Shaine's tone, and why he did not look at me directly now.

"I thank you, Lord Shaine," I said, as proper as if I had never dreamed of what his lips might feel like on on mine.

He nodded, and acknowledged his steward with a nod before they both went out to the castle's main hall. I watched them go, my spirit aching for just a few more moments with him, even if we could not have the contact I so desperately craved. And then I sighed, and turned, and went back in to Merime.

She died just after midnight, her breath strangling in her throat as she fought against the disease that slowly drowned her in her own mucus. Very gently I pulled up the blankets to cover her livid face. Black bruises girdled her throat, making it seem as if some invisible giant had placed his hands around her neck and squeezed until the life was driven out of her. And I knew she would not be the last, for as I sat wakeful at Merime's bedside, wondering whom I should call to come and help with the body, Raifal had come creeping in to tell me that Lady Yvaine, Auren's future mother-in-law, had begun to cough.

So soon? I thought, but that was how the accounts ran. One person would sicken, and then soon after a few more, and then more and more until sometimes entire villages died to the last man.

But not here, I vowed silently. *Not while I still live and breathe.*

I nodded at Raifal and told him that I would be up directly. He acknowledged my words with a slight nod, then turned and ran back out. Above the linen strip his face looked even more pale and pinched than normal, and I knew he must be wondering who would be next, and whether that person might be himself.

No point in faulting him for such thoughts; I myself had begun to worry as to when I would begin to show symptoms, and who on earth I could trust to look after the others if I did fall ill. The household had suffered a blow in losing Merime, for she had always been the linchpin around which the doings of the castle circled. And while I knew Ourrel to be steady and as trustworthy a man as I had yet met in three kingdoms, still he was not a healer. He would not know what to do.

No one would.

I will admit that I did not look forward to my examination of Lady Yvaine. She had made no secret of her dislike for me, although I still could not quite understand from whence her animosity came. Perhaps she was more perceptive than I gave her credit for, and had glimpsed some of my attraction to Lord Shaine. I supposed that might be basis enough, for one inclined to find trouble wherever she looked; after all, if the lord of Donnishold remarried and fathered a son, then Auren's inheritance would be greatly diminished, and Lady Yvaine's son Larol reduced to little more than a hanger-on in the household rather than its eventual lord.

But all that was a great deal of supposition based on what I guessed had been at most a few stolen glances in Lord Shaine's direction, and it was entirely possible that her dislike stemmed from seeing a slave—even a former slave—given the sort of authority that his lordship had bestowed upon me. At any rate, it did not matter overmuch what she thought of me, or how unpleasant she made the process. She was ill, and I was a physician, and I had a duty to fulfill.

The castle felt oddly deserted, even though at that hour it normally would have been quite empty. But something about it seemed forsaken, as if I could sense just from walking through its open spaces that no one had gathered that night for a shared meal. Earlier in the day I had overseen the making of a large pot of stew, aided by two of the kitchen slaves, but I had returned to Merime's bedside even as the slaves took the pot out to the hall, where people could fetch their portions one by one, or, in the case of Lady Yvaine and her family, have the food brought to them to be left outside the door to their suite. That precaution apparently had done no good, as the lady was the next one to sicken.

When I reached the suite the family shared in the east wing, I saw that the door was already open, and young Larol's head was thrust out into the corridor as he looked this way and that. His expression of relief when he caught sight of me might have been comical, had the situation not been so grave.

"Mistress Merys!" he gasped.

"Lord Larol," I said formally. But then I essayed a smile and inquired, "How are you, your lordship? Any fever, chills?"

"No, none at all," he said at once. "But Mother—" His breath caught a little, and he went on, "That is, my mother began to cough a short time ago. She says it's nothing—claims it's the drafts, if you'll beg my pardon. But we thought it best to call for you."

"You did very well," I replied. "And where is the Lady Yvaine?"

"In here." He led me through a well-appointed receiving chamber, one that had finer furnishings than Lord Shaine's private rooms. But perhaps he cared more for how he housed his visitors than for his own comfort. Off the main chamber were several rooms, one of which was the place where Lady Yvaine lay in an enormous canopied bed. In one wall of that chamber was a window, and there stood Lord Marten, his gaze fixed on the dark landscape outside. What he saw there, I do not know; perhaps he only wished to look at something besides his wife's face.

For it was clear to me at once that she was very ill. Raifal had only said she was coughing, and Larol had revealed little more, but the candles burning in the chamber told the story well enough. Like Merime, she was flushed and kept coughing into an oversized handkerchief she held before her mouth. And, also like Merime, she tried to insist that she was fine.

"It's this drafty castle," she wheezed, before bringing the handkerchief up to her face and coughing into it for the good part of a minute. "Haven't—felt—well—since I got here."

I only nodded and made what I hoped was a properly sympathetic noise. That her statement was patently untrue, I did not bother to mention. No one wants to face the truth that they are dying, but some handle it with more grace than others.

"I would like to listen to your chest, my lady," I said. "If I have your permission?"

She coughed again and made an impatient little gesture, which I took to mean that she would allow my humble self to approach her august person. I tried to remind myself of the vows of my Order, that all had a right to the same care, and that the physician's personal feelings and opinions should never enter into the matter. With some it was easier to follow these strictures than others.

So I went to her bed, and leaned my head against her chest. She was swaddled in a heavy damask dressing gown even underneath all the covers, and a good deal of warmth from the fire in the main room made its way in here, but she shivered and shook like one who had been standing naked in the snow. And from her thin frame rose a heat to rival the fire in the hearth, and from within her breast I heard only gasps and wheezes, and the faint ominous rattle of airways being continually restricted.

I straightened, and saw Lord Marten watching me with a pinched expression. The gods only knew what he had glimpsed in my face.

"I have some tea for her fever," I said calmly. "And a pack of mustard, I think, for the congestion in her chest."

"And that will help her?"

There was a terrible hope in his face, and I realized suddenly that he loved her despite her high-handed ways. It would be easy enough for me to say a few calming words, and pray that I would ease his mind enough so he could sleep. With any luck, she would pass in the night, and then the horror of watching his wife slowly choke to death might be avoided. But it was also not in me to lie, not even when it might have been the more politic thing to do.

"It will ease her suffering somewhat," I said, pitching my voice low as Lady Yvaine suffered another bout of coughing. I knew she could not hear me; indeed, her husband had to lean close to catch my words. "But there is nothing I can do save that."

"You can't—that is—I thought you were a doctor!"

"I am," I replied sadly. "But doctors are not gods, your lordship. We can only work with what we have. And against the plague even we can do very little."

He scrubbed his hands against his face, then passed a weary hand over his eyes. "I had worried it might be thus," he said, so quietly that this time it was I who had to strain to hear him. "But I had hoped—I had thought—"

"I am very sorry," I said. "But let me do what I can."

And so I bustled about, heating the tea and preparing the mustard poultice. In between I inquired as to both Larol's and Lord Marten's health, and asked after the daughter Alcia, whom I had not yet seen.

"We are all well, or as well as we can be," Marten told me. "Alcia is asleep. I made sure she had several cups of wine with dinner. This waiting and wondering has done none of us any good, and it is difficult for her, with us being away from our home and everything that is familiar to her."

I looked from Lord Marten's tired face to Larol's big-eyed one, and thought it was probably for the best. They would all do much better if they retired for the night and allowed me to watch over Lady Yvaine, but I guessed that would not happen. I nodded, then went to get her ladyship to drink as much of the tea as she could, and afterward laid the poultice on her chest.

"That stinks," she complained, her tone petulant, and she tried to push my hands away. But she had no more strength than a child, so I made soothing noises and did my best to get her to rest easily. It was not time for the poppy—and perhaps she would not need it, as Merime had not—but half a drop in the willowbark tea would have settled her down. Then again, I had only a limited store, and I did not know how much of it I would need before this was all done. Better to watch and wait. In the meantime—

"You must rest easy, your ladyship," I said, in my gentlest voice, the one I used to soothe colicky babies and fretful children with toothache. "I know the smell is not the most pleasant, but it should help with your cough."

As if to contradict me, her thin frame was overtaken by another spasm, and she had no breath for a reply. I took the opportunity to tuck her hands under the blankets so she could not interfere with the poultice on her breast. She struggled a little, but it was only a token protest, as all her will had already been directed inward, to the invader that was taking over her body. She coughed again, bringing up a quantity of green bile, and I went to fetch her a clean handkerchief and take the fouled one away. Knowing it would be of no use to anyone after this, I threw it into the fire, and then wiped my hands down with some of the alcohol from my kit.

The spasm seemed to have taken the last of her energy, though, and she subsided, her eyelids dropping from weariness. She would sleep fitfully, I thought, until the pressure to cough became too great, and she would wake herself by trying to clear the air passages in her chest. And so it would go, until her body had no strength to fight any longer, and she succumbed to the pneumonia that drowned her lungs.

I saw no need to say any of this to Lord Marten. Unfortunately, he would see for himself soon enough if he sat up with me through the night. To my relief, he did send Larol to bed, saying that the boy would do himself no favors if he deprived himself of sleep and thus made himself susceptible to the disease. That seemed to do the trick, for the boy bade me a distracted good night and then disappeared into his own room.

For a time Lord Marten and I sat quietly, I in a hard wooden chair next to her bed, he in a somewhat more comfortable one near the window. He had poured himself more wine and offered some to me, which I declined. It would not do for me to dull my wits thus, even though some part of me did crave the easing of care—however spurious it might be—that the drink might have provided.

Then he spoke, his tone musing. "Why do they do this to us, do you think?"

I turned halfway in my chair so that I could see him more clearly. "They who?"

"The gods."

Without really thinking—perhaps I was more tired than I had thought—I answered by saying, "I don't believe there are gods."

That shocked him, I could tell. His eyebrows lifted, and he took a quick gulp of his wine before shooting an uneasy glance behind him, as if he thought perhaps Inyanna or Mardon was hiding behind the worn velvet curtains and was about to reach out and smite me for my blasphemy. "You cannot mean that."

"I do," I said calmly. "That is, I believe there may be some greater force in the universe that brought about the world we live in and all the wonderful things in it, but I do not believe such a force has anything to do with our daily lives. This plague, this devastation—" I lifted my shoulders. "It is only an accident of—of nature." I had been about to say "of biology," but I did not know the Selddish word for such a thing, or whether one even existed. The teachings of the Order involved a good deal of specialized nomenclature.

He said nothing at first, but only sat silent, one finger running up and down the hammered surface of the pewter goblet he held. "You are a very strange woman."

I laughed then, but quietly, so the sound would not disturb the woman who slept so fitfully only a few feet away. "Perhaps I am, Lord Marten. You are not the first to say so. Even among my people some of my ideas were viewed as odd, or different."

A corner of his mouth lifted the smallest fraction, as if that were the most energy he could exert to smile. "In truth, I am not sure which is worse—to believe as I do, that the gods control all things and so have brought this pestilence down upon us, or to see the world the way you do, and think that all which happens is merely coincidence, or accident. I will confess that I do not wish to see all this as random. The gods bring pain, but they also bring comfort."

Perhaps that was true. I had seen it even in my own family. Worldly they might be, but I know my mother had invoked Inyanna's guidance when my oldest sister went to her childbed, and offerings had been given to Thrane, lord of the land beyond death, when my paternal grandparents passed away. I had viewed such things as simple following of custom, but perhaps it went deeper than that. And if these practices offered some measure of solace, then who was I to say they were wrong?

It might have been easier if I did believe in the gods. At least then I could have railed at them, or offered sacrifices, or done something to invoke their guidance and support. As I regarded Lord Marten's sad face and knew he was already saying his goodbyes to his wife, I felt only emptiness, and the sudden gnawing of fear. For I was alone in this, with no one to guide me, and I did not know what to do.

CHAPTER FIFTEEN

In the end, Lord Marten did fall asleep, head nodding over his empty goblet. I took it gently from him and set it down on the table. By some miracle his wife also continued to sleep. Her breath came in a harsh rattle, and seemed shallower with every passing moment, but at least she hadn't begun to cough yet. I wondered then if I should try to sleep as well. Over the years I had learned how to take short naps where I could grab them, and I had seen what looked like a relatively comfortable chair out in the receiving chamber, but somehow I couldn't force myself to go in there and lie down. Despite my lack of sleep, my nerves thrummed with anxious energy, and I could not seem to rest. I knew the seeming peace of the castle around me was but a mockery, and that death moved amongst us, even if none of us had the eyes to see it.

So I was not overly surprised when a furtive knock came at the door to the suite in the dead hours of the night, and a young female slave whose name I could not recall peered up at me with dark, frightened eyes. "It's Master Ourrel," she said simply.

I would be lying if I didn't say my heart sank, or that I felt a stir of irrational anger. First Merime, and now the steward? Perhaps Lord Marten was right, and the gods did have a hand in everything. It would be one of their caprices to remove all those who were best able to manage the castle and the people who lived within, and to leave behind only the terrified underlings who would have no concept of what to do.

But I knew I mustn't think that way. For Lord Shaine was still well, and I seemed to have escaped contagion for the nonce. And perhaps Master Ourrel had caught the less invasive form of the disease, and there was still hope...

Hope could be a treacherous thing, however.

I retrieved my satchel, then bent over Lord Marten and said quietly, "My lord."

His eyes snapped open, and his gaze immediately went to the bed where his wife lay.

At once I said, "She still sleeps, Lord Marten. But I have been summoned to see to the steward, who has also been stricken. Can you manage here for a time? You can send one of the slaves to fetch me if there is any change in Lady Yvaine's condition."

For a second or two he hesitated, and then he nodded once, very slightly. "Of course, mistress. She does seem to be doing well. Perhaps even a little better?"

I wished I could tell him yes, or even tilt my head to indicate my agreement. Instead, I touched his arm, gently, and then turned and went to follow the slave girl to Ourrel's quarters.

His rooms—for he had a small suite consisting of a study and adjoining bedchamber—were located in the east tower, and were in perfect order, of course. I caught a quick glimpse of a shelf of what were obviously much-loved books and a desk with papers neatly stacked to either side before I went on into his bedchamber, which I guessed would normally have been just as neat. Now, however, the clothes he had been wearing earlier in the day were thrown over the back of a chair, and I tripped over one of his boots as I entered the room. That mattered little, though, for immediately I heard him coughing, and knew that once again I was powerless to do anything.

Even from a foot away I could feel the heat coming off him, and indeed, he had pushed back the covers so that he was exposed to the chill air in the bedchamber. The fire in the other room had not been lit. What with the household in its current disarray, no slave would have come to tend it, and of course he was far too ill to do any such a thing. As I stood at his bedside, staring down at him in dismay, I heard the swift patter of light feet and knew that the slave girl who had brought me here had decamped, wishing to put as much distance between her and the sick man as she could.

Not that it would do any good.

"I'm here, Master Ourrel," I said, and pulled the covers up over his chest. The linen sleep shirt he wore had ties to hold it closed, but he had either never fastened them, or torn them open while in the throes of his fever. I caught a glimpse of dark hair before I brought the blankets to his chin, and experienced an odd stab of shame on his behalf. The steward was always so fastidious, so proper in his dress and manner, that I knew if he had been in his right mind he would have been quite discomfited to be seen in such a state. As it was, such things mattered little now.

"He's dead, isn't he?" Ourrel gasped, and then began to cough, horrible wracking spasms that seemed as if they must shatter his very bones.

"No one's dead," I soothed, pulling fresh linen from my satchel to hold against his mouth. That was one good thing—we might run out of everything else, but we would have enough linen on hand to supply handkerchiefs for every plague-stricken man, woman, and child in Donnishold. As for this rest, it was only a small lie. True, two of the stableboys were dead, but I somehow doubted their fate was what concerned Ourrel so. The mind does odd things when caught in the throes of a terrible fever.

"Yes!" Another round of coughs, and this time I thought I saw blood mixed in with the bile he left behind on the handkerchief. How hideous a disease it was, and all the more pernicious in its frightening speed. I had seen the steward less than twelve hours earlier, and he had seemed in the prime of health as he left the kitchen in the company of his lord.

Icy fear seemed to squeeze my heart then at the memory of the two men standing next to one another. True, they had both worn masks covering their mouths and noses, but that didn't seem to have done Master Ourrel much good. Why, even now Lord Shaine could be lying in his bed, coughing his way to a slow death…

I gave myself a little shake, and a warning to set my imagination aside. If the lord of the castle were ill, I would have been brought to his rooms posthaste, but I had received no such summons. I must focus on the matter at hand, and not let foolish fancies distract my attention.

As luck would have it, I still had willowbark tea left over from the batch I had brewed for Lady Yvaine, and so I poured some into the steward's mouth, even as I fought against an overwhelming sense of futility. What good did it do to bring down the fever, when the rising tide of mucus in his lungs would slowly drown him, fever or no?

But it was all I could do, even as Master Ourrel choked and gasped and muttered more incomprehensibilities about someone being dead, and how he was needed, and couldn't tarry here. For he attempted to rise from the bed, and even in his febrile state he was strong, so strong that I had to push back against him with every ounce of strength I possessed, my hands locked around his upper arms as I attempted to force him back down against his pillows.

Somehow I got him back down onto the bed, and this time I did spare the barest drop of the poppy to ease his ravings. He went limp almost at once, his breathing still coming in terrible rasps and gasps. I backed away from the bed, and noticed that my hands shook as I put the stopper back in the vial of poppy and returned it to my satchel. What would I have done if I hadn't managed to wrestle the steward back into his bed?

You would have called someone to help you, the practical part of my mind told me, but still I couldn't seem to rid my mind of the image of Master Ourrel sprawled on the ground, possibly with me trapped beneath him. And though he was tall and well-built enough, he was not an overly large man. What on earth would I do when confronted by a burly man-at-arms who could not be persuaded to take his rest?

All evils in their times. Perhaps I would have to face that contingency; perhaps not. For now, at least, the steward was quiescent, and I was more or less unharmed, although my apron would have to go the way of Lady Yvaine's handkerchiefs. I reached up to untie it from about my neck as I went into the study. At least there was a goodly pile of wood in the basket near the hearth, and a tinder box on the small marble mantelpiece. Kneeling down and concentrating on getting the fire started gave me something else to think about besides the sick man in the next room and the others in the castle who no doubt were beginning to display symptoms as well. Once the plague had begun to spread, it was as quick and merciless and all-devouring as a forest fire.

From behind me I heard the door open and slam against the wall. I jumped at the sound and turned at once to see who had entered so precipitately. To my surprise, I saw Elissa standing there, a dark shawl wrapped around her nightdress.

"Oh, mistress!" she gasped. "They said I could find you here."

"No," I said, shaking my head. I did not want to hear what she had to say. I did not think I could bear it.

"Yes, Mistress. It's Lady Auren. She needs you."

I could not get anyone to watch over Master Ourrel, for the simple fact that all around the castle, more and more people were falling ill. I would have to tend to all of them somehow, but no one could fault me for going to see Auren first. She was Lord Shaine's daughter; of course she would have to be seen to before anyone else.

The stairs up to her room seemed interminable. My

muscles ached, but I knew it was not from fever, nor the deep aches that came sometimes with the bubonic form of the disease. No, my current pain had everything to do with weariness and that little tussle with the steward, and nothing at all to do with the plague. And all the way there I could only hear the litany running through my mind: *Not the lungs. Anything but that. Let there be a bubo. I can lance that. I can do what I can, as long as it is not in the lungs.*

But then Elissa opened the door to Auren's chamber, and I heard the familiar thick coughing from within. A wave of despair washed over me, so deep and so dark that some part of me wanted to turn and run, run far away where I would never have to hear that sound, nor see the imploring stares from people who couldn't understand how someone who had cured their other coughs and chills could not give them the succor they so desperately needed now.

Of course I did not run. I clutched my satchel, and though I did not truly believe there were any gods to hear it, still I murmured a little prayer that somehow her cough was from something else entirely, that Auren did not have the plague after all.

A dark shape moved to one side, and I looked up into Lord Shaine's haggard face. Worry seemed to have more deeply imprinted every line and shadow in his visage, even with half of it concealed beneath that strip of linen, and I longed to go to him—although whether to comfort him, or to seek my own reassurance, I could not say. I recalled Elissa's presence, though, and also somehow knew that going to him in such a way would only cause him more worry. If we lived, perhaps…

It was easier than I thought to slip into the cool tones of the physician. "How long has she been coughing?"

"Not long," he replied. "I sent Elissa out at once. I do not know why it took so long for you to come." And with that he frowned at me, and his face might have been almost a stranger's.

I reminded myself that whatever his feelings for me—if any—Auren was his daughter, and so of course she must be first in his heart, and in his worry. Still, an edge entered my voice as I said, "I was on the other side of the castle, tending to Master Ourrel. Perhaps you do not know he is ill as well."

At once Shaine's expression altered, but if anything, he appeared even more troubled. "No, I had not heard that. A bitter blow, if he is to follow Merime."

"I fear he is." Somehow I could not find the strength to say anything more, but instead moved away from him and went to Auren where she lay in her bed. At once I was forcibly reminded of the first time I had been brought to tend her in this very room, but the circumstances were far different. Then she had lain quiet, seeming far closer to death than the girl who coughed and gasped before me now, but appearances meant for very little in such things. True, her face was not quite as flushed as Master Ourrel's had been, and her cough did not yet have the same horrifying rattle as Merime's or Lady Yvaine's, but that was most likely because I had come to see Auren before the disease was as far progressed.

"Stir up the fire, Elissa," I said, and the girl ran to do as I said, even though I could tell she was shaking and afraid. At least, I hoped it was fear that made her hands tremble as she knelt to grasp the poker and encourage a bit more heat from the flames. She and Auren spent a great deal of time together in close company. If the daughter of the house was so ill, I did not think Elissa—frail, delicate Elissa, who never seemed to have enough meat on her bones—could be very far behind.

I busied myself with heating some water and pulling out both the willowbark and the ingredients for the mustard poultice. Perhaps if the congestion were caught early enough, it could be broken up before it truly caught hold.

"What is it you are doing?" inquired Lord Shaine.

As I worked, I explained how the tea made from the willow's bark would bring down her fever, and how the mustard served as a powerful relaxant for mucus built up within the chest. Together, I hoped they would give her the fighting chance she needed to bring her own body's defenses to bear, and that because she was young and strong, she might have a better chance than Merime.

Or Lady Yvaine, or Master Ourrel, I thought then, and wondered if either of them had died in my absence. Again I was struck by the thought of so many people contained within the castle, all needing my help, and all so difficult to reach.

Shaine said nothing but seemed to absorb my words, and watched quietly as I tipped some of the tea down Auren's throat. It was true that she did not fight me as Merime or Master Ourrel had, and although she made a face, for once she did not complain about the taste or comment on how I must have become a physician because I certainly had no knack for cookery. And when I said I needed her to lie quietly as I applied the mustard poultice to her chest, she did as I bade her. From time to time she would cough, and then clench the blankets with her hand as if to show she had tried her best to keep the cough from disturbing me at my work.

These homely remedies did seem to help somewhat. As with Merime and Lady Yvaine, Auren slipped into a restive sleep a few minutes after I had finished with the poultice and laid a clean cloth across her breast to protect the inside of her nightdress from the mustard mixture. As I had told Lord Shaine, she was young and healthy enough. She might have a chance where others did not.

But she has been through so much already, I thought then, although I kept such thoughts to myself. *She is only lately healed of an injury that could have killed someone else, and her body has been overtaxed. How much more can it take?*

"She sleeps," I said briefly, and straightened and brushed a stray lock of hair away from her brow before I turned to face Shaine. At that moment I couldn't even remember the last time I had run a comb through my hair. I must look dreadful.

As if such things even mattered.

"And when she awakes?"

I could not meet his eyes. "It is too early for me to say."

"And what of Lady Yvaine? Master Ourrel?"

"They are dying."

Shock showed clearly in his eyes then. I saw his eyebrows lift, and he said, "You do not bother to equivocate, or say soothing things."

"What would be the point?" Before the lines of worry could engrave themselves any deeper in the skin between his eyebrows, I added, "But I cannot say that is the case with Auren. I have come to her sooner than the others, and her condition does not seem as acute."

He did not relax precisely, but his shoulders did appear somewhat less slumped. I wished I could say more to reassure him, but the truth was, our situation was quite as bad as could be, and not likely to get any better in the near future. Since my plan to keep everyone separate to avoid further spread of the disease seemed to have failed, it made the most sense to change course and arrange things so I could attend to as many people as possible. The only way I could make that happen was to beg for the lord of the castle's assistance.

"There are more, and will be more," I told him. "This is a disease utterly without mercy. I do not know how many I can save, or how much of a difference I can make. But with everyone isolated in their quarters, I can do hardly any good at all. We must set up the great hall as an infirmary, where I can tend to everyone at once."

"But won't that spread the disease?"

I lifted my shoulders. "Shaine, it has already spread. As I came here from Master Ourrel's rooms, on all sides people came to beg me for help—and I had to say I would see to them later. Which was only right," I continued hastily, for I saw the frown begin to crease his brows once again, "but it only serves to emphasize the fact that if I had everyone in a central location, I could see to many more at a time."

"You would have my daughter down with the slaves, with the men and my other servants?"

It would have made the most sense to move her as well, but although I had come to know Shaine as a good and thoughtful lord, I knew that in this I was asking too much. Every man has his breaking point, and I thought with his daughter he had found his. And really, it would not be so bad if she remained in her room as long as everyone else was brought to the hall.

"No," I said gently. "Of course not. I would not wish to move her, not when it seems as if she is resting quietly for now. But have I your leave to order the rest as I see fit?"

He paused. One hand went up to touch the linen that covered his nose and mouth, and his brows drew down as his gaze rested on the still form of his daughter in her bed. At length he nodded. "Do as you must, Merys."

I bowed my head and went, knowing that he would stay there to keep watch over his daughter. There was no point in my telling him to stay away, that it was not safe for him to stay in her room. It could not be easy, to see his beloved daughter so ill, and less easy still for a man used to command, to having his own way in things, to see himself rendered so utterly powerless by a disease that brought low both the great and the weak.

As I had expected, I encountered some resistance to the notion of gathering everyone in the great hall, but as I reiterated that these were Lord Shaine's express orders, eventually all who could move under their own power congregated there. They made a great jumble of motley bedsteads and cots and even pallets, but they all came—the boys from the stable, the women from the weaving and dyeing huts, the field workers from their dormitories. Even Master Wilys limped in, two of his stablehands lugging his bed between them.

"Ah, I am well enough," he said, in answer to my worried question as to his condition. "Indeed, I am wondering what I did to so please the gods that they would let me off so lightly."

I found myself wondering the same thing. As I laid my hand against his forehead, I felt no heat other than the flush which might have been caused by his walking over here. His pulse was strong, and the tenderness in his armpit had quite faded. Truly it was a miracle.

Miracle or no, I bade him to stay in his bed and not over-exert himself. A relapse would do neither him nor anyone else any good, and so he heeded my admonishments and clambered into his bed with nary a word to gainsay me. Of the boys in his charge, I was somewhat less sanguine: Two seemed well enough, but the third bore a hectic color and shivered overmuch, even for one who had walked through the snow to get to the hall. For the hearth was piled high with firewood, and between that and all the bodies packed into the space, it was quite warm—almost too warm, I thought, as I grimly untied my over-sleeves and rolled up the embroidered cuffs of my chemise.

All seemed as settled as it could be for the time. I had confirmed several new cases, and isolated them at the end of the room closest to the fire, and dosed them with willowbark tea. Thank goodness I had laid up a generous store against the coming of the winter months, with their various fevers and coughs. I would have to make up more mustard poultices, but luckily several of the women who still showed no sign of the illness had volunteered to help with that once I showed them the proportions of ingredients the treatment required. Everyone still wore the linen tied across their mouths and noses, and that was something, I supposed.

I deemed it safe enough to slip away to the suite where Lord Marten and his family were housed. I did not know whether he would accede to my request to come down to the hall, but I did know that Lady Yvaine was too ill to be moved. But at the very least I thought I should tell them what was happening in the rest of the castle, and let young Lord Larol know that while Auren had sickened, she seemed to be holding her own for the nonce.

The door opened in response to my knock, and I looked up at a red-eyed Lord Marten. From the little receiving chamber beyond him I heard the sound of a girl weeping.

"Lady Yvaine?" I asked quietly, but I knew the answer.

"Gone this hour," Lord Marten replied. His voice sounded thick with unshed tears—at least, I hoped the roughness in his tone came from unspoken emotion, and not from congestion induced by yet another case of the disease.

There was never any correct thing to say an these times, but I laid a hand on his arm and murmured, "I am very sorry, my lord. May I come in?"

He bowed his head and stepped aside. I saw Alcia, his daughter, wrapped in a dark blanket and sitting in a chair as she rocked back and forth. Larol stood behind her, patting her shoulder. His face was very white, but he looked calm enough.

"You have all suffered a very great loss," I said. Whatever I had thought of her—and she of me—it was clear that Lady Yvaine had been greatly loved by her family. "And I do regret not being here at the end. But I would say that Lady Auren, while ill, does not seem to be in any immediate danger."

Larol's eyes brightened at my words, but his sister continued to weep into a handkerchief, and Lord Marten's dull expression changed not at all. Well, I probably should not have hoped for anything more than that.

I continued, "Because there are now so many whom I must treat, all the residents of Donnishold have gathered in the main hall. I have come to ask you to join them, but of course I cannot compel you to do so."

"E - everyone?" inquired Larol. Again his expression lightened a little.

"Almost everyone," I said gently. "Lord Shaine does not want his daughter moved from her rooms, and I agreed that disturbing her as she seems to be holding her own is not the wisest course. But yes, everyone else is there."

"I won't!" Alcia burst out, emerging from behind the handkerchief. Her face was mottled red and blotched with tears. "I don't want to!"

Lord Marten said, "If we are well, I do not see the need for us to go among the others. Surely that is only further risking our health."

Some part of me wanted to tartly reply that staying in these rooms with the plague-ridden and now decaying body of the late Lady Yvaine was also not something conducive to their health, but I managed to hold my tongue. After all, they had just suffered a loss, and of course they were probably not thinking clearly. Still maintaining as mild a tone as I could, I replied, "Of course I cannot compel you to come down and join everyone else. But I must also impress upon you the fact that I may not be as available to you as you would like, should any of you fall ill."

"Is that a threat?" Lord Marten's face darkened with anger.

"Of course not." I did not bother to tell him that I had no need of threats when such a calamity had overtaken all of us. "Merely a statement of fact, my lord. But I must return to my other charges, now that you know how it goes within the castle. Would you like me to see if I can find someone to—to take care of Lady Yvaine for you?"

At those words the anger appeared to pass as quickly as it had come, and he lifted a shaking hand to his temple. "If you could. I—I do not think I could manage that."

"No one would expect you to."

And so I bowed my head and took my leave, wondering who I could enlist for such an unwelcome task. Truly, it would be easier to get some of the field hands to help with removing bodies from the hall, as no one would wish to share quarters with a corpse. But I could see how some of them might think little of having to remove the lady, as she lay dead far from any of them, sequestered in the rooms where her family had chosen to isolate themselves.

Luckily, though, I came upon Raifal and another of the kitchen slaves as I descended to the hall, and although they seemed less than enthusiastic at my request, still they agreed to it.

"Better than sitting in the hall and waiting to see who gets sick next," said Raifal, and I found I couldn't disagree with him.

I looked in on those gathered in the hall, and luckily no one else seemed to have sickened in my brief absence. The women who had volunteered to prepare the mustard poultices had gone ahead and applied them to those suffering from coughs, and I experienced a flash of intense but very welcome relief. I had thought I would have to do this all by myself, but I had forgotten that even though none of these people were trained physicians, still they had nursed one another through various illnesses over the years, and the simple tasks they could manage quite well on their own.

As they seemed to have the matter in hand for the nonce, I thought I had better run back up to Auren's room to see how she fared. It would only take a moment or so, and I thought my heart would be lightened to know that she still slept, and showed she might somehow fight off the disease, impossible as that might seem.

But I met Elissa on the stairs, her face pale above the candle she held. "Oh, thank the gods, mistress!"

"What is it? Has Lady Auren taken a turn for the worse?"

Her breath hitched, and for one horrible second I thought she, too, had sickened, and begun to cough. Then I realized it was only a sob caught halfway in her throat. "She has wakened and is coughing. I gave her more tea, even though it went cold, but it didn't seem to help. But oh—that's not the worst!"

"No," I said, and shook my head. "No." Surely if I denied it strongly enough, I could make it untrue.

"It's Lord Shaine," Elissa said. "He's come down with it, too."

CHAPTER SIXTEEN

I WANTED TO SCREAM, to fall to my knees and rail against—what? The gods? But I didn't believe in them.

As Elissa had said, Shaine had taken ill. Worse than that, I found him sprawled across the rug, face down. Heedless of all else, I flung myself down beside him and turned him over. His face was flushed, and even through the thick wool of his doublet I could feel the fever heat coming off him in waves.

"What happened?" I demanded of Elissa, who had paused a few paces away, her hands knotted in the folds of her nightdress.

"I—I don't know, mistress, truly I don't!" In the flickering illumination I saw glimmers of reflected light glint off her cheeks, and I realized she wept. "He had gone to look at Auren, touched her cheek. Then he put out his hand, and if trying to reach out to something in front of him, and he just fell. I didn't know what to do, so I came to find you."

He was still and slack beneath my hands. At least he was not coughing. With a feverishness that had nothing to do with the plague and everything to do with urgency, I tore open his doublet, felt of his body. There was nothing of desire or passion in my touch—I only wished to discern if he had a plague lump. And he did, rising in his left groin. As I passed my fingers over it, he twitched beneath me and let out a sharp little cry that did not sound as if it could have come from his throat.

"We cannot leave him here," I told Elissa. "Go down to the hall and look for Raifal. Tell him that his master has been taken ill and needs to be brought to his own bed." For I knew I could not risk having Shaine carried all the way into the hall, and yet of course he could not remain sprawled as he was on the Keshiaari rug I had thought so fine only a few months ago. Taking him down the one flight of stairs shouldn't put him in too much peril.

The girl fled, pewter candlestick clutched in one hand as if it were the only thing protecting her from the darkness that sought to swallow us all. Perhaps it was.

I sat there, Shaine's head cradled in my hands, as I fought the fear rising in me. Yes, he had the plague, but he was not coughing. He had the less virulent sort. Master Wilys had survived the thing, and Shaine would as well. I tried not to think of Grahm and Drym, dead of this thing, and with twenty years of vigor that should have been on their side. Obviously I had no way of knowing who would live and who would die, but I knew I would do anything to keep the man I loved alive.

In a very short amount of time, Elissa reappeared with Raifal and the red-headed slave whose name I had never learned. Because they had spent a lifetime in servitude, they did not waste time with expostulations or exclamations of dismay. They merely took up their fallen lord and took him down the narrow stairs, on into his suite and then his bedchamber. I hurried ahead of them, pulling down the bedclothes so the bed would be ready to receive its occupant. Once they had set him down there, I thanked them hurriedly and set about removing his boots.

"Stir up the fire, Elissa," I commanded, and she hastened to comply. It had burned down to almost nothing, but the coals were still hot enough that it blazed up again quickly enough, showing me her white face, and how she shivered in her nightdress with only the dark shawl to ward off the castle's chill. I hoped that was all which ailed her, but I asked anyway, "Do you feel ill, Elissa? Any fever?"

"No, mistress," she said immediately. "Only it's so cold, and I had no chance to put on proper clothes. Should I?"

"No. I can manage here on my own. Go on upstairs and keep watch on Lady Auren. If she sleeps, try to sleep as well. You will be the better for it."

She did not have the strength to protest, poor child, but only nodded her head and then fled the chamber. I returned my attention to Shaine, who had begun to toss and turn, the fever flaring even hotter. I had had no chance to make more of my willowbark tea, but I set about the procedure grimly, attended by an overwhelming sense of futility. It had helped Master Wilys, but that meant little, for far more than the single man who had survived had already perished.

But I would allow no further thoughts of defeat. As the water in the trivet over the fire heated, I pushed the covers away so I could examine Shaine further. The lump in his groin was large and well-developed, a whitish bulge surrounded by an angry sea of red. How it had gotten so large so fast, I had no idea. And I wondered then whether he had been experiencing symptoms for some time and had only concealed them so he would not be sent away from Auren's bedside. It would explain some of his odd shortness of temper earlier, when normally he would not have reacted to my suggestion in the way he had.

Even the lightest touch of my finger on the plague boil was enough to have him twitch violently away from my touch. At once I lifted my hand and stared down at the loathsome bulge, all the while trying not to pay attention to the expanse of well-muscled thigh below it, nor his organ in its nest of dark hair only a few inches away. Of course he was not the first man I had seen thus, but it was a far different thing, I was finding, when such sights belonged to the man you loved, whom you had hoped in the dark, wakeful hours of the night might make you his. But I had no time for such things. First, I had to make sure he lived.

Steam drifted up from the pan of water over the fire. I rose from Shaine's bedside to cast the leaves upon the water's surface, and somehow made myself wait as they steeped. I worried that he would fight me over swallowing the hot liquid, but to my surprise he did not resist at all. His head lay slack against my hand as I propped it up and poured some of the willowbark tea down his throat. Then he did cough, just a little, but I knew it was only a reaction to the tisane and not the deep, racking spasms of someone infected with the pneumonic form of the disease.

As if from a great distance, I heard a male voice say my name. "Mistress Merys!"

I did not look up, but only continued to wipe the sweat from Lord Shaine's brow. "What?"

"Mistress, we have many ill—we need you in the hall—"

"I cannot come!" I snapped. "Can you not see that I am attending to your lord?"

"Yes, but—"

"I will come when I can. If he will but sleep, then I will come. In the meantime, have Tresa and Lisane brew more willowbark tea for those who have fevers."

"But Harl is having fits—"

"I said I will come when I can!" I burst out, and then there was silence, followed by slow steps and the slam of a door.

How glad I was then that my masters in the Order were not there to see me come to such a pass. For our teachings plainly told that a physician could never allow the needs of one patient to outweigh the needs of many, and yet here I was shutting myself out to those suffering in the hall below, simply because the man who lay in the bed before me was one I had come to love, who was more precious to me than the whole castle of them put together.

Hot tears filled my eyes, and I choked back a sob. "Forgive me," I told Shaine, who lay there, heart racing as if he had just run up a mountain, his whole form shivering with a fever that the willowbark seemed unable to touch. "I must go to them, but how can I leave you?"

Of course he made no response, so I was left to console myself that somewhere within his pain and delirium he had heard me, and understood. Foolish, I know, but it was the only way I could force myself to stand and then descend the stairs.

What passed then was an hour—perhaps more—of going from person to person, watching the faces of those I had come to know and care about contort in pain or stare blindly in delirium, of watching some of them pass from this world, even as I fought to break the fevers that tormented them, or loosen the bile that choked them one by one. And those who had yet to fall ill watched with the weary resignation of the condemned man who knew that it would be his neck next in the noose.

Finally, though, I broke away, saying I must see to their lord, that they need only wait a few minutes and I would return to tend to them. Whether this was a lie, or whether I truly meant it, I could not have said. I only knew that I must be away, for in the time I had been gone he could have left this world as well, passing from me before I ever had a chance to tell him all that was in my heart. I took the narrow, treacherous stairs two at a time, my fear giving my feet a sureness they had never known before. And I burst into Shaine's room, dreading what I would see, and yet knowing I had to look.

And then I did weep, for he was much as I had left him, his tall form limp and quiet on the bed, although I could hear his frenzied panting from where I stood. An incoherent cry tore itself from my lips, and I ran to him, dropping to my knees beside his bed.

"Dearest," I whispered, for I knew then that he was dearer to me than anything or anyone I had known, the one thing in this world from which I did not dare to be parted. Surely it was safe for me to utter that word now, when his delirium would keep him from understanding what it meant.

"Merys," he murmured, his lips dry and cracked from the fever. "Hurts."

"I know, Shaine. I know." Although I wished I did not have to look, I lifted away the bedclothes so I could inspect the plague boil. It had risen some more, but it did not seem quite ready to be lanced. And the coward part of me was glad, for I would have to cause him more pain in doing so. If we could only last until the morning light—and truly, it was so very late that the sun should be rising in another hour or so—then I would feel more fit to attempt such a procedure. As to who I could possibly find to help me, I had no idea. Elissa was biddable enough, but I misdoubted she would last more than two or three minutes into the operation, even if I drugged Shaine so he lay quiescent through the ordeal.

The weight of weariness fell on me then, so heavy it was as if a real physical force somehow burdened my shoulders and caused my legs to ache. I could endure without sleep if I must, but sooner or later either I or one of my patients would pay the price. I might fall ill myself, or make a mistake that could cost someone their life. Shaine seemed stable for the moment, and if anything changed with Auren, I knew Elissa would come to fetch me. Surely just a quarter-hour or so would suffice; I had bolstered myself with such brief respites while nursing patients through the influenza outbreak in Lystare a few years back.

That justification seemed to be all it required. I blinked, then tried to shake my head, but somehow sleep fell over me in a dark cloud as my head fell upon Shaine's bed and my body slumped against the frame.

At first all was utter black, deep as a night without stars or moons, and then I saw a warm glow far off in the distance, one that might have heralded the rising of the sun, save that it came from the west. Within that golden light was a figure. As it came closer I saw that figure was the shape of a woman, one of my own age or thereabouts, save that she had a beauty which would have drawn notice even in the courts of my own king. Her hair was the rich, warm brown of the finest loam, and her eyes glinted with the pure blue of a summer sky. Her gown was also blue, the deep shade of a sapphire necklace I had once seen around the neck of the Duchess of Trelion.

The strange woman smiled at me, and held out her hand. "Merys Thranion."

Startled to hear her speak my name as if she had known me all my life, still I rose from where I had been crumpled against Lord Shaine's bed. My fatigue of just a few moments earlier seemed to have dropped away, and likewise I was surprised to look down and see that I wore my fine gown of wine-colored velvet rather than the crumpled brown working gown that had been on my back for the greater part of a day and a half.

"You have my name," I said, "but I do not know yours."

Her smile broadened, showing a dimple in the creamy skin next to her rose-pink mouth. "What is in a name? I have many, you know. But for simplicity's sake, you may call me Inyanna."

She must have been jesting, although there were many

who would have said that for a mortal woman to claim the name of a goddess was not a jest, but purest blasphemy. I met her gaze directly and replied, "Surely you do not think I will accept that."

"Accept it or not—it is the simple truth. You are a doubting one, Merys Thranion, and perhaps it will take more than simple words to convince you. But look about, and tell me what you see."

Then I looked away from her face, and saw that we stood not in Lord Shaine's bedchamber, but on a peak of the Opal Mountains, with all of Seldd spread out before us. Around glinted me fresh-fallen snow, and yet I felt no cold, not even through the low indoor slippers I wore. To the east the sun rose, spreading a false warmth over the land before us. All appeared peaceful enough, but I knew that within those dark clusters of villages and towns there must be many more struggling to live, many whom the plague had already claimed.

It seemed so real that I could reach out and touch it, and I told myself it must all be a product of my sleeping mind. "Is this a dream?"

"You can call it thus, if it will help. But it is much more than that."

She waved a graceful hand, and the picture before me changed, and showed me the familiar shapes and colors of Auren's room. I saw then the terrible struggle as she coughed and the air strangled in her throat. Elissa held a handkerchief for her, tears streaking down her cheeks. She glanced about wildly, as if she expected someone to come to her aid.

"I must go to her!" I cried.

"Why?" the woman who called herself Inyanna inquired.

I whirled on her. "Why? Because she is my charge. I should never have left her."

"You left her to watch over her father. You are a very capable woman, Merys Thranion, but you are only one. And even one as capable as you cannot stop the inevitable."

Even though I knew I must be asleep, still I took a few steps forward, urgency driving my feet against all reason. And then I fetched up against the edge of a cliff, as Inyanna's voice came to me,

"Where would you run, Merys Thranion? Even if you could somehow get down from this mountain, you would not be there in time."

"In time for what?" I asked, my heart seizing with dread. The strange woman's cool tones mocked me.

"You see."

As I watched in horror, I saw Auren choking, gasping… and then falling, finally silent and still, against her pillow. Elissa let out a little scream and burst into noisy sobs before climbing to her feet and running from the room, calling my name.

"And what will she find, when she goes to seek me?" I demanded. Anger kept the sorrow at bay, allowed me to ask the questions I must.

"She will find you asleep, your cheek on the bed of the man you love. And she will wake you, and take you to see her mistress, and you will mourn the dead."

This information was relayed in a cool, dispassionate tone, and Inyanna's placid, vaguely interested expression never altered.

"You are a monster," I said.

"A monster?" she repeated. "Hardly. What distorted views you mortals have, to think that all that passes in the world below is at our behest. We have greater things to concern us than your travails, especially since we know they are as nothing, compared to what comes next."

"And what is that?"

Inyanna smiled again, my obvious ire apparently of little import. "Watch, and see."

As little as I wished to turn back to the vision—or dream, or whatever it was—reluctantly I did as she bade me, and focused on the dim little chamber, one that had just begun to be touched by the rising sun. Auren's body was a still, dark shape against the white linen of her bedsheets. Then I thought I saw movement in the shadows of the room, movement that resolved itself into the tall form of a man in old-fashioned long robes. Over all he wore a dark cloak, but the hood was thrown back to show the face of a man in his prime, noble and cleanly etched. Even in the dim illumination of the chamber I could see the glint of his grey eyes.

He approached the bed. "Auren." His voice was low, seeming to shake the room, but rich as wild honey.

And then Auren's eyes opened, and she smiled and sat up in her bed. "Is it you?" she asked.

"It is. Are you ready?"

She nodded, and smiled, and flung the thick waves of her hair back off her shoulders as she stood. "I had hoped you would come."

"I always do."

He held out his hand, and she took it, trust and happiness shining out so clearly from her dark eyes. Then they moved away, and it was as if they slowly disappeared, growing fainter and fainter until they were gone completely.

"You see?" Inyanna asked.

Confusion sharpened my tone. "I confess I do not."

She sighed then, and for the first time I heard a touch of steel in her voice. "Come, Merys, even a skeptic such as yourself surely must have recognized what just transpired. You saw my Lord Thrane come to escort the young woman to the next place."

"The next place?"

"Don't be dull. You know very well that of which I speak. You may call it heaven, I suppose. As I said, we concern ourselves with what comes next, and not the struggles of the world in which you are so engaged."

"That does not change the fact that a young woman—girl, really—who should have had her whole life ahead of her had it taken away, all by the caprice of a terrible disease."

I had thought my words might anger the goddess—if that was really who she was—but Inyanna only laughed then. "Is it so difficult for you to understand? Death is not hard for those who die. A few moments of pain, perhaps, but then it is all done, and they can move on. No, death is difficult only for those who are left behind."

"And what of us? The ones left behind, that is. So our pain means nothing?"

"It may mean something to you, but it is transitory. What you mourn is the loss of what you had, not the person who is gone. Because that person is not gone, as I have just shown you. They have merely moved to a place where such things can no longer touch them."

If she had meant to reassure me, she had done quite the opposite. For even if I were to believe that she truly was the goddess, and that truly was Lord Thrane who had escorted Auren from this world to the next, still I and everyone who had known Auren would feel her absence each and every day we were alive. And if death truly were so simple, what did that say about my profession, and the work of all those who had gone before me and who were yet to come? Did we toil in futility, our efforts wasted because we lengthened lives that would have done better to end sooner, so that they might go on to this "next place" of which Inyanna had spoken?

I said as much, and she laughed again and shook her head. "You misunderstand me," she replied. "I did not say that you should not fight these things, because they are terrible and bring suffering even when they do not bring death. I only meant to tell you mourning those who are gone is an effort that should be spent otherwise, for sadness is misplaced when its object is bettered by that change. We do not seek to interfere, but rather to guide and inspire. And that is why I am here."

"Indeed? For I am not sensing much inspiration at the moment."

Another of those tinkling laughs. "This is why I have laid my hand upon you, Merys Thranion. For we gods have no need of worship, whatever your priests may say. But we do appreciate determination, and skill, and in those gifts you are doubly blessed. Have you never wondered how it is you can go amongst those suffering from disease, and yet never fall ill yourself? It was my protection, my doing, though you believed in me not. And I have tried to guide you in this, although you dismissed my suggestions as the vagaries of dreams, of troubled thoughts that had no meaning."

"Suggestions?" I repeated. Truly, her words had given me one of the answers I had sought in this life, even though I was not sure I liked knowing it had been the doing of a goddess I didn't even believe in that I had survived this long.

"The key to survival lies in your hands, Merys. It is sometimes from the simplest things, the most mean and lowly, that salvation comes. The gods did not bring this plague upon you—it was an unhappy accident of circumstances. The source of the disease lies many leagues hence, in the hot deserts of Keshiaar. When the conditions are right—or wrong, as some may see it—the carriers come forth, and spread the illness with them. So it came from the south into Purth, and from Purth thence to Seldd. And you, Merys Thranion, unwittingly brought it with you to Donnishold."

"I!" I cried. "How is that possible, when I took every precaution?"

"Your masters are wise, and much of your teachings are helpful, but you still do not fully understand how such things can come to pass." She spread open her graceful hands; on the palm of one of them I thought I saw the smallest speck of black, perhaps a flea or other small insect, before she closed them once again. "It came with you, riding along on the horses you brought from Lord Arnad's estate. You could not have known, of course."

Her tone was light, as if what she said was not of much import, but inwardly I reeled, thinking of how I had unwittingly brought so much death and destruction down upon the people I cared about. It was easy enough for a goddess to say that death was easy. I had not enough detachment to think such things for myself. And while I could not change what had already occurred, I knew I must do whatever I could to make sure no more deaths could be laid at my feet.

Willing my voice to remain calm, I said, "You told me that the key to survival lies in my hands. What meant you by that?"

"You must see beyond what you have been taught, Merys Thranion of Lystare." To my surprise, she stepped forward and took me by the hand. "See now, what you have overlooked."

And there I beheld the kitchen garden from my dreams, and the midden heap which sat in one corner of that garden, where the compost could be used for the crops. In winter, it did not crawl with flies as it might in the summer, and the pile was somewhat sparse—no strange thing, considering how haphazard meals had become of late. But beyond the dusting of snow I saw something pale gleaming against the dark heap. The end of a loaf of bread, now mottled with mold and far beyond its use. Merime would never have let such a thing come to pass when she ruled the kitchens, but she was far past such concerns now.

Somehow that discarded chunk of bread made its way to Inyanna's outstretched palm. "As I said, sometimes it is the mean and lowly things which can bring our salvation. Something smaller than you can see has laid you low, but here is the key to fighting it, now and forever." She took the moldy loaf and placed it in my hands. “You know something of this, Merys. We have seen how the members of your Order have defeated the pox, which once laid waste to as many as the plague. You have seen how to make the cure for that disease. Within this castoff loaf is the means to defeat the plague just as surely. Remember all you have been taught.”

For a long moment I only stood there, staring down at the bread, at the patches of green and blue that had spread across its surface. And then it was as if something in my mind shifted, and I recalled my days in the workrooms of the Order, carefully preparing the milder form of pox as an inoculation against the more severe smallpox. I thought also of the needle going into tender flesh, and all the lives we had saved.

I raised my head and met her eyes, blue as a mountain lake. Again her mouth lifted in a smile, and for the first time I saw something unearthly in it, a mixture of compassion and detachment that could have its place on no visage other than that of a god.

“You begin to understand,” she said. “I will not say that the road ahead of you is an easy one, but it has its end. And you have suffered, and lost, and yet I tell you that in the end you will be richer for it. Because while we do not meddle, we do observe, and if there is anything we can learn from the people of this world, it is that their capacity for love exceeds all else. Believe in that love, and let it guide you.”

And then it was if I began to fall, and yet that descent was a gentle one, almost as if unseen hands guided me from that lofty peak down to the place where my body had waited all that time. For a second all was darkness, and then I opened my eyes, and I saw I still sat on the floor beside Lord Shaine's bed. The first rays of the sun caught in the window in the far wall, and showed something pale against the age-darkened oak floor. I stared at it for a long moment, and then, somehow, I began to laugh.

It was a hunk of moldy bread.

CHAPTER SEVENTEEN

My laughter was abruptly stilled, however, as I got to my feet and gazed down at the limp form of Lord Shaine, and thought of his daughter lying dead only a floor above us. Almost as if that thought had been a signal, I heard the sound of Elissa's cry. My eyes burned with unshed tears at hearing that keen of distress once again, but I turned toward the doorway, bracing myself for that which was to come next.

The girl burst into the room. "Oh, mistress—it's—it's—"

"I know," I said calmly.

My words halted her, as she came to an abrupt stop a few paces away and stared at me as if I had gone mad. "You know, mistress?"

"I do," I replied. Somehow I knew that the best way to address her was simply, in words she would understand. "The goddess came to me—in a dream. She showed me all—and showed me what I must do next."

"She showed you?" Elissa's dark eyes widened in wonder and fear, but I saw no disbelief in her face. These people lived closer to the gods than I; perhaps they had had the right of it all along.

"Yes. And I would ask that you say nothing else in—in here," I finished lamely, with a quick glance over my shoulder at Lord Shaine as he lay half-comatose in his bed.

But she seemed to understand at once, for she nodded gravely. No doubt she thought it was the province of the physician to relay all such bad news, along with measuring out the proper doses of medicine and setting broken bones. And it was something I would have to do, but not now. Shaine was too weak, too caught in the illness, to be burdened with the news of the death of his only beloved child. How I would ever have the courage to tell him such a thing, I did not know, but that evil could be saved for a later date when he was better equipped to handle it.

In the meantime, there was much else that must be attended to, not the least of which was lancing the plague boil. He could not remain as he was. In my absence he had pushed away the covers, and the sweat beaded on his forehead. At least he was not coughing his way down to death as so many others in the castle had done and might be doing at this very moment, but time was still of the essence.

"I need two things of you, Elissa," I said, and at once she stood up a little straighter, even though I saw her worried gaze stray to where her lord lay sprawled on his bed.

"Yes, mistress."

Perhaps she, too, was a gift from Inyanna, this slight, frail girl who yet lived and did as I bade her without question. I could not ask now, and I supposed it did not matter one way or the other. One should accept such gifts without questioning where they came from.

"Send up one of the male slaves—Raifal, if he is yet well, or one of the others if…he is not."

She nodded again, and bit her lip. I wondered then if something had begun to grow between the two of them, as I thought I had noted a special closeness on Midwinter's Eve. That was a type of healing I did not practice, and did not fully understand, and yet it was as powerful—and as important—as the medicines and surgical implements I wielded.

"Once you have sent Raifal to me, I need you to go to the kitchens. Inspect all the bread, and set the moldy loaves aside."

"To send to the midden, mistress?" From her tone it was clear she thought this a foolish task, when all else in the castle was awry.

"No. Keep it for me—and go search in the midden as well, in case any has been thrown out there that might be of use. You may start with this one." And I handed her the partial loaf from my dream, which had not been a dream at all.

Gingerly she took it from me, her eyes still wide with questions. But she had seen me right too many times before to say anything, although I saw her give it a dubious glance before she transferred it to her apron pocket, where it made an incongruous bulge. "As you wish, mistress."

Then she was gone, running down the stairs, leaving me behind with the feverish master of the castle.

Once again I went to the fire and built it up, and once again I swung the trivet and its kettle over the flames to boil the water I would need. Only this time I would not be brewing tea, but setting my instruments in boiling liquid—the thin sharp knife to cut the flesh, and the forceps to hold the wound open while I washed the pestilence from within. I could only hope that Lord Shaine had the strength still within him to withstand such an operation.

I went to the chair that had been placed up against one wall and dragged it over to his bedside. He still writhed with fever, but withal his face was still the one I loved, although black hollows smudged the skin beneath his eyes, and a sheen of sweat covered all visible skin.

"You will live," I told him then. "You will live, because you must. If all else should perish and fail, yet I would have strength if I had you next to me. We will survive this, and our strength will lend itself to those others who have need of it. You will live, because I love you more than my heart can bear." And I leaned down and pressed my lips against his fevered brow, not caring for the disease that might come forth with his every exhalation. For had not Inyanna told me that her hand was upon me, and such things could not touch me?

I heard then a half cough from the doorway, and I straightened, only to see Raifal paused there. In the chancy light of the rising sun it was difficult to tell for sure, but I thought I saw a flush spread over his face that had very little to do with fever and plague. Well, if he had seen, I could think of no one better to keep my secrets, and I knew in the end it mattered little. If all went as I hoped, then perhaps one day soon I would be able to confess the truth of my heart to Lord Shaine, and he would reveal the truth of his as well.

"Are you well?" I asked, my tone a trifle sharp. For while I could tell myself it mattered little whether Raifal had just witnessed what had passed, still it was uncomfortable to know that such a moment of vulnerability might have been witnessed by another.

He straightened. "Quite well, mistress. Dran and I have a bet going, to see which one of us holds out against the plague the longest."

I almost laughed then, simply from amusement that they should bet over such a thing, and also that Raifal should have recovered himself so much that he could make light of such matters. "Well, then, as long as both of you are resolved to win, then neither of you should fear catching ill. But come, for I will need you to assist me."

At my words he inched a little closer, but I could tell he was reluctant to approach his lord's bed. "What is it you would have me do?"

Most of the other slaves would not have had the courage to ask me such a question, but Raifal knew me, knew my mettle, and so he knew I would not take him to task for such impertinence. Besides, I thought it only fair that he should know what lay ahead of him.

"Your master is lucky in that he has the bubonic form of the disease," I said calmly, as I rose from the chair and went to retrieve my now sterilized instruments and lay them out on a piece of clean linen. "But even so, the sickness has concentrated itself in a boil in his groin, and I must lance it to release the sickness from his body. Once I have done that, he has a much greater chance of recovery."

Raifal gulped and appeared a little green at my reply, but he said nothing, only cocking his head to one side as he waited for me to continue.

"Of course I shall perform the surgery. I will dose him with the littlest bit of poppy so it will dull the pain somewhat, but there is still a risk that he will jerk about, and of course that would jeopardize his life, if he were to lash out while I was cutting him. So I need you to hold him steady, and make sure he does not interrupt the procedure."

In response, Raifal went even more green, but I couldn't help smiling a little as he squared his shoulders and approached the bed. "I will do whatever you need, mistress."

"Very good. Then go to the head of the bed, and make sure you have a good grip on his arms. I can manage his legs." *I think*, I added mentally; even in his febrile state, Shaine was a strong man. But I had held down bigger men than he during surgery, and besides, I would have the poppy to help me. I retrieved the vial and tipped a drop into Lord Shaine's mouth. At once he went limp, and Raifal took his place as I had instructed, holding his lord by the upper arms so he could not twist away from my knife even should the pain penetrate through the poppy's haze.

Nothing for it, then. I pushed back Shaine's linen shirt so that I would have clear access to the area. And I saw it was time, for the boil had risen yet higher, the whitish mass underneath straining to push through the overtaxed skin. I picked up the sharp, tiny knife, and made the first cut.

At once a whitish-green pus oozed forth, and even though he had been well-drugged, Shaine jerked.

"Hold him!" I ordered, and Raifal tightened his grip, his gaze studiously fixed on the canopy above the bed. I did not know whether it was because the sight of blood made him green, as it did so many other men, or whether he was simply discomfited by the sight of his lord's nakedness. I supposed it did not matter much one way or another.

Luckily I had set aside a quantity of clean linens to aid me in my task, for the accounts I had read said that the plague boil could contain much putrescent matter. I mopped away as the pus seemed to rise ever forth, creating an ever-growing pile of filthy cloths at my feet. Sweat grew on my own brow as I worked away, and a knot of unease formed in my stomach. When would it ever stop? I had never seen such a disgorgement before.

At length the pus gave way to a watery yellowish discharge, followed by a gush of blood. Still I worked to clean it away, wondering all the time whether the supply of cloths I had laid in would be enough. At least the blood would help to clean the cut. And then at last it began to slow, and I judged it time to cleanse the wound.

If he had jerked when I made the first cut, Shaine positively convulsed as I poured alcohol over the incision. Somehow he managed to twist out of Raifal's grasp and strike at me, the bottle of alcohol falling from my hand to the floor.

"Catch him!" I commanded, and to Raifal's credit, even though he looked pale enough to faint away right then and there, he somehow managed to grab hold of Lord Shaine's arms and pin him back down.

The alcohol was quite gone when I bent to retrieve the bottle, but I knew I could get more from the stillroom if need be. At least I had gotten the wound clean before he knocked the bottle from my hands.

I did not want to stitch the wound closed; not yet, as there was always the risk of trapping some infection within.

Instead, I took up a quantity of clean bandages and bound them firmly against the incision in his groin. The pressure would keep the blood from flowing, and in a day's time I could reinspect the wound and judge whether any putrefaction had occurred.

If, of course, he lived that long.

For what I had done here was only half the fight. The goddess had given me the vital information I required, but it still lay in my hands to attempt the making of a cure, and to hope it would not come too late. She had given me no assurances, but had she not spoken of love, told me that it would guide me? If she truly were a goddess, then she knew of the love that I felt for Lord Shaine. Surely she would not be so cruel as to speak of love if it was destined to be torn from me.

As much as I wanted to stay by Shaine's side, I knew I must make haste down to the kitchen. I finished tying off the bandages, pulled down his shirt, and drew up the blankets. Then I looked up at Raifal, who still had his gaze fixed on some spot in the middle distance. "Raifal," I said quietly.

He jerked a bit, and turned his face toward me. I noticed a bit of relief pass over his features as he appeared to note that his lord was now safely covered up. "Yes, mistress?"

"You have done hard duty here, and it will not be forgotten, neither by Lord Shaine nor myself. But I must ask one more thing of you."

"What is it, mistress?" His voice sounded strained, but I was pleased to see that he met my eyes directly, with no fear. Perhaps he, too, had passed some test this night.

"I have work in the kitchens—I have an idea for some... medicine...that might help us. But I cannot leave Lord

Shaine alone. Will you stay here, and watch over him, until I can return?"

At once he nodded. "Of course, mistress."

Again I realized that, as alone as I had felt, I was not. Everyone who still drew breath was here to help me, to offer whatever limited aid he or she could. I could not have asked for more than that.

I thanked him and rose, then went to the door. Before I went downstairs I had one more duty to fulfill.

She lay in death much as she had in life, with no sign of the disease that had ravaged her. Whether she had died that way or whether Elissa had done so out of some gesture of respect before she came to fetch me, Auren's small hands lay crossed on her breast, and her dark-honey hair rippled down over either shoulder. Truly, from where I stood one could have thought she slept only. I knew better, however.

I stepped closer, breathed, "Oh, Auren," and shut my eyes for a moment, willing the tears away. All the weeping in the world would not bring her back. And should I mourn, I who had seen her rise from this very bed, whole and healthy, and smile as she laid her hand in that of Lord Thrane, who led her from this world to the next? The goddess had said I should not, and yet even I, who knew she had moved on to a better place, wanted nothing more than to fall down at the foot of her bed and weep bitter tears for the young life that was gone, with all its promises unfulfilled.

Very gently, I reached out to touch her forehead, to feel the smooth skin there that would never know a line or wrinkle. "Be at peace, lady," I said softly.

Perhaps it was only the way the morning light fell against her face, but it seemed that the corners of her mouth were curved upward slightly, in an echo of the smile she had given the Lord of Death as he reached out to take her hand. At some point I knew I would have to send someone up to retrieve her body, and yet it grieved me that she should be sent out to burn on a pyre with the rest of the household's dead before her father had a chance to make his farewells. But she could not stay here forever, and I had no idea when Lord Shaine would regain consciousness, and, even more, when he would have the strength to hear such unwelcome news.

"Suffice the evil," I murmured, in the words of the old proverb, and forced myself to step away, to move back to the staircase. No one else shared that room, and even with the sun rising it was very cold; she could remain there for some hours without a problem. In the meantime, I had much to do.

Head high, eyes burning but tearless, I descended the stairs and made a quick pass of the gathered people in the hall. Two more had passed during my absence—the elderly woman who had sorted the dyes, and who I guessed might not have lasted the winter, plague or no; and one more of the stableboys, who had succumbed to the airborne version of the disease. So poor Master Wilys only had two left in his charge, although at least the both of them still seemed to be hale and hearty enough. I looked on the stable master as well, who appeared mostly recovered, although there was a hollow look to his eyes that hadn't been there a few days before.

"I am well enough to get out of this blasted bed and help, mistress," he protested, as I told him that he must lie there at least a day more.

"You think you are well enough, but it would not do if you sickened again," I replied. "Relapse" was also not in my Selddish vocabulary. "I know it must chafe you, but we will need every able body to survive this, and I cannot let you take that risk."

My tone was stern, and after a bit more fussing he subsided, for I guessed he understood the wisdom of my directions even if he didn't much like them. "If you will it," he muttered, and I smiled and said,

"I do will it."

As I turned away from him, one of the women who had been helping to tend the plague victims approached me. I was glad to see that she still wore the strip of linen tied over the lower half of her face, but above the pale fabric her dark eyes were worried. "Mistress Merys?"

"Yes…" I cast about in my mind for her name. "… Ruanne?"

"I did not wish to have anyone disturb you while you were tending to his lordship, mistress, but I thought you should know that Lord Marten came looking for you, and I said you were with Lord Shaine and could not be interrupted. He swore at me then, lady, but I held my ground. But now—" She hesitated, and then continued, "I heard the girl say you needed to attend to somewhat in the kitchen, but perhaps you should see to Lord Marten, just in case…"

If Lord Marten had come looking for me, I feared the worst. But perhaps he only sought me out for news of Auren. Either way, I did not much look forward to seeing him, but I knew it must be done. Five minutes of my time I could spare for such an errand, no more.

"I will see to him," I told Ruanne. "You have done good work here, and I thank you for it."

She bobbed a curtsey, and the linen moved a bit, as if she smiled beneath the mask. But then someone called her name, and she hurried off, leaving me to go to the tower where Lord Marten waited for me.

Meeting with a goddess did not, I found, lend wings to my feet, nor had it given me any fresh stores of energy. Each step up the tower to the suite now occupied by Lord Marten and his children seemed higher and higher, and by the end I fairly had to drag myself up, foot by unwilling foot. Perhaps at the end of all this there would be a time when I could finally lay myself down and seek refuge in sleep, but that time was still as far-off and cloudy as the rest of my future. I could only concentrate on what I had to do now, in the time I had, and hope that my strength would be enough to carry me through it.

Even before I lifted my hand to knock on the door, I heard the hollow coughing from within. *Ah, goddess,* I thought. *And which one is it now? Will it be Lord Marten who follows Lady Yvaine into that next world, or is it young Lord Larol who will meet up with his lost betrothed in that place where mortals cannot reach?*

When the door opened, I looked up into the weary face of Lord Marten. As the coughing came from somewhere in the suite behind him, I knew it was not he who had fallen ill.

"You took your time, healer," he snapped.

"I was attending Lord Shaine, as I know Ruanne told you." If my own tone was curt, it was only from weariness.

The man had lost his wife; he should not have to face the loss of his children as well. "And I fear—I fear we have lost Lady Auren."

"Ah, gods," he sighed, all anger disappearing from his visage. He stepped aside so I could enter the suite, but I saw no one else. The coughing came from one of the open bedroom doors, but I could not remember which was Larol's and which his sister Alcia's. "Is that how it is to be? For my son to follow his lady from this world?"

"We do not know that," I said. "Let me see him."

As if he had not the strength to go within, Lord Marten merely raised his hand and pointed at the door to the left. I nodded and went in, fearing what I might find, and yet hoping it might not be so bad as I thought.

Alcia sat at her brother's bedside, wiping down his forehead with a damp cloth, although he tossed and coughed and, as I watched, reached up to push her ministering hand away. Like the women down in the hall, she had tied a strip of linen across her nose and mouth. Her eyes glinted with tears, but she ignored her brother's restlessness and continued to tend to him with a fierce determination that seemed to signal she was not going to give up any time soon. She must have heard me enter, for she looked up, and I saw a little frown pucker her brows.

"We needed you!" she burst out.

"I know, Alcia, and I truly am sorry I could not have come before this. But Lord Shaine was gravely ill as well, and I have just come from—" I cast about for the word for "operate" and instead substituted, "I have come from cutting open the boil, so that the disease could come forth. I came here as soon as I heard that your father had need of me. May I see your brother?"

She hesitated, then pushed her chair back so I might approach and bend over him. As with the others, he burned with fever, and his slender frame shivered and shook from the resulting chills, even though the door was open to the room with the blazing fire beyond, and a brazier burned in here as well. I bent toward him, and he coughed again, each spasm seeming to tear at his lungs. He did have enough strength to hold a handkerchief to his mouth, and so I did not see the discharge that he brought up, but I knew what I would find if I inspected the handkerchief.

Even in the throes of the coughing fit, he struggled to get out one word. "Aur - Auren?"

I feared what the truth would do to him. He had never seemed to be an overly strong boy, and now the disease had its merciless claws in him, shredding at his lungs, overwhelming his body's ability to defend itself. The news he desired could be the death of him. So I equivocated. "I have come from tending her. She is in her room." Not lies, not at all, but of course the most important facts had been withheld.

It seemed he guessed I did not tell the whole truth, for his brow furrowed, and he opened his mouth again, only to be interrupted by another wracking fit of coughs.

"Don't try to speak, my lord," I told him. The cough could be soothed temporarily by the tincture of coltsfoot I had prepared earlier; I turned from him to pull it from my satchel, glad that I always kept a pewter spoon for such purposes with the rest of my kit. And as he opened his mouth to attempt a protest, I poured a dose of the tincture down his throat. He coughed again, but not as deep—he was more surprised than anything else. "Keep watch over him," I told Alcia. "This should soothe his cough for a time, and I will come back to check on him as soon as I can."

"You're going?" she asked, the panic clear in her voice. I guessed she had thought she would only have to be his nurse until I arrived on the scene, and then she could be relieved of that duty.

"I fear I must, Alcia. I need to go to the kitchen, where I will be making what I hope is a cure. But I cannot help anyone if I do not go there now and tend to the process."

She nodded uncertainly, as if she hadn't quite understood what I had said but somehow knew better than to question me. That was sufficient; I sent an encouraging smile in her direction and went out to see their father, who paced in front of the fireplace as if he couldn't find the strength to sit down and be still.

"His fever is high," I said, "and the cough quite bad, but I have given him a tincture that should quiet the coughing for awhile, as well as tea that will help to bring down his fever. Alcia seems to be keeping good watch on him, but I must go. The only way I can truly help him—help anyone else in his situation—is to get back to the task at hand."

"And what would that be?" From his expression, it was clear that Lord Marten thought the only task I should have at my hand was caring for his son.

"The cure to this pestilence," I said, then turned and left him.

I hoped it would be that simple.

CHAPTER EIGHTEEN

At least Elissa had been diligent—when I arrived in the kitchen, I saw the table where Merime used to chop vegetables piled with all manner of moldy loaves and rolls. Truly, I had not thought we would have that much, but it was clear that housekeeping duties in the kitchen had fallen by the wayside without a guiding hand, and so food had begun to spoil that would never have gotten to that state under Merime's watchful eye.

Elissa waited for me there, with another of the kitchen slaves, a girl even younger than Elissa, named Alinne. They both looked up at me expectantly as I entered the room, and I felt more than ever the weight of need. I could not fail them, or the man who lay recovering from his surgery in the tower above. The goddess had said the answer lay here, but she had given little more information than that. I would have to bring all of my knowledge to bear, and hope it would not fail me.

"You've done well," I said. "Now what we must do is break off all the moldy bits, and gather them here." I found a bowl on the lower shelf of the work table and set it on the tabletop. "Try not to take any extra bread with the moldy parts, if you can. We want to concentrate the mixture as much as possible."

"The mixture?" Elissa asked.

"I'm going to brew a sort of—well, I suppose you could call it beer, for lack of a better word."

"From this?" Her eyebrows lifted. She was not the type to contradict me, but I also knew that every village and hamlet across my homeland made its own brew, and very likely she knew far more about the process than I did.

"Yes, from this. I know it sounds strange, but in that mold is medicine that can help us to fight the plague. But we have to concentrate it, make it into a drink we can give to those who are sick."

Alinne, whom I did not know well, slanted me a frankly dubious look. But as she had been raised to obey orders, she set about removing the moldy portions of the bread and popping them into the bowl. Since she was small and slender, and her fingers delicate and nimble as well, she proved well-suited to the task. Elissa set to work as well, picking out the bits of mold as deftly as she once used to braid Auren's hair.

That thought brought a certain choking sensation to my throat, and I swallowed and turned away from them so they could not see the tears starting in my eyes. I could not think of that now, nor could I think of Lord Shaine, lying upstairs with only Raifal to look over him. The sooner I set about this task, the sooner I could bring him the help he so desperately needed.

I located a large, deep pan and went to the pump to fill it with water. Afterward, I set it on the trivet and swung it over the fire, which at least had been well-tended. Probably Elissa had seen to it merely to ward the morning chill from the kitchen, but whatever her reasons for building it up, it helped me now. The water must be hot enough to increase the fermentation process, but not so hot that it would break down the mold and render it ineffective. How precisely any of these mechanisms worked, I could not say—I could only rely on my years of working with herbal remedies and the procedures my Order used to compound them. I didn't know how they would translate into this new and strange ingredient I had never worked with before.

"Is this enough?" Elissa asked, and held up the bowl, which brimmed with bits of moldy bread in various shades of green and blue.

It will have to be, I thought, but I only nodded and said, "It will do. Bring it here."

She came around the table, holding the bowl in front of her with all the gravity of a temple acolyte bringing an offering to Inyanna's altar. I took it from her and carefully tipped its contents into the pan of hot water. "A spoon, please, Elissa."

At once she dashed away to fetch the requested utensil, while Alinne also sidled around the corner of the table and peered suspiciously into the pot. Her nose wrinkled. I had to confess the mixture didn't look particularly appetizing, as the bread and its accompanying mold had begun to break down in the warm water, turning into a green soupy mess that looked rather like blended pond scum.

"Here, mistress," Elissa said, and handed me a large wooden spoon. I took it from her with a nod and began to slowly stir the contents of the pan, keeping the viscous fluid moving so that the heat would be distributed evenly through it. When I compounded my tinctures, I usually tried to keep them at a simmer for at least an hour so the ingredients could mix properly, but I had no idea whether the mold would react the same way as the extracts of the various herbs and plants I used. Then again, mold did tend to like the heat, which was why it could thrive in a kitchen even in the heart of winter, as the kitchen hearth was usually the one fire that was never allowed to go out.

"What are you going to do with it?" Alinne asked. Apparently she had no great fear of me, or perhaps she had already seen so much that a woman physician was no longer the fearsome thing she might have once been. She was a pert little thing, with a sharp nose under its linen swathing and tilted dark eyes. In fact, she reminded me rather of an inquisitive little rat, although I supposed she was pretty enough, in a pointed sort of way.

"I'll heat it, and then strain it. And then I shall give a measure of it to everyone to drink."

"To drink!" she exclaimed. "How will you get anyone to swallow that?" And she pointed at the soupy greenish mass in the pan.

Well, then, that was always the question. I'd encountered many over the years who had no desire to take their medicine, even when they had evidence all around them that it would do them good. But I rather thought there wouldn't be many at Donnishold who would refuse the concoction, not when the alternative was almost certain death—Master Wilys' almost miraculous recovery notwithstanding.

"I'll simply ask them if they would rather have the plague, if they give me any trouble," I replied calmly, still stirring away at the mold mixture.

That seemed to mollify her; she appeared to swallow, and bite her lip, and suddenly seem very interested in the tips of her toes in their scuffed low boots. I guessed that, like Raifal and his comrade—and most likely everyone else in the hall—she had been counting the minutes and wondering when it would be her turn for the hollow cough to descend, for her forehead to flush with fever.

"You can test it on me, mistress," Elissa said in stout tones, with a sideways glance at Alinne. I got the impression she didn't have much use for the other girl.

I smiled then, and said, "As to that, I always taste my tinctures first, so that I am not inflicting anything on my patients that I would not take myself. But you should have the first dose after that, so I know you are protected."

"How does it work?" She peered over my shoulder into the pan; despite everything, she still smelled good, of the chamomile and peppermint hair wash I had mixed up earlier in the fall.

A very good question. One might as well ask how the plants grow, or why the sun rises in the east. To these and so many questions, neither I nor the members of my Order had the true answers. Oh, we knew that a cough could be soothed with coltsfoot, and a fever with willowbark; that packing a wound with honey speeded its healing, and that peppermint—besides adding a sweetness to soaps and hair tonics—was a sovereign cure for an upset stomach. But why these things worked, how they interacted with the body and effected these cures, we still had very little idea.

I knew, though, that to confess my ignorance would only bolster Alinne's suspicions, and would of course set Elissa somewhat less at ease, and so I attempted to manufacture a reply that settled the matter to both their satisfaction. "In my order, we are taught that disease and contagion are carried in the air, and in the blood, by tiny specks one cannot see with the naked eye. And there is something in some cures that fights these specks, and drives them forth from the body. Not all cures work for all ailments, which is why I would not dose Merime's weak heart with feverfew, nor give a patient with plague an infusion of foxglove. And because the plague is so rare, and so pernicious, it requires a very special medicine to treat it."

Elissa seemed to accept this explanation without question. She nodded, and returned to watching me swirl the greenish mold mixture. Now, after some time over steady heat, the bread had almost broken all the way down, and the solution had taken on the consistency of very watery oatmeal. Alinne seemed rather less convinced, as her eyes had narrowed when I spoke of the tiny specks that carried disease, but she forbore from saying anything else.

"Alinne, do you know if Merime had a strainer?" I knew it was better to ask her, as she had been assigned to the kitchens, whereas Elissa had spent very little time there. It was something that the laboratories and stillrooms of the Order took for granted, but I knew it was not the sort of thing one might readily find in every kitchen because of the expertise required to make such fine screens. These things were easily procured in Lystare, whose factories churned out an astonishing amount of useful items, but in Seldd they did not have such resources.

As I feared, Alinne hesitated, then shook her head. "I do not know what that is. When Merime wished to strain something, she used a length of cheesecloth."

It made sense, I supposed. After all, linen in all weaves was the one thing of which there was no shortage in Seldd. "It will have to do. Please bring me several lengths of it, and several clean pans."

Pert or no, the girl was used to following orders. She stepped away from the hearth and went to a cupboard at the far end of the kitchen, from which she drew forth a pile of the thin, open-weave cloth. On her way back to the fireplace, she stopped and retrieved two more pans, both of which looked clean enough, although I would still have to make sure they were thoroughly cleansed. It would do those suffering from the plague no good to be introduced to more illness because I could not be bothered to make sure all my pans were clean.

To that end, I set Elissa to fetching another large pan of water, and moved the trivet to one side so she could set it over the fire on a second trivet. As it heated, I bade Alinne continue stirring the mold mixture so I could steal a few minutes to look in on those in the hall. All around me was the sound of coughing, and haggard, hollow-eyed faces. But the women there seemed to still have things in hand, and I could do little except administer some more tea, and murmur a few reassuring words. At least no one seemed materially worse than they had been a half-hour before, and I prayed they would hold on long enough for me to administer the brew I was concocting.

And you hold on as well, I thought then, looking up at the dark stone ceiling and seeing again the shape of Lord Shaine on his bed, his pallid face, the fearful slackness of his mouth.

When I returned to the kitchen, the water was at full boil, and I instructed the girls to wash the two new pans I had brought out in it, and then dip the cheesecloth in it as well. Afterward they draped the dripping fabric across the openings of both the pans, preparing them to receive the sludgy batch of mold broth I had prepared. Because the liquid was so precious—and because I was taller and stronger than either of the girls—I lifted the pan from the trivet myself and brought it over to the table where the prepared receptacles waited. Slowly I tilted the pot so the liquid could pour out. Somehow I found myself holding my breath as I did so, so fearful was I of splashing even a single drop. But it all transferred easily enough, and I was relieved to see that most of the bread had been broken down enough that it passed through the cheesecloth. Only a fine grit remained on the surface of the fabric, which meant that almost all of what I had prepared could go straight into the mouths of the people who needed it.

I repeated the procedure with the second pan, and then instructed the girls to boil three pewter mugs, one for each of us to carry into the hall. Although I would administer the broth myself—I did not want either Elissa or Alinne to deal with recalcitrant patients—still I knew it would go more quickly if we didn't have to keep returning to the kitchen to replenish our supply. Likewise we cleansed a quantity of spoons, as many as we could find, so that each plague victim could have his or her own utensil and not risk further contamination.

But first Elissa must have her dose, which she took meekly enough, although she couldn't help wincing as I had her swallow two large spoonfuls of the concoction. Her face screwed up in disgust, and she coughed a little as she tied her linen mask back in place.

"That's awful!" she exclaimed, once she recovered her breath.

"Yes, I suppose it is," I said cheerfully. Somehow now that I was done with the brew, I felt immeasurably lighter. Although Inyanna had said the gods did not meddle in human affairs, but only stood back and observed them, I wanted to believe that because I had done as she bade me, she would allow the medicine to work, and drive back the sickness that had threatened to take away all within Donnishold's walls. At any rate, I had done the best I could. Now only time would tell if those efforts had been for naught.

And then it was Alinne's turn, and her reaction was much as Elissa's, although I guessed she exaggerated somewhat for effect. After spluttering a bit, she, too, retied her mask, and then we all went out to the hall, bringing our little pot of hope with us.

Because they had done so much for me, and because they had yet to show any sign of the disease, I gave doses to the women who had been acting as nurses first. Made of sterner stuff than the girls, they swallowed the medicine without complaint, although I saw one give a brief shudder afterward before she stoically replaced her mask and moved on to provide fresh handkerchiefs to a young woman from the dye hut who was coughing incessantly. And from that point it was only a matter of going from bed to bed and cajoling or persuading everyone to take their dose—or in the cases of those so far gone that they barely knew who they were or why they were there, simply pouring the medicine down their throats. By my count there were some forty souls gathered there in the hall, and each of them was given the gift of the precious liquid. By the end I was down to a few inches in one of the pots, and the other was quite dry, but it would be enough. All who were left were Lord Marten and his family, and Lord Shaine and the watching Raifal.

I told Elissa and Alinne that I would go upstairs to tend to those few remaining, and that they should remain in the hall. "And if anyone should show a reaction," I added, "come and fetch me at once."

"What kind of reaction?" Elissa asked, her eyes widening above the linen mask. It was obvious that she had expected once everyone had their medicine, then the cure would begin and we would have nothing else to worry about.

"Some people are sensitive to certain substances—I've known some who could not eat nuts, or who cannot ingest honey. So there is always a chance that someone might react in the same way to the mold. They may develop hives, or become nauseous, or even have convulsions. Although I hope it will not come to that."

They both looked similarly worried, if not downright alarmed in Elissa's case, so I assured them that such reactions were very rare, and then hurried away, carrying the last of the mold broth with me, although I had transferred it into a smaller receptacle that I also rinsed with boiling water. No need to lug one of the heavy pans all the way upstairs when I only had half a flagon's worth left at best.

It seemed I had climbed these stairs too many times already, although now they appeared somewhat different with the wintry morning light coming through the tower's slit-like windows. Candles still burned in their sconces, however; most likely no one had thought to make the usual rounds this morning to put them out. I stood on my tiptoes and blew out the flames before continuing on my way.

All was silent at the suite when I paused outside the door. Uncertain as to whether this was a good or a bad sign, I raised my hand to knock, and then realized that the door stood slightly ajar. I saw Lord Marten then, sitting in a chair by the fireplace, his head in his hands. He did not look up as I said his name, but through the entry to Larol's room I heard a faint cough. So perhaps I was not too late after all.

That hope died, however, as I entered the room and beheld the still form of Larol in his bed, covers pulled up to his nose, and the huddled form of his sister next to him. It had been she who was coughing, for even as I moved toward here she began to hack again, her thin frame shaking with each spasm.

"Alcia," I said softly.

She looked up at me with red-rimmed eyes, a handkerchief pressed to her mouth. As if unable to utter a word, she only shook her head at me and turned away.

I knew she was angry with me for what she saw as an abandonment of her brother, for not coming up with the miraculous cure everyone had been expecting. And I had no words, nothing to say to soothe the pain she must be feeling. Perhaps I had the cure now, but it had come too late to help Larol, or Lady Yvaine.

"I have some medicine for you," I told her then. "That is what I have been working on." Whether my words were an explanation or an excuse, I did not know, but I felt I had to say something. And as she still spoke no words, I added, "And you need to go lie down. Let me tend to your brother."

"As you did before!" she burst out finally, and then broke into another fit of coughing. "What good are you?"

What good, indeed? Well, I hoped time would tell that tale, but at the moment my only concern was to tend to the girl before she went the way of her brother and her mother. "Alcia, please," I replied. "Your father does not want to lose you as well."

That had an effect, as I thought it would. She straightened a little and shot me a glare of pure hatred before she rose, if somewhat unsteadily, and stalked past me out into the receiving chamber, and then on into her own bedroom. Still Lord Marten did not look up to regard what we were doing, and I could not spare him a glance at the moment. Time enough for him, as the only apparently healthy member of the family. At the moment, Alcia was my main concern.

As she had still been wearing her nightdress with a shawl draped over it, she merely flung the shawl into a chair and then climbed into bed. Once she was lying down, she began to cough again, but with her head turned away from me, as if she could not bear to let me see her weakness. Her distress of mind I could do nothing to ease, but merely hope that time might work its healing magic on her. In the meantime, I must tend to her ailing body.

"Can you sit up, just a little?" I asked. "I need you to swallow all of this."

For a few seconds she did nothing, but then rolled over onto her back and made a show of wriggling up against her pillows so she was in a halfway sitting position. Even this mild exertion caused her to begin hacking and wheezing again, and I waited until the fit passed before I poured a measure of the mold broth into a spoon and held it out to her. It did not have much of an odor, but even so she wrinkled her nose—probably at its less than appetizing appearance. But at least she did not fight me, but opened her mouth and let me administer the medication. She spluttered a little and coughed again, but she managed to keep it down, although she sent me another one of those baleful stares. Perhaps she thought I was trying to poison her.

"Sleep now, and let the medicine do its work," I told her. "That will be best for you, if you can manage it."

Although she halfway appeared as if she wished to argue with me, she only nodded and slid down onto her back, then shut her eyes. I doubted she was asleep; more likely she thought that was a good way to dismiss me.

As it was. I had done what I could, and now I must let the medicine do its work and hope, as I had with all the others I had dosed earlier in the hall, that some good would come of it. Nor did I think it would be as simple as that—one dose would help them along the way to health, if what Inyanna had told me was true, but we would need more the next day, to continue with the treatment until the last sign of plague was erased from Donnishold. I would have to set all the able-bodied to work to make more yeast mixtures, and hope for the best.

I went back out to the receiving chamber and looked down on Lord Marten for a long moment. At length he raised his head and said, in the monotone of one who has lost all hope, "I suppose she is gone as well."

"Not at all," I said gently. "She is resting, and I have given her some medicine. And I must give you some as well, for though there are no signs of the plague in you, still you have been exposed to it, and I would stop it before it ever gets a chance to start."

He looked at me with dull eyes, uncomprehending, and my heart was wrung, for I had a flash then of how he had looked on Midwinter Eve, hale and hearty, pleased to see his beloved son engaged to the daughter of Donnishold. As Larol was the middle son, I knew Lord Marten must have another son elsewhere, most likely back at his estate, but I could see he had either forgotten such a thing in his despair, or believed his own household had succumbed to the plague as well. As to that, I could give no reassurances. It could not be expected that the people of his estate understood modern quarantine procedures. And even one such as I who did could still make a mistake, like the one that had proved so fatal to many who lived within Lord Shaine's walls.

But at least he made no protest, not even when I retrieved a fresh spoon from my satchel and gave him a dose as well. I then bade him to rest as well, but he only shook his head and turned to look back at the dying fire. I did not have the strength to force him to his bed, so I quietly said I was going to check on Lord Shaine, but that I would return within the hour to see how Alcia fared. He did not respond, not even with a shrug, but I knew I had done what I could. At least he showed no sign of the plague, and I hoped the medication would do its work to kill whatever traces of the disease might have begun to bloom in his lungs and in his blood.

After that I left, and finally made my way back to the tower that housed Lord Shaine's rooms—and my room as well, although I guessed it would still be some time before I could avail myself of the rest I so desperately needed. By that point I was putting one foot in front of the other through sheer willpower. I had been in similar sleep-deprived situations once or twice before, and now, as then, it seemed that I floated through a dream world, that everything around me had somehow lost part of its substance, and might disappear like mist in the sun if I stared at it too long.

In that otherworldly state I ascended the stairs and then opened the door to Shaine's suite. In some detached part of my mind I wondered what I would do if I found him dead, as I had so many of the other souls housed beneath this roof, but I refused to acknowledge such a possibility. He would be alive. The goddess had spoken of love, and I would take her words as acknowledgment that the man I loved would somehow weather this storm along with the rest who still managed to survive.

When I opened the door to the chamber where he lay, I found myself holding my breath—and yet nothing seemed to have changed. Raifal sat wakeful by Lord Shaine's bedside, his head nodding as if he struggled to stay awake, but the morning light pushing past the heavy curtains showed that

Shaine's color had improved, and I could see the rise and fall of his chest.

A flood of relief went through me, so great that I stumbled as I entered the room. At once Raifal looked up, and began to rise to his feet.

"No, stay," I said. "You have done very well. His lordship looks…well."

"Yes, mistress. He has slept most of this time, thank Inyanna."

I must thank her as well. Perhaps it was she who had sent this healing sleep upon Lord Shaine, though I guessed she would deny such a thing if I were ever given the opportunity to ask her. But whatever the reason, it seemed that my desperate surgery had done some good. I had left off dosing him with more willowbark tea, even though his fever had concerned me, for I could not risk thinning his blood so soon after making such an incision. Even without that measure it seemed clear that his fever, if not broken, had lowered itself to safer levels. To reassure myself, I stepped close and laid a hand on his forehead; it was warm, but not hot, and I nodded. And then I lifted my hand at once, even though I would fain have left it there if I could.

"I have brought medicine for you and his lordship. Everyone else has already taken theirs, and so I hope there will be no more new cases, and that those who are already ill may have the signs of the sickness lessened. Here." And I opened the satchel and brought out the flagon that contained the last of the mold mixture.

As with everyone else who had been well enough to notice its appearance, Raifal gave the substance I poured into the spoon a dubious look, but he took it readily and without complaint.

I told him, "And I can take over watch from here for a while, so you can rest."

"And what of you, mistress?" Raifal asked, relief over the prospect of getting some sleep warring with worry for me on his features. "You have been awake all night as well."

Too well I knew that, felt it in every muscle and bone in my body. But I would go without sleep for longer than I already had if it meant the safety of the man I loved. I could not tell Raifal that, of course, but I said, "And not for the first time. It is part of my training, to go without rest when necessary, and to make sure the needs of others are met before I tend to my own. I will do well enough here—you should go to the kitchen and see about getting some food, and then as much sleep as you can manage."

Still he hesitated, but then he lifted his shoulders. "I am hungry."

"Well, there you have it. If you see Elissa, tell her that I bid her get some sleep as well. She has been a great help to me this night."

At the mention of Elissa's name, something in his eyes lit up, just the smallest bit, and I thought again that some regard had begun to grow between the two of them. I could only hope that they would both be able to live, and thrive, and go on to learn something more of one another.

In the meantime, though, I was content to see Raifal give me a little bow and then go as I bade him. For myself, I took the chair he had vacated and drew it a little nearer to Shaine's bedside. I knew I should wake him and give him the medicine he needed, but he slept so soundly that I was loath to rouse him. Slumber has its own healing properties, that mysterious time when the body can draw in upon itself and use its own resources to combat whatever ailed it. Surely it would not hurt to give him a little more time. For if he woke, and was lucid, I knew I would have to tell him of Auren, and that I did not wish to do. Not yet.

So I sat there, with the light of the morning sun painting his fine jaw and cheekbone with its golden brush, and waited, and called myself a coward.

CHAPTER NINETEEN

I WILL NOT LIE AND SAY I did not doze from time to time; I felt my head fall down toward my breast more than once, and on each occasion I jerked upward, startled at how easily the dark cloak of sleep had attempted to spread itself around me. And still Lord Shaine slept, and again I wondered if I should wake him. At least no one came to disturb me, and so I thought that perhaps the medicine had begun to do its work, and the need for me was not as great as it had been a few hours earlier.

But then his eyes opened. He blinked against the morning light, and stared upward as if not sure of where he was. After a pause he shifted ever so slightly, and I saw his eyes fasten on me. "Merys."

His voice was hoarse, but I could discern no trace of a cough, and none of the frightening slurring of the night before. All good signs, I told myself.

"Some water, my lord?"

He nodded, although a slight frown etched his brow. I rose from my seat and went to pour him a half-mug of water from the pitcher that had been sitting on a side table. I did not recall bringing it out. One of the slaves must have brought it up at some point during the night. As I tilted the pitcher, I noted that my hand trembled. Weariness, or nerves?

Whichever it was, I knew I could not delay. I crossed the room and took my seat once again, and helped him to a semi-setting position so he could drink without spilling the liquid down his front. When he had swallowed a few much-needed sips, I said, "And I have some medicine I would like you to take. You're the last—everyone else has had their dose, but I thought it best to let you sleep while you could."

When he spoke, the words sounded less rough than before. The water must have done him some good. "Medicine? I thought there was no treatment for the plague."

I hesitated. It was one thing to speak of goddesses to Elissa, who was young and credulous. I did not know how Shaine would take such tales; he had never been one to speak much of the gods. In that way we had been much alike. Perhaps we would have time later for me to tell him the whole story. Whether he would believe me or not, I had no clear idea, although he did know that I was the level-headed sort not much given to fancies. Physicians could not afford to think in such ways—we must focus on the here and now, and what will work best for our patients.

"It is—something I wished to try, based on some of the treatments we developed at my Order," I said after a pause of several seconds. "It will take some time for me to know for sure how it is working, but I've had no new reports of anyone else sickening since I gave everyone their measure."

For a time he was silent, staring down at the shape of his

legs beneath the layers of blankets. He placed one hand on his groin, as if to feel the blanket there, and his lips thinned.

"Is there much pain?" I asked. I needed to inspect the incision, to make sure it had stayed clear of infection, but that could wait a bit more.

"Not much. You cut the boil, I assume."

"Yes, my lord. There was nothing else I could do, and I thought—"

"You did what you had to, as always." He shifted on the pillows and made an odd impatient gesture with one hand. To be laid up again, so soon after he had recovered from that knife wound, probably chafed, but of course his temporary incapacitation was far better than the alternative. "How many?"

"My lord?"

"Stop that, Merys." The dark blue eyes caught mine, and held. They were clear enough, with none of the glassiness of fever. "With all that has happened, you still call me 'lord'? If it comforts you to do so in front of others, then do not abandon the practice immediately, but you have no need of such things when we are alone."

"Yes...Shaine."

"How many have we lost, Merys?"

I took in a breath. If I stopped to count them, then I would guess that roughly half of Donnishold's denizens had not survived the night. No one had had time to take a formal count, however—we had all been too busy trying to keep those who were yet alive from succumbing as well. But I knew I must answer him as honestly as I could. Somehow I managed to hold his gaze and said, "Ourrel is gone, and

Merime…but you knew that. Four of the boys from the stable, and roughly half the dye hut workers, as well as the field hands. Lady Yvaine, and young Lord Larol." At that Shaine shut his eyes, his mouth tightening to a narrow line.

"That is a blow," he said. A few heartbeats passed, then, "And what of my daughter?"

It was the hardest thing I had ever done, to not look away. Once again tears stung my eyes, and I replied, in barely a whisper, "She is gone, my lord. We all did what we could, but she had already been through so much these past months, and—"

"I understand." The words might have been spoken by a stranger, so harsh they sounded. He turned away from me then, to stare up at the swaths of dark fabric that hung above his bed. "Tell me nothing more, Merys. I do not wish to hear it."

"She—she did not suffer overmuch—"

"I said I did not wish to hear it!" This time he forced himself up on his elbows, and then winced at the pain the movement must have caused him. Still looking away from me, he added, "Give me this medicine, and then go. I wish to be alone."

There were times when I found it necessary for me to push my suit, and others when retreat was the best option. From his tone I knew that any more comments or protests would be met with more anger, and so I said quietly, "If you wish it," and retrieved the mostly empty flagon of the mold mixture from my satchel and poured him a measure with my last clean spoon. He took it without saying anything else, but only gestured toward the mug of water I had set down. No doubt he wished to wash the taste of the tincture from his mouth. I handed him the mug, waited for him to drink the rest of it, and took it from him. Afterward I stood and returned it to its place on the side table, and busied myself with replacing the flagon and spoon in my satchel.

As I gathered it up, however, I ventured, "I do not think it a good idea for you to be alone—"

"Oh, I am quite out of danger," he cut in. "See to the rest of your flock, Mistress Merys. They have far more need of you than I."

There seemed to be little I could say in reply to that. I only murmured, "As you wish," and left him staring up at the ceiling. Still there remained the matter of checking the dressings on his wound, but that would have to wait. At least he had taken the medicine.

Somehow it seemed more difficult for me to descend the stairs than it had been for me to climb them. The dreamlike state was gone, replaced by the cold realities of the morning after. Grief came in many shapes and forms; I had seen enough of it over the years. But it had never struck so close to home before. It was always a sad thing to lose a patient, but it was also a reality of a physician's life. I could not save everyone. But those I had watched over in my time since leaving the shelter of the Order's house in Lystare had never been as close to me as those here in Donnishold. Every death was as a loss in my own family, and if it pained me that much, I couldn't begin to think how it must be for Shaine, who had lost his only child—the daughter who had survived, when all her siblings and her mother had left this world far too soon.

It would take some time, I tried to tell myself. Of course he could not be expected to react in any sort of rational way right now—he was still recovering from a severe illness himself, and although I guessed he would never have been able to accept the death of his beloved daughter with any sort of equanimity, it was all the more difficult now when so much of his strength should have been devoted to his own recovery.

So I tried to convince myself, and it must have worked. Either that, or I was so weary myself that I did not have the strength to begin to understand what his words might have meant. Did he blame me, as young Alcia blamed me for the death of her brother and mother? It was not completely unexpected, I supposed. People tend to think that healers, once they have cured one ill, are somehow magically able to cure them all. But in the end, there was very little I could have done. Perhaps if I had grasped what my dreams had meant earlier, and created the medicine as soon as I got back from Lord Arnad's estate. I was not a priestess or a seer, though. How could I have known those dreams were anything but the normal jumble that passes through our minds as we sleep?

I stumbled a little as I stepped off the bottom stair and entered the hall. At once Ruanne came to me, her steady hand guiding me to a nearby chair. "You must get some rest, mistress. You are not ill?"

"No." *Sick at heart, and weary beyond endurance, but not ill.* "I have just told Lord Shaine of his daughter's passing. He...did not take it well."

Her dark eyes glittered with companionable tears. "A tragedy, mistress, but he'll come to accept it. But now you should sleep."

I shook my head. "I cannot. There are so many thing I must look into—"

"What?" she inquired, tone skeptical. "No one has sickened, and most of those who were given their medicine are sleeping. True, Master Wilys is fretting, and he seems so hale I'm of half a mind to tell him to get out of bed and go help in the kitchen, only I misdoubt he'd like to hear such a thing from a slave. So the best thing you could do for everyone is to sleep—and eat something," she added, giving me a critical glance. "You look as if you're about to fall over, begging your pardon."

"No need for that," I replied. Something in her friendly, no-nonsense words made me very much want to burst into tears. It felt wonderful to have someone worrying about me, and inquiring as to my welfare. I knew if I began to articulate these thoughts, however, most likely I would begin sobbing, and that would only alarm her and force me into explanations I wasn't sure I could begin to make. I continued, "I do feel as if I am about to fall over, to tell you the truth. Is there a spare corner where I could curl up for a bit? I confess that I am not sure I could climb all those stairs back to my room." *And pass Shaine's rooms...and the room where poor Auren sleeps forever.*

Sympathy was clear in her lined but still pretty face. "No need for that, mistress. I've a spare bed here that hasn't been used—someone brought it in for one of the dye girls, not knowing that the poor dear had succumbed before she ever made it in here. You sleep, and let us manage for a bit."

Something in me wanted to argue with her, to protest that I should not lie in sloth while there was so much yet to be done, but I found I had no strength for any further protests. She led me over to the pallet, and helped me down onto it. I had barely placed my head on the pillow and shut my eyes before darkness washed over me, and the hall and all its inhabitants disappeared in a deep flood of slumber.

If I had hoped that sleep would lead me to another meeting with the goddess, then I was to be disappointed in that hope, for I had no dreams at all, only a period of deep blackness that might have resembled the slide into death itself. The indifferent observer might be amused by what would seem from the outside to be an abrupt about-face, from skeptic to believer. In answer I can only say that those who have not had an encounter with Inyanna—or indeed, any of the gods—cannot know what it is like, to be faced with something one had not thought to exist, and to realize that there are far greater powers at work in the world than one might ever have guessed.

But although I had relented in my disbelief, I was not to be rewarded with a return visit. Whatever advice and guidance the goddess had seen fit to grant, it appeared she was not inclined to give me anything else. And when I rose from my pallet some hours later—almost twelve hours, to be exact, with the next day well begun—I did so not knowing what was to come next.

As it turned out, those slaves who were able had joined Ruanne in the kitchen, and had set about following my instructions to force another batch of moldy bread. From that it was simple enough to concoct another batch, and once again dose the castle's inhabitants, most of whom appeared to be on the mend. Those who were not I treated with the same homely remedies I always used to assuage a fever or quiet a cough, and I gave them more of the broth, hoping that the repeat application was what they needed to send them on the road to recovery. But no one had died, and no one else had come down sick, so it seemed the goddess's hand had guided me truly in this. I should have been feeling relieved.

Perhaps I was, in some part of my being, but now my unease lay in a new quarter, in the coldness I had heard and seen in Shaine's voice and visage. I told myself not to be put off by this, that the news of Auren's death was fresh and raw, and no one could be expected to recover quickly from such a thing. Logic has its purposes, but it is often not of much use when applied to affairs of the heart. So my steps were heavy as they took me once more up the steps to his rooms, to give him his second dose of the medication as well.

When I entered, at first it seemed that he slept, but as I approached his bed I saw that he was awake after all; a glitter of eyes showed beneath the fringe of dark lashes. This was where my training became unexpectedly useful, for I had been taught how to be cool and calm and professional even under the most trying of circumstances, and that rigor supported me now when I otherwise would have found it difficult to approach him.

"How is your leg?" I inquired. "Any swelling or pain?"

He shook his head, but said nothing.

"Fever?"

Another head shake, this one even slighter than the last.

"And no incidence of a cough?"

"Blast it, woman, I am fine!"

Well, there was a response, although perhaps not the one I would have wished for, given the choice. It was not like him to lose his temper thus, but he had been through more than any man should have to endure. "I am pleased to hear it," I said coolly. "I have your next dose of medicine."

He did not reply, instead staring up at the canopy above his head. Since he had not given me an outright refusal, I decided that meant he would not argue the point with me. "It seems to be working quite well," I continued. "Most seem to be getting better, and we have had no new cases. I believe we may have turned the corner." Since he continued to gaze, stony-faced, toward the ceiling, I went ahead and poured a measure of the mold broth into a spoon and extended it to his mouth. As before, he swallowed it without protest, his mouth closing firmly afterward. I could see the movement of his throat as he swallowed, but it appeared I would get nothing else out of him.

"Have I your leave to inspect the dressings on your wound?"

Again I was given only a short nod, and I tried not to sigh as I stepped closer and reached out to pull back the blankets. Once I had his voluminous shirt pushed away from the wound, I was able to carefully undo the wrapping and get my first look at the incision site since I had made it. I could see no redness or puffiness, which meant it had begun to heal cleanly, with no hint of infection. If he had been in a better mood, I would have made some comment on his recovery, but I guessed he cared little at the moment how well the wound might be doing. So instead I only fetched clean bandages from my kit and set about covering the wound once again. I had thought perhaps it would need stitching, but it appeared to be knitting itself together on its own. I would let it alone to do its work.

"It is doing well enough," I said then, more because I felt I needed to say something to fill up the terrible silence that stretched between us. "I will keep checking it daily, but I see no reason for concern."

"Hmm."

Some part of me wanted to shake him them, to tell him he was not the only man who had lost someone—there were many in the castle who had suffered as much as he, or more, and yet they hadn't turned into surly, cranky children. *Well, not all of them*, I reminded myself, for Lord Marten had also not handled his losses very well. But he at least answered me when I spoke to him, although when I had looked in on him earlier, I had very much gotten the impression that he had answered me by reflex, and not because he put any thought into his replies.

"They are making barley broth in the kitchen," I went on, doggedly, because I had information I must relay, and at the moment he was my patient first and foremost, not the man I thought I loved, and who I hoped had begun to feel something for me in return. "I'll see to it that some is sent up."

Silence was my only reply…not that I had expected anything more.

Briskly I gathered up my kit, and avoided looking at him as I lifted the satchel and left the room.

I did not expect a miracle—that is, I had been given one already. It would have been presumptuous of me to ask for any more. And yet, as the days stretched on, with those under my care gathering their strength, I wondered when things would change, when Shaine would once again look upon me with warmth.

That is not to say we did not have our little tragedies. One of the women from the dye hut passed in the night, a week after I had first dosed her with the mold medication; her heart, as far as I could tell. She had been convalescing, but slowly, and I supposed the strain was too much for her. The ground was still frozen, so we sent her off as we had all the rest, in a pyre that used firewood we could ill afford to spare. But neither would we stack the bodies to wait for the spring thaw, and so another bonfire blazed away into the night.

Shaine did attend her farewell, as by then he had begun to limp about with the use of a cane. I tried to tell him to stay in bed, but he only looked at my with those stranger's eyes and informed me that he had been a sluggard long enough, and that it was time to resume his duties. To be sure, we had need of every willing pair of hands, for although I had saved many, we had lost almost half the household, and the chores, perforce, were distributed among those who were left. There was no question of asking the lord of the manor to scrub the floors or muck the stables, but he had taken Wilys and some of his men-at-arms who had survived and went forth to hunt what game they could. I did not think it wise for him to be riding, but I also knew that any protests on my part would fall on unhearing ears, and so I only admonished him and his men to stay far away if they should spot any other people.

That they did not, in all the times they went forth from the castle, and I began to wonder whether we were the only ones who had survived, a tiny island of life and warmth in an otherwise dead land. But surely it could not be that bad. Surely it was only that the other survivors were huddled in their own castles and keeps, unwilling to venture forth in case they should come across others still infected with the dread disease. And even if everyone in the immediate vicinity was gone, it still did not mean that all of Seldd had been laid waste. There had to be some left. Even the accounts I had read of the last time the pestilence spread across the continent spoke of some few who had survived. There were always some who never sickened, no matter how dread the disease. Perhaps the goddess had laid her hand on them as well, so that some might live to recount what had happened and leave a record to guide those who would come after.

And one day I awoke in my cold bed to hear a dripping sound from outside my window, and I went to the window to see the icicles that had hung there all winter melting, their forms beginning to evaporate in a warm wind that had come up from somewhere to the south. It would not last; these false springs never did. Yet it reminded me that, as with all things, this winter of death would come to an end, and the roads would be open once again.

And that I was now a free woman.

The thought had flitted through my mind from time to time that I should pack my things and go. For Shaine of Donnishold had shown that even if he had once been inclined to think of me with some warmth, it had been extinguished the night Auren died. I had no doubt he blamed me, though I heard no recriminations from his lips. Indeed, I had begun to blame myself, even if in my heart of hearts I knew there was aught I would have done differently, given the opportunity. There are hard equations that must be made in times of extremity, and I had been trained as much in those as setting limbs and delivering babies. I could not sacrifice the care of many so I might sit with Auren all night. And even if I had, there was no guarantee my presence would have changed anything. When the body decides it wishes to succumb, even the most accomplished healer has not the skill to bring it back from the brink.

So it seemed I had no real reason to stay, although as the days stretched on and that false sign of spring turned to a true one, I kept wondering why I lingered. If I had asked, I knew Lord Shaine would have gifted me with a horse, a payment of sorts for the services I had rendered, even if I had failed at the one thing that truly mattered to him.

But still I remained, even as the sadly dwindled number of field hands returned to till the soil now that it was no longer frozen, and a creeping carpet of green covered all that had been snowy waste. I tried to tell myself that my presence was not completely useless—even with the plague now apparently behind us, still there were coughs and colds and the odd sprained ankle and burned finger. If any wondered why I stayed, they kept their questions to themselves. Shaine did not ask my intentions, and I did not voice them. Indeed, I myself did not truly know what they were.

I was, however, the only guest who stayed, for not long after the true thaw Lord Marten and his daughter left us, desiring to see what had come to pass on their own estate. We had had no word, and although Shaine asked if they would stay a little longer, he did so gently, as if he knew they were set on their decision. Donnishold had been a place of death for them. Both the Lady Yvaine and young Larol had burned with the rest of the casualties, but they had a stone set in the graveyard to mark their passing, along with all the other plague victims. I found a bouquet of early wildflowers, forget-me-nots and crocuses, placed across the earth in front of their marker the day after Lord Marten and Alcia left, and guessed it was Alcia who had done so, her final farewell before she returned home. We had no word of how they fared after that, and could only hope that they had not gone home to desolation.

A gentle wind blew from the south on a day not long after the new seed was sown on the freshly tilled fields, and a week since our guests had left us. I had gone to assist in the dye hut, as no one required my other services, and I found the process of coloring the fabric to be quite interesting, a novel use of the herbs and plants I often utilized for far different reasons. Ruanne and I were pinning up a length of rosy linen, and laughing because the fresh breeze kept catching the fabric and trying to lift it from our fingers as we raised it to the drying line.

The gates to the keep stood open. We had not had visitors for months, and it was easier for the field workers to pass back and forth from their labors to the hall where they shared their meals if that entry was not shut. Guards stood there, of course, and there were two more up in the tower immediately above the gate.

I heard one of them call out, "Rider!" and almost dropped the cloth I held.

Ruanne had heard him, too, of course, but she maintained a better grip on the fabric. "Mind the cloth, mistress.

Even if they have seen someone, he won't be here for a few minutes."

She was right—the guard had a much better vantage point, and anyone he spied was most likely still almost a mile away. But I couldn't help feeling a shiver of mixed anticipation and fear run along my spine. Who would be coming here, after so many months of isolation?

Somehow I managed to get my side of the cloth pinned up, and then wiped my damp hands against the apron I wore to protect my gown from any errant splashes or drips. Then I moved toward the gate, wishing to see who it was that approached Donnishold. I was not the only one giving in to her curiosity, as Ruanne was only a few steps behind me, and ranged beyond her were some of the other workers from the dye hut who had emerged after the lookout had shouted his warning.

By then we could all see the stranger: a lone rider coming at an easy canter, apparently not driven by any urgency. He wore a dark cloak with the hood down; the bright morning sunlight caught in his fair hair. I caught sight of that hair and frowned, for I had yet to see tresses that flaxen anywhere in Seldd. Even in Farendon hair of that particular shade was rare. One of my fellow members in the Order, Brahn Landisher, had hair that color, but—

I broke into a run, bursting out through the gate even as he brought his horse to a standstill a few paces away from me. His eyes, pale grey to match his silver-gilt hair, gleamed as he looked down into my face.

"Well, Merys," he said, "it seems we've found you at last."

CHAPTER TWENTY

Despite his heartache, Lord Shaine was ever the gracious host, and although we could not offer anything terribly fine, he had the kitchen prepare a hearty meal of smoked meats and creamy turnip soup. We sat at the high table, and if both Shaine and I tried to dissemble and show we did not note the empty places at that table, well, I think few would fault us for that.

"You have done well here," Brahn told us, as he broke off another piece of bread and washed it down with some of the young wine Shaine had ordered brought up from the cellar. "Much of Seldd is—gone, I suppose you could say. That's the only reason why I was able to make my way here so easily."

Lord Shaine lifted an eyebrow, but said nothing. I supposed he did not much care for Brahn's tone, which seemed to imply that the only way to escape the depredations of the slavers was to have most of them dead from the plague.

To cover up the uncomfortable silence, I asked, "And how did you know where to look?"

"Ah, that's a tale in itself." Brahn smiled, teeth flashing even in the dimly lit hall.

I recalled how easily he had been able to charm everyone back at the Order house, from Lhiare, the musty old librarian, to Selcy, the girl who fetched and carried firewood and anything else the masters could think of. Somehow I had been able to mostly evade that charm; I had never cared overmuch for those who used easy smiles and graceful words in place of hard work. But I supposed I must revise some of my opinion of him, for he had undertaken an arduous task by coming here to Seldd at all, let alone in the aftermath of the plague.

"Well, let us hear it, for there is plenty of wine," I returned, somewhat recklessly, even as I caught Shaine's brow furrowing briefly before he said,

"Yes, I think we would all like to hear how you found us."

Thus encouraged, Brahn held out his goblet so that I might refill it, and then helped himself to a hearty sip before continuing, "At first we were not unduly concerned, for you had often been away from the Order for some time. But the weeks bore on, and winter began to approach, and there was no word of you. Then one day a man who claimed to be a farmer from Threnlyn appeared, and said he'd been told to pass on word from another man, an innkeeper named Frin, that one of our healers had been stolen from his village by slavers."

"Frin," I murmured, surprised despite myself. So he did manage to get the message through.

"You knew him?" asked Brahn.

"Only slightly. He was the innkeeper in Aunde, the

village where I had been treating an outbreak of tertian fever when I was taken. He tried to hide me."

Lord Shaine shot me an odd look. "You never told me any of this."

I lifted my shoulders and replied, "You never asked me."

Brahn looked from Shaine to me and then back again, and drank more wine. It was hard to say what he saw in our faces. He had been surprised to find me a free woman, and perhaps even more surprised by the way I made free of the household, but he had accepted my status with equanimity. If he thought some of that status might have been conferred by a not entirely professional physician/patient relationship, he was too well-bred to say so. I recalled then that he was the son of minor nobility, a baronet or second son of a viscount, and so possessed perhaps more knowledge of how to navigate such potentially tricky social situations than most of the members of my Order would have been able to.

"At any rate, we knew then you had been taken, but before we could begin to plan how to recover you, we received word that the plague had begun to spread across Seldd. The masters said it was far too dangerous for any of us to undertake such a pursuit." Once again Brahn surveyed the hall—the quiet forms of the slaves who came to remove empty trays and plates from the table, the surviving men who could still take their place at the high table: Master Wilys, Master Breen. "We were lucky in Lystare, for the masters went at once to the king and counseled him to close the city gates, so that there was no risk of the disease spreading within the population. And because then it still had only touched the outlying provinces, we headed it off before it could get a grip on the city. But safe as we were, there was no question of anyone riding forth, not while the plague ravaged the countrysides of both Purth and Seldd." His manner uncharacteristically grave, he added, "I will not detail what I saw as I finally made my way here. Suffice it to say that this is the only estate I have yet come across that shows any sign of resuming a normal life. I assume it must be because of the careful stewardship of Mistress Merys here?"

Lord Shaine's mouth tightened a little, but he replied in cool, even tones, "We are indebted to Mistress Merys. I have no doubt that none of us would have survived if it had not been for her hard work and quick thinking."

That was the most praise I had ever received from him for my labors during the plague. I would have taken more comfort from it had I not known that he spoke thus for Brahn's benefit and not mine.

All I said, however, was, "We were lucky," and sipped at my wine.

Brahn would not be put off, though, and said, "I misdoubt it was luck and guess that it was more your training. You were ever modest, Mistress Merys."

His words, rather than cheering me, only served to make me feel more uncomfortable. Truly, at that moment I wished I could rise and go hide in my rooms. Since that option was not available to me, I instead asked, "But how is it you were able to discover where I was, once you determined it was safe to leave the walls of Lystare?"

"Ah, that." He settled back in his chair and raised his goblet, but did not drink. Somehow I had the feeling it was a posture he affected often in the taverns of our capital city.

Men like him always did better when they had an audience. "Well, we did have to wait the better part of the winter, but then Charis and Millarn and I decided to ride south, to see if we could heat up the trail again, so to speak. We did not much fear the plague, as it has a tendency to burn itself out. I will not say that Farendon did not suffer, but the word had spread out from Lystare that the safest course was to isolate each village and town as much as possible, and so we fared better than some. And when we reached the southern marches we began to ask for word of the slavers who roamed in those areas."

"And were they so easy to find?" inquired Lord Shaine. "I had always been told that their success lies in stealth, and in possessing secret strongholds whose location no outsider may know."

"You would know the truth of that better than I, my lord," Brahn replied, and this time he did not make quite such an effort at politeness.

Even an undiscerning listener would know right away what Brahn's personal feelings on slavers and slavery were, and Shaine was far from undiscerning. His mouth tightened somewhat at the corners, but his voice was mild enough as he said, "As to that, I only know what I have been told. I have had no direct dealings with such people."

I wondered if that somehow made it better, to have his slaves brokered by a steward, so that he never had to dirty his hands by going to the slave markets of Myalme and arranging for a fresh batch of workers there. Then I thought that was uncharitable of me. Lord Shaine could not help the customs of the land where he had been born, and he did well by his slaves compared to most, for they had comfortable quarters and plenty of food and clothing that was strong and serviceable. True, they did not have their freedom, but I knew I was expecting much if I thought he should throw off the traditions of his land and free all of them, and collect rents from them while he paid them a wage to work the fields or the dye houses or the looms. Truly, how different was it in Farendon, where I knew many peasants beggared themselves to maintain the rents on their properties, and so might as well have been slaves? Yes, they had the freedom to gather their meager belongings and leave when they so desired, but in practice that happened very rarely.

Brahn seemed to pick up the hint, and adopted a breezy smile. "Lucky you are, then, my lord, for I would not say they are the most pleasant people to be around. However, they suffered this winter, along with everyone else. The news seemed to be that most of the bands had dissolved, having lost most of their men, and those few who remained could be found washed up in various taverns. So it was that I chanced upon a fellow in Chondley, who—after I had bought him several rounds of ale—went quite melancholy in his cups, and informed me that he used to be such, but that the trade had all dried up. 'And,' he said, as he embarked on his fourth mug of the innkeep's best porter, 'I wish I had kept one, and not taken her to Myalme, for with a doctor such as her perhaps I would not have lost so many men.'

"This piqued my curiosity, as you can well imagine, and I pressed him for more information. So it was that I learned he had taken you, Merys, from Aunde, and sold you in a private transaction to the steward of Donnishold. From there it was a simple enough matter to come south in search of you." He shook his head, and his smile began to look a little shopworn. "Well, 'simple' is a relative term. I mean that I was not challenged along the way, though it was a grim journey. Days passed where I saw not a single soul, and I began to wonder whether all of Seldd was dead. I avoided Myalme altogether, knowing that the plague could hide itself within a city and linger there far longer than in a small village or estate. But I continued on, and here I am."

"Yes, here you are," Lord Shaine said. "And great joy Mistress Merys must have in your arrival." With that his gaze slid toward me, but those dark blue eyes were unreadable, and I could not guess what he thought. Most likely that I had been given a graceful way to make my exit, and I could leave and take my painful memories with me.

"I am very glad to see you, Brahn," I said, and it was not a complete lie. For there was something in seeing a familiar face after so many months, and to hear the accents of someone from my homeland. "And I very much appreciate the labors you undertook to find me."

He gave me a little half-bow while seated, obviously happy with my praise. I doubted that he even noticed the omission, that I had said nothing about plans for leaving.

But if Brahn was oblivious, Shaine was not. I saw his eyes narrow slightly before he gave the slightest shake of his head. "And I am sure you are weary, Master Brahn," he said. "I have had one of the guest chambers made up for you. No doubt you wish to rest after such an arduous journey."

"I do, very much." If he sensed the undercurrents swirling through the hall, he gave no sign of it, but only rose from his chair and bowed to Lord Shaine, and then to me, before the pert Alinne appeared to guide him to the rooms that had been prepared. Her dark eyes fairly danced, and I guessed she thought it a very good duty, to be able to show such a handsome guest to his suite. And Brahn grinned down at her as well, no doubt pleased to have found someone who seemed happy to see him. Very likely he thought my response more than a little lackluster. He knew me well enough to realize I was not the sort of woman who would fling herself into his arms to show her thanks, but I guessed he had expected a little more show of appreciation than what I had displayed.

Master Breen and Master Wilys had not participated much in the conversation, apparently content to listen, but after Brahn had gone, Master Breen turned to me and said, "So you will be leaving us, mistress?"

I did not dare look at Lord Shaine. I somehow managed to turn to Master Breen and reply, "Yes, it appears I am."

No visions of Inyanna came to me that night, no soothing dreams to guide me and tell me what my path should be. Instead, I was haunted by broken jumbles of faces and voices, of those I had lost. I saw Lady Yvaine's accusing eyes, and heard Merime's chiding tones, and then the boys from the stable, and finally Auren, who stood on a low rise I recognized as the one just south of the castle walls, where we had gone to gather the last of fall's wildflowers together. The wind whipped at her dark blonde hair as she stood facing away from me. I reached out to touch her arm, but as I did so she shifted, and her face was not Auren's at all, but Dorus', his features contorted with anger. Then it was his hands on my throat, and I sat up in bed, gasping and choking, and realized I was safe in the room I shared with Elissa.

Her voice came to me in the darkness. "Mistress Merys? Is something amiss?"

Oh, it most definitely was, but I knew I could never begin to explain the cause of my unrest. "No, Elissa," I said gently. "Nothing is wrong. Go back to sleep."

Silence then, but after the space of a few heartbeats I heard her shift on her pallet, as if she settled herself back down to sleep. I realized then that she had no real reason to still stay here, as of course she was now no one's lady's maid, but Lord Shaine had not requested that she move into the slave's quarters, and I had remained silent on the subject as well. She was too fragile for such work, I thought, but I had lately begun to show her how to make simple tinctures and healing draughts, and I hoped they would allow her to continue after I had left. The girl could never be a healer, but I believed in time she would be a worthy successor to me in the stillroom.

These thoughts were pleasant enough, and allowed me to settle myself down in bed and contemplate a hopeful future for her, and for all the residents of Donnishold. I could not stay, it seemed, but at least I could send forth my wishes that they would all do well and prosper. Nothing else remained here for me.

I was awake at dawn, although not because I wished to hasten the day in any way. No, I slept restlessly for the remainder of the night, and arose early because it seemed slightly more appealing than lying in bed and pretending to slumber.

I moved quietly, so as not to wake Elissa. Normally even a household slave would have been required to rise earlier than that, to start the fires and heat water and begin the preparation of breakfast. But though Lord Shaine had taken over as much of the management of his household as he could, still there were things that were let slip, and Elissa, because of her dubious status, was one of them.

After all, I had very little to pack—my satchel with its complement of medicines and surgical implements, my two gowns and clean chemises and underthings. In fact, it seemed I took nothing away that I had not brought with me in the first place.

Only a broken heart, some maudlin part of my mind put in, but I dismissed the thought as self-pitying and instead set about braiding my hair and putting it into its customary coil at the back of my head. Broken was a bit extreme—sprained, perhaps. I would heal, and go on, and do the work I had spent years training for. Someday I might even forget the sound of Shaine's voice, or the calm regard in those dark blue eyes as he told me I was a gift from the goddess.

I gasped then, feeling the pain of it as a knife wound in my midsection. I put a hand to my mouth and forced the tears back, choked them down like the bitterest of wormwood extract. Tears would avail me nothing now; better that I should descend the stairs and make my goodbyes with the dignity that befitted a physician of the Golden Palm. I did not want Shaine to see me with red eyes and a blotchy face. If he did not love me, there was nothing I could do about it, but at the very least I wanted him to respect me.

So caught up in my own thoughts had I been that I did not realize Elissa had risen from her pallet and thrown a shawl over her shoulders. She stood a few paces away, watching me with a grave expression on her delicate features. I had told her the night before that Brahn had come to fetch me home, and so she knew why I had my satchel out, and all my things neatly packed away. Even so, her eyes shone with tears, and her voice trembled as she said, "Do you really have to leave?"

I could not give her the truth—not the whole truth, at any rate. My feelings for Shaine of Donnishold were my own concern, and I would not burden her with them. "This is how the life of a physician of the Golden Palm is ordered. I am a free woman, and I must return to the work for which I was trained. I did not leave ere this because I wanted to make sure we were all out of danger, and then travel still would have been treacherous because of the weather. But now spring is here, and I can tarry in Donnishold no longer."

She nodded, although I saw her bite her lip and look away, her eyes unable to meet mine. I suppose I had been her mainstay during all her months here—with me gone, there would be no one to protect her. Not that I expected any ill to come to her, but the life of a slave is a difficult thing even in a household as civilized as Lord Shaine's, and of course she did not know what was next intended for her.

Speaking more gently than I thought I could manage, given the circumstances, I said, "I will speak with Lord Shaine before I leave, tell him of the good work you are doing in the stillroom. I am certain he will allow you to remain in the house, and not go to the fields."

Obviously this was the fear that had been preying on her, for she grasped my hands then and breathed, "Oh, thank you, Mistress Merys! It is too much—but if you would!"

I assured her that I would see she was taken care of. Then I picked up my satchel and left to descend the stairs for what I guessed would be the last time.

Despite the early hour, I found Lord Shaine in the hall before me, Markh the overseer at his elbow. Spring was a busy time at the estate, what with the preparation of the fields, the plowing, the sorting of the seed. No wonder Shaine had been up even before me. Of Brahn, however, there was no sign.

"Mistress," Lord Shaine said formally. I had expected no less, but still that painful tightness rose up in my throat, and suddenly I found it difficult to reply.

"Good morning, Lord Shaine," I managed, and somehow gathered the strength to force a few breaths into my lungs.

"Eager to be away?" he inquired then, with a glance down at my satchel.

That was not the word I would have used. Rather, I had approached my departure as any other unpleasant task—something I wanted to get over with quickly. "It is always best to get an early start when one is faced with a long ride."

"Ah. Yes, I suppose it is. You may take Surefoot with you—he is a good and sturdy mount, and will bear you safely home."

"Thank you, my lord." I replied. That was all I trusted myself to say, for although I appreciated the gesture, it seemed only another means for him to rid himself of me as quickly as possible.

"It is the least I can do, considering the service you have rendered here."

As he spoke, I thought I glimpsed the slightest flicker in

his eyes, the smallest tightening of his mouth. Was he regretting his coldness to me over the past few weeks? Impossible to say, and I did not have the strength to press the issue. A clean break always heals the easiest.

Then I heard Brahn's voice as he called out, "Good morrow, Lord Shaine—and Mistress Merys. Ready for the journey, I see!"

I looked away from Shaine and saw Brahn descending the last few steps into the hall, the pert Alinne darting away with a giggle. No mystery as to where she had spent her night. I had the feeling she might regret those hours of pleasure. While Lord Shaine did not meddle in the affairs of the slaves, it was quite another thing for one of them to take a tumble with an honored guest while under his roof.

"We have a long day ahead of us," I said simply, choosing to ignore Alinne, who had already slipped off to the kitchen.

"Ah, that is true enough," he agreed, although he appeared less than eager to be off. Most likely he would have preferred to stay a night or so more to enjoy Donnishold's "hospitality" before he set forth again.

"Allow me to send a guard with you, to see you safely to the border," Shaine said then, and I noted yet another of those diffident glances before he shifted slightly toward Brahn.

"No need of that, my lord. As I said, most of the population appears to be gone. There are always some few survivors, of course, but I encountered no one bold enough to approach me. And of course, I took my own precautions." And his hand rested briefly on the long dagger he wore at his waist.

Some of the Order did ride armed. I had never done so, save for the knife I used to cut my meat—although I supposed in a pinch my scalpels could have also served as weapons.

Lord Shaine nodded, but his eyes narrowed slightly, as if he were not wholly convinced. He said nothing more, however, but only bade us accompany him to the table, where we broke our fast together on fresh bread and honey and some of the last rashers of bacon. What we spoke of, to this day I cannot recall—inconsequential things, I believe, the weather, and the condition of the roads. I said very little, glad that Brahn loved the sound of his own voice so much. It saved me from having to put forth much effort.

Afterward the horses were brought around, and we were given packs filled with as much food as Donnishold's larders could spare. Lord Shaine said only, "Goddess go with you, Merys, and guide you on your journey."

I believe I mumbled some thanks before I turned the horse around. The courtyard dissolved into a wash of tears, and I blinked against the brisk wind as we rode forth, glad the horse knew his way, for I was unable to guide him. I could only sit in the saddle as each step took me farther from Donnishold, farther from the man I loved.

I did not allow myself to look back.

Blessedly, we rode for some time before Brahn spoke. "You must be glad to be away, Mistress Merys."

I blinked, and kept my face forward as I replied, "Brahn, there's no need for the 'Mistress.'"

He chuckled. "Very well, then, Merys. What an ordeal that must have been for you!"

Oh, yes, quite the ordeal, although that which had caused me the most suffering was a matter I would never discuss with him. "It was…trying…at times."

"Trying!" The word came out as almost a snort, and his mount tossed its head a little at the sound. He patted the mare's neck. "Only you, Merys, could describe living through the plague while a slave at a Selddish estate as 'trying.'"

"I was not a slave," I said at once. "Lord Shaine freed me on Midwinter Night."

"He did, eh? Why?"

"I had saved his life, and the life of his daughter. I suppose he thought he owed me that much."

"Never knew a Selddishman to be so honorable. Daughter, eh?" Brahn shot me a sideways, silver-tinted glance. "I didn't see her."

"She died of the plague," I said shortly, almost biting out the words.

He appeared to take the hint and looked off into the distance. We rode at an easy pace, for we had a long way to go, and no place to obtain fresh horses if we tired these ones overmuch. Despite my heartache, I could not help glancing about me, as this was the first time I had ventured farther than a few hundred yards outside Donnishold's walls since the plague had swept over the countryside.

Truly it did seem as if Lord Shaine's estate was an island of life in an ocean of desolation. I saw no other human soul, and not even signs of life such as smoke rising from chimneys. From time to time I spotted the bones of plague victims along the side of the road or lying in a field; the birds had long since stripped the flesh away. And I saw as well the skeletons of horses and cattle, who must have perished in the harsh winter weather with no one to care for them.

The enormity of it all came to me then, and I felt once again the useless tears stinging at my eyes. What good would my tears do, after all? Weeping would not Brahng back the dead. I wondered, though, how Seldd could ever continue after such devastation. We had heard nothing, so I did not know whether the king and his family survived. I did know that Myalme had been decimated, but the true seat of government was farther north and west, in Tyrlanne, and perhaps it had fared better than the regions of the country closer to the disease as it spread out from Purth.

Despite all that, the day was finer than it had any right to be—birds called riotously from all sides, and wildflowers blossomed in yellow and blue and pale pink from either side of the roadway. The land would heal, although whether its population could manage to do the same was still unknown.

From behind us I heard a dull thudding sound, and at first could not guess what it might be. Then it resolved itself into the rhythm of a horse being ridden at a hard gallop, and Brahn cried out, "Someone is coming!" He dug his heels into his horse's sides, spurring her to a gallop, and after a brief hesitation, during which I finally understood that anyone coming toward us in such a fashion most likely meant no good, I did the same.

We had barely picked up speed, however, before I heard a familiar voice call out, "Merys!"

I yanked on the reins, so abruptly that my mount half-reared. Somehow I managed to cling to the saddle and then wheel the horse around, so that I faced Lord Shaine.

His own stallion breathed hard, flanks shining with sweat. They must have ridden the whole way at a gallop.

Uncertainly, I said, "My lord?"

By that point Brahn had stopped as well and had begun to turn his horse toward us. He was still almost a furlong away, however.

Blue eyes met mine, and held. Shaine opened his mouth, paused, shook his head, and then spurred his horse closer. "Call me a fool, Merys."

"I would never do that, my lord." Somehow I kept my voice steady, but an unreasoning joy had begun to blossom in my heart. Surely there must be only one reason why he had ridden after us.

"If you will not, then I must." His gaze did not waver. "I have been a fool all these weeks, and all because I did not want to accept what fate had sent my way. I have wronged you, and I will understand if you cannot forgive me. But when I watched you ride off, it was as if the truth of my heart was finally revealed, and I knew I could not live without you. Don't leave me, Merys. Tell me you'll stay."

Somehow words seemed inadequate. Instead, I leapt down from my horse and ran toward him, even as he dismounted as well. And then I was in his arms, feeling them around me in an embrace I thought I would never know, as his mouth rained down kisses on my hair, my cheeks, my brow. And his mouth was on mine, and my body pressed against his, as an astonished Brahn paused a few feet away and stared at us in bemusement.

At last I regained my breath and pulled away—just a little—so I could meet his eyes as I gave him my answer. What would come next I did not know, but one thing was truer than all the rest, and it was that I loved him, and he, by some miracle, had realized he loved me in return. As the goddess told me once, love must be the guide.

"Yes, Shaine of Donnishold," I said. "Oh, yes, I will stay with you."

The End

14697863R00205

Made in the USA
Charleston, SC
26 September 2012